A sister in trouble

He goaded her, he prodded her, but
Shannon O'Connor couldn't remember a single
thing about the night she almost died. So Nick had
to keep her safe and protected...around-the-clock.
Till Shannon couldn't bear to let him go.

A brother incommunicado

Joanna Stanton didn't want to head to her
ex-husband Ryan O'Connor's island. But when
you're looking for a safe hiding place, there isn't
always a lot of choice. And she certainly didn't
want her fourteen-year-old son anywhere near
Ryan, who might notice a certain resemblance....

Two heart-stopping romances from
master storyteller
Karen Young

RITA and *Romantic Times* Award winner **Karen Young** is known for her groundbreaking stories in romance fiction. She is the author of more than seventeen novels published by MIRA, Harlequin and Silhouette Books, and is highly acclaimed as a "spellbinding storyteller." Karen, the mother of three grown daughters, recently moved to Jackson, Mississippi, from Louisiana, which means that Karen—a native Mississippian—has come home.

Karen Young

The O'Connors

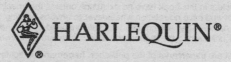

HARLEQUIN®

TORONTO • NEW YORK • LONDON
AMSTERDAM • PARIS • SYDNEY • HAMBURG
STOCKHOLM • ATHENS • TOKYO • MILAN • MADRID
PRAGUE • WARSAW • BUDAPEST • AUCKLAND

HARLEQUIN BOOKS

by Request—THE O'CONNORS

Copyright © 1999 by Harlequin Books S.A.

ISBN 0-373-83413-6

The publisher acknowledges the copyright holder of the individual works as follows:

ROSES AND RAIN
Copyright © 1994 by Karen Stone

SHADOWS IN THE MIST
Copyright © 1994 by Karen Stone

Visit us at: www.romance.net

Printed in U.S.A.

CONTENTS

ROSES AND RAIN

PROLOGUE

THE BATHROOM WAS STEAMY, heady with the smell of rose-scented bath gel. With her eyes closed, Shannon O'Connor let the warm, tingling spray cascade over her body, wishing that more than the grime and fatigue of her trip to Atlanta could be washed away. It would be nice, she thought, to have an elixir that zapped the nasty details of a murder.

Unfortunately, they were clear and stark in her memory.

When a story was beginning to come together for her, her mind teemed with angles to present it. The words circulated in her journalist's brain like alphabet soup until she had them arranged precisely as she wished to tell the story. She imagined its impact on the *Sentinel*'s subscribers as they read it over morning coffee. It wouldn't be tomorrow morning's coffee because she still had a few loose ends to tie up, but within a day or two...

"Yes!" she whispered fiercely, shutting off the water. This one was definitely front page stuff. Her editor would be overjoyed. She had allowed Ernie Patton to expect something extraordinary, and boyohboy, he wouldn't be disappointed when she tossed this one on his desk. She probably should have clued him in before now, but she loved to spring these things on him.

Sliding the glass door open, she stepped out of the tub and reached for a towel. She went still suddenly, thinking that she heard a sound. She waited a second, then with a little click of her tongue, she resumed drying herself. She was getting spooked over nothing. But after what she'd seen in Atlanta...

She wriggled into an oversized T-shirt and a pair of string bikinis and left the bathroom. She was tired, depressed, actually. Who wouldn't be? She looked at her journal lying open on her desk. Things sometimes took on another perspective when she put her thoughts in writing. With that idea in mind, she sat down, picked up a pen, entered the date in the upper left-hand corner and began writing.

From a tiny, almost overlooked seed of suspicion, I have uncovered a story of deceit and obsessive ambition that is almost unbelievable. I won't go into details until the story is in print. I can only say that I will always be amazed at the secrets people carry around. Does everyone, even the most unlikely among us, live life safeguarding secrets of mistakes made, of wrong turns taken? And does that make us prisoners in jails just as formidable as those with real iron bars and locked doors? The story I'm working on is a sad commentary on a number of issues: a person can be imprisoned by fear; excessive ambition can be contaminating; love gone wrong can be—

She hesitated, uncertain how exactly to express her thought. There was something about this story, about this particular victim that drew from her intense empathy. It was almost as though she somehow sensed the depth of humiliation, of pain and degradation suffered, before the finality of death brought deliverance. Why she should feel so personally involved in a story baffled her. It was unusual enough to give her an uncomfortable feeling, and she attempted to shake it off as she stared at the half-written sentence.

For no good reason she could think of, she suddenly felt afraid. The hair on the back of her neck prickled. She had the crazy feeling that she was not alone. Had she actually heard a sound earlier, or was it her neighbor's cat? Sometimes he slipped inside when she unlocked her front door. She'd been loaded with take-out Chinese, her carry-on, her tape recorder, her jacket for the chilly March nights. The cat could easily have snuck inside without her knowing it. She glanced at the telephone on her bedside table. She could call 911. But what if it *was* just the cat? Or the wind? The weather was blustery tonight. Sort of.

Standing, she moved to the bedside table and picked up her portable telephone. She could always punch out 911 if she needed to.

The hallway was dark as a tomb. Naturally. She hated the dark. It was a juvenile phobia and she'd worked hard to overcome it, but it was still there. Fearless in pursuing a story, she'd interviewed serial killers and exposed crooked politicians, she'd badgered burly union demonstrators and skulked in back alleys getting information from snitches who would just as soon slit her throat as look at her. But she was still scared of the dark.

She moved toward the light switch and flipped it. Light illuminated the hallway and the shape of Clarence, her neighbor's cat. Arrested in the act of washing a paw, he gave her a disinterested look and went back to grooming himself. Shannon swallowed the obstacle lodged in her throat, laughed a little shakily and leaned for a moment, weak as water, against the wall.

"Out you go, rascal," she told him softly. Setting the phone down, she scooped up the cat and started down the stairs, grimacing a little to find that area dark, too. She usually left a night light on near the bar that separated the kitchen from her family room, but she must have forgotten it. Her foot nudged something bulky—her carry-on bag. It lay on the floor where she'd dropped it when she first got home.

She touched the light switch on the wall and nothing happened. Instantly she went cold with fear. That light should not be out. Clarence stirred in her arms, struggling to get down. She released him and he darted away toward the kitchen. One leap and he was up and out.

He had jumped through a hole in the door.

Frozen where she stood, Shannon stared at the sight. A panel was shattered near the lock. Glass shards covered the floor. Cold air was seeping into the room. A split second was all it took for her brain to compute the danger. She whirled, thinking to run for the front door. And that was when she saw him.

Her heart exploded with terror as he came at her out of the shadows. She had no time to act, no time to scream. With his first blow, her body slammed into the wall. With his next, a shower of stars burst inside her head. The next drove her to her knees. Then she was down.

Pain was a white-hot knife in her middle, in her limbs, in her head. He meant to kill her. She had enough awareness left to know that. And he was shouting. As consciousness faded, the words were just that…words. Sounds with no meaning. And then he closed his hands around her throat. Light and sound fluctuated and shifted into a bizarre kaleidoscope. Her struggles became more feeble. Only the pain was real.

Then, just as she had always feared, the darkness claimed her.

CHAPTER ONE

THE LATEST CASE was waiting for Nick Dalton when he got back from Atlanta. He studied the single sheet clipped to the front of the file, forcing down frustration and the surge of weariness that nearly always came now when he got a new one. The first words steadied before his eyes. "Melissa Ann Morgan, juvenile female, white, age thirteen, missing December 23, 1993…"

Nick dropped his head back. He did not need this. He'd already lived through one hell of a day. Up at dawn for the drive to Atlanta, then six tiring hours combing through state and federal files for something, anything, that might even remotely link Savannah—or someone in Savannah—to the sleaziest operation ever to come down the pike, at least on his watch as chief of detectives. He'd come up empty.

He swallowed another gulp of bitter black coffee, grimacing at the taste. It was past 10:00 p.m. now, long past time to pack it in. He should go home, leave it until tomorrow. God knows, this one wasn't going anywhere. But then, he didn't have anything much to go home to. Just Jake, and it would take more than a hard-bitten, dog-eared alley cat to cheer him up. He knew from experience that nothing would take his mind off the grim reality of the case. With a sigh, he blinked the report back into focus.

"…Blond hair, blue eyes, four feet, eleven inches, multiple scars left and right wrists—"

With a muttered curse, he shoved his chair away from his desk and scrubbed a hand down his face. Both wrists scarred.

This thirteen-year-old, this…this…little girl had tried suicide at least once, maybe more.

From the window behind him, gusts of cold March wind rattled the ancient casings. The forecasted cold front had arrived with a vengeance. Twisting around, he turned his brooding gaze to the rain-sparkled windows. What would drive a child to attempt suicide? Was it before or after she'd been lured into a life of prostitution? How terrible was the home she'd fled compared to the hell of the streets?

Rolling his chair back up to his desk, he pulled a black-and-white photograph from the file, then added it to the string of photos laid out in a straight, even line in front of him.

Melissa Ann Morgan. Thirteen. *God.*

Where are you, Melissa Ann? Does your mama know what you're doing, little girl?

Rising to his feet, he stared down at the photos. Eleven female juveniles. Eleven children missing from six Georgia towns. Two from right here in Savannah. Reports of sightings on every one of them, now obviously engaged in teenage prostitution, but no success in apprehending them. And not a single atom of solid evidence to begin building a pattern. God, it was enough to drive him—

"Hey, Nick, you're back."

Ed Raymond came through the door, bringing with him the scent of rain and the outdoors. Shrugging out of his wet raincoat, he tossed it across one of the two green plastic upholstered chairs that faced Nick's desk. "Did you see the paper?"

In the act of scooping up the photos, Nick looked up. "The *Sentinel*? No, what about it?"

"You're gonna be royally p.o.'d, boss. Shannon O'Connor's done it again." Ed headed back across the hall to his own office, sending out a flurry of raindrops as he rubbed a hand across his short hair. He came back holding a folded newspaper which he dropped on Nick's desk. "Her timing on

KAREN YOUNG   15

this one is incredible, Nick. Does the woman have a crystal ball or what?''

With a grunt, Nick took it, but was forced to work out the folds before he could read the headline. In the time it took to absorb the first paragraph, he was swearing softly, incredulously. By the time he finished the article, he was enraged.

"How did she get hold of this?" he asked, nailing Ed with a laser-sharp, gray-green stare.

"Your guess is as good as mine," Ed said with a shrug.

With one short, vulgar word, Nick stood up, sending his chair crashing back against the wall. "Do you realize what this means, damn it! She's destroyed months of work by telling the whole frigging world that we may have a teen prostitution ring working out of Savannah."

"I guessed you'd see it that way." Ed dropped into the empty chair and crossed one knee over the other. "Since you were in Atlanta, I went by to see her. I knew you'd want to know her source."

"Who the hell is it? I'll have his—"

"She wasn't home, Nick. But even if she was, we both know Shannon wouldn't reveal a source...no-how, no-way."

Nick pinned Ed with another glare. "You got any ideas?"

"None."

Stopping at his desk, Nick picked up the paper again. "Why didn't she talk to anybody about this before spreading it all over the front page? Is her precious career all she thinks of? Hell, her grandma owns the whole newspaper. If she wants a Pulitzer, they can just buy it for her."

"Come on, Nick. Shannon doesn't work that way."

"That's right, take her side," Nick growled, crumpling the paper and hurling it in the direction of his trash can. "I keep forgetting you're tight with her."

"We were classmates, Nick, not soul mates." Ed shifted and stood up. "To give her the benefit of the doubt, maybe she didn't realize the damage she did by running that story without clearing it.''

Nick's response was a disbelieving snort.

"We've got a couple people working this undercover. We'll have to pull them off. With the major players alerted by the article, they may be in some jeopardy. You can bet they'll be looking for Shannon's source.''

Nick swore again. "Pull them. Now.''

"Right.''

"It'll be back to square one,'' Nick grumbled, adding sarcastically, "thanks to the woman's knack for screwing things up.'' He made a face. "Reporters.''

"Yeah, but as reporters go, she's in a class by herself,'' Ed said, reaching for his raincoat. "It's one step back, two forward, as they say. How about a drink?'' He gestured to the file on Nick's desk. "You ready to quit for the day?''

Nick slipped the photographs into a large manila envelope, stacked it on top of Melissa Ann Morgan's file and opened the side drawer of his desk. "This makes eleven, Ed,'' he said, dropping the folder and envelope into a space in front where he could pick it up first thing in the morning. "I don't want the count to go to an even dozen.''

"We're bound to get a break soon,'' Ed said, putting on his raincoat.

Nick closed the door behind him, then headed with Ed down the dim hallway toward the front desk. A couple of uniformed cops were at the counter, drinking coffee and killing time. It was cold outside and still raining. Behind the sergeant manning the front desk were the two 911 stations. Both operators were occupied with calls. One wore an expression of pained patience; the other frowned and repeated an address, obviously having difficulty trying to make sense of whatever she was hearing. Beside Nick, Ed checked his pace when he heard the address. It was 611 Magnolia Place, Breckenridge Apartments.

"Breckenridge Apartments. That's where Shannon lives.''

He looked at Nick. "Six-eleven. Jeez, I think that's her apartment, Nick."

Nick squinted at the screen, reading the information taken from the caller. Reporting from the scene was a neighbor, almost incoherent with panic. An apparent assault had taken place. Victim unconscious. Female, mid-twenties. The description fit Shannon O'Connor. Dread darted through him, but he suppressed it. Who else but Shannon would be at her address?

Swearing, he turned away, digging into his pocket for his keys. "Let's go," he said to Ed, heading to the rear exit of the station where his car was parked. "We're as close as the nearest black-and-white."

Heedless of the rain-slicked street, he pulled out into the traffic and accelerated. He could easily beat the EMTs to her apartment. He wasn't sure why it suddenly seemed so urgent to get to her.

The SPD unit was drawing up to the curb as he whipped around the corner and screeched to a halt. Jacoby and Miller, two veterans. Good. Still, he was out of his car and halfway up the stone-paved walkway before they even realized who he was. Behind him, he heard Ed's explanation to the two cops, but Nick was intent on getting to Shannon.

He wasn't sure what he was feeling. Shannon O'Connor had been a thorn in his side ever since they'd met. She was forever nosing around the police department or the city hall looking for material for the *Sentinel*. Or she was poking into other areas of Savannah's shortcomings, business, political, cultural or social. Nothing was too insignificant or too big for her pen. And she wielded that pen with swift and deadly accuracy too often for Nick not to feel wary and defensive around her.

Their last run-in had been about two months ago. She'd wanted to ride along in a squad car for a couple of weeks to get a "real feel" for law enforcement. He had rejected the idea out of hand and recommended to the chief that he tell the *Sentinel* and Shannon O'Connor where to go. He didn't have a lot of patience with ordinary citizens riding shotgun with cops. That was the way people got hurt. No cop could function at his best with a reporter badgering him with questions and recording everything as it happened. Besides, when a willing ear was sitting right there, some cops talked too much.

Unfortunately, both he and the chief had been overruled by the mayor, and Shannon had accompanied a couple of black-and-white units for several days. Nick had admitted, grudgingly, that the series in the *Sentinel* had been fair to the police department, on the whole. But there'd been a couple of zingers in it for city politics. The mayor had fumed and cussed to the chief and Nick when he saw that part, but he had only himself to blame.

And Shannon O'Connor.

He felt other emotions when he was around Shannon, as well. She was a beautiful woman, smart and sassy and challenging. Her dark fiery hair and green eyes were sexy as hell. Taken altogether, she was dangerous. Trouble personified. Since he wasn't in the market for trouble, he invariably kept his distance.

But he didn't want to see her hurt.

A dark-haired woman met him at the door, her anxiety melting into overwhelming relief at the sight of him. From her garbled words, he guessed she was the neighbor who'd made the 911 call.

"She's hurt horribly!" the woman exclaimed, pulling him inside. "Who would do such a thing? I heard sounds, and she'd given me a key one day, just in case, thank heavens. So I let myself in and there she was. Oh, where are the EMTs? She's really in bad shape."

"Where is she?" Nick snapped, his gaze slicing over the empty living room. A lamp was overturned and chairs upended. The pale sand carpet was strewn with glass shards from a smashed coffee table.

"There." The woman pointed to the small bar situated in

an L that led to the tiny kitchen. On the floor behind the bar, one foot was visible. Nick swallowed. There was something about that small, feminine foot. So still. Too still.

"I did what I could, but..." The woman moaned. "Oh, where are they? *Where are they?*"

"They'll be here real soon, ma'am." His words came automatically. He had rounded the bar and looked at Shannon. A deep, sick dread lodged in his chest as he dropped down beside her. She had been savagely beaten. Her face was battered and grotesquely bruised. Blood matted her beautiful auburn hair and stained one cheek. She lay sprawled on her back, her arms at her sides, palms up, her fingers curled helplessly like a baby's. They were bruised and her nails were broken. He'd seen it before. A woman without any other defense using her hands to fend off her attacker. From the look of her throat, he had tried to strangle her, too.

Grim-faced, Nick put two fingers against her carotid and found a thin, thready pulse, then bent his ear close to check that she was breathing. Above him, he heard Ed consoling the neighbor, handing her over to one of the uniforms. Then Ed was hunkered down beside him, one look telling him how bad she was.

"Where the hell are the paramedics?" Nick growled.

"On the way. Four minutes, tops. They'll be here."

"Damn! She's—"

"Yeah, in bad shape."

Both men stared at her helplessly. Nick felt the familiar frustration and rage that was always with him at times like this. But he couldn't remember ever feeling this sense of...connection with the victim. He didn't like the sound of her breathing or the look of those bruises on her neck. "Her trachea is damaged," he muttered. "She might not have four minutes."

Ed looked at him. "What'll we do?"

"I don't—" He broke off as Shannon made a sudden small, choking noise and then there was no sound, nothing.

Nick swore. "She's stopped breathing!" Instinct and training suddenly took command. Patting his pocket for his ballpoint pen, Nick quickly unscrewed it and handed it to Ed. "Hold this." He plunged a hand into his pants pocket and pulled out a small pocketknife. Opening it, he wiped the blade with his handkerchief and prayed that the need for disinfectant was outweighed by the urgency of what he was forced to do to save Shannon's life.

"Jeez, Nick…" Ed's tone was incredulous as he realized what Nick intended. "You aren't going to use that? Do you know what you're doing?"

Nick gave him a fierce look. "Do you have a better idea?"

"No…no…just…be careful, will you?"

Closing his eyes for a second, Nick composed himself. Above him, Jacoby and Miller stood stoic and silent. Hovering a few feet away, Shannon's neighbor wept without making a sound. Opposite him, Ed picked up Shannon's limp wrist. His fingers curled around the delicate bones, feeling for a pulse.

"You'd better hurry, Nick," he said softly.

She was not breathing. Nick knew that. Felt it. She had what, three minutes? Four? What if he missed and severed an artery? What if she survived but couldn't speak? What if she survived but was mentally impaired? Questions came and went like rapid gunfire, but no answers. Should he wait and let the paramedics do it? Already, a couple of precious minutes had passed.

With all of his concentration centered on one small spot on Shannon's throat, he touched the tiny blade to her pale, white skin and, taking a deep breath, made the cut.

There was not as much blood as he expected. Ed quickly offered the cylinder from the ballpoint pen and, praying again, slipped it past the slit he'd made in Shannon's throat into her trachea.

"Breathe, Shannon," he urged quietly, but fiercely. "Breathe, damn it!"

Above him, Jacoby and Miller were both shaking their heads, accepting the inevitable. The neighbor's sobs were audible now. Opposite him, Ed released a shaky, emotional breath.

"Jeez, Nick…it's too late. I can't get a pulse. She's dead."

"*No!*"

THE PAIN IS GONE.

That was Shannon's first impression. The second was the incredible sense of peace that pervaded her whole being. She floated somewhere above her body, beyond all things physical. She felt no inclination to think or reason it out. It was good not to have any demands upon her. And no pain. Nothing seemed substantial enough to be real. Everything was… otherworldly, as though she drifted in an ethereal realm. It was a timeless, utterly tranquil existence. She accepted it, no questions asked.

Such calm and tranquillity were rare for her. No, not just rare, but new. She had never felt so peaceful. Even more wondrous, she'd never known such a soul-deep sense of joy and well-being. Her body seemed weightless, like a shadowy, fragile ghost of itself.

Wasn't that odd? Her curious mind nudged tentatively at that. It was basic instinct for her to question and wonder. Especially in this time of…of what? Looking around, she viewed a tabloid of urgency and desperation. People milled over her fallen, bruised body. Harsh commands came from two paramedics. Their hands were prodding her, intrusive. She watched impassively as they went about their business. In the crowd of onlookers, another man crouched beside a paramedic. Something about him spoke to her. His face was anxious. His fear was a tangible thing. He put out a hand to touch her, silently urging her to fight.

She hesitated, floating backward to distance herself from the frenetic activity. Ah, good. Now everything appeared tinted in soft, pleasing hues. Like a picture barely out of focus. And overlaying all that was a sort of shiny, mystical glow, as though illuminated by special energy. Spiritual energy.

Of course. A silver lining. Every cloud had one. The whimsical thought amused her. She liked that. No problems, no deadlines, no pain. Yes, especially no pain. And no darkness. She definitely liked that. She would be more than happy to stay here. Maybe forever.

Except…there were those voices. Urgent, strident voices that kept on at her, pulled at her, urged her, prodded her. That deep one in particular kept on and on and on. Why didn't he stop? And why did it sound so desperate? What was it to that man if she…if she…what?

Beyond it all, Shannon contemplated the situation. Momentarily, she became aware that there were two scenes, one in sharp focus where people milled and voices called, where movement was urgent and purposeful. The other was that soft, peaceful place. She probably should choose that one, but something pulled her back to the other. There were unfinished things there. And him. He was so insistent. Looking at one and then the other, she wavered for a time. Then with a sigh, she moved forward, leaving the special place for another time, and reached for his hand.

NICK HELD HIS BREATH, not daring to believe the tiny flutter of Shannon's fingers against his palm. Beside him, the paramedic bent over Shannon with his stethoscope, listening intently. With a start, he looked up into Nick's eyes.

"She's back!"

"Good girl," Nick murmured, closing his eyes as relief spread through him in a rush.

Now that the crucial moment was past, both paramedics were galvanized into action. The ambu-bag was replaced with an oxygen cup slipped over Shannon's face and an IV inserted in her arm before they turned their attention to the makeshift tracheotomy.

The medic wore a name tag. Jerry. He looked at Nick. "This your work?" At Nick's nod, he whistled. "Couldn't have done better myself. This little lady owes you big time, buddy."

"She couldn't wait," Nick said shortly.

With a nod at their clasped hands, Jerry said, "You can let go now. We need to get her on the stretcher."

With reluctance, Nick gently tucked her hand by her side and backed away. "Will she be all right now?"

"Hard to say." Jerry studied her ravaged throat for a moment as his partner fastened the straps on the stretcher. "She's not out of the woods yet, that's for sure." He shook his head. "I've seen battered women before, but this is one of the worst. Somebody was really mad at this lady."

"Yeah." With a brooding look, Nick watched them wheel the gurney through the door and out to the waiting ambulance. Across the room, Ed was talking to the uniforms. A couple of Shannon's neighbors hovered just outside. They'd have to be questioned, but Nick was ready to bet nobody would have seen anything. This wasn't something a man would do in front of witnesses.

Renewed rage rose in him. Judging from the marks on Shannon's throat, somebody had meant to kill her. But he'd taken his time about it. Had he enjoyed brutally beating her first? Nick hadn't seen this kind of cold-blooded viciousness in a long time. It shook him. He fooled himself most of the time, thinking his years as a cop insulated him against such heartfelt reactions. Then he'd see something like this and his immunity was snuffed out in an instant.

Taking in the shambles that used to be Shannon's living room, he swallowed once, hard. Only the timely intervention of that neighbor had saved her life. If she survived. It wasn't a sure thing, even now. He rubbed an unsteady hand over his mouth, recalling his crude, unsterile invasion of her throat. No, there was no guarantee yet that she would survive.

"What d'you think, Nick?"

"What?" He looked at Ed, missing most of what he'd asked, something about the crime scene.

"Hey, you okay?" Ed studied him narrowly.

"Yeah." He forced down the shakes by drawing in a deep breath. "I guess we'd better see what the neighbors know."

"Nobody saw a damn thing," Ed said, looking around at the devastation of the living room. "He got in by breaking the glass panel in the back door, but nobody heard it. Hard to believe that some scum-bag could enter a woman's house, manhandle her, destroy everything she owns, break a sheet of three-eighth-inch glass in the act, and nobody sees or hears a thing, isn't it?"

Nick stared at a scrap of blue on the carpet. From Shannon's T-shirt. It had been practically torn off her. "He meant to kill her, Ed."

"Sure looks like it."

"Why?"

"Well—"

"Her journalism?"

"It's the most logical answer. But which story? If I know Shannon, she's probably working on half a dozen articles."

"Maybe, but I intend to find out, Ed. I intend to find out."

CHAPTER TWO

"SHANNON...SHANNON O'CONNOR...wake up, Shannon."

"Can you hear me, Ms. O'Connor?"

She existed somewhere in a dark void, aware but unresponsive to the disembodied voices plaguing her. She made no sense out of their torment. Her every nerve ending screamed with excruciating, white-hot, unrelenting pain. Her body was saturated with it. Her brain vibrated with it.

And then, just when she felt she couldn't endure another second, the blessed relief would come, sweeping through her veins, washing pain and voices away in a rushing, oblivious tide. She turned to it eagerly, embraced it, gave herself over wholly to sweet, blissful escape. Then she knew nothing until the next time.

And yet voices pestered her, badgered her unmercifully. Over and over again, they forced her from her deep, safe cocoon into hellish awareness, a half-conscious state of wakefulness that she she had no choice but to tolerate. She resisted, but there was nothing she could do to keep the voices at bay.

Besides, if she stayed, there was darkness and danger....

Invariably, moments of awareness increased, as the intervals between painkillers extended. She realized eventually that she was in a hospital, although she could make little sense of what was going on around her. Some fragments of conversation were almost meaningless.

"...concussion, and we won't know with any certainty until..."

"...a miracle that...survived...brutal..."

"...helluva thing with a ballpoint pen...too much TV, you ask me."

At other times, she comprehended all too well.

"...her family...concerned for her."

"...some kind of security...hospital not equipped for patients who need protection."

"...a detective...haunts the place. Gonna move in here next thing we know..."

"...wasn't raped. Little string bikinis. Didn't touch her. Go figure."

Memory flickered, a small flash, not quite substantial enough to see clearly, to *know*. But still her heart began to beat faster and the machine linked to her shrieked a warning.

"Something's wrong. *Nurse!*"

"Shannon, can you hear me?"

"What do you expect her to say with that...that thing taped in her mouth that way? Can't you remove it?"

"Can you hear me, Ms. O'Connor?" Brisk, efficient, the voice demanded a response.

"She's scared, can't you see that?" Another voice, deep, grim, accusing.

"Darling, we're right here. You're going to be all right." That voice. Soothing. Safe. Granny Kathleen. The blips on the machine slowed dramatically.

"Can she hear me, do you think?"

I hear you, Gran. Don't leave me.

"I'm not sure. But she's definitely aware of you. She responds positively. She's quieted down now. I think she'll wake up fully soon."

"But when, Doctor?"

"No one can answer that, Mrs. O'Connor."

"SHANNON...WAKE UP NOW."

"Is she conscious? I saw her eyelids move."

"She's been conscious, more or less, for a couple of days, but we want her to come all the way out of it."

"Come on, Shannon. I know you hear me. Shannon…"

Deep, husky, persistent, the voice coaxed her up from the depths. She knew it was no use trying to sink back again. When she came this far, it was always a while before they let her escape into the soft, pain-free mist.

"Ah, Ms. O'Connor, it's about time."

She recognized that voice. Brisk and efficient. A doctor, probably. He never wasted time trying to cajole her into the real world. He left that to—

She didn't know who it was trying to bring her back into the land of the living, but there was someone. Not just her grandmother. Gran was there, yes. She talked gently and constantly to Shannon. *Maman* was there sometimes, too. Had Michelle come all the way from Paris to be with her?

Giving in finally, she struggled to open her eyes. With a flutter of her lashes, she managed it.

"Good girl."

Light, sharp and penetrating, struck her pupils, making her whimper. She closed her eyes again.

"The light is painful to her, isn't it, Doc?"

There. That voice. The deep, compelling voice that had been with her throughout. Who was he?

Her eyes fluttered open again and she found the room dimmer. With an effort, she focused on the people peering at her. Her grandmother, a man in green surgical garb, a nurse at his elbow and…another man. Standing slightly apart, he was big, silent and still. He was the one.

She closed her eyes again, trying to figure out what had happened to her. Why was she in the hospital? She wanted to move, but her body didn't seem to belong to her anymore. How badly was she hurt? Was she paralyzed? Fear swamped her, accelerating the blips on the machine beside her. The doctor made a move toward her.

"She's frightened and confused," Kathleen O'Connor said from the opposite side of the bed, and moved swiftly to take Shannon's hand. "You're in the hospital, Shannon," she said, softly reassuring her. "You've had...an accident. But don't worry, everything's going to be just fine."

Shannon blinked twice. Something hovered at the edge of her memory, something that sent a dart of fear through her. She pushed it away, unwilling to deal with it just now.

"Your *maman is* here, she just left to grab a bite for lunch. And your brother, too. Will has been so worried." Her eyes bright with tears, Kathleen gently stroked her granddaughter's hair. "We've all been worried, Shannon, but that's over now. Just rest, darling. We want you to get well and come home."

Shannon tried to speak but couldn't. Renewed panic streaked through her. Her heart pounded.

The doctor bent over her. "You have an airway," he explained. "I'll remove it soon—today, actually—and then you can talk all you please."

Why? She looked at him fiercely.

He smiled with professional detachment. "A tracheotomy was necessary at the scene. Don't worry, nothing that happened will leave any permanent damage."

She knew that was not true, but her memory was blocked by a thick, impenetrable curtain. Later, maybe, she would sort it all out.

Fatigue swept over her like a dark, heavy cloud. She was aware of someone in white fiddling with the IV tube dangling above her. Her eyes glanced around at the group, stopping at the tall, silently watchful man at the foot of her bed. Oddly, the sight of him calmed her. Then the magic elixir was once again rushing through her veins, pushing aside pain and fear and questions. Her lashes fluttered weakly, and she sank gratefully into deep, soft nothingness.

NICK DALTON WAS a good cop. Cautious, conservative, he played it strictly by the book. In carrying out his duties as a detective, he sorted through the facts of a case with methodical care. He took meticulous notes. When he was away from his desk, he wrote them in the pocket-sized tablet that he kept tucked in his shirt pocket.

Nick liked things neat. He worked best that way. The very orderliness of good police work appealed to something basic in him. His desktop was always clear except for the case he was working on. There was not even an ashtray; he'd given up smoking six years before. Ed hassled him about it, but his partner wouldn't know how to function if his paperwork wasn't strewn over every available inch of his desk. Even the pens Nick used were neatly stored in a black coffee mug that proclaimed I'd Rather Be Fishing. Which wasn't necessarily so. Nothing intrigued him as much as a difficult case.

Shannon O'Connor's assault was a difficult case.

"Any ideas yet?"

As his partner strolled into his office, Nick turned from the window where he'd been contemplating the pigeons in the parking lot. "A dozen, but nothing that makes much sense until I can talk to Shannon."

"The doctor hasn't consented to let you question her?"

"Not yet. Tomorrow, maybe."

Ed eased his bulk down into the green plastic chair. "What is it now—five days?"

"Six."

"Yeah, six."

They exchanged a look. It hadn't escaped Ed's notice that Nick was keeping close watch over Shannon O'Connor. He had followed the ambulance the night she'd been admitted, then stayed well into the next day. Every moment away from his desk he spent haunting the ICU, waiting to talk to her. He told Ed it was because he couldn't get his investigation off the ground without answers from Shannon herself, but he had admitted he wasn't even certain about that anymore.

With a muttered oath, Nick left the window and sat back down at his desk. "The woman is incredible, Ed. According to her editor, she's working on no less than half a dozen stories."

"That sounds like Shannon."

Nick felt in his shirt pocket for his notebook. "Listen to this. Rival teen gangs in Savannah's ghetto. Proposal to legalize riverboat gambling. Suicide in the Victorian District. Battered women…" He shook his head over that one without looking up. "Legal uses for confiscated drug money. Teenage prostitution."

Ed crossed a leg and leaned back. "My money's on the prostitution thing."

"It's logical. Her story on it came out in the paper that morning, and he was waiting for her when she came home that evening. So it makes sense that somebody might have retaliated. But why eliminate her? The story alone effectively kills recruiting for teens in Savannah."

"In Savannah, yeah. But what if the operation is bigger than Savannah?"

Nick didn't reply. He'd thought of that, but he needed to talk to Shannon before he could be certain.

They sat in silence for a few minutes, pondering. "Have you found out what she was doing in Atlanta for two days?" Ed asked.

"A good question," Nick said. "And one her editor wishes he could answer."

"It's not like Ernie Patton not to know everything his staff is working on," Ed said.

Nick grunted. "Patton said she badgered and cajoled him until he authorized the trip, promising him that she wouldn't disappoint him if her suspicions panned out."

"What suspicions?"

Nick scowled at his notes. "I plan to ask her that as soon as she can talk."

Ed shifted in his chair, squinting beyond Nick to the window behind his desk. They'd been partners for two years. Ed was twenty-six and single, with a face that was good-natured rather than good-looking. He was big, twenty-five pounds overweight, with the hands and feet of a pro ball player and a face that looked as if it had been recycled at least once. He was the most un-yuppie looking yuppie Nick had ever known. His privileged, Ivy League background made him an unlikely cop. He was soft-spoken to the point of gentleness, which fooled a lot of people when it came to his job. On a case, Ed was single-minded, tenacious and tireless, like a bulldog with a bone. He and Nick made a good team.

Nick eyed him narrowly. "You got something on your mind, say it."

Ed sucked in a deep breath, his hands resting on his huge thighs. "I had a call a few minutes ago from Will O'Connor."

"Shannon's brother."

"Yeah. The family's getting a little anxious."

"Then why didn't they call me direct?" Nick snapped. "Or the chief." Meeting Ed's eyes, he tossed his notebook onto his desk. "Forget it. As a friend of the family, naturally you'd be the one they'd pressure. What'd he say?"

"He believes that Shannon's assault was attempted murder. If that neighbor had been a minute later, the O'Connors would be in mourning this week. So, Will and the old lady, Kathleen O'Connor, want to be kept informed of our investigation. They all want to be assured that Shannon is protected while she's in the hospital. Otherwise, what's to keep the sleaze who did this from finishing the job while she's most vulnerable."

Because Nick had been worrying about the same thing, Will O'Connor's criticism hit a nerve. "We don't need concerned family members telling us how to do our jobs, dammit!" he said. "I've got round-the-clock uniforms stationed in the Intensive Care Unit. Nothing can get past them." He glared at Ed. "What else do they expect?"

"They're just afraid, Nick." Ed studied the toe of his battered Dock-Sides. "It's not hard to understand. One look at Shannon is all it takes. Anybody who'd hurt a woman that bad has got to be a certified nut case, so her family expects us to take extraordinary measures to protect her and apprehend him."

"Nobody wants to nail him more than I do," Nick growled.

"Right. Exactly what I told Will."

"Fine."

"Right after we discussed just how important Shannon's safety is to you, of all people."

Nick was up and at the window in a heartbeat. "What does that mean?"

"You saved her life, Nick."

"I was just doing my job."

"I don't recall an emergency tracheotomy being covered in my training at the academy," Ed said dryly.

"It was just that, an emergency."

Ed got to his feet. "Maybe so, but the O'Connors consider themselves lucky that it was you who got to Shannon first. They'll be wanting to tell you that in person, Nick."

"They already have. And nobody was lucky that day, especially Shannon." He raked a hand through his hair. He still tried to block out those agonizing minutes when he had feared Shannon was gone forever. When he closed his eyes, he saw her fiery hair fanned out beneath her head like spilled blood and her face deathly pale. Except for the bruises.

"You went above and beyond to save her, Nick," Ed said quietly. "And it was more than just the tracheotomy. I still don't understand what went down in that few minutes, but I know something did. Even the paramedics thought she was gone."

It was true. At the window, Nick recalled the way they'd taken one look and written her off. He remembered yelling at them, threatening them. Whether they thought it was hopeless or not, he'd demanded the whole nine yards of their expertise. He'd hated the obscenity of the paddles on her breast. His own heart had jumped with the jolt of electricity that had resuscitated her. And he would never forget his feelings when her fingers had finally stirred in his. He'd felt in that second that she was going to make it, and he'd never experienced anything like that in his whole life. From that moment, he had not been able to think of Shannon O'Connor without some odd feeling he couldn't identify rippling through him. Her family didn't need to request extraordinary effort from him for Shannon. She was going to get it simply because he couldn't give anything less.

Still at the window, he said, "Tell me about her family, Ed."

"Her grandparents are legendary here," Ed said, settling back into the chair. "Patrick O'Connor was a penniless Irish immigrant who came to Savannah in the mid-twenties. He'd met Wade Ferguson, a Savannah shipyard owner, in New York. Folks say he saved the old man's life on the docks one day, and Ferguson offered him a job on the spot, brought him to Savannah, and within just a few years, O'Connor was part owner of Ferguson Shipyard. I guess it didn't hurt that within that first year, he married Ferguson's only daughter."

"That would be the old lady, Kathleen."

"No, Miss Kathleen, as she's known around here, was a journalist for the *Sentinel* at that time, a legend in her own right. She exposed child labor abuses, political scandals, women's rights, you name it. She even took on the Leland Corporation, which had acquired the Ferguson Shipyard by that time. She was something else."

"And Shannon, her granddaughter," Nick said softly, almost to himself, "is simply following in the family tradition."

"Exactly. And it's no secret to anyone who knows Shannon that she admires her grandmother. Miss Kathleen is her mentor, her guiding star. She prides herself in following in her footsteps. Maybe if you and Shannon get a little closer, she'll give you the straight skinny. There's quite a story there," Ed said with a sly smile.

Nick scowled. "When I finally get an audience with Ms. O'Connor, we won't be talking about her family history."

"I hear you, boss." Ed stood up, hiding his smile, and crammed his hands into his pockets. "Meantime, any more family phone calls on this case, I refer them directly to you." Nick's phone rang just then, and he grabbed it with a feeling of relief. He could sit here for the next two days and deny that Shannon O'Connor was just another case history without convincing his partner.

"Dalton," he barked into the receiver.

"Nick, this is Dr. Webster. Shannon O'Connor is fully awake. She can talk to you now."

SHE MADE THEM KEEP the blinds closed. Her excuse was that daylight hurt when she opened her eyes. The truth was that the light bared the full horror of what used to be her face. They had not allowed her to have a mirror even though she'd begged to know the worst. But she knew how she looked. She had the use of her hands and she'd explored her face. Besides, her injuries had been too painful not to have done extensive damage.

Her grandmother appeared at her bedside. "You have a visitor, Shannon."

She moistened her lips slowly, and sipped the ice water Kathleen offered from a cup with a straw. The aftereffects of the tracheotomy were diminishing. She could swallow relatively painlessly now. She could even speak without feeling as though acid was being poured down her throat. The trouble was, she didn't want to speak.

"No," she said, turning her face despondently to the window. She could barely tolerate Kathleen and her mother, and she certainly didn't want to see anybody else.

Or to have anybody see her.

"Yes."

She froze, knowing that voice. Rich and deep, low-pitched and masculine, it was somehow as familiar to her as her grandmother's. She fumbled for the edge of the sheet and pulled it up, forcing it with a soft cry when it caught and she could not cover her face.

She felt her grandmother gently squeeze her hand. "Detective Dalton needs to ask you some questions, darling. It's necessary, you know that."

"Hello, Shannon."

She stared stubbornly at the closed blinds, but she knew it when he reached her bedside. She *felt* it. The pain that was with her constantly was nearly forgotten. "Go away, Nick."

"I know you don't want to deal with this, but you have to," he said, speaking quietly. "I'll go easy, I promise you. Five minutes, I'm out of here."

"I believe you," she said after a moment. She turned then, and drawing a deep breath, looked him straight in the eye. "You probably won't be able to stand the sight of me for any longer."

Watching him for his reaction, she thought with a flicker of black humor that he was probably used to ghoulish sights. She knew he'd been with Alcohol, Tobacco and Firearms, and before that, with the FBI. He'd had a lot of experience at keeping his cool.

"Dr. Webster tells me you'll be as beautiful as ever when you get well," he said, moving closer.

Damn him, he was studying her as dispassionately as though she was a bug in a glass jar. "See anything interesting?" she demanded.

"Yeah." His gave her a slow half smile, and with his finger, touched a spot just to the left of her mouth. "Did you have this dimple before?"

To her consternation, her eyes filled with sudden tears.

"Ah, Shannon…" With his thumb, he wiped the moisture that streaked down her cheek. "You've been through hell, haven't you?"

Kathleen O'Connor spoke up. "It's all right, Detective Dalton. She's a little weepy sometimes. The medication, you know. And the trauma. She's perfectly aware that she must answer your questions. After all, we want to put this whole thing behind us, and we can't until we have the fiend who did this behind bars.

"Yes, ma'am."

"I can fight my own battles, Gran," Shannon said with a sniff. She looked at Nick. "So, let's get on with it."

He studied her a long moment, then took a small notebook from his shirt pocket. "Right. As a journalist, you've interviewed enough witnesses to crimes to know that every detail is important. I want you to tell me exactly what happened, what you saw, what you sensed or felt from the moment you got out of your car that night and walked up the steps to your front door."

"In that case, this really will be quick," Shannon said. She took a deep breath, wincing with the pain in her windpipe, then, looking directly at Nick, she said, "Nothing."

"What?"

"Nothing," she repeated. "I don't remember a thing."

For a few seconds, Nick was silent. He glanced at the old lady and found her watching Shannon intently. Outside in the halls, routine hospital sounds could be heard. A phone rang somewhere. A burst of applause came from a TV blasting in another patient's room. Nick drew in a deep breath. "Come on, Shannon."

"It's true," she said, and her eyes filled with tears again. It was a bizarre sight. One eye was almost swollen shut. The other was nearly obscured by the bandage from her broken left jaw. She was lucky, though. Nick remembered Dr. Webster saying only the lower jaw was broken, consequently he wouldn't have to resort to wiring and immobilizing her for six weeks while she healed. Lucky, yeah.

"I've been trying to remember," she said hoarsely. "It's no use. No matter how hard I try, nothing's there. I don't even remember getting out of my car to go into my house."

"What was the purpose of your trip to Atlanta?" Nick asked.

"I don't remember going to Atlanta."

"Don't try to con me, Shannon," he said, losing patience. "You won't be out of the hospital for weeks yet. You can't just sit on this until you're able to resume your job. You're going to have to sacrifice this chance to pull off another journalistic coup. There will be others."

"That's not what I'm doing, Nick. I'm telling you, I don't remember anything."

"Shannon, somebody tried to kill you!"

She shrank from him then, folding into herself as completely as though she'd walked into another room. Her grandmother gave him a chastising look before bending over Shannon and wrapping her arms around her granddaughter.

"I think you'd better go now, Detective Dalton," she said. "I believe Shannon has had all she can take for the moment."

"Yeah." Nick sighed and tucked his notebook back into his pocket. In her grandmother's arms, Shannon looked small and vulnerable and lost. Even her fiery auburn hair seemed less vibrant. Her hand, resting on her grandmother's sleeve, was bruised, the nails torn where she'd fought her attacker. If Nick was any judge, from the looks of Shannon's apartment and the forensic evidence collected on the scene, she had not succumbed easily to the man who assaulted her. It had taken a lot of courage to put up that kind of resistance. She was a real survivor.

At the door, he stopped and turned back, studying her gravely. Faking amnesia wasn't something he expected from a woman like Shannon. So, if her amnesia was genuine, where did they go from here?

IN A WAITING LOUNGE on the third floor, a man sat with his face buried in a newspaper, pretending to be part of a family awaiting word about a loved one who had had a severe accident. Instead of reading the paper, his attention was on the room midway down the hall where Shannon O'Connor had been transferred out of ICU. By keeping his ears open, he had learned that she was going to survive.

What a rotten screwup.

The bitch had the luck of the Irish. Literally. Six days and he still felt like killing somebody when he thought about it. A practical man, he accepted the blame, but it was difficult not to kick the hell out of that nosy woman whose appearance had cheated him out of the two minutes it would have taken to finish the job. He hadn't forgotten the rush that came over him as his fingers had tightened around Shannon's interfering little neck. She was as good as dead, he'd felt it. But then that dumb-ass neighbor had knocked.

He ducked behind his paper as Nick Dalton came out of the room. That was another headache he had to contend with. He knew Dalton's reputation, and the cop was no pushover. What he couldn't figure was all the attention she was getting from Dalton. No problem, though. Dalton wouldn't be able to piece anything together right away, not with her amnesia. Crossing his legs, he settled back again. He would simply have to make certain she was shut up permanently before she remembered anything. He smiled behind the newspaper.

Your days are numbered, you nosy bitch.

CHAPTER THREE

SHANNON WAS IN a courthouse. Two lawyers were arguing heatedly. She couldn't tell what they were saying, but whatever it was, it made her anxious. There was no jury, and no others were seated in the courtroom. Just her. She looked at the woman in the witness box and felt deep sympathy. The woman was weeping. Shannon sensed her pain. As the lawyers hassled between themselves, Shannon got up from her seat and went toward the woman in the witness box. But just as she reached for the small gate that would bring her close enough to touch the woman, the judge roared at her and brought his gavel down with a mighty crash. Shannon dropped her hand from the gate, and with a startled cry she turned and ran.

She tried to wake up before the dream pushed her over the edge, but it was like fighting her way through a thick fog. Her heart was racing as though she'd actually been running when she finally opened her eyes. The echo of her own cry lingered in her mind. But only in her mind, she realized with relief, closing her eyes again and drawing in deep gulps of air. This time, thankfully, the nightmare was private, since for once her room was empty. She hated the moments when she was dragged from sleep to find someone at her bedside watching her with concern. The questions would begin then and she would have to admit yet again that she didn't remember.

Just to prove that she was still sane, she recited the facts she did know. Her name was Shannon O'Connor. She was twenty-seven and unmarried. She lived in Savannah, Georgia. She had a degree in journalism from Duke University. Her mother, Michelle, was an artist living and working in Paris for a year. Her father, Cameron, was dead. She had two brothers, Will and Ryan. She was a reporter with the Savannah *Sentinel* and she was good at her job. Damn good. The story she was working on was—

Nothing. She moaned in frustration. Her memory always ended there. It was like taking a drive down a familiar road, then turning a corner expecting more trees and grass and sky and instead finding a stone wall.

Why? Why couldn't she remember? She'd asked herself that question a thousand times. A person didn't just blank out a whole period of time and then pick up and carry on as though nothing more important than a pair of socks was missing. This was a chunk of her life, a vital link to something, and someone believed it was significant enough to kill her over it. That explained the frantic beat of her heart and the cold sweat that seeped through her nightgown when she reached the point where her memory stopped.

She shuddered and wished for pain medication. That magic potion that lifted her out of herself and transported her to a place where nothing mattered. But her battered body was healing, the pain diminishing, so there would be no more magic potions. No more escape.

A soft knock drew her eyes to the doorway. Her grandmother entered, smiling. "Hello, darling."

Shannon's heartbeat quickened. With Kathleen O'Connor was Nick Dalton. He was tall and broad shouldered, with an uncompromising jaw and straight, dark eyebrows over gray-green eyes. He was studying her face intently as he nodded and greeted her in his deep, dark voice.

The room suddenly felt crowded. Nothing to do with her grandmother's presence, she realized, or the profusion of paraphernalia that had sustained her life for more than two weeks now. It was Nick Dalton. Looking at his firm mouth with its full bottom lip, she was suddenly aware of his latent sensuality, when she should have been thinking only of him as the straight-edged, focused cop she knew.

Nick kept his distance while Kathleen O'Connor moved to the bed. Her eyes were bright with tears as she touched Shannon's hair. "It's so good to see you awake and alert, sweetheart," she said softly. "How are you this morning?"

"I'm fine, Gran." Even to herself, her voice sounded gravelly, unfeminine. But having the voice of a frog was a minor flaw when compared to her other injuries. She should be grateful. Hadn't they told her that a hundred times? "When can I get out of here?"

It was Nick who answered. "Your granddaughter is as headstrong as ever, Miss Kathleen."

Miss Kathleen? He made it sound as though he and her grandmother were old friends. She searched her murky memory of the past few days. Mixed with other vague impressions of that time was the clear recollection of Nick Dalton. Funny how that stood out in her mind when all else was shrouded in a mist of pain and lurking terror. He'd questioned her once before when she'd first recovered consciousness, and she recalled he'd been skeptical about her memory loss.

She gave him a dark look. "How is it headstrong to want out of a hospital?"

"It isn't if you're well." He started forward, stopping at the foot of the bed. "You haven't been strong enough to walk unassisted to the bathroom, yet you want to walk out of here?"

"He's right, darling." Kathleen gently stroked the back of Shannon's hand. "You have to be patient and let the healing process begin. You were so badly hurt, Shannon. When I think—"

"Don't think about it, Gran," Shannon told her quickly, squeezing the fragile bones of her grandmother's hand. She glanced at Nick and her tone firmed. "I don't."

Nick left the foot of her bed and closed in on her. Shannon watched him warily. She thought briefly about sending him away as she had the last couple of times he'd been here. She'd been able to get away with it because she was still partly disoriented from medication and pain. But Nick was a tough, single-minded cop who usually got what he wanted. She sighed. Sooner or later, she was going to have to deal with what had happened. And it looked as if Nick was going to be the instrument of her torture.

"I think I'll just run into the visitors' lounge and brew myself a cup of tea," Kathleen announced brightly, and Shannon knew that if her grandmother was abandoning her, the moment had arrived. "Bye for now, dear. I won't be long." She glanced at Nick. "You'll join me when you and Shannon have talked, Nick? It's Earl Grey."

"In a minute, thanks," Nick said, smiling. As Shannon looked, she blinked at the charm revealed in his smile. If he'd been spreading that around in the hospital, it was no wonder her grandmother was eager to offer him tea.

"Earl Grey?" Shannon repeated after Kathleen left.

He shrugged. "I like it."

"And here I had you pegged as a coffee or nothing type. If I recall, that stuff you folks keep on hand at the station is black, chicory-flavored sludge. I assumed you were all addicted."

"Yeah, well, after sixteen hours on a hotplate, that stuff *is* sludge. Fresh-brewed anything is a treat."

Shannon studied his face. The man was was not exactly movie-star handsome, but she bet he didn't have any trouble getting dates. She realized that even though she'd known him longer than a year, she knew nothing about him except his career moves. She was suddenly very curious about Nick. The reporter in her must not be completely subdued. Or was it the woman in her?

"Beautiful day outside," he said, nodding at the window where Gran had opened the blinds to let the sunshine in.

She withdrew her gaze from him to look outside. "Yes. Can you blame me for wanting out of here?"

"You wouldn't be afraid?"

And like a dash of icy water, reality returned. "I've been assured I'm safe with one of your men stationed at my door around the clock. Should I be afraid?"

"No, not at all. We've taken all necessary precautions to keep you safe," Nick said.

"Thank you."

Moving to the window, Nick stared at the activity below for a few moments before turning back to look at her. "Got anything to tell me?"

"No."

"Not even a glimmer?"

"*No!*"

He took a deep breath. "I'm on your side, Shannon, just in case that's something you've forgotten, too."

For a few seconds, they simply stared at each other. She was suddenly conscious of the way she looked. There was no getting around it, she admitted inwardly; there had always been something about Nick Dalton that made her conscious of herself as a woman. Even when they had been sniping and biting at each other, there had been something there. Feeling naked and exposed, she wished that her face wasn't battered and sporting all the colors of the rainbow, and that she didn't have these obscene tubes and bandages everywhere.

In the course of their relationship, they must have disagreed over a thousand and one things. But that was when she had had the option of one last potshot and a quick escape. Now, trapped in her bed, she simply had to ride it out when he showed up, notebook in hand, pen poised to hear an eyewitness account of the moment of her near-death.

If only she could remember it.

She took a breath, knowing the time had come to say what she'd been rehearsing for two days. "I haven't been able to remember what happened that night, Nick, but I do know that I wouldn't be here today if it hadn't been you who answered the 911 call. You saved my life. I—"

"I did my job," he said quickly, heading her off. "I'm a cop. Serve and protect, that's what cops do."

She looked at him. "My heart stopped and I couldn't breathe."

"Shannon—"

"I would have died—I did die."

"No."

"Yes. I saw you when you performed the tracheotomy." He made a low, abrupt sound and she glanced up to find him rigidly still, but his features were hazy to her as she thought back to that night. "I watched from somewhere above it all. When the paramedics worked over me, it seemed remote, somehow. Nothing they did made a difference."

"They pulled out all the stops," he said, defending them. "I don't know what you've been told, but they worked like hell to save your life. One of them was on the phone to the hospital trauma surgeon the whole time. He relayed everything as though your life depended on it. I—"

"My life didn't depend on that," she said, with quiet certainty. "It depended on you."

He swung away, ramming both hands deep into his pockets. Shannon watched his big shoulders move as though he wanted to shrug off her words. "I could hear you," she said softly, squinting as she recalled the scene. "You kept calling to me, swearing, demanding. You—"

"Shannon—"

"Held my hand and begged me not to die."

"They made me turn you loose to use that…those…" He swallowed, still shaken by the memory.

"The defibrillator, the electric shock."

"Yeah."

"But you were right back when they stopped."

"We didn't think it worked."

"It didn't. You reached for my hand and I thought a long time before deciding to take it."

"*Christ!* Shannon, I don't think—"

"Those paramedics didn't save my life, Detective Dalton. You did."

Watching him, Shannon realized he was completely at a loss. It threw her off. The Nick Dalton she knew was seldom emotional, but that was the only word to describe him now.

"I just wanted to say thank you," she told him.

"I don't want your gratitude."

"You have it, anyway. But relax, if it makes you that uncomfortable, I won't mention it again."

"Good," he growled, prowling restlessly around the room. Taking a seat, he pulled his notebook from his pocket.

She groaned. "I take it you're here to grill me some more?"

He didn't exactly smile, but for a moment his features weren't quite as relentlessly grim. "I promise to be gentle. No chains or rubber hoses."

"It doesn't matter. I can't tell you what I don't know."

"Then tell me what you do know."

"Why doesn't anyone believe me!" Shannon exclaimed, turning her face from him. "I'm not lying about this. I don't remember—can't you accept that? I don't remember!"

AFTER A STOP at the nurses' station to check whether anything new might have been added about Shannon's condition, Nick made his way down the hall toward the visitors' lounge. He knew the whole O'Connor clan was waiting and he dreaded it. What was he going to tell them? That he didn't have a clue as to who did this? That not a trace of evidence had been lifted from the scene? That he and Ed were as baffled now as they'd been since it happened?

Hearing voices inside the lounge, he guessed wearily that

he was going to pay dearly for that cup of Earl Grey. Hesitating only a second, he entered.

The whole O'Connor family was waiting, and, as one, they all looked at him. Except for Kathleen, there was not another friendly face in the room. Will O'Connor, the eldest, who managed the family's shipping interests, looked the fiercest. He was tall and lean and as tough and uncompromising as everyone else he'd met whose name was O'Connor. He was not going to be pleased to hear the department's investigation into his sister's assault had turned up exactly nothing.

"We want some answers, Dalton," Will said, going directly to the point. Low-pitched his voice might be; friendly it wasn't. "It's been two weeks since my sister was nearly beaten to death. You're supposed to be the best, according to the mayor and Chief Harding. I don't think we're being unreasonable to expect some results."

"There's been little change from the last time we talked, Mr. O'Connor," Nick said coolly. "As I told you then, we're following up every lead, no matter how insignificant. We've interviewed dozens of people in Shannon's neighborhood and at the *Sentinel.* We've spoken to her friends, we've contacted everybody in her address book, we've questioned people at the grocery store where she shops, at her bank, her beauty shop, her church, the health club where she works out. You name it, we've been there."

"And you haven't turned up anything?" Will's reluctance to accept what he was hearing made his features more harsh than usual.

"Very little."

"Then you've found something?"

"Only that Shannon is neat, pays her bills on time, arrives at appointments a little late. She has dozens of friends, male and female. She dates, but no one who could be considered special." He gave Miss Kathleen a quick, apologetic look. "She has no lover, or at least we've been unable to find one.

She has her finger on the pulse of this town, and, as a journalist, she is surpassed by no one. At least, no one at the *Sentinel*. Questions about the material on her computer for future articles revealed nothing unusual.''

"Detective Dalton, how can this be?" Michelle O'Connor asked in her husky, French-accented voice. Shannon's mother had dark hair worn in a sleek chignon and near-violet eyes. Nick had it from Ed that Shannon's father, Cameron, had met and married the talented artist while reporting the war in Vietnam. "How can something so... so...savage occur and the perpetrator simply vanish?" she asked in distress.

"We're trying to figure that one out ourselves, Mrs. O'Connor," Nick said, hating to admit it.

Will swore impatiently. "This is a hell of a note, Dalton! You've got to do something. As long as that son of a bitch is still running around loose, my sister's life is in danger."

"Don't you think I know that?" With his eyes on his notebook, Nick flipped the pages one after another. "I've got dozens of interviews here and every one is a dead end." With a frustrated sigh, he crammed the thing in his shirt pocket. "Shannon's amnesia is a major problem. It's difficult to focus when she can't recall any details about what she was working on. We're all over the board trying to piece together what might have been going on in her life."

"I don't buy it," Will snapped. "If that son of a bitch had killed her outright, you wouldn't have her memory to rely on."

"Now, Will..." Nudging Nick gently, Kathleen O'Connor offered tea in a plastic cup. "This has been terrifying for us. We're all worried and anxious to find the person who did this to Shannon. However, Detective Dalton is right. With nothing to go on, the police can only do so much. Without her to guide us, we have nowhere to start. I'm hoping her amnesia is temporary." She paused, looking thoughtful. "Assuming, of course, that it's genuine in the first place."

In the act of swallowing tea, Nick studied her with interest. "Is there some reason you think she's pretending?"

Kathleen set her cup down carefully. "I don't think she's pretending, at least, not consciously. But it wouldn't be surprising for a young woman who's been subjected to such senseless brutality to need to protect herself from the trauma that recollection might bring while her emotions heal along with her body."

"You're suggesting hysterical amnesia," Nick said, his tea forgotten.

"Shannon wouldn't do that!" Will said emphatically. "She's too up-front, too honest."

"She's human, too," Nick said, but it was an absent reply. Hysterical amnesia? It was an interesting possibility, especially coming from Kathleen. Shannon's grandmother probably knew her as well as—even better than—anyone else in the room. Her mother had been away for a year. Something about Michelle O'Connor suggested to Nick that her work as an artist took precedence over her maternal role. It was definitely Kathleen who was Shannon's idol, according to Ed. She had the same talent for journalism as her grandmother, and they shared personality traits. Shannon even looked like her grandmother, same green eyes, ivory skin, exquisite bone structure. In the days Nick had come to know Kathleen O'Connor in the hospital, he had sensed other, deeper similarities. Things he couldn't quite put his finger on. But they existed.

Crushing his cup, Nick tossed it into a lined trash can and centered his attention on Kathleen O'Connor. "If what you say is true, Miss Kathleen, it's a complication I wouldn't wish for. I was hoping her memory would return sooner rather than later. Basically, what you're saying is that she's using her amnesia to hide from the truth."

"Not purposely," Kathleen said, quickly coming to Shannon's defense.

"Not purposely," he agreed. "But the result is the same.

We may have a long wait ahead of us. We'll just continue the investigation without Shannon's direct input.'' His gaze connected briefly with all three. ''I don't have to remind you that as long as she's in the dark about what happened, the danger to her is multiplied.''

''Without Shannon around to accuse him, whoever tried to kill her is sitting pretty,'' Will said, instantly following Nick's logic.

''Which brings up another subject,'' Kathleen said. ''We want Shannon to convalesce at home as soon as her doctors feel she can be released, Nick.'' Spotting the hesitation in his expression, she hastened to explain. ''Your department has done a wonderful job protecting her here at the hospital, but surely you agree that maintaining security at Wilderose House will be far less complicated.''

She gave him a smile that she had perfected after fifty years of matriarchal status in a powerful family. Wisely, Nick said nothing. Besides, Shannon's security was something he and Ed had already discussed. He had expected them to send her to a small private clinic somewhere close by, but Wilderose House was probably better. Protecting her behind the iron fencing at the O'Connor estate shouldn't present too many problems if they were willing to be guided by his suggestions.

''We need your advice about security at the house, Nick. What do you think? Should we hire someone?''

''You're not suggesting that SPD is out of this, are you?'' he asked.

''Certainly not.''

''Good, because we're working this case. There's manpower assigned, but—'' he assumed an apologetic look ''—we don't have the resources to assign round-the-clock surveillance. Since you've mentioned private security types, there are a couple of people I can recommend. I'll pass their names on.'' Again, his look included all three O'Connors. ''Actually, the best way to keep Shannon safe is to hire a bodyguard.

Preferably a woman—someone who could go undercover. A woman could spend all her time with Shannon.''

Kathleen looked interested. ''That sounds reasonable,'' she said after exchanging a look with Shannon's mother and Will. ''Is there someone you'd like to recommend for the job?''

''Matter of fact, yes. There's a former Savannah policewoman who will do a good job for you on this. She's a private investigator—the best, in my opinion. She was once on the force at SPD, which means she's a fully trained law enforcement officer. Since Shannon's life would be in her hands, I don't think you'd want to settle for anything less.'' He stopped, waiting for their verdict.

Will nodded in agreement. ''Sounds good to me.''

''And to me,'' Kathleen said, receiving a nod when she arched an elegant eyebrow at Michelle.

Nick set his cup and saucer carefully on a small table. ''Cheryl's bright and tough and very good at what she does. Playing private nurse and companion will be a piece of cake for her.''

''Cheryl?'' Will said sharply. ''Are we talking about Cheryl Carpenter?''

''Do you know her?'' Nick asked, picking up something in his tone.

''I know her.''

Studying his closed expression, Nick decided not to ask questions. After a gently inquiring look at her grandson, Kathleen addressed Nick. ''As soon as Dr. Webster says Shannon is out of danger, we'll bring her home. You'll want to know the details, of course. And you might even want to accompany her yourself.'' She gave him an expectant look, to which he nodded. ''Fine. Then it's settled. If she continues to respond as well as she has been, we'll have her out of here within a week. Can you have Ms. Carpenter ready to go?''

''She'll be ready.''

CHERYL CARPENTER DID NOT appreciate Nick's glowing referral. "Isn't there somebody in the department who can do this?" she asked Nick.

"Former law enforcement officers who just happen to be female and qualified for this job aren't exactly growing on trees around here, Cheryl," he said, tossing his pencil on top of her open file. "Especially *women*."

Her reluctance puzzled him. He had her file, pulled from inactive records, in front of him. There were several citations for bravery, consistently superior efficiency ratings, and she was quick, intelligent, hard-working. In short, perfect for the job.

"Do you know Shannon O'Connor?" he asked.

She sat down on the edge of the chair. "Only slightly. Everybody in Savannah 'knows' Shannon. Her byline is in the paper nearly every day, and besides that, she's the darling of one of the most prestigious families in Georgia. You could probably get half a dozen people who would jump at the opportunity to work for the O'Connors."

"But not you."

She met his eyes. "Not me." When Nick appeared unmoved, she looked imploringly at Ed, who sat in the only other chair in Nick's office. Ed hadn't said anything so far, which struck Nick as odd since he had agreed readily that Cheryl was the best person to guard Shannon. The job called for a woman. She would need to spend practically every waking minute with Shannon, eating with her, sleeping close by, running errands with her.

Her excellent record aside, Cheryl Carpenter would fit well in Shannon's world. She was slim as a model, with long, shapely legs. In her simple straight black skirt and white blouse, she looked trim and neat and classy. More significantly—according to her file and her former fellow officers—she was extremely proficient in the art of self-defense.

"Am I right, Ed?" Cheryl asked. "There have to be PIs up

the kazoo who'd jump at a chance to hobnob with the O'Connors.''

"True," Ed said in his slow drawl. "The problem is that Nick wants the best for Shannon, and you're the best, Cher.''

Cheryl looked suddenly at Nick. "Has this been cleared with Shannon's family?''

Nick nodded. "Yes, and they agreed to go along with it.''

"You told them my name?''

"Yes, Cheryl, I told them your name.''

"You told Will O'Connor it was me you were considering for this assignment?''

Suddenly recalling Will's reaction when he first mentioned Cheryl, Nick looked first at Ed, then back at her. "What's up here? What's going on that I need to know?''

He got an impassive look from Ed. No help there. Cheryl got up from her chair and went to the window. "Will O'Connor hates me. I don't believe he would welcome me to put out the garbage for the O'Connors, let alone place the life of his sister in my hands.''

"I told you he did just that," Nick said, exasperated and suddenly out of patience. "So give it to me straight. What's with you and Will O'Connor?''

"He thinks I killed my husband," Cheryl said.

Nick tossed his pen on his desktop and leaned back in his chair. "He thinks you killed your husband. What the hell are you talking about?''

"It's true.''

"Well, did you?" he asked, letting a little sarcasm into his tone.

"Boss..." Ed rolled his eyes.

Nick didn't know anything about Cheryl Carpenter's personal life except that she was a single woman. That was usually the case for women in her line of work. Not many husbands sat idly by while their wives chose a career that put their lives in jeopardy on a regular basis.

"Help me out here, you two." Nick closed the file with a snap. "Unlike both of you, I haven't lived in Savannah all my life. I didn't know Cheryl's husband. If there's a solid reason why that has any relevance to this assignment, I expect to hear it." He drilled them both with a look. "Now."

With her hands clasped low behind her back, Cheryl said, "I was married to Andy Welles...Andrew Welles. He was chief engineer at the shipyard Will manages. He and Will were cousins...and blood is thicker than water, as they say. They were very close. When we separated, Will came to see me because Andrew asked him to. He wanted me to reconsider." Her smile twisted with bitterness. "Actually, he demanded that I reconsider, because the way he saw it, there couldn't possibly be any good reason for me to divorce Andrew. I refused."

"And..."

"And that night, Andrew ran into a bridge abutment at about ninety miles an hour."

Nick swore softly.

"Will called it suicide. I'm sure he thinks I drove Andy to it. As cousins and co-workers, they were close. Andy confided in Will, who naturally heard only one side of the story. Our marriage was over and Andy knew it. But apparently his friends thought otherwise, including Will. Incidentally, Will was the first on the scene that night. I don't know what Andy said to him before he died, but Will has hated me ever since."

Leaning back again, Nick surveyed her thoughtfully. He made it a point not to get involved in the personal lives of his people. But he sensed more to the story than Cheryl had volunteered. Whether it concerned Will himself, or something bad about her marriage, her husband's suicide had happened a long time ago. Cheryl was still the best woman for the job. "If you feel you can't handle this assignment for personal reasons," he told her, "say so and I'll look around for somebody else. The decision is yours, Cheryl."

Put in those words, her professionalism was on the line, and everyone in the room knew it. The people she'd worked with on the police force were valuable contacts. She couldn't jeopardize that, not if she wanted to continue getting referrals. Nick had her over a barrel on this one. With a sigh, she nodded. "When do I start?" she asked dryly.

Nick smiled. He didn't smile often, but when he did, it was a killer. For a second or two, Cheryl felt the full benefit of it.

It was rumored that Nick had a special feeling for Shannon O'Connor. As Cheryl left his office, she reflected to herself ruefully that playing nurse-companion to Shannon might have its moments. It would be interesting to watch whatever was developing between the toughest cop on the force and the reporter who used to drive him crazy.

Interesting, that is, if she could avoid Will O'Connor.

CHAPTER FOUR

April 12—Mercy Hospital

SHANNON O'CONNOR DIED. *The person they resuscitated and sent to the hospital to be patched up and coddled back to health is not me. I'm different. I'm not sure about all the changes, but I am sure about this: I'm not the person I was before I was assaulted. I'm less. I'm damaged.*

The fear is the worst thing. Every day, I live with terror hovering just at the edge of my consciousness. The least thing sets it off—a sudden noise, a footstep outside my hospital room, the instant before someone speaks when I pick up a ringing telephone. Added to that, I'm teased by momentary flashes of...something. And I'm tortured by one recurring nightmare. Not a dream, a nightmare. I don't remember and I don't want to remember. And yet, I don't know how long I can hold everything at bay. Which, of course, is the worst fear of all: that I might remember.

Damn you! Whoever you are, I hate you. I hate what you did to me. And what you took from me. I hate the pain and suffering you brought me and my family. I hope you rot in hell!!!

"YOU HAVE A VISITOR, dear." Kathleen O'Connor took the hairbrush from Shannon, who went suddenly still except for the flutter of her pulse. She knew it was Nick. She heard his deep, low voice as he spoke to someone in the hall. Jacoby probably, or Miller. Whoever was on duty as her bodyguard.

And another feminine voice—a nurse—laughing flirtatiously. Was every female susceptible to his unique brand of charm?

She slipped out of bed instantly. Even though she couldn't walk far because of her IV, she still wanted to be on her feet to see Nick Dalton. Besides, the room seemed even smaller lately, and she couldn't stand lying in bed with time creeping by at an agonizingly slow pace. But neither could she bring herself to leave the sanctuary of her room to walk in the corridor.

She looked hastily into the mirror, checking her appearance. The peignoir she wore had been a gift from *Maman* to cheer her up. Lavish with yards of peach silk and ecru lace, it was designed to make a woman feel beautiful. Unfortunately, she was still hopelessly ugly.

With a moan, she leaned close and examined her face. Although the swelling was reduced, it was still puffy and distorted. The discoloration was hideous, especially the skin over her broken jaw and beneath her right eye. With the fingers of her right hand, she fluffed her hair forward so that it fell in a deep curve over her right cheek. The IV was still in her left hand. Fumbling through the items on her side table, she located large sunglasses and quickly put them on. Only then did she turn and face Nick.

They looked at each other in silence as her grandmother slipped out behind him. He didn't close the door. Instead, he propped his hand on the edge, holding it open. "Hi," he said, after running a quick look from the top of her head to the tip of her toes.

"Hi."

His features gentled with the hint of a smile. "I leave you alone for two days and you're practically out of here."

"I wish." Shannon went to the bed and sat down, folding her hands tightly together in her lap. "The truth is, I'm going stir-crazy penned up in this room tethered to this IV pole."

She gave the contraption a baleful look. "But I can't seem to get up enough courage to venture into the hall. Stupid, huh?"

"Not stupid. Just a natural reaction from someone who's been through a lot. You'll get beyond it."

Would she? The way she felt now, Shannon doubted she would ever be the carelessly confident, independent person she had been before that night.

Nick pushed the door to and moved into the room. "You met with Cheryl Carpenter today. What did you think?"

"She's a nice person. I've always liked her." Her gaze went to the window as she thought back. "She was married to my cousin Andy, you know, but that was when I was away at college. I never knew her very well. She seems a very private person, don't you think so?"

"I don't think about the personal lives of the people I work with at all," Nick said, settling back with his notebook in his hand. "I only asked to be certain that you felt comfortable with Cheryl. You're going to be spending a lot of time with her."

"I'm sure we'll get along just fine."

"Good." He flipped a couple of pages in his notebook. "So, if we've got that behind us, how about answering a few questions?"

Shannon rose abruptly from the bed and turned her back to Nick. "I told you I can't give you any answers, Nick. Nothing's changed. My memory is just as blank as it was when I first woke up."

"I know, but bear with me for just a minute." Nick spoke calmly, as though she was a fractious child who needed to be pacified. "There may be another way to get what we need to know. We can talk about what you've been working on currently. Maybe something will trip your memory."

"I've already tried that with Ernie. He—"

"Ernie Patton? Your editor?"

"Yes. He came by this morning with a printout of projects

on my computer at work, and the result was nothing. *Nada.* Zip.''

''Indulge me, anyway.''

Her attempt to shrug ended with a wince, but she settled back, looking resigned.

''What can you tell me about the exposé you did on teenage prostitution?''

She felt a headache coming on. It was a dull, heavy feeling now, but it could blossom into a real killer with incredible speed. Just as it had earlier when Ernie Patton had been here. Talking about her job was stressful. No, it was more than stressful. It was another of those areas in her life that sent terror coursing through her. Why she felt threatened by talk of her job, she wasn't certain, other than the obvious. Someone had tried to kill her because of something she was working on in her job. Supposedly.

''Shannon?''

''Hmm?''

''The prostitution thing.''

''Everything I had went into the story,'' Shannon said. ''At least, I assume so. You read it.''

''Everything except your source.''

She nodded carefully. ''Everything except my source.''

''Who was—'' Nick looked at her questioningly.

She closed her eyes wearily. He knew she could not reveal a source.

''Okay. Let's back up. Since you were assaulted the same day the story hit the paper, it makes sense that somebody you might have ticked off felt mad enough and mean enough to silence you forever. Do you have any idea who that could be?''

''No.''

''Were you aware that I had a months-long undercover investigation going that was blown sky-high when you let the cat out of the bag?''

"No." She laughed weakly. "Maybe it was one of *your* guys." Her smile died as she looked into his eyes. Clearly he didn't consider her remark funny.

"How did you stumble on the story in the first place?"

"Would you believe purely by accident. Through another story I was doing involving teens."

"Teen gangs?"

"Uh-huh."

"What about those gangs? Did you talk to anyone in particular? One of their warlords?" He used the term as though referring to smelly garbage.

"Yes, but he wasn't the link to teen prostitution. And don't ask me to reveal a name. If I did, my source would be targeted for something a lot worse than what happened to me."

"There is only one thing worse than what happened to you, Shannon."

"I know, and I don't want to be responsible for it happening to a sixteen-year-old."

"Sixteen-year-old male or female?"

She gave him another impassive look.

His breath came out in an explosive sigh. "Okay, but do you get anything, any...feeling when you think of him? Or her?"

"No, Nick, I don't."

After a short, silent survey of her face, he looked again at his notes. "Offshore riverboat gambling. You don't shy away from the big ones, do you?"

"I don't think the people who are interested in riverboat gambling feel it necessary to kill me to accomplish their goal," she said dryly. "Eventually greed will bring gambling to the state."

"Humph." Nick flipped another page. "A suicide in the Victorian District."

"I don't remem—"

"I looked it up. Marion Chaney, reclusive, rich, divorced,

in and out of substance abuse clinics for years. Did the job with a bottle of pills. No surprise there.'' Nick looked up at Shannon. ''Ring any bells?''

''No.''

''Why would you have thought Marion Chaney interesting enough to do a story on her?''

''What kind of question is that!'' Shannon demanded. ''Maybe I felt sympathetic about a woman desperate enough to commit suicide. Maybe I thought it odd that a woman with money, possessions, status…that's a lot to live for. Besides, I don't remember doing a story on her.''

''You think it was a human interest thing?''

''Could be. Probably was.'' She shrugged, shaking her head. ''I just don't know.''

''Okay.'' He flipped another page. ''You had a few notes on the woman who's heading up the new shelter for battered women. Georgina Frazier.''

''Gina is fabulous. I remember doing some preliminary stuff, but I hadn't even thought out the direction of the piece.''

''At least you remember something.''

''That's it, though. Not much, huh?''

''I talked to her. She couldn't come up with anything either. Incidentally, she sends her love.''

''Thanks.''

''Last, but not least, confiscated drug money and possible legal uses for it.''

''Drug rehab and more cops on the street,'' she quipped.

''Does the subject ring a bell?'' Nick demanded evenly.

She rubbed her forehead, looking away. ''No.''

Nick drew a deep breath, watching her sit back down on the bed. ''That's it…unless…'' He paged backward in his notebook. ''Was there anything not listed on your computer, any story you were working on that, for reasons only you know, you were keeping close to your chest?''

''No, Nick. At least, nothing I can recall.'' Something—a

thought, a feeling—flickered and was just as quickly gone. She rubbed the center of her forehead where the dull ache threatened to blossom into something worse. These brief flashes that came and went with no rhyme nor reason had to mean something. She didn't know what. But they were significant. They were always accompanied by a stab of fierce pain as though her mind was trying to goad her into seeing...seeing what? And then the momentary half memory faded into nothing. She leaned back against the pillows, seeking relief.

"What is it?"

"Nothing." Her gaze wandered to the large window. Outside, it was night, and the windowpane made a dark mirror, clearly reflecting her image in the bed. And beside her, looming tall and solid and protective, was Nick.

And, as she stared, something else.

The ache behind her eyes suddenly became blinding pain, and instantly a scene materialized. It was as sharp and clear as though the window was a movie screen. She saw a courtroom, a judge, clad in a voluminous black robe, and two contentious lawyers. While they wrangled back and forth, the judge studied papers in front of him. In the witness box, ignored by all, a woman wept tragically. Then, just as abruptly, it was gone.

With her face turned from him, Nick did not realize her distress until she suddenly buried her face in her hands. His move toward her was involuntary, as reflexive as when he'd saved her life on the floor of her apartment. He fumbled for the remote control to call a nurse. He finally found it, and with a muttered oath, pushed the button.

"I'm okay," she whispered in response to the nurse's inquiry over the intercom. Beside her, Nick made a protest, but her look silenced him. "It'll pass. It always does."

Looking anything but convinced, Nick let her have her way, but he held on to her hand and gently rubbed his thumb across her bruised knuckles. "What happened? You went white as a sheet, Shannon."

She was shaking her head. "It's nothing. Just these… flashes."

"Flashes of memory?" His tone was sharp.

"No! I told you I don't have any memory of that night."

"Then what?"

She breathed in deeply. "Just…pain, Nick. My head hurts and it…it scares me." She wasn't ready to reveal to anyone that she was having hallucinations. Maybe it was the drugs. She'd had a ton of them. Maybe—

"Does it happen often?" he asked, studying her intently. He breathed easier now that a trace of color was back in her cheeks. Still holding her hand, he sat down.

"No. Yes…" She laughed weakly. "Well…enough to keep me humble." It wasn't drugs, she thought hysterically. It was the dream. The recurring courtroom dream. But how? Why? She wasn't asleep. For some bizarre reason, the dream had materialized in the window, in full color, as sharp as a movie. Was it related to something she and Nick had been discussing?

She lay with her eyes closed, struggling not to reveal her agitated thoughts, until she became aware of Nick's gaze fixed on her. "I'm all right, Nick. Really."

"Webster says it probably won't help much to try to force your memory back, and he's the expert. I was out of line trying to push you. I'm sorry."

Shannon waved away his apology. "You were only doing your job."

"What about yours?" he asked, studying the fading discoloration on her cheekbone.

"My job?" She gave a tiny movement of one shoulder. "Funny you should ask. I've been thinking about that. Ernie and I talked about it today. I'm thinking about giving it up altogether."

Nick snorted in disbelief. "You mean resigning?"

Turning her head, she looked at him. "Yes."

He released her hand. "Tell me another one."

"I'm serious."

She held his gaze until he stood up, pushing his chair back with an impatient scrape. "I don't believe you, Shannon. Forget about chasing this story on your own, whatever it is. It's crazy, it's dangerous. And pursuing it after what happened is the most harebrained idea you've ever had. How long do you think it would take this guy to corner you again? And next time, your neighbor just might not conveniently knock on your door."

"I'm not planning to chase any story," she told him quietly. "I told you that before and I meant it. Besides, have you forgotten that I don't even remember what story it was? You don't have to remind me how stupid it would be to keep on after the kind of warning that guy gave me." Her mouth thinned bitterly. "One near-death experience was enough to convince me, thank you very much."

He watched her from his position at the window. "You're serious about leaving the *Sentinel*?"

"Yes. No...oh, I don't know." She made a disgusted sound. "I seem incapable of any decisions right now. I really don't know."

"Why would you? You don't have to chuck your career because of this. Hell, if anything, you should be ready and raring to help us find him, to make him pay for what he did."

"I don't want to think about him. I just want to forget all of this and get on with my life. If I can."

"Journalism is your life, Shannon."

"Maybe. Maybe not."

Funny that telling her editor that she was thinking of quitting had been a lot easier than defending her decision to Nick Dalton. Ernie Patton had been surprised and unenthusiastic, but he hadn't argued. He'd even shown sympathy. Not Nick.

Instead, she felt she had disappointed him on some fundamental level.

"What does your grandmother think about this?"

"I haven't discussed it with her."

He moved away from the window, rubbing the back of his neck. "I can't believe you're serious."

"I thought you'd be relieved. I've been a pain to you ever since I pushed that series where I went with two cops on patrol for a month."

"You went over my head to the chief, and when he said no, you went over his head to the mayor. You don't exactly endear yourself to Savannah's finest that way, lady."

"Well, all of you can breathe a sigh of relief now. I'm out of your hair."

She lay very still, feeling as brittle as old parchment while Nick studied her in silence. It struck Shannon that since her accident Nick Dalton had been at her bedside more than any other single person with the exception of her grandmother. Maybe he was here only to pry out the answers locked in her memory, but she was quickly becoming used to having him around. His strength and size and sense of purpose made her feel safe. Almost. Deep inside, she wondered if she would feel completely safe and secure ever again.

She sighed softly. "I wish—"

"Yeah, what do you wish?"

"I wish I could turn back the clock to the day before this happened."

"Seems to me that, in a sense, you've already done that."

She looked at him sharply. "What do you mean?"

"By losing your memory, it never actually happened. It could be that you have stopped the clock sometime before the assault so that you won't have to deal with it."

She looked away from him. "That sounds very shrink-ish."

"It doesn't take a trained shrink to see what's happening

here, Shannon. The bastard who did this hurt you badly. Why give him even more power?"

"Have you been talking to my *maman?*"

"No."

"Gran?"

She could see that he had. She huffed with exasperation. "Do you both really think that I would resort to such a sneaky thing as feigned amnesia?"

"I don't think you're pretending, Shannon, at least, not consciously. You were brutally assaulted. Your body's healing just the way it's supposed to. But something else deep inside you also took a beating that day. Maybe your amnesia's a safeguard that you need just now. Maybe not. Time will tell."

She hated it when people did that. First her family, then her editor, and now Nick Dalton. All of them dispensing advice like jelly beans to a six-year-old. Did they really think that she could just wake up after what had happened to her and pick up right where she left off? What would they say if they knew that just the thought of leaving her room was terrifying? That she was afraid of being alone in her hospital room without a night-light?

"Walking away from your career seems a drastic decision," Nick said. "I'm just suggesting it might be good to wait until you've had a chance to put all this in perspective."

She held up her hands, which were still marked with bruises. "How do you put this in perspective, Nick? And this?" With a quick, jerky gesture, she snatched the sunglasses off and indicated her battered face and broken jaw. Kicking at the hem of the peach silk, she bared her wrapped ankle, which had been brutally twisted. "I'll never be the same person I was before this happened to me, so if that's what you mean by putting it all into perspective, then perspective be damned to hell and back!"

Her emotion vibrated throughout the room. Being savagely beaten, she had discovered, brought out latent bad temper in the victim. It was the third time in as many days that she'd lost it, first with *Maman,* then with Will, now Nick. Her doctor had assured her it was normal, that her nervous system had suffered damage along with her body. But it did not make her feel good to lose control.

"I wondered when you'd get mad," Nick said quietly.

She threw him a grudging look. "What does that mean?" she demanded.

"Just that as long as you're scared and hiding behind amnesia, your assailant is as safe as a slug under a rock."

With his taunt, she felt a new surge of fury. "How dare you! How *dare you!* I'm not hiding behind anything, you... you...arrogant...cop! If that's not just typical male—"

"Take it easy, Shannon. I—"

"You think you can come in here and poke and prod at me over something that you know nothing about, insult me by not believing a word I say, then expect me to just lie here and take it? Just who the *hell* do you think you are, Detective Dalton?"

"I'm the arrogant cop trying his damnedest to find out who tried to kill you," he told her flatly. The contrast between his tone and hers made her seem childish and demanding, but she was still furious.

"Then get out and start searching," she returned hotly. "No matter what you or my family think, I'm not withholding anything. For the last time, get this through your head—" with her nose close to his, she pinned him with her green eyes "—I ... don't ... remember ... a ... damn ... thing ... about ... that ... night!"

The room hummed with the energy of her anger. And something else. Whatever it was, she was in no condition to deal with it. Dear God, would she ever be herself again? Turning suddenly, she slipped back into her bed and pulled the sheet up high. When she looked up, she found him watching her intently, but there was nothing in his tone when he spoke to explain it.

"I have a suggestion," he said.

"I can hardly wait."

"Counseling."

"Counseling?" She stared at him.

"I'm sure you think you don't need it," he said, stealing her protest before she could say it. "You think only pansies or neurotic women or pitiful victims of spouse abuse need counseling after surviving an assault. You don't think there's anything a psychologist, or other women who've gone through the same thing, could say or share with you in a group that could possibly make a difference to the way you feel right now."

"Of course not. I know the value of psychological counseling..." She paused. "For people who need it."

"As I said, you think you don't need it."

"Look, Nick, I know you mean well, and there's just no polite way to say this, but...butt out. Please. Just...mind your own business, okay?"

"This is my business, Shannon. The sooner your memory is unlocked, the sooner I can get a fix on the sleaze who hurt you." He let that register before adding, "Just think about it."

THE NURSE'S NAME was Sherry Carroll. Shannon saw it on the blue name tag pinned above her breast pocket. She shifted slightly to allow the blood pressure cuff to be slipped beneath her arm and then wrapped snugly. With her stethoscope and a smile in place, Nurse Carroll performed the task.

"Perfect," she said, jotting the result on Shannon's chart. "With a BP like this, you'll live to be a hundred. Now...the temp. Open wide." With the thermometer poised, she waited for Shannon to comply. "And how are we tonight?"

Why did nurses do that? Shannon wondered irritably. With a thermometer stuck in her mouth, she could reply only with her eyes. She rolled them, indicating…what? She was fine? She was not so fine? Was it okay to be terrified every waking moment of the day? And night. But she couldn't say that. If she did, Nurse Carroll would launch into a soothing monologue about how safe she was here in the bosom of the hospital. And how lucky she was to be alive. And how devoted her family was. And how fast her body was healing. And how soon a woman like herself would be able to put this behind her and get on with her life.

How I wish it was that simple.

She watched as the nurse jiggled the IV cord, checked the various machines blipping and beeping, surveyed and adjusted the fluids dripping away. Shift change for the hospital staff was less than an hour away. With a final check of her patients, she would settle them down for the night with vital signs taken, fluid intake and output noted, and then Nurse Carroll would walk away, out of the hospital to her car, and on to her house or apartment, which she would enter with casual, thoughtless lack of fear.

The thermometer was whipped from her mouth. "Hmmm, normal. You'll be on your feet and out of here before you know it," she said, tucking the chart back into its special niche. "I know one man who'll be happy when that happens."

"Who?" Shannon asked curiously.

"Nick Dalton, of course. If you don't hurry and get well, we just may have to find a job for him, he's here so much." She pulled the side rail up with a brisk movement. "You're very lucky having someone like Nick taking such a personal interest."

"It isn't personal," Shannon said with irritation. Great. Just what she needed, the whole hospital gossiping about the attention she was getting from Nick Dalton. "*Detective* Dalton wants to take the person who did this to me off the street before he hurts someone else."

"Of course," Nurse Carroll murmured in a tone that made

Shannon feel like a first-grader. "And that's why he's still pacing outside your door at—" she glanced at her watch "—10:49 p.m."

Still smiling, she headed for the door. "Is there anything else I can get for you tonight?"

Just a one-way ticket out of here. "No, thanks."

"Good night, then."

"Oh, Nurse…"

But it was too late. With a quick flick of the light switch, Nurse Carroll was gone, plunging the room into darkness. Panic burst inside Shannon like a shower of fireworks. With her heart in her mouth, and cold terror like a stone in her stomach, she pulled the covers up to her chin and focused blindly on the ceiling.

There was nothing to be afraid of, nothing, nothing, she chanted silently. She was safe. Protected. She didn't think Nick was still outside her room, but Jacoby was. Or Miller. Nobody could get to her. Nobody. She was safe.

She knew it was irrational, but logic didn't help to banish the terror she felt. Before the assault, the problem had been bad enough. Now, her fear of the dark was a full-fledged phobia. A few days before when Shannon had freaked out completely upon awakening to a dark room, the doctor had assured her that it would not be that way always. Breathing deeply, she closed her eyes and forced herself to lie still. Her body was well on the way to healing, and as soon as her emotions were mended, she would be able to face a darkened bedroom. A deep shudder racked her body.

But not tonight.

Groaning softly, she threw her covers aside and maneuvered herself past the rail until she was on her feet. Every nerve in her upper body screamed with the effort. Forgetting her broken jaw, she clenched her teeth and nearly bent over with renewed pain. She had luckily escaped having any serious fractures in the attack, but her ribs were still stiff and sore, and it was sheer agony to shuffle toward the door.

She stopped and took a few cleansing breaths. Outside her room, she could make out the familiar sounds of the hospital— voices, low-pitched, whining, moaning, the rattle of glass bottles, the squeak of an IV "tree" as it was wheeled down the corridor, the muted laughter of TV emanating from someone's room.

She was not reassured. Clutching the edge of the tray-table, fighting dizziness, her eyes darted around the darkened room. She made out the outline of a chair in the corner. It was occupied! No, of course not. She whimpered as terror swirled through her, sweeping away logic and reason. Oh, God, her eyes were playing tricks on her. Her *mind* was playing tricks on her.

With her heart thudding in fright, she turned away in blind haste and slammed into the bathroom door, slightly ajar. With terror-filled eyes, she looked inside and saw him. She screamed.

"He's in here! He's in here!" she cried wildly, scrambling to reach the door. Her injuries forgotten, she focused only on escape. The IV cord, stretched beyond its limit, pulled the needle from its shunt, ripping the flesh on the back of her hand. The pain barely registered.

Sobbing, shrieking in abject terror, she stumbled over the chair, flailing both arms, trying desperately to stay on her feet, but weakness and fright combined were too overwhelming, and she pitched forward to the floor, scraping both knees and sustaining a glancing blow to her cheek from the edge of the bed.

The door flying open with a crash was like the sound of a shotgun blast. Cursing with fear, Nick made for the small, whimpering heap on the floor and swept her up into his arms as though she weighed less than nothing. Heedless of the blood dripping from the dangling IV, totally uncaring of Nurse

Carroll clucking and an intern's bewilderment, he sank onto the bed and held Shannon close.

"It's okay, it's okay." His hand cradling the back of her head, he whispered to her, reassuring her with words that came from somewhere deep inside him that he never knew was there. "You're safe. No one's going to hurt you ever again, I swear it. It was a bad dream, just a bad, bad dream."

"No, no, it wasn't. He...he was...h-here." Sobbing, her breath jerking in and out through her chest which felt on fire, Shannon clung to Nick. He was big and solid and safe. It was the most natural thing in the world to turn to him. She didn't think she could bear to leave the haven of his arms ever again.

"He wasn't here, Shannon," Nick said, his lips firm against her temple. "Nobody was in your room. Jacoby was right outside your door, just as he's been from the start. Miller, too. He's early to take the midnight shift." His palm moved caressingly up and down her spine. "Not even a tomcat could get past those two, lady, believe me."

"Ah...sir...Detective...ah..."

Nick gave the intern standing at the foot of the bed a fierce look. "Dalton," he snapped. "What is it?"

"She's bleeding, Detective Dalton." He glanced at the wound on the top of her hand where the shunt had pulled away. "We'll need to fix that."

"No, no more," Shannon sighed. "I don't think can—"

Nick pressed her face into his neck. He'd never empathized with another person's pain the way he did with Shannon. "You can do it, a tough little cookie like you. You can't just crawl back into bed with all that blood and those scraped knees. Let these people do their job." He felt the shudder that racked her whole body and closed his eyes, squeezing her a little closer.

"Don't leave me, Nick."

"I won't."

"I mean..." Her glance at the dark window seemed almost

fearful. "You don't have to stay all night or anything like that," she said, looking embarrassed. "But if you could...just for a little while..."

"You got it."

"Until..."

"Until you feel safe again."

UNTIL YOU FEEL SAFE AGAIN.

Nick stood staring into his well-stocked pantry, seeing nothing. Cans on the shelf at eye level, boxes one shelf above that, cat food at the bottom. At his feet, his yellow tomcat, Jake, wound in and out between his ankles in a fever of feline impatience.

He wasn't thinking of cat food. Or of feeding himself. He was thinking of his reaction when Shannon had screamed. Something in him had reared up in desperate denial. It was true, a man's heart could actually stop dead. His began beating again when he picked her up and found that she was okay. That the killer hadn't somehow breached security.

"Meow."

"Sorry, buddy." Removing a can, he went to the counter and opened something with liver and bacon in it, then dumped it into Jake's dish. Now that dinner was served, the cat pretended he wasn't famished. He sat down, not too far away from his dish, and began leisurely grooming himself. It was a nightly ritual—the cat's statement to prove he didn't really need anybody—and Nick pretending he bought it.

"If you could figure a way to open the damn can, you'd probably ignore me completely," Nick murmured, watching Jake amble over and begin to eat.

Jake was a stray. He'd appeared one day just a few weeks after Nick moved into his house. Nick had never had a pet, which was just as well. From the cat's behavior, it was obvious he'd never had a home. Now they were both used to each other, Nick thought, stroking the sleek, soft fur. Two solitary, slightly jaded, thoroughly cynical survivors.

Nick straightened abruptly. It wasn't the first time lately that he'd felt an emptiness in his life. Tonight when he had stepped inside his house where everything was just as he'd left it that morning, where everything was his and his alone, he had wondered—just for a moment—what it would be like if someone waited inside for him.

He was lonely and the realization shook him.

God, he had to stop thinking about Shannon O'Connor. She, of all the women in the world, was the last one he should be thinking about. He'd been burned once. He'd been taken to hell and back by a woman like Shannon O'Connor.

He went to the freezer and rooted around until he found a TV dinner. Chicken divan, whatever that was. He yanked the box open, tossed the dinner into the microwave and grabbed a beer while he waited.

Waiting gave a man time to think.

It had been a hundred years ago when he'd fallen for a woman just as beautiful, as wealthy, as willful as Shannon. At twenty-three with a fresh degree and plans to go to law school, he had considered himself a pretty good catch, even for a girl with everything. Because he loved her, he would give her the world—just as soon as he began to practice his profession. He hadn't lacked for conceit in those days. Head back, he drained the beer and set the can down hard. He could still feel amazement at the naiveté of the boy he'd been then.

At the ding of the microwave, he removed the plastic container and slapped his meal onto a plate. Just as amazing was the fact that her betrayal could still hurt. The marriage had lasted three years. It had taken Nick that long to acknowledge the mistake. It had taken Leslie half that long to line up Nick's replacement—the man she should have married in the first place, he guessed. A man with far more in common with her than he could ever have had. Plunging a fork into the rubbery chicken, he wondered whether Leslie's second marriage had stood the test of time.

The divorce had soured his outlook for a while. Midway through law school, when an opportunity came to join the FBI, he took it. A job with Alcohol, Tobacco and Firearms had followed. It was several years later, after he was transferred to Atlanta, that he met Tracey Semmes, a fellow agent. They had similar jobs, similar family backgrounds, their politics were alike, and they were pretty good in bed together. The magic was missing, but he'd been burned by magic. They moved in together, but by mutual consent had never considered marriage.

Nick, at least, had never considered marriage.

His life rocked on a more or less even keel until that fateful day when Tracey was taken hostage on an ATF sting. When the press got involved, the whole thing blew sky-high and she was killed. The guilt he felt was almost overwhelming. Only when he was alone in the deep of the night did he ever admit that he felt guilty over Tracey's death because he hadn't loved her enough.

The cat jumped into his lap, and Nick pushed his unfinished meal aside and began idly stroking while Jake rumbled contentedly. Glancing down, he saw bloodstains on his pants. It was the second time in as many weeks that he'd come away from Shannon O'Connor with her blood on his clothes. If he was a superstitious man, he would think that fate was telling him something. Good thing he wasn't. Good thing he wasn't going to dwell on how right it felt to hold her and comfort her. Good thing he wasn't going to even think about how good she smelled. Like roses. Or how soft she was. Or the look of her breasts in that peach-colored silk thing she wore. Good thing he was too damn cynical to believe in whatever it was she made him feel.

He got up, dumping an outraged Jake without a thought.

What he needed to remember, he reminded himself, was who he was—a cop with a mission. Somebody had tried to kill Shannon O'Connor, and it was his job to find out who it was before he tried to do it again.

CHAPTER FIVE

SITTING IN HER ROOM with her door ajar, Shannon listened to hospital sounds that had become too familiar—the soft tone of the paging operator, the squeak of stretcher wheels, occasional moans from the elderly patient two doors down, a mix of television shows, voices, laughter, ringing phones, bumps and scrapes and rattles...

Twenty-one days. It seemed like months, years. But today— finally!—was the day. Within the hour, she would be out of here. On her way to Wilderose House. With Gran and Will and *Maman,* who had to return to Paris that evening. And, of course, Cheryl Carpenter. With a twist of her mouth, Shannon dropped her head back against the chair. Everything in her wanted to deny the need for a bodyguard, but the truth was, the threat to her since the assault was still there. Along with her own barely manageable fear.

She was patched up and mended everywhere that counted— on the outside. Dr. Webster had removed the bandage from her left hand just that morning, leaving only a strip across the back where she had ripped out the IV needle the night she had seen the intruder. No, imagined the intruder. How many times would she have to repeat that to believe it? There really had not been anyone in her bathroom that night. It was a delayed reaction to stress caused by her trauma. It wouldn't happen again. At least, probably not.

She still cringed inside with embarrassment over the way she'd reacted with Nick. Even as she'd clung to him, sobbing like a baby, she had known somehow, with whatever was left of her sanity, that her mind had played a vicious little trick on her. But she'd been so scared. And Nick had been...there. So solidly, securely there to rescue her. Even when there'd been nothing to rescue her from.

She'd made such a fool of herself. It had been hours before she'd quieted down and fallen into a restless sleep. Even then, when she'd partially awakened a couple of times, he'd still been sitting there. Just...sitting. As he'd promised. A promise she'd wrung from him unfairly. He was too nice a man to renege on his word. She had learned that much about him in the twenty-one days of her incarceration in this place.

He'd been as good as his word that night, but she hadn't seen him since. And she couldn't get up nerve enough to ask about him. Had he given up on her? It hurt to think so. Twenty-one days ago, she wouldn't have believed she could be hurt by Nick Dalton in any way.

She came alert suddenly as footsteps in the hall neared her door. With a quick knock, Cheryl Carpenter entered, pushing a wheelchair and wearing her usual polite smile. One of these days soon, she was going to find out why Cheryl's smiles at her never held much warmth.

"Ready to go?"

"Are you kidding?" Shannon returned, rising to her feet as fast as she could. She was still stiff and sore and unsteady, but she was making progress. If it weren't for hospital regulations, she wouldn't be wheeled out of this place. She would walk out.

When Shannon was seated in the wheelchair, Cheryl took a quick look around, then lifted the small overnight bag sitting on the bed and slung it over her shoulder. "Is this everything?"

"Yes, Will took everything else earlier." As Cheryl wheeled her out of the room into the busy hall, Shannon tried to find her brother. "Where *is* Will?"

"We persuaded him to let us manage this," Cheryl said.

Something in her tone made Shannon wish she weren't faced away from Cheryl. Any mention of her brother's name made the woman turn as cool as springwater. What was it about Will that turned her off? Literally. What about the next few weeks at Wilderose House when they wouldn't be able to avoid each other?

Jacoby was waiting at the elevators. "All set, Miss O'Connor?"

"I guess so."

"Okay, ma'am, we're out of here."

Now that they were inside the elevator, Cheryl stood where Shannon could see her. She made a face at Cheryl. "Even after twenty-one days, Jacoby and Miller still call me ma'am."

"Orders," Cheryl said succinctly.

"Orders?"

"From the man himself," Jacoby said.

"The man? Nick?" Neither Jacoby nor Cheryl changed expression. Shannon huffed and settled back in her chair. "Well, he isn't here and I don't think a little lessening of the rules on the last day of our...association...is going to threaten security."

Neither gave any indication whether they agreed or disagreed, and as the elevator opened to the lobby, both were suddenly quintessential professionals. Miller was waiting for them. He did not have his gun drawn, but he seemed to thrum in readiness for...what? Shannon looked around fitfully.

Cheryl nudged her and when Shannon looked up, the bodyguard slipped an oversized pair of sunglasses on her face. "There. Try not to look so much like yourself," she ordered as Shannon settled back.

Outside, the day was sunny and benign, but Shannon's mouth was suddenly dry. Would he try to kill her in broad daylight? "I feel like a rock star," she grumbled, bracing as Cheryl rolled the wheelchair over a bumpy place in the side-

walk. "Complete with sunglasses and three...count 'em...
three bodyguards."

Jacoby held up his hands in mock innocence. "Hey, we got
a job to do, Miss O'Connor. You want to register a complaint,
like I said, see the man."

Shannon winced as the wheels hit a small rock. "How? I
haven't seen 'the man' in nearly a week."

Miller, bringing up the rear, was noted for his wit and his
weight. "Hey, Cheryl, you want to come back here a minute?" he said, finishing off a jelly doughnut. "I think you
missed a pothole in the pavement."

"Cute, Miller," Cheryl muttered, stopping in front of a van.
"Cease with the remarks, both of you, and stand back while
I help my patient into this van."

"I'll help myself in," Shannon said, lurching unsteadily to
her feet. She needed no encouragement to get in the van as
fast as possible. Being outside for the first time was even
worse than she'd expected, but she tried to contain the fear
that licked at her like tiny flames seeking tinder.

There is nothing to be afraid of. Nothing. Nothing.

"Hey..." Jacoby sprang forward, catching her by the elbow
as she tried to stand.

"Whoa!" Miller grabbed at the wheelchair to keep it from
scooting backward.

"Stop, both of you!" With her hands on her hips, Cheryl
glared at the two cops. "You want to help, guys? Just let me
do this the way I learned to do it."

"No." Shannon braced herself on the van. "I'm sick of
being treated like an invalid. I can get in this thing by myself—" closing her eyes, she swayed slightly "—as soon as
somebody opens the door."

A strong arm went around her waist, drawing a startled gasp
from her. Before she could find the breath to scream, she was
lifted with dizzying speed and settled against a broad, masculine chest. "All of you back off!"

"Nick…" Shannon said weakly, melting into his hard heat. Her body reacted this way to no one else. For one horrible moment, she thought she would actually burst into tears of relief.

"What the hell do you think you're doing?" he muttered for her ears alone, shooting her a fierce look before shoving the wheelchair sideways with a foot. At his side, Cheryl scrambled to collect the overnight bag. "I don't believe you were actually going to try to get into the van by yourself, Shannon. Jacoby!"

"Yes, sir." Jacoby slid open the door.

Nick snapped orders right and left. "Cheryl, you drive. I'm riding back here with Shannon. Miller, you follow us until we get to Wilderose House. Jacoby, you go ahead and meet us at the gates. Use the radio if you see anything suspicious. Anything, you got that?"

"Yes, sir."

"Yo, boss." The jelly doughnuts had vanished.

With the ease of strength and purposefulness, Nick braced half in, half out, of the opened van with Shannon. From his expression, she expected to be dumped onto the seat, but in spite of his irritation, he was surprisingly gentle. Taking care with her injuries, he placed her in a nest of pillows that someone had thoughtfully arranged beforehand, then he propped her ankle high. The bruises looked obscene in the harsh light of day, Nick couldn't help but notice.

"Are you comfortable?" he asked.

"Fine," she told him, keeping her eyes away from him. Oddly, it wasn't easy. She wasn't quite certain what she was feeling. For one thing, she was still half intoxicated by those moments in his arms. The scent of his skin, spicy with after-shave and just plain healthy male essence, still swirled in her head like a small cyclone. Oddly enough, the security of being enveloped in his strength had left her feeling shaken and strangely vulnerable.

"Where's Will?" she asked, to turn the tide of her thoughts.

"Here." Will materialized at the door of the van. Cheryl, already behind the wheel, looked straight ahead. "I'll see you at home," he said to Shannon.

"It's not necessary, Will." She leaned her head back against the headrest. "As you see, I've got bodyguards galore."

"I'll see you at home," he repeated evenly.

Recognizing the I'm-big-brother-and-I-know-best tone, Shannon waved him away, sighing when the door was closed and locked.

For the first few minutes once they were under way, no one spoke. Beside Shannon, Nick looked through the side window. From the set of his jaw, he clearly wished he was anywhere but here. It surprised her how much that bothered her. She had never asked for special attention from Nick. She had no illusions about why he had spent so much time with her after her attack.

"No questions for me today?" she asked, eyeing his rugged profile.

It was a moment before he turned to her. "Why? Do you finally have some answers for me?"

"Not really. It's just not like you to give up."

"How do you know what I'm like?"

She thought about that. "As a reporter in Savannah, I'm hardly a stranger to the way you do things, Detective. It has to bug you like crazy having a known assailant loose on the street."

He grunted, not revealing what he thought. "I haven't given up, Shannon," he said quietly. "Far from it."

"You haven't been around for a few days."

He looked startled, then the hint of a smile touched his mouth. "Missed me, did you?"

She swallowed a short comeback. She didn't want to fight with Nick today. "I guess I did," she said, dropping her eyes to her hands, then forcing herself to look at him again. "I know how you hate gratitude, so I'll be brief. I never had a chance to say thank you for what you did the night I had the nightmare. So, thanks. I don't have to tell you how scared I was when I saw him—I mean, when I *thought* I saw—" She stopped altogether with a short attempt to laugh. "Am I sounding like an idiot?"

"No, you sound like a woman who's been brutally attacked and who's intelligent enough to be concerned because we still haven't found the man who did it."

"I wish I could force it, Nick. I'm trying. I spend hours doing nothing but trying to break through the...the brick wall that seems to stand between me and my memory of that night." She looked at him. "Do you believe that?"

"Yeah." Before he could help himself, he touched her cheek. "Relax, it'll come."

Shannon covered his hand with her own, closing her eyes. "When? How long do I have to wait? Until he tries to kill me again?"

He shifted on the seat so that he faced her directly. "He won't get a chance at you again, Shannon. That's why Cheryl is going to be living at Wilderose House. And Will is no slouch when it comes to self-defense. He was a marine. He'll back Cheryl up, if it comes to that." His hand had fallen to her neck, where his fingers curled warmly around her nape. The feel of her hair was soft and downy. Her skin was silky smooth, like ivory, Nick thought with bemusement, sunwarmed ivory.

"I'm still scared, Nick," she whispered, her eyes wide and green as glass. "I'm terrified all the time. I know it's silly, but—"

"Have you thought any more about counseling?"

She withdrew from him instantly, and Nick cursed silently at the loss even as he mocked his increasing need to forge a special bond with her. Staying away from her for days after those moments when he'd held her, trembling and vulnerable from an imagined threat, had been nearly impossible. If he didn't lighten up soon, he was going to drive his staff to request wholesale transfers. Ed had already threatened to take all his accrued vacation and come back only when Nick was sane again.

"We're here, Nick." Cheryl turned off the road at the entrance to Wilderose House, waving to Jacoby, who stood at the wrought-iron gates. Slowing, she waited until they were opened enough to drive through, then the van, followed by Miller in a squad car and Will in his Jeep, began the drive up to the house.

It was the first time Nick had ever seen Wilderose House up close. It was a beautiful, rambling structure, utterly southern in character. Fronted by eight square cypress columns with twin staircases in the shape of an inverted horseshoe curving up to a second-story gallery, it was like a genteel southern lady, complete with an air of feminine mystique. Looking at the house, Nick blinked to shake the feeling of awe.

"Why would anyone choose to live in an apartment in town over this place?" he asked with genuine bafflement.

Looking at the house the O'Connors had inhabited since the twenties, Shannon laughed softly. "It is gorgeous, isn't it."

"Yeah."

"I've always loved it myself," she admitted.

"Then why don't you live here?"

From the window of the van, she surveyed the familiar, beloved grounds of Wilderose House. Standing on the upper gallery, the view was truly breathtaking. A dozen or more ancient live oaks and magnolia and pecan trees studded the vast front and side grounds. Scattered around in a profusion of color were azaleas and wisteria, bridal wreath and redbud. And from the rear of the house, through more trees and shrubs, it was possible to catch a glimpse of the Savannah River.

"It took us over twenty minutes to drive here from the

hospital," she told him. "When I first went to work for the *Sentinel*, I realized that was too long if I didn't want to miss out on a breaking story." She shrugged. "So, I leased the apartment, but I still spend a lot of time here. I'm almost always here on weekends or holidays."

"It was a Saturday night when you were assaulted," Nick said, instantly forgetting the wonders of Wilderose House for a chance to tap into her memory. "He was waiting for you at your apartment. If you were not in the habit of being there on weekends, why do you think he thought otherwise that night?"

She rubbed her forehead wearily. "I don't know, Nick. Do we have to talk about this now?"

"When is a better time? Tomorrow? Next week? Next Christmas?"

"I want to go inside," she said quietly. "Cheryl—"

"Nick, she's tired," Cheryl said.

"Right." Although he'd already opened the door, he didn't move. He waited a few seconds until Shannon was forced to look at him through dark, smoky eyes. "Just think about it, okay?"

He noted that her spurt of temper had already faded, leaving her pale and strained. Any time she was pressed to recall details of that night, she retreated in a mist of pain. He hated being the one to force her. Feeling like a bastard, he hauled himself out of the van. Not waiting for Cheryl, he reached for Shannon. She came to him with complete trust, settling against his chest with a sigh.

With no one to see, he breathed in the rose scent of her shampoo, tasted the silky strands of her hair that caught on the midday growth of his beard. He turned and headed toward those incredible curving steps that beckoned like something from another time. He had a job to do, and lusting after Shannon O'Connor was not getting it done.

If only she didn't feel so right in his arms.

THE MIDSIZE GRAY CAR cruised slowly by the gates of Wilderose House. With a twist of his mouth, the man cursed viciously, slamming the heel of his hand against the steering wheel.

The bitch was safely back in the bosom of her family.

The high walls surrounding her seemed to mock him. It was all he could do to maintain a sedate pace past the property lines of Wilderose House. Then, hissing obscenities, he pushed his foot down hard on the accelerator and the rental sedan surged forward. In seconds he reached the legal limit and beyond. Oblivious, he vented frustration and rage in a blind, reckless orgy of temper.

She had run to ground at the family estate. She was like a goddamned princess, coddled by everybody who knew her, lavished with tender loving care, finally bundled up and hustled off to her own personal ivory tower. Of all the places he didn't want her to be, Wilderose House topped the list. He knew the drill. He'd seen it before with the wealthy. Let something threaten one of their own and they pulled out all the stops. Whatever it took to protect her, that's what the O'Connors would do.

And Nick Dalton would be at the center of it.

A glance at the speedometer drew another savage curse from him. The needle nudged the ninety mark. A ticket for speeding would put him in the bitch's neighborhood on the very day she'd arrived from the hospital. Stupid to take that kind of chance.

He slowed, although it was an effort when the urge to ram his foot down on the gas and crash through the pretentious iron gate was almost irresistible. He could aim the piece of crap he was driving straight at the front door and watch their faces before he took them all down. See how they liked that. Excitement at the thought curled through him, bringing a gleam to his eyes. Calming himself by drawing in a deep, deep breath, he concentrated on his next move.

He probably couldn't get inside the grounds, let alone inside the house. Unless somebody got careless. Watching the place, that was vital. Waiting for a stupid mistake. No problem there. To the lackeys guarding her, the duty was just a job. Some of his anxiety eased and he nodded to himself. It was simple enough, actually. Just watch and wait. That's all he had to do. Watch and wait.

And be ready when the chance came.

THE MEMORIES that assailed Cheryl in the first few minutes after entering Wilderose House house had been firmly suppressed. She had never been inside, but her ex-husband had talked about it many times. Taunted her about it would be a better way of putting it, she thought, drifting toward the oval doorway leading from the living room where Nick was settling Shannon. Thinking that her help was not needed, she ventured out into the huge entry hall.

"What big eyes, Ms. Carpenter." Low and controlled, Will O'Connor's voice close to her ear sent tiny prickles scudding over Cheryl's skin. Turning her gaze from Nick and Shannon, who were once again arguing, Cheryl braced to meet the mockery in Will's eyes. But when she looked at him, she saw only a cool politeness. "I thought you might want a quick tour of the house. Wilderose is full of nooks and crannies and—"

"Things that go bump in the night. I know."

Will was silent a moment as though reining in some fierce emotion. "Andy always believed there was a ghost that prowled the outside porches at certain times of the year."

Cheryl stared at her hands. Here it was. Only a dozen words exchanged between them before he had to mention Andrew. Well, she might as well meet the challenge head on, clear the air right away. Taking a breath, she met his look directly. "Do you?"

"Believe in ghosts? No."

"Good," she said, taking a step toward the stairs leading

to the lower level. "Then I won't have to hold my breath waiting for accusations from you...or worse, an interrogation about my dead husband, will I?"

He caught her by the elbow before she took another step, whipping her around to face him. "You cold-hearted bitch! Andy worshiped you. He worked like a mule to give you that house he couldn't afford and that car that cost over half his annual salary, not to mention the jewelry and trips—which you took alone, more often than not. Every thought in his head was for you, Cheryl. But it was never enough, was it? You told him that, didn't you? You didn't love him when you married him and you soon let him see it. He wrapped his truck around that abutment out of despair, Cheryl."

"He slammed into that bridge because he was drunk!" she said, jerking her elbow free.

"He was drunk because he was miserable...over you!"

"He was miserable, all right."

He stared at her a long moment. "I don't understand you, Cheryl," he said finally. "How can you slough off a marriage—even a brief one—to a man like Andy just like that?"

Her mouth dipped with disdain. "With 'a man like Andy,' believe me, it was easy." He could make of that anything he wanted, she thought furiously. He already despised her, anyway.

"Now, are you going to show me around Wilderose," she asked quietly, "or am I going to have to ask Miss Kathleen to do it?"

He stood for several moments as though weighing the question, and suddenly Cheryl had had enough. She could check the sprawling layout of the house later. If Miss Kathleen wasn't willing, there was nothing to say she couldn't do it on her own. Or ask a maid. She wouldn't for a second admit it would have been...interesting...seeing it in Will's company, even though he probably would have peppered every moment of the tour with a new insult. Slipping around him, she started back to the room to Nick and Shannon.

"Wait…" As she brushed past him, he caught her arm again. "We have to call a truce, Cheryl. While you're here for Shannon, we can't let our feelings jeopardize her safety." She pulled free again, looking straight ahead. "I couldn't agree more," she said coldly.

"Fine." He seemed to hesitate. "Well, I guess you need to see Shannon's room and check it out…do whatever it is a bodyguard does." He said the word "bodyguard" as though it tasted sour in his mouth.

"Yes, I guess I do."

"You'll be staying in the bedroom next to hers. They connect with a bathroom."

"I know. Nick and I studied the floor plan."

He still waited, looking at her. "Did Nick tell you that I would be around after hours…when I leave the shipyard, that is…if you have plans. You certainly don't have to spend twenty-four hours a day here."

"We want the world to believe that I'm an around-the-clock nurse-companion, so as distasteful as that may be to you, it's necessary to be just that."

"Do you do this kind of thing often?"

"You mean, go undercover?"

"Yeah."

She shrugged. "It's my job."

"What about your personal life?"

"What about it?"

He must have realized how extraordinary his questions seemed, because his face was suddenly ruddy with color seeping from his collar up to the harsh slash of his cheekbones.

"Right," she said dryly. "It's none of your business how I manage my personal life and my career, Will O'Connor. Now, about that tour."

"Sorry," he murmured, stepping back for her to start up

the stairs again. "Down the stairs, take a left. You recall that we entered the house at the upper level by way of the outside stairs. Like many old southern plantations, the layout of Wilderose House is designed as though the original owner expected the Savannah River to flood the ground floor one day. Fortunately, it never has." Speaking like a tour guide, he began pointing out various characteristics of the house. He wasn't going to insult her, Cheryl realized. She'd guessed wrong about that. Instead, he was treating her like a perfect stranger.

Wherever you are, Andy Welles—and I hope it's hell—I'll bet you're laughing. I'm finally getting to see inside Wilderose House, but not as family. As hired help. Isn't that a hoot?

Her heart aching, she took the tour and pretended to be a stranger.

"CHERYL, HERE YOU ARE." Shannon smiled as Cheryl approached the sofa where Nick, with Kathleen's cooperation, had set her up as a full-fledged invalid—ankle elevated, back braced, telephone within reach, pain pills close at hand. "We were wondering where you had run off to. Did Will show you where to put your things?"

"Yes, I'm all settled."

"Did you get a chance to familiarize yourself with the rest of the house?"

Cheryl smiled stiffly. "As much as possible in a ten-minute tour. Wilderose is lovely," she said, turning to Kathleen O'Connor. "You must love the house very much."

"I do, dear. And, please, make yourself at home while you're here."

Shannon frowned as Cheryl murmured a thank you. "Surely you've been here before, haven't you, Cheryl? I was in college while you were married to Andy, but—"

"No, I was never here."

Her tone was polite, but reserved. Why hadn't Andy

brought his wife to Wilderose House during their marriage? Shannon wondered. The O'Connors had an annual New Year's Eve party, and Andy as a distant relative would have been on the invitation list. Barring that, he would have been invited because he worked for Will as chief engineer of the shipyard.

"Where is Will?" she asked suddenly.

"Outside with Jacoby and Miller, I believe," Cheryl said coolly.

At that moment, Nick's beeper went off.

"May I?" he asked, reaching for the portable telephone on the coffee table in front of Shannon.

No one spoke as he dialed the number. Shannon watched him make the connection with his office. He listened briefly, swore once, broke off with an apologetic look at Kathleen, then barked out a question.

"When did it come in?" He rubbed the back of his neck, nodding occasionally. "Any hope of a quick ID?" He released a sound that Shannon guessed would have been a string of profanity except for her grandmother's presence.

"I'm on my way," he said, and crashed the phone in its cradle.

"What is it?" Cheryl asked.

"Another teenage girl," Nick said, clipped tone. "This one's dead."

AFTER SAYING GOODBYE to *Maman,* Shannon went up to her room. It felt good to be in her old bedroom at Wilderose again. She spent a long time just walking around, touching familiar things, childhood treasures, mementoes of other times. Picking up an antique perfume bottle that had been her grandmother's, she passed the glass stopper under her nose. Roses. Gran had given it to her the night she graduated from high school, and because it reminded her of her grandmother, she'd never put a different fragrance in it. Drifting to her bed, she sat on the side of it and looked at her reflection in the old cheval glass mirror standing in the corner. She had not truly lived at Wilderose House since then, she realized now. Even so, nothing much was changed.

Only you.

A wild, utterly alien feeling came over her. She felt like a stranger to herself. Getting up from the bed, she moved closer to the mirror and looked intently at her face, almost expecting to see someone else. Someone different. The swelling was down, the bruises healing, but there was a telltale lavender beneath the skin on her cheekbone, and her eye was surrounded in pale green. It took time for the evidence of a brutal assault to fade away entirely.

But at least it *would* fade away. She thought of the newest teenage casualty. Unlike that young girl, Shannon, at least, would live to work and laugh and love another day.

With a frown, she studied what appeared to be the illusion of movement in the old glass. It was like looking through a veil of mist, but it seemed so real. *No.* She resisted it fiercely. She was alone in her bedroom, so it could not be. Tight, impenetrable security kept any intruders from Wilderose House.

Nevertheless, as she stared transfixed, a scene materialized out of the murkiness in unmistakable clarity. The place was crowded and public, and smelly with a mixture of perfume and overheated bodies, baby diapers and fast food. She sensed the weariness and irritation of the people in the crowd. A bus station, she finally decided. She was seeing a bus station.

This is a dream. She held fast to that thought, but her resistance was futile. The scene continued to unfold.

A dark-haired teenage girl—Becky—suddenly got up from a chair and headed for the door and the newspaper vending machines just outside. She intended to look for a job. She was fifteen years old, but she planned to lie and say she was eighteen. She prayed someone would believe her.

A man watched her.

Paralyzed with dread in front of the mirror, Shannon moaned, silently urging the girl to go back inside. But even as she sent the plea, she knew she could not intervene. She could only see this.

And then the girl was being approached, gripped by the arm with menacing strength, dragged in the direction of a waiting car. If she didn't get away, the future awaiting her was too ugly to survive.

Watching in frozen horror, Shannon saw the girl pushed into the car, then driven to a house where she was thrown into a tiny, dirty room and the door closed behind her with a crash that resounded inside Shannon's head like an explosion. With every atom of her being, Shannon resisted the events that began to unfold. But there was no respite. With her eyes fixed in dread on the girl's face and her own heart locked in painful empathy, she witnessed everything.

Dropping the perfume bottle, Shannon screamed.

CHAPTER SIX

CHERYL WAS THROUGH the door in seconds. Weapon drawn, she looked around wildly, searching the room for an intruder, then, seeing no one, rushed to Shannon, who leaned against the antique dresser, her head down, breathing as though she'd run a marathon.

"My God, what happened, Shannon? You're shaking like a leaf."

"I'm okay," she told Cheryl, sinking down onto the edge of the bed. "I...I had a...a nightmare."

Cheryl glanced at the undisturbed bed. "A nightmare?"

With a broken-sounding laugh, Shannon shook her head. Grabbing one of the pillows, she wrapped her arms around it, then looked into Cheryl's concerned face. "Cheryl, this just may be the most bizarre assignment you've ever had."

Cheryl carefully laid her weapon on the top of the dresser and then leaned back against the edge. "You want to explain what you mean by that?"

"I'm doing things that don't make any sense. I jump at the least little sounds, I freak out for no reason. Today, for instance, when we made the trip from my hospital room down to the van, I was petrified. I tried to hide it, but I was so scared."

"You did hide it," Cheryl said quietly. "You should have said something, Shannon."

"When you took this job, I'll bet you didn't count on having to baby-sit a neurotic, did you?"

"I don't think you're neurotic. But what I think isn't important. Why do *you* think that?"

Cradling the pillow, Shannon struggled not to cry. "Ask Nick. This is the second time I've had a...a hallucination, I guess you'd call it. My mind plays tricks on me. I seem to be seeing things." She glanced furtively at the old-fashioned mirror and shuddered. "Scary things. Ugly things."

Cheryl frowned. "Things related to the assault? Or just... anxiety attacks in general?"

"I don't know." Shannon rubbed her forehead. "My memory—"

"Do you see the man who assaulted you?"

"No!"

"Okay," Cheryl said calmly. "I'm not trying to force you. I just want to try and understand what we're dealing with. If you aren't getting flashes of the assault, maybe your memory is trying to return. Maybe your 'patch memory'—isn't that what they called it in the hospital?—maybe those patches are trying to..." She shrugged, at a loss. "I don't know, maybe become restored." She smiled at Shannon. "Or something."

With a curious look, Shannon shifted until she was propped against the head of the bed. Still holding the pillow against her, she said, "Would you answer a question for me? You may consider it personal, but...since it looks like we're going to see a lot of each other for a while, I'd really like to know."

"Sure," Cheryl said, but she seemed suddenly wary.

"Just now, you gave me the first genuine smile I've ever received from you. In fact, from the beginning, I've had a feeling that you're on this job reluctantly. If I'm wrong, please tell me. Don't I have a right to know?" She searched Cheryl's face, but it was as though she wore a mask. "After all, Cheryl, I'm putting my life into your hands."

"I'm sorry," Cheryl murmured. "I never meant to give you that impression."

"You thought I wouldn't notice that you freeze up in front

of everyone named O'Connor except possibly my grand-mother?''

Cheryl did not meet her eyes. ''I guess I'm not very accom-plished at hiding how I feel.''

''What a crock!'' Shannon laughed. ''You're excellent at hiding how you feel. I have it from Nick—who ought to know—that you're tops in your field. And Ed agrees. You were SPD's best female undercover agent. Those two don't hand out compliments like that to just anybody. So, since you're so good at hiding how you feel in every arena except with the O'Connors, then it must be something personal.'' Looking at her directly, Shannon asked, ''Have I ever of-fended you in any way?''

''No, of course not.''

''Does it have something to do with my brother?''

Cheryl pushed away from the dresser and went to a small cherrywood shadow box and began studying the miniature treasures tucked inside. ''Shannon, I really don't want to talk about this.''

''It *is* Will, then.'' Shannon watched her lift a tiny crystal bell and shake it to hear the soft tinkle. ''I can't imagine any-one disliking my big brother. He's one of the nicest people I've ever known.''

''I don't dislike him. He dislikes me.''

''He doesn't appear to, at least from where I sit. He's every bit as aware of you as you are of him,'' Shannon said. She watched with interest as color rose from Cheryl's throat all the way to her hairline.

''Shannon…'' she begged, sounding distressed.

''Okay, okay. I can see you really don't want to talk about whatever is between you and Will, but—''

''There's nothing between Will and me!''

''Uh-hmm.'' There was something going on here and the reporter in her was dying to know what it was. ''I never knew Andy very well. He was Will and Ryan's cousin, not mine.

The connection comes through my father's first wife. You weren't married to him very long, were you?''

"Two years."

"Will said he was an excellent manager at the shipyard."

"Your brother's respect was…very important to my ex-husband." Cheryl replaced the crystal bell with care, and Shannon sensed that she was choosing her words just as carefully. "He was very good at making other people like him."

"But not you," Shannon said quietly.

"What?"

"You didn't like him well enough to stay married to him."

"No."

After a moment, Shannon tossed the pillow aside and swung her legs off the bed. "Okay, end of inquisition. Now you know why reporters are reviled by so many." She made a face. "We're so damned nosy."

"You certainly are," Cheryl said, but her tone was wry, without any real malice. She turned and picked up her weapon from the dresser.

"Whoa! I get the message." Shannon put out her hands playfully. "You don't have to shoot me to shut me up."

They both laughed, and with the sound of it, their eyes met. Shannon realized with sudden insight that there was a sense of camaraderie that hadn't been there before. The barrier between them was crumbling. "I guess we have more in common than we thought," she said. "We both have things we'd rather not talk about. Or even think about."

"I guess."

"Well…thanks for checking on me," Shannon said.

"No problem." Cheryl shrugged. "You don't have to thank me. I'm just doing my job."

"Now, where have I heard that before?" Shannon said with mild exasperation. "Nick is just as prickly as you when I try to thank him. This is a losing proposition. I guess I'll just have to give it up. Or maybe send flowers instead."

"Don't!" Cheryl laughed outright. "I can't speak for Nick, but I don't think I'm the type. Let's just hope there won't be a next time."

"I certainly second that."

After checking the safety, Cheryl slipped the gun into the pocket of her thick terry bathrobe. "If you're sure you're okay, I'll go back to my room."

"Do you have everything you need?"

Cheryl nodded. "And then some. I'll be spoiled rotten by the time I leave here." At the connecting door, she stopped and looked back when Shannon called her name. "What is it?"

"Nick thinks I should have some counseling." She bent over and picked up the perfume bottle that had hit the floor when she panicked. "You've seen women who have been... hurt or...or... well, women who have gone through something like what happened to me. Do you think counseling is the answer? Or do you think my problems will just go away if I give it enough time?"

"I'm hardly an expert, Shannon."

"I'd like your opinion, anyway."

Cheryl stuffed her hands deep in her pockets. "Have the counseling. Contrary to what folks say, time does not heal all wounds. Take it from one who knows."

AFTER CHERYL LEFT, Shannon stripped and took a long bath, making liberal use of fragrant bath crystals and a sinful amount of hot water. After fifteen minutes, some of her aches and pains had diminished, but she was still nervous and unsettled over the dream. Or whatever bizarre occurrence she'd experienced looking in the mirror. She wasn't about to tell Cheryl that she'd seen a teenage girl abducted and that she'd known the girl was going to be abused and then murdered. She really would recommend counseling if she knew half of what went on in Shannon's head nowadays.

Staring into space, she acknowledged what had been nagging at the edge of her mind for weeks. The flashes of insight, the moments of near discovery, the feeling of impending danger—all were linked to something she knew about from reading her grandmother's journals.

Gran was clairvoyant. Bits and pieces of her strange 'Dream Sight' were sprinkled throughout her journal. She hadn't liked possessing such a strange ability, but Patrick, her husband, had revered her powers. Strangely enough, Shannon and Kathleen had never actually spoken about it. Reading about it in the journal, it seemed like a novel, a fantasy novel at that. Still, Shannon had often felt envious, and yet even a little fearful. She thought now that Kathleen probably knew that. A person with such powers of perception would surely be extraordinarily intuitive about other people. She would surely know the feelings of her own granddaughter.

With a sigh, she stood up in the tub and reached for a big bath towel. Counseling would mean leaving Wilderose House. Nick would be concerned about security. Even though he'd pushed her to do this, she knew there was no way he was going to let her go alone.

With sleep a distant wish, she left her bedroom, thinking that some hot chocolate might take the edge off her anxiety and make her drowsy enough to fall asleep. Making her way down the dark and shadowy hall, she set her jaw against her fear of the dark and headed down the stairs to the kitchen. She'd taken only two steps down when she saw a male figure standing in the oval opening just off the foyer.

"Don't scream, it's only me."

Almost faint with relief, she sank down on the stairs and dropped her head into her hands. Taking the steps two at a time, Nick crouched beside her. "Sorry," he said, touching her shoulder reassuringly. "For a second, you looked ready to scream the house down."

She tried a laugh. "You don't know the half of it. I thought for a minute he had managed to get inside." She didn't have to explain who "he" was. They both knew.

His fingers began gently kneading the taut ligaments in her neck. "Still don't trust Savannah's finest, hmm?"

She shivered, closing her eyes. "My head says yes, the coward inside me says no."

"I know some cowards, lady, and you aren't one."

His hands were warm and skillful on her neck and shoulders. For a few long, luxurious moments, she allowed herself to revel in the sheer pleasure of his massage. "I thought you would probably be at the...the crime scene all night," she murmured.

"I was...almost. It's nearly 4:00 a.m."

"Was it bad?"

His hands faltered, then began moving again. "Yeah."

A fifteen-year-old poised on the threshold of life was gone. As a reporter, Shannon had seen more than her share of death. Children were the worst. Even a veteran of Nick's experience could be unraveled by the death of a child.

"Her parents, have they been notified?"

"Yeah."

"Who had to tell them?" But she knew.

"Me." His mouth twisted. "It's my case. Along with eleven others," he added with angry frustration. "Unsolved."

"What are you doing here?" she asked with soft sympathy. Nothing she could say would ease what he felt about the missing teens, and she didn't even try. "You should be grabbing some sleep while you can."

He gave a short, softly violent laugh. "Yeah, sure."

"I know. I could never sleep after—"

He squeezed her nape gently, silencing her. "Which reminds me...why aren't *you* sleeping? Why is my star witness doing something dumb, like wandering around this house alone and unprotected?"

"I'm not alone." She moaned as he found a sore muscle

in the curve of her neck and shoulder. "Cheryl and Will are upstairs."

"Sleeping, obviously. Otherwise, they'd hear us."

"I do hear you." Cheryl's response came softly from somewhere on the landing above them.

"Go back to bed," Nick told her gruffly. "I'll see Shannon back to her room."

With a murmur, Cheryl melted back into the shadows. In a second or two, they heard the soft snick as her bedroom door closed.

"I couldn't settle," Shannon murmured, for some reason having difficulty keeping her voice on an even keel. "I thought maybe some hot chocolate would help."

"Maybe this will help." And his hands continued to massage her, soothing yet exciting her in some strange way.

Shannon sighed when his hands stilled after a moment, but neither of them was inclined to move. The old house was quiet and peaceful. The only light was moonshine glistening through the beveled glass of the front door. It made for intimacy, Shannon thought. False intimacy. Like Cheryl, he was only doing a job. And she was only reacting to moonlight and near hysteria. "A full moon," she murmured.

"Free license for the crazies," Nick replied, following her thoughts easily. Shifting until he was on the step beside her, he leaned back on his elbows. "When I caught sight of you on the stairs, I actually wondered for a second or two if there really was a ghost at Wilderose House."

"The ghost only roams the outside porches. Didn't Ed ever tell you that?"

He hesitated a moment, then leaned backward so that his face was lost in shadow. "How do you know that Ed told me anything about Wilderose House?"

"Because he's almost a fanatic when it comes to local history," she said, unconsciously edging closer. He smelled like the spring night, cool and fresh and masculine. "And because he told me you asked."

"Ed talks too much."

"He's nice."

"He probably wants permission to poke around in your attic."

"It's too late. I've already done the poking around. It paid off, too. I found the old family journals."

He gave her a quick look. "Family journals? You mean, like picture albums?"

"No, there must be some genetic quirk that compels some of us in the family to record our thoughts and experiences for posterity. Or for sheer egotism, I'm not sure which. Gran's are really wonderful—meticulous and emotional accounts of her life from the time she was a girl in Ireland."

"Nice," he murmured.

"Yes. Then there was Cameron, my father, who as you know was a war correspondent in Korea and Vietnam. Following right in his footsteps is my brother Ryan, who's a journalist based in New York. Right now, he's in some Middle Eastern country."

"How about you? Do you keep a journal, too?"

"Uh-hmm."

Sensing her withdrawal, he chose his words carefully. "And did you write in it your reason for being in Atlanta the night you were assaulted?"

"No."

He studied the pale profile visible in the moonlight, and felt a surge of desire so strong that it shook him. Instead of trying to probe the secrets hidden somewhere in her mind, he was thinking about swinging her up and striding down the hall to her room and spending the rest of the night with her. It was the damnedest thing, this near obsession with Shannon O'Connor. Very unprofessional, yet he seemed helpless when it came to this sexy Irish beauty.

Doggedly, he went back to the business at hand. "I don't suppose you would let me read it...just to decide for myself that there's nothing there?"

"It's...too private, Nick. I'm sorry."

He swore, softly but with real frustration. Sexual and professional. With his outburst, the mood was shattered; both realized it at the same instant. Shannon straightened and stood up. Nick followed, keeping a steadying hand on her arm.

"Up or down?" he asked. In the pale wash of the moon, she seemed more vulnerable than ever. Had a woman ever had whiter, more delicate skin? And that glorious auburn mane. He let go of her. "Do you still want that nightcap?"

"Not really. How about you? The bar in the family room is pretty well stocked. You're welcome to help yourself."

A double Scotch would be good. Anything to blot out the memory of a lifeless Rebecca Berenson, age fifteen, blond, blue-eyed, once beautiful. But if he started, could he ever quit? "I think I'll pass."

"Nick..." Drawing a cautious breath, Shannon tilted her face to his. Nick thought that she looked like she was bracing herself for bad news. "What was her name?"

"Rebecca."

"Becky..."

"Probably. At least to her folks. But she was ID'd as Rebecca. Rebecca Berenson. We managed to put it together fast because her family had filed a missing person's report a couple of months ago."

Shannon looked beyond him to the bright moonlight pooling inside the foyer. "Such a waste."

"Yeah. We've been lucky. This girl is the only fatality...at least, the only one we know of. The others...well, we'll just have to wait and see."

"Do you have any leads?"

"Nothing. Not a thing. Her body was found in the warehouse district of the city. Run-down, inadequate lighting, no

witnesses. At this point, we're working in the dark. Maybe—''
He broke off as Shannon bent her head and with a little moan,
rubbed the spot between her eyes.

"What is it?'' He swore, the quick explosion directed at
himself. "What the hell am I doing? I shouldn't be talking to
you about this.'' He reached for her. "Here, let me—''

"No.'' Her head still bent, eyes closed, she waved him
back. "Nick, she wanted a job, but she was only fifteen. She
planned to lie and say she was eighteen.''

He stared at her. "What are you talking about?''

With the fingers of both hands, she now rubbed her temples.
"Becky...she left the waiting room to go outside and get a
newspaper. To read the want ads.''

Nick's fingers wrapped around her upper arm with the
strength of steel. "What the hell is going on here, Shannon?
What waiting room? I came here straight from telling her parents. They didn't even know she was in Savannah. Nobody
knew.''

"I...I...'' Squeezing her eyes closed, she swayed. Nick reacted instinctively, reaching to sweep her up into his arms.
Shannon resisted.

"No, I'm not going to...I'm all right.''

"You look like death,'' he growled. "Pale as a ghost. At
least let's find someplace besides the stairs to sit down. You've
got some explaining to do, Shannon.''

He caught her by the arm and turned her, urging her upstairs. Once inside her room, she sank down on the side of
her bed, and after a moment of indecision, Nick crouched on
his haunches in front of her.

A few moments passed before he spoke. "Now, what's this
about a waiting room? And what makes you think she was
looking for a job? And why do you call her Becky? Did you
know her?''

She sighed with weariness. "One question at a time,
please.''

"Fine," he snapped. "You choose."

She shook her head. "You're not going to believe it."

"Try me."

"I saw it in my mirror."

"You're right. Try again."

"I told you you wouldn't believe me. But it's true, Nick. I was standing in front of that mirror right there—" she pointed to the long cheval glass mounted in an ornate frame "—and suddenly a scene began to unfold before me. It was Becky."

Nick surged up, raking a hand through his hair. "Damn it, Shannon, do you take me for a fool?"

"No. I know it sounds...I know it's a stretch of the..." She shrugged helplessly. "It sounds ridiculous to me, too."

"Okay, let's start again. Where did you meet Becky?"

"I've never met her. I don't know her. I've never heard of her."

"You know her name, her age, you claim to have personal insights about her. But you've never met her."

She just looked at him.

He drew in a deep breath. "You saw all this in your mirror."

"Uh-huh." She glanced at it, and following her gaze, Nick did, too. It was beautiful, old, cherrywood, he thought, carefully preserved, but still only a mirror. From her bedside, both were reflected in its murky shine. "It's a family heirloom," she said inanely.

"Passed from one witch to another?" he asked sarcastically.

She turned in a huff, facing away from him and the mirror. "This isn't a joke, Nick. You asked me and I told you the truth. I was standing in front of that mirror thinking about...about Becky—although I didn't know her—and suddenly these pictures and...thoughts, I suppose you'd call them...came to me." She frowned, recalling the moment, and absently touched her finger to a spot between her eyes. "This sharp pain came first, just as it did a few minutes ago when I gave you those facts.''

''Does this have something to do with your amnesia?''

''I don't know. Maybe.'' She looked at him beseechingly. ''Probably, but I really don't know. This is as strange to me as it sounds to you. More so.''

''A concussion can cause any number of side effects.''

''What if it isn't the concussion?''

His look narrowed. ''What else could it be?''

She studied the shape of her bedroom slippers for a few long seconds, then gazed up at him with uncertainty. ''Don't laugh, but...what about when I died?''

''You didn't die!''

''I did, Nick, and you called me back.''

Nick raked an unsteady hand through his hair. ''What does that have to do with anything?''

''Strange things happen to people after near-death experiences.''

''They become witches?''

''Stop calling me that!''

He swept a pleading glance at the ceiling. ''I don't believe what's happening here. We're arguing over whether or not you're a witch, whether or not you died and came back. If they overheard this at the station, they'd take my shield and suggest early retirement.'' When Shannon said nothing, he hissed out a long breath and began again. ''Look, just give it to me straight. Do you know anything about Rebecca Berenson? Anything factual, I mean.''

''I guess not. When you put it that way.''

''How else would you put it?''

''I was standing in front of my mirror and—''

''Okay. *Okay!*'' A few seconds ticked by while he reined in his temper. ''Just tell me what you...saw, and I'll make up my mind whether it's legitimate or not.''

''She was in the bus station here in Savannah.'' She gave

him a chastising look when he opened his mouth, and with a
grunt, he subsided. "I don't know how I knew that, I just did.
I saw the crowd. I even recognized the smell of the place—
you know, people and old plastic and the hot dogs behind the
snack bar. Becky—" Shannon frowned, trying for total recall
"—she was scared. I picked up on her fear instantly. She was
hungry, too, but she didn't have any money. She was obsessed
with finding a job. She got up and made her way through the
crowd and went outside. The newspaper machines were out
there and she was going to grab one...steal it, actually...when
the next person's money tripped the door."

She glanced at Nick and found him watching her with a
look that was impossible to decipher. "She never got the
chance. A man approached her and struck up a conversation.
She was cautious, but he smiled a lot. He asked her if she was
hungry and she thought he meant he would buy her a hot dog.
She said yes, and he started hustling her toward his car, which
had pulled right up to the door. The driver...I couldn't see
him. Or her."

"How did they get her in the car in a public place like
that?" Nick asked for the sake of argument, not because he
believed what he was hearing.

"No one was outside at the moment he made his move."
She looked at Nick. "He's done this before."

"Come on, Shannon." Nick walked a few steps away and
turned back. "Do you realize how preposterous this sounds?"

"You asked. I'm telling you what happened. What I saw."

"In your mirror."

"Yes. In my mirror."

He made a mocking half bow. "Then continue, by all
means."

"He shoved her inside the car, got in behind her." The
emotion vanished from her voice. She began speaking in a
low monotone. "They drove to a house and locked her in a
bedroom. They made a call to somebody. Becky was terrified,

trying every way she could think of to get out of that room. They came in and gagged her to shut her up. That's when the one who abducted her decided to rape her. She fought him. She had a small knife and she managed to inflict a cut or two—one on his face, another on his palm. It infuriated him, not so much because she hurt him, but because she dared to fight back. He hurled her against the headboard of the bed. She died there.''

"Not in the warehouse district where we found her?''

"No. They just chose that site to dump the body.''

Nick felt prickles on the back of his neck. The forensic specialist said her body had been moved after death. "She hit her head when he threw her against the headboard, right?''

"No, it broke her neck. That's what killed her.''

He sat down abruptly. "Damn it, Shannon, how are you doing this?''

Her eyes filled with tears. "I don't know. I don't want to.''

He got up and went to her. The bed sagged with his weight as he hauled her into his arms. "I'm sorry, it's just so…''

"Unbelievable?'' She sniffed, turning her face into his shirt. "I know.''

"If I go back to the station and file a report like this, it'll cause a ruckus neither one of us will ever live down.''

"Uh-huh.''

"But I can't just ignore it. There's no way you could have known she didn't die where her body was found. Or that her neck was broken.''

She didn't reply. What was there to say? he thought, resting his chin on the top of her head. "I don't believe I'm asking this, but do you think you could find the place where they took her?''

"I don't think so. I only have a feeling for the inside of the house. If I were taken there, I believe I would know it.'' Lifting her head, she gazed up at him in apology. "I'm sorry.''

"How about the guy at the bus station?''

"I'd know him if I saw him again."

He sighed with disgust. "That leaves only the entire population of Savannah to pick him out of."

"Half the population," Shannon said, wanting to lighten the conversation. "He's definitely not female."

"But the driver might be."

"Maybe. Maybe not."

Somewhere deep in the heart of the house, a clock chimed the half-hour. Through the window, the first pale, near-pink hint of dawn had banished the darkest shadows of night. Nick was achingly aware that Shannon wore no bra. With his arm circling her midriff, her breasts were a soft, sweet weight on his forearm. Feelings he ought to be fighting rushed through him, hardening his body and heating his blood. Before his thoughts made him do something stupid, Nick abruptly set her aside and stood up.

"Are you leaving?" she said, unconsciously smoothing her hands down the front of the T-shirt, stretching it over her breasts. The motion tightened Nick's groin to the point of pain.

"I need to grab a couple of hours of sleep." He knew he sounded irritable, but better that she think him rude than lusting after her body. "I'll see myself out."

"Nick…"

He turned back to see her reaching for a pillow. The T-shirt hiked up, revealing a long, satiny length of thigh. Desire coursed through him hotly, setting up a thick, heavy pounding. "Yeah?"

"I've reconsidered about counseling. Tonight…after seeing…all that in the mirror, I can hardly keep on believing that time will take care of all the…changes in me. I'm calling tomorrow for an appointment."

The pillow slid to the floor. She had to get off the bed to pick it up, and when she did, he saw not only thigh, but the luscious curve of her derriere and a flash of French-cut bikinis.

God, his hands ached to strip them off, but this woman was

off-limits. It wasn't only that she was everything he knew to be unsuitable for a man like him, but he was charged with her protection. Her emotions were already in turmoil. Her body was still recovering from deep trauma, her mind was playing tricks on her and somewhere out there a savage animal wanted her silenced. The last thing she needed was for him to come on to her.

And the last thing he needed was to get mixed up with a woman too much like his ex-wife.

"Counseling," he repeated, dragging his thoughts back into line. "Good. It's a smart decision."

"There is a victims' encounter group," she said, hugging the pillow close against her. "I rejected the idea at first, but maybe it's the best thing. That way, Cheryl can go with me. Pretend to be just another victim. What do you think?"

"It sounds workable. What does Cheryl say?"

"We talked about it." She frowned, thinking back. "She seemed positive about the idea...at least I think so. Of course, I don't know how she'll react to actually being forced to go with me." She lifted a shoulder with a rueful look. "Why would anybody like being forced to listen to a bunch of people trot out their troubles?"

"She's a professional. If it takes attending a victims' encounter group to protect you, then she'll do it."

"Probably. Even so..." She turned and added the pillow to the others plumped up at the head of the bed, flashing him a smile over her shoulder. "I think I'll let you be the one to tell her."

He wanted to taste that smile so much that he almost took a step forward. Only the striking of the clock at 5:00 a.m. brought him to his senses. Muttering a hoarse good-night, he got out of Shannon's bedroom before he did something that could cost him his job.

CHAPTER SEVEN

THE SMALL CLOCK on the mantel in Shannon's room softly chimed the half-hour. Slipping the ends of a bright woven belt through the loops of her denim skirt, she pulled it snugly around her waist. Smoothing nervous palms over the slim lines of the skirt, she hoped she was dressed right for the first session of the victims' encounter group. How did a victim look? Stupid question. She didn't want to look like a victim. It was bad enough that she acted like one, cowering in the house, afraid most of the time to venture beyond earshot of Cheryl or her grandmother.

Hallucinating.

She didn't want to think about that right now. Her anxious look was reflected in the old-fashioned cheval glass that now seemed somehow to dominate the room. With slightly unsteady fingers she finally managed to fasten her beaten silver earrings. Seeing movement behind her in the mirror, she turned to find Cheryl watching her from the door of the connecting bath. "How do I look?"

"If you mean, are the bruises obvious, no, not at all. You look fine."

"Well, that's a relief." If Cheryl thought she was worried about the look of her bruised face instead of the fact that she was leaving the sanctuary of the house, then her fear must not be too obvious. "Let me just find my shoes, then I suppose I'm as ready as I'll ever be. How about you?"

"The truth?" Cheryl laughed a little uneasily. "I didn't feel nearly this nervous posing as an aging teen prostitute."

Shannon frowned. "Why are you nervous?" Alarm flickered in her eyes. "Is it security? Do you think—"

"No. Nick has patrols on this road day and night. You're safe. You know he would never agree to this if he thought otherwise."

"Then why the nerves? This is just another undercover role for you, and you're so good at what you do, nobody will guess you aren't a victim yourself."

"Right."

Tucking tissues and a lipstick into her small purse, Shannon missed the wry tone. "You can wing it, Cheryl. When we get to the encounter group, just make up something."

"Uh-huh."

Distracted by her search for the sandals she wanted to wear, Shannon was more focused on her own problems than Cheryl's lack of enthusiasm. "Don't even think of backing out. I'm too close to choosing that option myself. The truth is, Cheryl, I'd rather face a street gang on a rampage than do this."

"You've already done that, and Savannah missed having a night of unparalleled violence by a hair," Cheryl said dryly.

"Now you sound like Nick," Shannon said, quick to defend her part in an incident that was nearly a year in the past. "It was a turf war between rival gangs. They were going to have it out if we didn't do something. Interviewing them together and putting it on the front page was a good idea, I don't care what Nick says. It worked, didn't it? Mario and Abdul have co-existed peacefully ever since."

"Those two hoodlums don't know the meaning of peaceful co-existence, Shannon. Nick put the fear of God in them, and that's what keeps them from stepping over the line."

"Maybe. But I still think the dialogue did some good. Besides, it's ancient history now." Going to the closet, Shannon began rummaging among the shoes on the floor, still looking for her sandals. "How did we get on this subject?"

"You tell me." Cheryl shrugged. "Anything to keep from thinking about the next hour, I guess."

Sitting back on her heels, she looked at Cheryl. "You sound as if you're the one who's going to be psychoanalyzed. I'm the patient, remember?"

"Hmm." Busy with the contents of her handbag, Cheryl did not look up. Finding her weapon, she withdrew it and carefully checked the clip.

As always, Shannon shuddered just looking at the thing. "You're as comfortable handling that gun as most people are handling their car keys," she observed.

"Just like you and your typewriter."

"Computer."

"Whatever." Satisfied, Cheryl stowed the gun deep in her handbag, then said to Shannon, "Are you about ready?"

Shannon nodded slowly, still watching Cheryl. "As soon as I find my sandals."

Cheryl closed the flap of her handbag and anchored the strap securely on her shoulder. "I'll meet you at the car, okay?" She was already through the bathroom and heading for the door of her bedroom.

"Right," Shannon murmured, her eyes on the straight line of Cheryl's backbone. Something about their brief exchange bothered her, but she wasn't sure what. She had never met anyone as difficult to read as Cheryl. "Give me two minutes."

WILL O'CONNOR STEPPED out of his room and halted Cheryl with a look. "I want to talk to you."

Glancing quickly at Shannon's door and finding it ajar, she replied quietly, "Not here." Without looking at him, she led him toward the porch. He followed, closing the door quietly behind him.

"I'm against this and I told Nick that I was," he said, coming bluntly to the point.

"Good morning to you, too."

He looked discomfited momentarily. "Sorry, I didn't mean any offense, but I—"

"Didn't you?"

"Of course not. I wanted—"

"Is it just me, or do you treat all the hired help at Wilderose House this way?"

"What—"

"You don't have to answer that," Cheryl said, clamping her mouth tight too late. It irritated her that she'd said anything to Will that even hinted at being personal. She turned her back to him, resting her hands on the railing, and looked out over the gorgeous grounds of his grandmother's house. "I know you're polite, even warm and friendly, to everybody else who sets foot in this house."

"I—"

"But after four days, it just gets a little tiresome, that's all. I suppose I—" Coming from behind, his hand suddenly covered her mouth. Startled, her eyes flew to his. She hadn't realized how close he was. Or how big. And strong. Her heart racing, she reached to clamp her hands on his wrists.

"Will you shut up and let me finish a sentence," he growled in her ear. "Just once?"

She could easily escape. One well-placed elbow and a quick kick and he'd never grab her again. But even as she thought of self-protection, she knew Will was not a violent man. He wouldn't hurt her. Not physically, at least. He was all hard male angles against her softness. Fresh from the shower, he smelled of soap and after-shave. Closing her eyes, she fought his roughly soft hold on her and her rioting senses. "Let me go!"

He stepped back slightly, allowing her to turn. When she looked up at him, he was still dangerously close. "Let me know when I can get a word in," he said, crossing his arms over his chest.

"Why do you object to Shannon having some counseling?

She's been through a horrible experience. It can only help."
She didn't look at him while she spoke. She knew her voice
sounded slightly breathless, but hoped he wouldn't notice.

"I don't have any problem with the counseling. Actually, I
approve. It's the fact that the clinic is nearly eight miles from
here, down a two-lane secondary highway. It's not safe."

She met his look. "Did you tell Shannon that?"

"No!"

"Then don't. She's already more than half ready to back
out, as it is."

"I'm not telling her anything," Will said grimly, shoving
his hands in his pockets. "I'm telling you that I think it's too
risky. I'm saying come up with another plan."

"Have you forgotten what I do for a living?"

"I don't give a damn what you do for a living," he said
implacably. "As far as I'm concerned, it doesn't make a par-
ticle of difference. You're a woman, too, and just as vulnerable
as Shannon."

Stung, she put her hands on her hips. "Are you suggesting
I can't do my job?"

"I'm suggesting that two women on a lonely highway are
no match for the kind of lowlife who might be out there looking to finish the job he started on Shannon. I told Nick—"

She gasped. "You discussed this with Nick Dalton?"

"Since I hold him ultimately responsible, yes. I told him
you need backup on that highway. It's nothing to do with you
being able to do your precious job."

She propped her hands on her hips and spoke sweetly.
"And would you be pushing for extra backup if I were a man,
Mr. O'Connor?"

"This isn't about sexism, Cheryl. It's common sense, damn
it! I want a couple of men to ride shotgun and that's the end
of it."

"If you had any problem with hiring a *woman* to protect
your sister, you should have mentioned it when Nick recom-

mended me. But I'm hired now and I decide when and if I need extra help. One thing I don't need is your advice on how to do my job, Will O'Connor.'' Fuming, she turned on her heel to go. This was personal, she knew it. Anybody else hired to protect Shannon wouldn't get this kind of harassment from him, she'd bet on that.

She had her hand on the door when he caught her arm and whirled her around. ''You may not need my advice, but you're damn sure getting it,'' he said through gritted teeth. ''You expect me just to stand by and watch you jeopardize Shannon because you're too stubborn to ask for help?''

Her reply was a firm jerk that broke his hold on her arm. ''Nick expects you to need help from time to time,'' he argued. ''He's willing to send a unit from SPD. But you have to ask, Cheryl.''

Still silent, she snatched the door open.

''Damn it! If I have to put a call through to Nick and make a formal complaint, I will. How will that look on your precious résumé?''

She gave him a look that would sear steel. ''You mean you'll make a formal complaint?''

''We're doing this my way, Cheryl. I expect you to have extra backup when the two of you leave Wilderose House.''

''But I don't!''

''You stubborn female!'' His body rigid, he glared at her. ''I can see what Andy meant now. If you don't have any concern for your own safety, then think of Shannon, for God's sake!''

''Andy?'' Blank confusion gave way to sudden understanding. ''I might have known,'' she said softly. ''This is not about Shannon or protection or my ability to do a job at all, is it? This is about my ex-husband.''

''Not that it ever mattered to you, but he used to worry himself sick over your casual attitude toward your own safety. He hated the way you took unnecessary chances, endangering your own life and probably the lives of others, and if your behavior here is anything to judge by, I'm thinking he didn't exaggerate one bit.''

"How dare you, Will O'Connor! Bringing up Andy's name, throwing his words back at me when you know it's not possible to defend myself against a dead man. Who the *hell* do you think you are?''

"I'll tell you who I am! I'm the man who had to listen to him day in and day out for most of the two years you were married.'' It was as though the mention of her ex-husband's name had pushed some invisible button inside him. "One of the reasons your marriage failed was your stubborn disregard for Andy's feelings. A man has a basic need to take care of his wife, Cheryl. Maybe if you'd respected that, Andy would still be alive today.''

Cheryl was so furious that she actually felt like launching into him tooth and nail. Or maybe a shove off the balcony to the bricks twenty feet below might bang some sense into his head. Instead, she had to bite her tongue and put up with the self-righteous, condescending hogwash he was dishing out. Her lip curled with cynicism. "You know him so well, right?''

"I think so.''

"He had a basic need to take care of me.''

"You were his wife. Any man would...if he loved her.''

"Exactly.''

He frowned. "What does that mean?''

For a moment, she simply stared at him. Her silence was long enough that a seed of apprehension began to grow in him. With less hostility, he said, "Look, I'm willing to listen to your side.''

"Oh, you're willing to listen, are you?'' she said, her tone a little too quiet.

"Well...''

With a sigh, she let it go. "It doesn't matter, Will. My marriage is behind me. Andrew Welles is dead. Do what you

like about extra backup for the trip to the clinic. If Nick wants
to send a unit, tell him to make it snappy. Our appointment's
at ten.''

Turning on her heel, she was through the door and gone
before he had a chance to object.

"I'VE BEEN MEANING to ask..." From the passenger side of
the car, Shannon glanced over her shoulder. The Jeep driven
by her brother was so close that a sudden stop was hazardous.
"What was going on with you and Will? When I walked outside, the air between you two could have been cut with a knife.
Not that it's any of my business," she added hastily as Cheryl
pulled into a parking space and squeaked to a stop.

"It must run in the family," Cheryl muttered, glowering as
Will wheeled the Jeep into a space two cars over.

"What?"

"Butting into business that doesn't concern you," she replied, giving Will a chilly look as he got out of his vehicle
and started toward them.

"Will is butting into your business?"

"Telling me how to run my business is a better way to put
it," Cheryl said darkly.

"Ahh." Shannon hid a smile. "You didn't want him tagging along acting as backup bodyguard, right?"

"He's an amateur, and having an amateur around is the best
way to screw up an operation. If we had to have somebody,
we could ask Jed Singer, the private security guard who patrols
at night. He'd stay on if I asked him." She bumped the steering wheel with her fist. "This is so irritating. It isn't necessary!
I'm perfectly capable of handling this assignment, just ask
Nick. *He* doesn't have a problem with the way I work. It's
your brother who's locked into nineteenth-century thinking."

Correctly reading Will's grim features through the wind-
shield as he approached, Shannon had to agree. But with the
vast parking lot between her and the safety of the building,

she couldn't help feeling a craven unfeminist relief for the additional protection her big brother represented. Still, loyalty to her sex made her lean over and pat Cheryl on the knee. "Blame his overprotectiveness on me. He knows I'm scared of my own shadow lately. It's no reflection on you." She gave Cheryl an apologetic look. "I know you're the best because Nick says so, and that's what counts."

"Thanks," Cheryl said, but her smile was forced.

"So…" Drawing in a fortifying breath, Shannon looked at the entrance to the clinic. "We've got our stories straight just in case anybody seems suspicious? We're friends who have both been victims of violence. I don't think I'll have any trouble telling the truth, as long as I can get beyond talking about it in the first place." Shannon turned to find Cheryl nervously biting her lower lip. "Have you made up something that sounds…well, believable?"

"No, but when the time comes, I'll wing it, as you say."

"Cheryl, you don't have to do this, you know."

Cheryl studied the landscape from the window on her side before speaking quietly. "I have a job to do, Shannon," she said with only the barest tremor in her voice. "If that means attending an encounter group for victimized women, then I'll do it."

Shannon made a mental note to try to resume the conversation later. Right now she was too worried about getting from the car to the relative safety of the clinic to think about why Cheryl should be reluctant to sit in on a victims' encounter group.

The car door on Shannon's side was wrenched open. "What's keeping you two?" her brother demanded. "If you were going to spend the morning talking, you could have stayed at Wilderose House."

"Coming." Shannon scrambled out, chalking up Will's rudeness to his worry about her safety and to whatever was going on between Cheryl and him.

Even though she was flanked on both sides by Cheryl and Will, her hands were icy cold and her stomach in a knot as she started for the entrance to the clinic. Movement caught her eye suddenly from the far side of the building and she almost tripped over her own feet. Two people approached from the opposite direction. Holding her breath, she waited for them to reach her. They did. Deep in conversation, they didn't even glance her way. Her breath fluttered out.

Beyond them, a lone man in sunglasses stood in the open door of his car. Her stomach coiled tightly again, causing her to press her palm over her middle. For just a fraction of a second, they looked at each other. Then he got into the car—a Jaguar, she thought—backed out and accelerated quickly into traffic. She nearly shuddered in relief.

She was perfectly safe, she assured herself. It was her first trip away from the house since leaving the hospital. She was just nervous. Cheryl was a professional. She even had a gun. Watching the car disappear around a curve, she wished for Nick.

The instant she had the thought, she squelched it. She could not continue to lean on Nick. She hadn't lied when she said she trusted Cheryl. This fear that was with her constantly was unreasonable and neurotic. Somehow she would have to learn to deal with it. That was why she was here. To talk out her fear. To neutralize her anger at having her body brutalized and her life wrenched from her. Seeing every strange man as a threat was a trick of her imagination.

o

THE THERAPIST for the encounter group was a woman. Shannon admitted to herself that she was glad. Dr. Susan Levinson was tall, dark-haired, soft-spoken and intuitive. Watching her skillful handling of the motley group of victimized women, it was difficult for Shannon to imagine her being unsettled over anything. Or angry. Or frightened. Or uncertain. Shannon knew herself to be all of the above.

The sessions were informal, another plus to Shannon's way
of thinking. The eight women introduced themselves by first
names only. Shannon had done a feature on Alcoholics Anonymous a year ago and had attended some AA sessions. The
meeting reminded her of that. Some of the women had been
in counseling for a long time, others just weeks. Some were
victims of rape, assault or domestic violence. Some had been
mugged on the street, or in the case of the young mother of
two seated on Shannon's left, right in her own driveway as
she returned home from grocery shopping in the middle of the
afternoon. The woman sitting next to Dr. Levinson was being
stalked by an ex-boyfriend after ending a relationship that had
grown increasingly violent.

"Hello, I'm Francine," she said, hands tightly laced in her
lap. Her gaze was fixed on the feet of the women across from
her in the semicircle. "I was afraid to come back after he
found out I was attending this meeting. He said he would kill
me if I did. We had a terrible fight over it." The muscles in
her throat worked convulsively as she swallowed to control
her tears. "I think he would have 'taught me a lesson' right
then—" the words came with bitter irony "—but my fourteen-
year-old daughter was in the house and he knew Kelly would
call 911 if he got violent."

As the women spoke in turn, counterclockwise in the circle,
Shannon noted that few named names. Most referred to "he"
or "him" to identify the men responsible for their being here.
Anger and fear and pain poured from them in disjointed sen-
tences, through choking tears and bottled-up frustration or
flashes of rage as they described the violence perpetrated
against them.

A petite blonde with lackluster blue eyes and obscene green-
ish-purple bruises on the side of her face spoke so softly that
if she had not been seated so close, Shannon would not have
been able to hear her. "Hello, I'm Sissy. I don't think I will
be coming here anymore. It's not helping any. I'm still too

scared to go back to work or to the grocery store, or even to church. No matter where I go, I have to get in my car and drive, and that's where he...he..." Gulping, she crammed the fingers of her hand against her lips. "I don't think I can ever forget the feel of the gearshift gouging me in the back as he...he..."

"He raped you, Sissy," Susan said quietly. "You can say it. Say it and get beyond it." But with Sissy shaking her head and tears pouring down her face, it was obvious she had a long way to go.

After a long silence, Susan looked at Cheryl. "It's your turn, Cheryl—that is, if you'd like to talk."

Shannon had the odd feeling that Cheryl almost got up and ran. She glanced sideways at her, concerned to find her face pale and strained. Impulsively, she touched her hand. It was icy and limp. She squeezed it once reassuringly, wondering why Cheryl had agreed to come here if it brought her this kind of pain. It was difficult to tell from her shuttered look, but something about her screamed pain. Shannon knew that look.

"Hello..." Cheryl cleared her throat. "Umm, my name is Cheryl." Her voice was low, nearly inaudible, totally unlike the self-possessed woman who had been a rock of security from the moment Nick had introduced her and left Shannon in her care. Cheryl licked her lips, looking upward as though searching for the right words. "Ummm, I'm a widow. Well, actually, we were separated when my husband, uh...my ex-husband died in a car accident." Dropping her eyes to her hands in her lap, she stared at the finger where she had once worn a wedding ring. "It wasn't a very good marriage, but you never know that before you get married, do you? They say all the right things and then they do all the wrong things."

The seconds ticked by until a full minute passed. "What wrong things did he do, Cheryl?" Susan asked softly.

She made an effort to laugh. "Oh, you know—stay out late, drink too much, criticize, lie...the usual. I mean—" she sent a quick look around the group ''—isn't that how most men are? Critical and undependable and bullying and...generally obnoxious?''

Silence followed her outburst, then she seemed to realize that she had said more than she intended. With an uneasy look into Susan's face, Cheryl said, ''I'm finished, okay?''

''Fine. We don't do word counts here,'' Susan said with a smile. She looked at Shannon. ''How about you, Shannon?''

''What?'' Cheryl's ''story'' had sounded a little too heart-felt to be fiction. But surely it was. She had said she'd make up something. She couldn't have been talking about Andy Welles, could she?

''Do you want to tell us your story, Shannon?''

Shannon swallowed once, hard. No, she wouldn't like to tell her story. She would much prefer to think about the mystery of Cheryl Carpenter and just forget her own story. That's what she'd been working on since the day she woke up in the hospital—forgetting it. She closed her eyes, and in her lap, her hands curled into fists. The problem seemed to be that she couldn't forget. Like Sissy, she was locked into a tangle of emotion and freeing herself seemed beyond her.

A touch on her knee interrupted her thoughts. It was Francine. Shannon guessed that something of her distress must show on her face to prompt Francine to offer support. With a weak smile, she drew a deep breath. ''Hello, my name is Shannon.''

Beside her, she felt a tiny reaction from Cheryl. More support? Sympathy? She didn't look to identify it. ''My job is reporting. I never used to be afraid, but I am now.'' She hesitated, looking around the group. ''Afraid, I mean. I'm afraid all the time. I feel like I live in a cage. I used to have a life, a promising career, friends, goals. Now I don't have the courage to drive to the grocery store by myself. Or the library. I'm even afraid to go to church. I hate myself because I've become such a coward!''

When she managed the courage to do it, she looked up to see the reaction to her confession. She didn't see disgust or pity. No one seemed shocked. No one seemed critical. They all seemed simply...accepting. As though every one of the women listening to her knew firsthand what she felt.

Across from her, Susan spoke. "Perhaps it would help if you would talk about what actually happened to you, Shannon."

The familiar ache began between her eyes. "I don't remember what happened."

"Nothing?" Susan said softly. "Absolutely nothing?"

A snip of memory clicked in her mind, like the quick flash of a light in a dark room. Dark. She remembered the dark. She shivered, and beside her, Cheryl reached out to touch her. "It was a very dark night and I had arrived home only an hour before from Atlanta. I'm not sure if I remember that or if I just know it because I've been told I was in Atlanta that night." Closing her eyes, she saw herself holding a white paper sack. "I bought Chinese take-out on my way home. The boxes were found in my kitchen. I took a shower." She frowned, recalling something, but it slipped away. "I must have gone downstairs, because..."

"Because..." Susan's voice prodded gently.

"Because someone was in my apartment." Her eyes flew open with the first certain memory she had ever had. "He was waiting in the dark for me. He was tall and he wore a stocking over his face. He hit me." Her voice quivered. "Without warning. I just barely had time to look up and see him, and then...blam. His fist..." Seeing the moment again, she touched her cheekbone unconsciously. "I just remember it coming at me and then an explosion of pain."

"It's all sort of vague after that," she said, focusing on her inner nightmare. "He wasn't satisfied with just the one blow. He kept hitting me and hitting me. He seemed in a fury. He was so mad at me. Even after I was down, he kicked me, then slammed me into the wall, all the while screaming threats. I guess I didn't comprehend them because I was so terrified and in such pain. Then, the worst part.'' Her hand crept to her throat. ''He meant for me to die. He tried to strangle me. The last thing I remember was him looming over me, his hands around my throat, his wrist…''

She sat back with a small gasp. ''He wore a very expensive watch!'' Impulsively, she turned to Cheryl. ''He must be someone who's successful, Cheryl. He was—''

At the warning squeeze on her arm, she closed her mouth with a snap. But her smile could not be contained. ''Oh, I hope I didn't break any rules, but this is the first time that I've managed to recall so much of what happened.''

''We don't have any rules except confidentiality,'' Susan reassured her. With a glance at her watch, she indicated that the session was over. ''All right, everyone, see you on Thursday, same time, same place.''

CHAPTER EIGHT

NICK WAS WAITING in the hall outside the office. At the sight of him, Shannon checked her footsteps. Their eyes met, Nick's shuttered, giving away nothing, Shannon's wide with surprise at first, and then vividly green. Without thinking, she left Cheryl's side to go to him, the only thought in her head to tell him what she had finally remembered.

He smiled at her and her breath caught. When had she begun having this kind of response to Nick Dalton? she wondered, pulling herself up short. For several moments, she forgot what had been a vital discovery only two minutes before. She had the idiotic impulse just to stand and look at him.

"Nick..." She found herself staring at his mouth, but quickly glanced away. Beyond Nick, she met a pair of amused eyes. "Oh! Ed, too. Hi." She smiled and tried to still her whirling thoughts. "I didn't expect to see either of you this morning."

"I didn't expect to be here, either," Ed said with a mild look at his partner. "You know how it is, the boss speaks, my plans don't count."

"You said something about a cup of coffee." Nick's comment was issued in even tones.

"I did?" Ed bumped his forehead with the heel of his palm. "Oh, yeah, I did. Slipped my mind for a second, how thirsty I am."

Nick closed his fingers around Shannon's arm. "Cheryl wants a cup, too. Cheryl?" He gave Shannon's bodyguard a keen look. "What is it?"

Cheryl was searching the hall and beyond the foyer to the entrance of the clinic. "Oh, nothing. Just...ah...Will O'Connor followed us on the trip in. I just wondered..."

"He went on to the shipyard," Nick said.

"Reluctantly, I'll bet," she said, her expression unreadable.

"I managed to convince him that we had the problem under control," Nick said dryly.

"No easy task, right?"

"He's concerned for his sister."

"Sure."

Nick touched Shannon's arm. "We'll meet you both back at Wilderose House in about an hour."

Ed saluted, still wearing a grin. "Good to see you out and about, Shan."

"Good to see you, too, Ed," she said, calling the words over her shoulder as Nick urged her toward the door. They were out of the clinic and crossing the sidewalk, heading for his car when Shannon realized she felt no fear. It wasn't a miraculous cure after only one session with a psychologist. It was Nick. She felt safe when she was with Nick.

At the car, he helped her inside before going to the driver's side, his expression alert. Nothing seemed to escape his keen-eyed survey of the area, she thought. It was understandable that she felt safe with him. Sliding beneath the wheel, he started the car, but instead of pulling away, he turned to her. "Well, how did it go?"

"Good. Surprisingly."

"Did you remember anything?"

She was half turned in the car seat, facing him, the words she wanted to tell him trembling on her tongue, but at his curt question, she eased back and reached for the seat belt. The moment she had walked out of that session and seen Nick, she had wanted to share that recaptured scrap of memory with him. Not as a witness in a case he was investigating, but as a friend. It was dumb to set herself up for a letdown.

"Haven't you forgotten something?" The seat belt snapped as she clicked it into place.

"Like what?"

"Your little notebook." Disappointment put a hard note in her voice. "You always have it out and ready when you grill me."

He stared at her in silence for a minute. Then, turning so that he leaned against the door and faced her fully, he said, "You want to explain what the hell you mean by that?"

What *did* she mean by that? Shannon watched a pair of squirrels dart across the limb of a massive oak tree. Just seconds ago, she had been admiring Nick's professionalism. The man wasn't obligated to treat her in any special way. He was supposed to question her. She was supposed to cooperate. To save her life, it was imperative that she *did* cooperate.

"Forget it," she said. Still watching the squirrels, she managed a halfhearted smile. "Just the stress of baring my soul in front of all those women, I guess. It takes a toll."

"Bull."

That drew her head around fast. "What?"

"You're ticked off because I asked what you remembered, and I'm trying to figure out why."

"It's nothing, Nick. It's my problem, not yours." She held his searching look for a beat or two. "As for that little notebook of yours, get it out because I really did remember something."

His eyes narrowed. "A name, a face, what?"

"Nothing that good. Just...vague stuff, a watch, his belt buckle."

"Then will it keep?"

She shrugged, confused. "I guess so."

"Good. Because I want to drive you through a couple of neighborhoods to see if anything looks familiar to you."

She watched him buckle up, then back the car out of the parking space. "Familiar in what way?"

At the street, he checked both directions, then pulled out

before replying. "Most of what you told me about the teenage runaway, Becky, turned out to be true."

Shannon said nothing. Although she'd known all along that she had not been hallucinating or dreaming, to hear it confirmed was like a punch in the stomach. Propping her elbow on the ledge of the window, she rubbed her forehead wearily.

"Most of it?"

"Actually, all of it."

She nodded.

"No comment?"

"What can I say? I saw it. I didn't make it up. I just hope it helps find whoever murdered her."

Nick turned at a major intersection and eased into traffic heading up a ramp to a bridge. When they were speeding along with the rest of the traffic, he glanced at her. "I've been thinking whether or not to mention your...ah...input. Officially, I mean. It would be better not to, I think. Most people wouldn't believe it, anyway, but the killer just might, if it got out. And it would. Something like that..." He stopped, gazing through the car window as though afraid to say the word "psychic." "Anyway, it's a chance I don't want to take. If the killer just happened to believe...well, you never know. It would put you in even greater jeopardy."

"You're assuming Becky is somehow linked to the teenage prostitution thing that was exposed in the last article I wrote before I was assaulted."

"She was, or at least the evidence we've uncovered so far makes it look like she was. A girlfriend in her hometown received a couple of phone calls from her while she was on the road. From remarks she made, they believe she was targeted. She mentioned being pressured by some unsavory types, which was why she decided to move on, so her friend says." His mouth twisted bitterly. "She was very pretty. She would have been a definite asset in their sleazy operation, at least for a few years."

All Shannon had to do was close her eyes and Becky was

there, like a picture etched permanently in her mind. What set her mental pictures of Becky apart from other ordinary memories was that she knew Becky's thoughts, felt her hunger as she'd eyed the hot dogs warming on the grill, shared her terror as she had trembled in that dingy bedroom in the dark. She shuddered now, thinking of it.

"Where are we?" she asked suddenly, looking around blankly.

"From something her friend said, we think Becky might have cruised this neighborhood a day or so before she died."

"She did, I think." Shannon's heart began to flutter. "Make a left turn at the intersection ahead," she told Nick. With one quick, penetrating look at her, he did as she directed, driving slowly through a neighborhood that had clearly seen better times. Poverty and the ravages of years had taken a toll. Tired row houses lined both sides of the street. Relics of the fifties, most were identical with only a few alterations to distinguish them—a porch here, a carport there. Shutters sagged, windows were dingy, broken-down toys littered patchy brown lawns.

"What a dismal place," Shannon murmured, watching two small boys trying to replace the chain on a sorry bicycle.

"Yeah." Keeping an eye on her and trying to drive at the same time, Nick drove slowly down the street. Shannon glanced at him and realized that he was waiting for a reaction from her. His expression was hard to define, as though he couldn't quite believe he was doing this. "Do you get some kind of feeling in this neighborhood?" he said, slowing at a seedy convenience store on the corner.

Shannon suddenly turned away from the window, stifling a gasp. Reacting automatically, Nick swerved to the curb and stopped the car. "What? What is it?"

"I...nothing. I just felt for a minute..."

Nick frowned, looking from her shocked face to the store. There were several people in sight, mostly male. One man went inside, another walked out. With a casual glance at them, he ambled toward an aged pickup truck, pausing before getting inside to peel the wrapper from a pack of cigarettes.

"Do you know him, Shannon?"

"No."

"Any of the others?"

"No, of course not. How could I?" But her heart was pounding and her mouth felt dry as dust. "I want to go home, Nick...please."

"Is there somebody I should question?"

"How should I know!" Feeling tired and beset with too many grim images and vague premonitions, she rubbed her forehead where a jackhammer was going full force behind her eyes.

A minute passed. Nick sat ominously silent, watching with a dark look while the driver of the pickup backed up, then peeled out in a screech of nearly bald tires. Beside him, Shannon winced.

"I can't believe this," he said finally.

Shannon sighed and leaned her head against the backrest. "Believe what?"

"That I'm actually sitting here asking a psychic to help me find a killer."

"I am not a psychic."

"What else would you call it, then?"

"Clairvoyance," Shannon said with a shrug. "Sort of. Because I think it's temporary. I think what's happening to me is just a...a fluke, something that is a result of my head injuries and amnesia." Nick made a low sound, but she ignored it. "I've told you before that it has something to do with—"

"Don't say it, Shannon," he warned.

"Dying."

He started the car and pulled away from the curb almost as aggressively as the driver of the pickup. "We're heading home," he muttered, zipping through a caution light as it turned red. "I shouldn't have done this, anyway. It was a bad idea. I did some research about psychics assisting in police

work and the statistics stink. The chances of getting anything—''

''It's my grandmother who truly has a gift.''

He stared straight ahead stonily.

''It's true, Nick.''

He sighed. ''Okay, I'll bite. Tell me about your grandmother.''

''She's been clairvoyant all her life. She has often seen
things, known things...sometimes before they happened,
sometimes when they were happening. She calls it her Dream
Sight.''

''Then how come her 'Dream Sight' didn't tell her that
somebody planned to kill her granddaughter?'' The question
was out before he thought, steeped in sarcasm. Glancing at
her distressed face, he swore softly. ''Forget I said that,'' he
muttered. ''I always seem to—''

''It's okay,'' she said softly. ''I don't know why she didn't
see it. Maybe I'm going crazy. Maybe—''

''Come on, Shannon. You're one of the sanest people I
know.''

''I used to be sane. Now...''

''You're still recovering from a major trauma. And you're
probably right thinking that this...clairvoyance you've developed could stem from your injuries. The fact that your grandmother filled your head with such nonsense makes it even
more understandable.'' She started to protest, but at his look
she subsided. Nick was a realist. He wouldn't be persuaded
by anything she could say. Seeing her expression, he eased up
and a smile tugged at the corner of his mouth. ''It's no big
deal. A little kid hearing that stuff from a lady like Miss Kathleen from the cradle...who wouldn't believe?''

''She never told me anything.''

''What?''

''Not one word.''

''Then how do you know she—''

''Her journals. And before you say that's the same thing,

hear this. I never even knew about the journals until about six months ago when I discovered them in a trunk in the attic.''

He remained unmoved for a few moments, then released a long breath. ''Hell, it beats me, Shannon. I don't know what to make of it, other than to say we'll just play it by ear.'' Then, with a resolute sound, he turned and gave her an authoritative look. ''Just don't be talking about this to anybody else, okay?''

She settled deeper into the seat and crossed her arms. ''I hear you.''

''Good.'' He pulled up at the entrance to Wilderose House where Ed and Cheryl were waiting beyond the closed gates. At Nick's signal, the gates swung slowly open. He drove through, motioning for the two officers to follow.

''Now…'' He ignored the exasperated sound she made. ''Let's talk about what you remembered in the session.''

''It wasn't much.''

''Let me decide what's much and what isn't.''

''Don't you need your little notebook?''

He gave her a curious look. ''What is it about my notebook that bugs you, do you mind telling me that?''

Good question. But she knew the answer, Shannon thought as the car wound slowly through half-wild grounds that were far more appealing than clipped, formal landscaping could ever be. The answer was that Nick's meticulous notetaking was a reminder that their relationship was strictly business. Cop and witness. As it should be. Staring into the tangled wild roses bordering the lane, she wondered what exactly she wanted it to be.

''Your notebook does not bug me,'' she told him as they stopped in front of Wilderose House. ''I know you have a job to do.''

He looked as if he wanted to say something, but in the end he simply pushed the door open with a muttered oath and got out of the car. Behind them, Cheryl and Ed were already out, both eyeing the house and grounds with the same alertness that she had observed in Nick. On the lookout for a madman. She felt the familiar tension settle between her shoulders. Her jaw clenched, she stepped out onto the driveway. She heard Nick instruct Ed and Cheryl to wait, then he put his hand under her arm and urged Shannon up the steps. "Come on, we'll talk inside."

He would get her statement, then see her safely into Cheryl's keeping and go. She would soon be alone again with her fear.

"HE WORE A ROLEX, the kind that has a steel band with gold in the middle." Too restless to sit, Shannon paced the huge front room, moving from window to window, from the archway entrance back to the fireplace, then back to the window again.

"Anything else?" Nick asked, watching her without expression.

"His face was covered with a stocking."

"Original," Nick said dryly.

She stopped. "Do you want to hear this or not?"

"That was a comment about him, not you. Here..." He patted the space beside him on the tapestry sofa. "Sit down. I'm tired just watching you."

Hesitating only momentarily, she sat, then wilted suddenly into the deep cushions as though the strength that held her backbone straight had suddenly disappeared.

Eyes closed, hands linked in her lap, she murmured, "I bought Chinese take-out..." She frowned, trying to recall. "I went upstairs after eating it and took a shower. Something made me go back downstairs."

"Did you surprise him, or do you think he was waiting for you?"

Nick cursed himself when he saw the impact of his question. Shannon paled, touching her cheek. "You mean, was he a casual intruder, or was I his preferred victim?" She gave a humorless laugh. "He had time to slip out the way he came in, I think. No, he must have been waiting for me."

"You lost consciousness?"

"No..." She closed her eyes. "I don't think so. He—"

"You saw him?"

"He came at me..."

"Physical attributes, Shannon."

"I'm not sure."

"Was he tall? Short?"

"Ahh..."

"Fat? Skinny?"

"I don't... He... Fat!" Her eyes widened. "He was overweight! His belly bulged over his belt buckle." She looked at Nick. "And there was something on his buckle." She frowned, trying to see it. "A crest? A symbol? An initial..." She shook her head. "I'm not sure."

"Try. What else?"

"It's hard, because he kept yelling at me."

"The words, Shannon. The words."

"I don't know! He was...crazy...screaming, but I don't remember the exact words, Nick. It's all scrambled, the noise and the p-pain." Her voice trembled, dropping. "I just know that he was hitting me with his fists. Over and over and over. How can you expect me to tell you what the dialogue was!"

Her eyes swimming with tears tore at him. Feeling lower than a snake, he pocketed the notebook and stood up, ramming his hands deep into his pockets. Better that than what he wanted to do. He ached with the urge to pull her into his arms, to wrap her as tightly against him as he'd ever held a woman. To keep from doing just that, he muttered an apology and told her he'd find his own way out.

Pulling the door closed behind him, he leaned against it, his heart thudding like a piston. What the hell was happening to him? He had never veered so far off course in conducting an investigation. From the moment he had intercepted the 911 call and rushed to Shannon's apartment, he'd seemed to be caught up in forces beyond his control, beset by feelings of lust and possessiveness and fear for her safety until he hardly knew whether he was coming or going. Without warning, he suddenly thought of the moment on the floor of her apartment when he'd held her hand and felt her life force waning. He'd known the instant everything was reversed and she'd come back. Was Shannon on the right track in thinking that that was the source of everything happening now? Had his life become irrevocably linked with Shannon's in that moment?

Every atom of his experience as a cop rejected that idea. But why else had he haunted her bedside? Why did he drive by Wilderose House every night just to check on her? Why did he feel so protective of Shannon O'Connor? Taking the front steps of Wilderose House two at a time, he put distance between them as though getting away from her would put a stop to what he was feeling.

AT THE POLICE CAR, Cheryl looked up, instantly concerned by something in his eyes. "What's wrong, Nick?" He was saved from the necessity of making a reply by a squawk from the radio. Ed was in an urgent exchange with the dispatcher.

"We've got a hot one, Nick."

He nodded and started around to the other side of the car. "Shannon's upset," he said to Cheryl over his shoulder. "Stay close to her for a while, will you? Whatever happened in that encounter group, it tripped a switch in her memory. Not much of substance, but it's a beginning."

"I'll try to do better next time," Shannon said curtly, appearing at the top of the steps.

Nick swore before looking up at her. "You know I didn't mean it that way, Shannon. I—"

"We haven't got time, Nick. We gotta move it." Ed replaced the transmitter and reached for the ignition. "A crazy is shooting up the Dilly Burger, holding a woman customer and the manager hostage. An accident on the interstate has several units occupied. Dispatch is issuing a call for anybody in the area.''

"Wait!" All three turned to look at Shannon. A hostage situation was a cop's worst nightmare, but it was a media event. It was drama and danger personified. In a town the size of Savannah, it could possibly be the news event of the year. First on the scene... Shannon chewed her lip anxiously. To a reporter, it was a dream opportunity. "I..." She could feel her heart start to pound with fear. "I mean...I think..."

From over the roof of the car, Nick looked at Shannon. "Do you want to go?"

"Jeez, Nick!" Ed stared at him in amazement. Cheryl was equally astonished.

"You'll be safe. Cheryl will see to that."

But not Nick. She would not be able to stay with him. He would be caught up in the drama.

"For a journalist, it's the kind of story that only rolls around once in a blue moon." Nick's voice was soft, almost singsong, a trainer coaxing a thoroughbred to attempt a higher fence.

"I know." The words were barely a whisper. Before her assault, they would have had to tie her down to keep her away. She didn't have to close her eyes to imagine the scene. Chaos and danger; a man with a weapon; fear and anger and violence; excitement; people, hordes of people, the good indistinguishable from the evil. Including the man who'd hurt her. Who wished to kill her. Fear washed through her in a deadly tide.

"I can't."

Nick held her gaze another long and silent moment, then at Ed's urging, tapped the top of the car, nodded once and climbed into the car. With a spray of gravel, the vehicle was off.

Shannon watched it disappear around the curve in the lane with her fingers pressed against her mouth. Then, with a crushing sense of despair, she turned and dashed inside to the sanctuary of Wilderose House.

A FEW MINUTES LATER, Cheryl rapped softly on the open door, then stepped inside the small sitting room where Shannon sat gazing through the French doors watching the antics of two blue jays tormenting a squirrel. "Want some company?" Cheryl held up two tall glasses of iced tea sprigged with mint. "And something to drink?"

"Sure, have a seat." Shannon took the glass. "Thanks."

"I can't believe Nick put you through that," Cheryl said, finding a comfortable seat in the corner of the sofa. "He knows you haven't been cleared to go back to work yet."

"He also knows I had a tiny breakthrough in that session this morning. A big story breaking right on the heels of that might have triggered even more." Looking into her tea, she said wryly, "Striking while the iron is hot, I think it's called."

"He's not a psychologist! I don't know what he was thinking," Cheryl said indignantly, "but pushing you into something like a hostage situation is going too far. He knows nothing's more dangerous than a crazed gunman, plus you have the hostages—you never know what frightened people will do. Unless he's disarmed right away, within an hour there will be TV cameras and reporters, people gawking..." She shook her head. "It's the last place you should be."

"It's the only place I should be, Cheryl."

"Oh, Shannon..."

"It's true. Nick knew this was just the sort of thing I would have reveled in before the assault. And he was right. When I heard Ed tell him about it, I wanted to be there so bad I could taste it, but..."

"But what?"

"I was too scared. Nick knows that, too, but he hoped my instincts as a reporter would overcome my fear." Shannon rubbed a hand over her face wearily. "He was wrong."

Cheryl leaned forward and touched her knee. "Don't worry, it'll come. You just have to give it time, Shannon."

She gazed out through the French doors for a moment, then

gave a bitter laugh. "Ernie will kill me if he finds out I had a chance to be first on the scene and I chickened out."

"Your editor? He will not. *He* knows you're not ready."

"And my grandmother," Shannon said, shaking her head. "She would never have ducked an assignment, no matter how risky."

"Nobody ever threatened your grandmother's life!" Cheryl protested.

"Actually, I think that is precisely what happened once."

"Shannon..." There was sympathy and understanding in Cheryl's tone.

"Then there's my brother Ryan, a foreign correspondent somewhere in the Middle East. He dodges bullets and car bombs on a daily basis."

"Which isn't the same as a deliberate attempt on his life," Cheryl pointed out flatly.

Shannon studied her bodyguard's face for a moment or two, then bent forward and set her iced tea on the coffee table. "I guess I sound like a whiner, huh?"

"Well..." Cheryl's mouth tilted in a half smile.

"Or a spoiled brat."

Cheryl studied the wallpaper intently.

"A pain in the backside."

Her topaz eyes dancing, Cheryl covered her mouth, and they both laughed out loud. As it had once before, the laughter touched a chord in both of them. With a warm feeling, Shannon realized that Cheryl had become a friend. A very good friend. When all this was behind her, at least she would have one good thing to show for it. Maybe two, if she could make Nick see her as anything except a citizen he was sworn to protect.

She watched Cheryl reach for her glass. "I wish—"

"This is neat," Cheryl said, squishing mint leaves into her tea. "Nobody but Miss Kathleen thinks of this anymore."

"Cheryl, is Nick... Is he involved with someone?"

Her glass suspended halfway to her mouth, Cheryl's face

registered her surprise. "If he is, he's managed to keep it under wraps. Of course, that's what Nick would do anyway if he was actually interested in a particular woman. He's a pretty self-contained individual, a loner, almost." She sipped her tea thoughtfully. "I think he was married once, but he's never mentioned his ex-wife that I recall."

"So you don't know if he has children...or...anything."

"No," Cheryl said, watching her intently. "But I think he'd make a wonderful father."

Shannon stood up and went to stare out the window. "He thinks I'm withholding information, Cheryl."

"Why would he think that?"

"I'm not sure. Maybe it has something to do with our relationship before the assault. We were natural adversaries. You know how it is, cops hate the press, and I suppose I was guilty of pushing Nick in the past. But as somebody once said, that was then and this is now. He saved my life, Cheryl. He hates for me to mention it, but it's true. Still, every time we spend more than three minutes together, we wind up sniping at each other, or disagreeing about something. I've always been able to get along with people. I don't know what it is about Nick and me. One minute we're close—you know, almost...well, just close. Then the next minute, we're...not."

"What do I know?" Cheryl said, earnestly studying her nails. "But it sounds a lot like plain old-fashioned sex appeal to me."

Shannon whirled around. "I'm serious, Cheryl!"

"Me, too. It would go a long way toward explaining Nick's foul disposition lately."

"Foul disposition?"

"Let me put it this way. If Nick's temper gets any more uncertain, his staff is going to put in for transfers. Even Ed is running out of patience. Only two things make a man that crazy—sexual frustration and job stress."

"I'm sure he's worried about his cases," Shannon murmured.

"Yeah, and if you combine the two—I'm talking about you and the man who hurt you who's still at large, as well as the missing teenage girls and Becky Berenson...well, I rest my case."

"Nick doesn't think of me that way," Shannon said, unaware of the bleakness in her eyes. "To him I'm just someone withholding information. Until I recall the details of my assault, another criminal walks around unapprehended. That's the way Nick thinks. That's all he thinks."

"Then why was he at your bedside around the clock the first few days after your assault?"

"He was waiting for me to recover enough to answer his questions. To nail the perpetrator."

"Why did he go personally to your apartment when the call came in on 911?"

"I don't know."

"And what about showing up here at Wilderose House in the middle of the night?"

"He said he couldn't sleep." That was the night Becky had been killed, Shannon thought. He had been tired and discouraged and he had not hidden it from her. Why?

"And wasn't it actually Nick who persuaded you to go to the victims' encounter group?"

"To prod my memory," Shannon murmured, but she wasn't as certain as she once was.

"No. He wants to see you overcome the trauma. He wants to see you healthy again."

Deep in thought, Shannon stood at the window. She wanted to believe that Nick's interest was more than professional. She wanted to think that he felt the same connection between them that she'd felt since he'd literally pulled her back from the jaws of death. But the truth was, Nick hadn't given her any hint that he wanted anything from her except information.

With a sigh, she left the window and came back to the sofa. Scooting back in the corner, she made herself comfortable. "What did you think about the encounter group?"

Cheryl studied the mint leaves floating in her tea. "It was interesting."

"Uh-huh. Some of those women have been terribly unlucky in their personal lives, haven't they?"

"Yeah."

"I admire them for reaching out and getting help. I know how hard I resisted taking that first step."

"You did just fine. You hit pay dirt on the first try."

Shannon nodded. "I know. I'm actually looking forward to the next session." She gave Cheryl an apologetic look. "It's twice a week, you know. I feel awkward forcing you to sit through it, but you carried it off just fine. I couldn't tell that you weren't actually a victim yourself. You're really good at this undercover stuff."

"Yeah, I fit right in."

Something in her tone drew an intent look from Shannon. "It *was* all pretense, wasn't it, Cheryl?"

Cheryl's laugh was a travesty of the genuine thing. "You mean you didn't recognize the man I was married to in my monologue?"

"It didn't sound like the Andy Welles everyone thinks you were married to," Shannon said slowly. "But I've gotten to know you better than I ever knew Andy Welles, and something about your words today sounded a little too intense to have been pulled out of thin air."

Avoiding Shannon's eyes, Cheryl set her glass on the coffee table and got to her feet. "I don't really like talking about my marriage, Shannon, do you mind?"

"I'm sorry," Shannon said instantly. "Was I being nosy again?"

"No, you were being kind. It's me who's a little screwy about the subject. So..." She cleared her throat suddenly. "I think I'll just make a routine check of the house and grounds. Can't do my job sitting around drinking iced tea. Okay?"

"Cheryl?" At the door, Cheryl stopped, reluctantly, Shannon thought. "Just so you'll know...I'm a good listener."

THE HOSTAGE SITUATION made headlines in the *Sentinel* and every other major newspaper in the state. CNN in Atlanta carried it live after the first three hours. Only after darkness fell did the hostage negotiator finally talk the former Vietnam veteran into laying down his weapons and giving himself up. His estranged wife died in the hospital. He had coolly shot her from a booth in the fast-food restaurant as she entered to order a hamburger. Although two others were wounded, no one else had been killed.

They talked about it at the next meeting of the victims' encounter group. To the astonishment of Shannon and Cheryl, the dead woman, Mary Ellen Kirk, had been a regular participant in the group.

"What happened?" Shannon demanded, her question directed at Susan. It seemed to Shannon that as a professional she should have anticipated the explosive rage that provoked Mary Ellen's husband to murder her in full sight of the whole world. "I thought this whole group was about speaking out. If Mary Ellen did that and was ignored, what kind of justice system do we have?"

"She was not ignored," Susan said gently. "She filed half a dozen complaints with the police. She called repeatedly to tell them that she feared her husband was nearing a breakdown and that he could be violent. She had the scars to prove it."

"And they did nothing?" Shannon said, scandalized.

Cheryl, not Susan, answered. "They can't do anything until he actually commits a crime."

"Threatening to kill your wife isn't a crime?"

"Not really," said Susan. "And neither is psychological abuse. Husbands and wives can say just about anything they please without fear of prosecution. We're working to change that."

"I wish you luck," Cheryl said dryly. "As long as men are in charge, I can't see the system making any dramatic changes."

"I hear a lot of anger in your words, Cheryl," Susan said. "Would you like to talk about that?"

"I'm not angry anymore," she said shortly.

Her statement was so patently untrue that Susan waited. Finally, she said, "Because he's dead?"

Cheryl shrugged. "Well, it hardly helps being mad at a dead man, does it?"

"So long as your anger doesn't keep you from other good things in another relationship, then go ahead and be mad."

"The last thing I need is another relationship," Cheryl said bitterly. "I've managed just great without a man for the past five years."

"And you're never lonely?"

She gave a mirthless laugh. "I was ten times more lonely married to that bastard." She seemed to realize suddenly that everyone's attention was riveted on her and what her words revealed. "Hey, it's no big deal. He's out of my life and, as they say, I'm free at last."

Susan smiled, but it was a sad smile. "Are you really?"

WITH A CURSE, the man rammed his vehicle into gear and pushed the gas pedal to the floor. The neat, well-manicured landscaping of the clinic was a green blur as he accelerated to a speed well beyond the legal limit, then wrenched the wheel to a hard right that took him up the ramp and onto the interstate.

The stupid bitch was seeing a psychiatrist.

Through a red haze, he overtook the eighteen-wheeler in front of him, swerving back into his lane a second too soon. He ignored the loud blast of the truck's horn, barely noticing that the driver missed a guard rail by a single inch. A bunch of women sitting around bellyaching about life in general and men in particular, he knew what went on in those sessions.

He gave an outraged driver a vulgar signal with his finger. Getting the name of the shrink was the first priority. He didn't know how long it would take. Several possibilities occurred to him, but he discounted them. Too risky. He couldn't afford mistakes now, or delays. Fury was a hot ball in his throat. Just the thought of the O'Connor bitch was enough to make his blood boil. He hated women complicating his life. When he finally got his hands on her...

Another long blast from an aggrieved driver cut into his internal tirade. With a long breath, he fought to bring his rage under control. It wouldn't help to get stopped by the highway patrol. He was not scheduled to be in Savannah today, and he didn't need to fabricate any more lies about his comings and goings. His secretary was already suspicious.

Another pushy broad.

But nothing like Shannon O'Connor. Damn her! With a professional counseling her, she just might recover her memory, and when she did, she might put it all together. She had already come very close once.

His fingers now drumming on the wheel, he frowned darkly as the rushing lines of the interstate spun out in front of him. He had to figure out a way to keep her from ruining everything. He had to figure out a way to silence her. And this time, it would be forever.

The picture of how she would look once he'd finished with her was vivid in his mind. Focusing on it, he calmed somewhat and settled deeper into the leather seat. His smile was almost one of sexual satisfaction.

CHAPTER NINE

May 29—Wilderose House

I'M GOING BACK to work. I have been out of the hospital for almost five weeks. There have been no threats, no attempts to hurt me. I'm still afraid, but I can't spend the rest of my life doing nothing. Cheryl will accompany me to the office and back and to other assignments away from the newspaper. There was a time in my life when I would have fought having a bodyguard beside me all day long. "Protection" would have been far more of a threat to my independence than any crazed assailant could ever be. But...never say never. I know I have a long way to go to heal, because I accept the presence of Cheryl and others. More significantly, I'm glad they're there.

The victims' encounter group was a good decision. Since the assault, I seem to be on a roller coaster of emotions— fear, anger, hatred—you name it. I never knew I had the capacity for such passion! Like Cheryl, I can't be truly free until I can put it all behind me. It's mostly fear that keeps me walled in. Somehow, in a way I don't yet comprehend, my feelings about the man who did this to me are also linked to my inability to function as a whole person again. When I've worked through that, I will be free. I'm working on it. There are jails and then there are jails.

SHE'D HAD THE DREAM again last night. The courtroom, the weeping woman, the two lawyers carping back and forth and, as usual, no jury. She could see now that the woman wore a hat with a veil, a heavy, dark swathe of net that obscured her face. But it could not conceal her sobs. She wept brokenly, begging for help. Shannon had jerked awake, the sound of the woman's weeping echoing within her, and filled with the woman's fear.

Today was to be her first day back at the *Sentinel* and the dream unsettled her. Having to dredge up the energy to cope with another bizarre symptom of her assault was almost enough to make her back out. But of course there was no other option. She had to face down her fear. It was the only way to take charge of her life again.

For a while, back at her desk in the familiar, disorderly newsroom of the *Sentinel,* she managed to pretend that things were back to normal. That her life was under control again. Opening her computer, she looked at headings for the features she had been working on before the assault. One of them interested her more than ever now. She highlighted Battered Women, tapped a command and waited.

Several women in the encounter group were victimized by men who claimed to love them. Listening to them week after week, she was appalled by their stories and baffled by the choices they made. To stay. To hope. They rationalized. They kept on keeping on. God knows how they managed, since they had so little support from law enforcement.

Mary Ellen Kirk had been a prime example. A week after Mary Ellen had been shot to death by her abusive husband, Shannon had still been fuming over a system of justice that had only rallied around the woman when it was too late.

"How could something like this happen?" she had asked Nick Dalton when she finally managed to question him about the case. She was in his office waiting while Cheryl took care of some personal business. "The woman begged for protection. She did everything she was supposed to do to safeguard herself. Why didn't it work?"

"The judge had granted a restraining order," Nick said. He used a quiet, reasonable tone, but his jaw had a rigid look.

Shannon guessed he'd been forced to explain the department's position on this one before. "It was supposed to keep Kirk away from her, or at least no closer than five hundred feet."

"He was ten feet from her in the restaurant when he shot her," Shannon countered.

"We can't keep a customer away from a fast-food restaurant, Shannon, and we can't keep tabs on a single individual twenty-four hours a day."

"Not even when he's threatened to kill his wife?"

"Not even then."

"You keep pretty close tabs on me."

"Yes, but the man who attempted to kill you is still at large."

From the defensive way he answered her questions, she sensed he felt the shortcomings of the system as much as she did. Thank God her own family was in a position to hire additional protection for her. Unfair, yes, but lucky for her.

"Some justice system we've got, " she said, pacing the room. "We bend over backward to protect the rights of criminals, while innocent women are left to cope the best way they can."

"You know that's not true, Shannon. The same rights you speak of are the cornerstone of our legal system. They protect criminals, yes. But they also protect you and me and the innocent everywhere."

He was right, of course. After years of reporting, she knew the law on the subject as well as he. But the injustice of it was infuriating. The encounter group had made her all too sensitive to the problems of abused women. Why were their complaints so often ignored? Why were "domestic disputes" considered unimportant?

"Can't you do something?" she cried in frustration.

"Can't you?" Nick shot back evenly.

She stared at him, her thoughts churning. Before becoming a victim herself, she would not have hesitated to pull out all the stops to expose the shortcomings of a system where women like Mary Ellen Kirk had been forsaken. Inside her head, she had already composed the first paragraphs of a feature. It would carry her byline. What if she inadvertently provoked the man who had attacked her?

She had sighed and dropped wearily into her chair, her shoulders sagging. She wasn't as intrepid as she used to be. And maybe never would be again.

Someone else would have to write Mary Ellen Kirk's story.

She blinked when with a click and a series of blips, the screen in front of her revealed her notes on battered women. Because of her amnesia, almost all of her activity in the week or two before her assault was blocked from her memory. Maybe she would tap into something that would miraculously restore something today.

"Shannon! I heard you were back." Liza Westfall stopped at Shannon's desk, studying her with a look that conveyed more curiosity than sympathy. Petite, dark haired and stylishly clad in canary yellow and black, Liza was the society reporter for the *Sentinel.*

"Hi, Liza. How are you?"

"Oh, I'm fine. I should be asking about you." Shannon didn't kid herself thinking Liza had missed her. Her assault had opened a prime slot at the *Sentinel.* Liza had often complained in the past that she was underutilized writing social fluff and obituaries. From time to time, she managed to wheedle a human-interest assignment from Ernie, but she wasn't satisfied with occasional soft pieces. With Shannon out indefinitely, she had seized the opportunity to try reporting hard news. She was talented, but there was an edge to her reporting. Shannon had sometimes wondered exactly how far Liza would go to get a story. Aware of her ambition, Ernie often cautioned her for her tactics in putting a story together.

"When I heard what happened..." Liza shuddered dramatically. "Well, it's just every woman's most *awful* fear, an intruder waiting in her apartment." She gave Shannon a wide-eyed look. "I suppose you must have been *terrified!*"

"Yes, I was," Shannon murmured.

"And what a piece of luck that the EMTs got there so fast!"

"They saved my life."

"With a little help from Nick Dalton." Liza settled herself on the edge of Shannon's desk. "At least, that's what we heard."

"Nick was there, yes."

"I suppose he's trying to figure out who did this to you and why," Liza said.

"He's heading the investigation, yes." Staring at the woman's face, Shannon wondered why she got the feeling she was being interrogated. She knew how Liza's mind worked, but it mystified her how her assault could be used to the reporter's advantage.

"How's it going? Has he turned up anything interesting?"

Linking her fingers on top of the desk mat in front of her, Shannon studied her co-worker thoughtfully. "What is this, Liza? Are you planning on writing a book?"

"Heavens, no!" Liza dismissed that with a tinkly laugh. "It's just that it's all so *incredible!*"

"Only if you've never had an intruder break into your house," Shannon said dryly.

"I can only imagine how you must have felt." Liza thought a minute. "I wonder if he was just some run-of-the-mill nut case or whether there was something personal in his attack on you. Of course, you always have a lot of feature ideas working at once. That could be his motive. Do you think he could have been trying to give you a message?"

"Possibly. If that was his aim, he can consider his effort a success. I got the message."

"What does that mean? That you're sticking to less controversial topics from now on?" Without waiting for a reply, Liza bulldozed ahead. "Hey, if you still have your notes, I would be happy to—"

"Liza, please." Shannon bent her head, inhaled slowly, then looked up at the woman. "I've just gotten back to work.

I don't know what I'm going to do. I haven't made up my mind about anything. My notes are disorganized. I think I've even lost a couple of tapes from my portable cassette. I had it in my bag...at least I think I did. There are lapses in my memory. I've only just begun studying my computer notes. Any decisions are on the back burner until I figure out what to do with—'' she shrugged, suddenly overwhelmed ''—everything.''

"Gee, I'm sorry, Shannon." Straightening away from the desk, Liza gave her a sympathetic look. "If I can do anything to help you, just let me know, okay?"

"Okay, thanks, Liza." Shannon looked again at the computer screen. "Now, if you don't mind..."

"Sure, you have a lot to catch up on. I'll see you later."

Even before Liza was through the door, Shannon was focused on the words before her. This was a feature about violence. About the absence of options for some women. About the depths of despair some women lived in day after day and the appalling ineptitude of the justice system in their plight.

It was interesting and gritty and just the kind of thing she had delivered brilliantly in past articles in the *Sentinel.* She read one case history and was left with a vague sense of unease. After reading another, she realized she was tense. Her stomach was curled into a knot. By the time she began a third case history, her heart was beating too fast. Anxiety was spiraling through her body. Sweat broke out on her palms. Inside, she was in turmoil.

What is happening to me?

She stared at the screen, so disoriented that she could hardly make sense of what was there. With trembling fingers, she punched and fumbled at the keys until she hit the command to exit. Then, breathing harshly, she gritted her teeth and sat back, counting slowly, desperately, both hands locked on the seat of her chair to keep from lunging up and running wildly to...

Where? Wilderose House? To hole up like a mole, coming

out only for the sessions with the encounter group? She couldn't live that way. She couldn't!

It was several minutes before the crisis passed. Resting her head in trembling hands, she wondered bleakly whether she would ever be the same again. God, there was no sanctuary for her. She had to stay. She had to fight this. She was nobody if she didn't work. And if she couldn't handle the kind of features that had distinguished her as a journalist with a future, then she would work at something else. She had to. Otherwise, he would still have control of her life.

"COME AGAIN, SHANNON?"

"You heard me, Ernie. I want the city hall beat."

With his arms crossed on the top of his desk, the editor of the *Sentinel* studied her the same way he might look at an interesting piece of art. Modern art, which Shannon knew he thought was a joke perpetrated on society at large. Ernie Patton was a short, squat man with a pug nose and impressive chin. His usual attire was rolled shirtsleeves and baggy, wrinkled khaki pants. His only concession to neatness was the carefully combed straggly hairs that scarcely covered the large dome of his head. A journalist from the old school, his standards—standards set first by her grandmother, and maintained by him and Jessica Howell, the publisher of the Savannah *Sentinel*—were high. One look from his small, beady brown eyes could skewer a reporter who failed to live up to them.

"You want the city hall beat," he repeated flatly.

Shannon sprang up from the chair opposite his desk and began to pace. "I don't know why you're not pleased, Ernie. Nobody ever wants the city hall beat. It's the assignment from hell. You use it for punishment. You always have to threaten to get anybody to take it." She gave him a defensive look. "I'm volunteering."

"You're right about one thing—nobody ever wants it." He transferred a chewed cigar stub from one side of his mouth to the other. "It's hard to make raising taxes and grousing about water and sewage rates interesting. And we certainly don't unearth enough political scandal to utilize your particular skills, sugar.''

"I've asked you a hundred times not to call me that.''

He shrugged, grinning. ''I bounced you on my knee, honey-bunch. I'm your godfather and Jessica's your godmother. If I can't call you sugar, then who can?''

"Oh, Ernie.'' Shannon sank back into the chair. ''I can barely function as a person anymore, let alone as a reporter. I know the city hall is boring, but it's also nonthreatening. I want to work, but I don't think I can handle the assignments I used to do.''

"That bad, is it, honey?'' He studied her in silence, a Buddha contemplating a troubling supplicant. ''Well, God knows, as you pointed out, it's not easy getting anybody to cover the city's politicos, but I'm a selfish bastard. I hate to give up the dynamite you're famous for. Readers will wonder.''

She shrugged. ''Maybe I'll write under a pseudonym.''

He smiled. ''Like your grandmother?''

"Do I look like a William Collins?''

"No more than Miss Kathleen did in her day, but she sure turned out some great stuff in the twenties and thirties.''

Shannon's spirits sank again. ''I don't think I'm made of the same stuff as my grandmother.''

He sat back and gave her a stern look, his eyes snapping. ''Now, just hold it right there, my girl.'' The cigar stub was rolled to the opposite corner of his mouth. ''You are as good or better than Kathleen O'Connor. You've hit a bad patch right now, but you'll overcome it, you hear? You'll overcome it. I'll stake my spot here at the front desk on that, Shannon.''

Fiercely, he warmed to his subject. ''Matter of fact, my girl, I figure one day you'll occupy this desk.'' At her instinctive protest, he held up one hand. ''Now not, not yet. I'm still firing on all cylinders and you've got a few more laps to go before that happens. But that's the way it'll turn out, sugar. Mark my words.'' He nodded his head, looking satisfied. ''You'll sit here one day fulfilling the O'Connor family tradition. And you'll be good. You *are* good. Damn good."

He scooted his chair back abruptly and stood up. "Now, there's a meeting of those boneheads at the city hall tonight at seven. Hell, I don't know, maybe you can write something about it that'll be worth reading about it. Now get outta here. I got work to do."

"AND SO I ASK YOU to put yourselves in the shoes of one of these kids. It's up to you."

Finally, Shannon thought, staring at the skimpy notes on the pad in her lap. Councilman Taylor seemed to be winding down a long-winded, deadly boring appeal to the governing body of the city to approve funding for a jogging track in a neighborhood that he represented. The vote was called for and the funding was denied. As she jotted the results on her pad, someone sat down beside her.

"Good call," Nick said, settling back and crossing one ankle over his knee. "We had two muggings and a rape in Taylor's district this month. It's unsafe to live in that neighborhood, let alone jog."

Shannon's pulse fluttered, and as always when she was near Nick, she felt a sudden keen awareness of herself as a woman and Nick as a man. The boring meeting was suddenly infused with zest. Her impatience slipped away as though it had never been.

"Public parks are needed more in those neighborhoods than elsewhere," Shannon said, gamely defending Taylor's proposal.

"Yeah, but what we don't need are any more muggings."

She chuckled, secretly in agreement. Keeping her voice low, she asked, "What are you doing here? Somehow I don't see you as a regular at city council meetings."

"Three guesses."

Still smiling, she glanced up and was startled to find him looking at her with an expression in his eyes that made her catch her breath. The gavel banged, ending the meeting. Flustered, she bent over to lift her shoulder bag from the floor, but Nick picked it up. He got to his feet and handed it over, watching enigmatically while she crammed in her notebook and a couple of flyers that had been passed around for the general public.

"I've got a better question," he said, guiding her away from the crowd to an exit at the side of the council chambers. "What are you doing here?"

"Working. Wait, Cheryl will wonder—"

"I sent Cheryl back to Wilderose House. Come on, the car's right outside."

"'Scuse me, ma'am." Shannon turned to find a man offering her an envelope. She took it, frowning. "Somebody back there passed this note up front to you. Said it was important."

"Wait! You don't know—"

Before Nick could stop her, she ripped it open and read the first words. Horror drained her face of all color as the note fluttered from her fingers. Nick made a grab for it, and with a ferocious expression, read it.

Amnesia is a good trick, but just in case your memory returns and you decide to tell what you know, be warned, bitch: next time nobody will be able to save your nosy neck.

She was still trembling when they reached the car. Nick helped her inside, then walked around, stripping off his coat as he went. His face thunderous, he tossed it into the back seat, then flicked open the top button of his shirt and loosened his tie. Watching the uniquely male ritual, Shannon was aware only of an overwhelming need for reassurance. Thank God for Nick. Nobody made her feel safer.

"Don't tell me," she said dully as he slid in behind the wheel. "Nobody saw a thing."

"Nothing," he said curtly. "Not a damn thing." With a squeal of tires, he pulled away from the city hall.

She knew the feeling. As a journalist, she'd run up against the same frustrating dilemma time and time again. A whole roomful of people, a letter passed from hand to hand, and then…a dead end. Nobody had noticed who originated it. Glancing at Nick, she suspected there was more to his anger than that.

"Why would he take a chance like that?" she said, watching his grim features highlighted in passing neon lights.

"Arrogance, audacity, tweaking the tail of the cops just for the hell of it," Nick said in mechanical tones. Shannon realized that he was as tense as a guy wire. Although his wrist was draped over the wheel, nothing about him was relaxed.

"You make him sound like a mental case."

"It's very possible that he is a mental case."

She pressed her fingers to her mouth. "That scares me even more, Nick. I've reported enough crime to know that it's next to impossible to profile an unbalanced criminal. Guessing his next move is strictly chance. Unless he makes some stupid, fatal error, we just have to wait for him to strike again."

"Leaving that note tonight was stupid. He'll do something else just as stupid, Shannon."

"But what if he doesn't?" She huddled against the door, her arms wrapped around herself. Glancing over, Nick swore, then slowed at the intersection. Instead of taking the county road that led to Wilderose House, he turned left.

"Where are we going?" she asked faintly.

"To my place," he said shortly. "I don't want to be too far away tonight just in case your tormentor decides to be even more stupid, but I need to do a couple of things at home. Okay?"

She closed her eyes as he turned into a quiet, dark street. "I don't care, Nick. I'm just so scared."

"Yeah, understandable. Looks like this guy doesn't stop with physical brutality. He's into psychological stuff, too."

"What am I going to do?" she whispered.

"We're going to go through your records with a fine-tooth comb," he told her firmly. "We're going to scrutinize every scrap of an idea you were working on before the assault. We're going to retrace every step you made. We're going to—"

"We've already done all that!" she cried, her voice high.

"We'll do it again." He pulled up in front of a tall town house and stopped. "And again. And again, if necessary. Until we nail the bastard." He pushed open the door. "C'mon, we'll talk inside."

He took her hand as she climbed out of the car. "God, you're cold as ice." Without thinking, he pulled her close and just rocked her against him for a few seconds. It was exactly what she needed. Tears welled in her eyes, and she buried her face in his shirtfront. It was heaven to be wrapped in Nick's arms, even out in the open with his neighbors watching. It felt safe. *She* felt safe. For the first time since reading that note, she drew a deep breath.

"I'm sorry," she whispered. "This is so—"

"Nice," he murmured against her hair.

"But you shouldn't have to—"

"Hush." He moved, slipping his arm around her waist to guide her up the walkway. "What are cops for?"

Not for this, Shannon thought, oddly dissatisfied with the reminder that he had held her and comforted her only for professional reasons. Since Nick had literally dragged her back to life, her feelings had been changing, expanding, deepening. Just exactly where she was headed, she wasn't yet sure, and she didn't like not knowing. Already she was in danger of needing Nick, and she'd never needed anyone before. He wasn't a cop who had become a friend. He was a man who could become everything.

Feeling decidedly shaken, she followed him silently up the steps to his front door and then stepped into his world.

She had wondered more than once about his personal life,

but their relationship before her assault had been too adversarial to even pretend friendship. He found her journalistic zeal trying and he'd never made any secret of it. Fascinated, she went inside his town house, not about to pass up a rare opportunity to see where he lived.

His foyer was lighted by a floor lamp with a stained-glass shade. "This is very beautiful," she said, admiring the intricacy of the dragonfly design.

"I like it," he said, and then to her amazement, he bent down and scooped up a big yellow tomcat. "Hiya, big Jake," he murmured, rubbing the animal behind its ears, chuckling at the cat's loud meow as he bumped his battle-scarred head against Nick's chin.

"I think he's trying to tell you something," Shannon said, smiling inanely. Nick Dalton, a cat lover!

"Say hello to a nice lady, Jake," he told the cat.

Shannon stroked Jake along his sleek back, but her eyes were on Nick's face. "Do those guys at the station know you're a sucker for beat-up alley cats?"

After lowering Jake to the floor, he gave her slow grin. "You mean you haven't ever noticed that little frame on my desk? The one with Jake licking his birthday cake and wearing a kitty hat that reads C'mon, Make My Day?"

"You're kidding!"

He chuckled, grabbing a cat-food can and feeding it to the electric can opener. "Yeah, I am, actually."

She slanted him a look to see if that teasing note in his voice was real or if she'd imagined it. Nick Dalton, teasing and protective, was a dynamite combination. And dangerous.

He was a private, self-contained man, she already knew that. Looking at him sometimes, she had seen things in his eyes, heard nuances in his voice, that told her there were depths to Nick that he kept carefully hidden. She wondered if there would ever come a time when he would open up to her.

After feeding the cat, he rinsed his hands and grabbed a bottle of wine on his way out of the kitchen, urging her ahead

of him. "How about a drink? Beer, or I've got wine...." He
held up the bottle. "Soft drink? Coffee?"

"Wine's good," she said faintly, realizing suddenly what
Nick was doing. He knew she had had the daylights scared
out of her tonight with that note, and he was trying to help.
To distract her. Which he certainly was doing. Glimpsing this
side of him was…something else. When he produced a cork-
screw to open the bottle, she reached for a couple of wine-
glasses in a rack overhead, but he only filled one, then grabbed
a beer from the refrigerator for himself.

He handed her the wine, then nudged her in the direction
of his den. They passed the cat, who was sitting beside his
untouched dinner, calmly grooming himself. "He didn't eat
anything," Shannon said. "Maybe he doesn't like Seafood
Fest."

"Don't you believe it. Come back in ten minutes and that
stuff will be history."

When she sank down onto the sofa, he sat beside her,
spreading one arm across the back. She looked around with
undisguised curiosity. Except for the stunning stained-glass
lamp in the foyer, Nick's house was curiously Spartan. It was
also scrupulously clean and tidy. What few magazines she saw
were collected in a neat pile on the plain coffee table. Nick's
house reflected the discipline that made him a good cop. She
couldn't imagine him rumpled and half dressed. Or hot and
sweaty after mowing the lawn, shirtless and wearing cutoffs.
Those strong thighs of his would— On second thought, she
could imagine it. All too easily.

"Do you have any idea how he knew where to find you?"
Nick asked in his low, deep voice. "Nobody's been following
you or watching the house, Cheryl's sure of that."

She drew a blank momentarily. Oh, yes. The note.
"No…no, I don't. I just got the assignment from Ernie today,
and since it was my first day back at the *Sentinel*, I don't have
a clue how anybody knew, except Cheryl, of course."

"You think Patton would keep it to himself?"

"Absolutely." She added thoughtfully, "Maybe whoever it is has been waiting for me to show up there. He seems to think I know something. The only thing is—" her mouth compressed ruefully "—I simply don't remember what I know."

"Which reminds me..." He leaned forward and set his beer on the coffee table, then settled back, his hand behind her on the sofa again. "You never answered my question earlier tonight. Why were you working the city hall beat? You haven't been stuck with an assignment like that since your first week with the *Sentinel,* and that was only to acquaint you with the city fathers. I'm surprised Patton made the assignment."

"He didn't. I volunteered."

"You volunteered."

"I opened my computer when I got to the office this morning, and the first notes that came up sent me into a panic, Nick." Closing her eyes, she leaned her head back, forgetting for a second that his hand was there. His fingers moved in her hair and the little chills that coursed through her felt good, reassuring. Almost sensual. "I don't know why, I just know I couldn't handle the...content of my research. It was about battered women. I actually had an anxiety attack."

"Well, that hardly requires a psychiatrist to explain," he said quietly.

"I don't know. I just ran into Ernie's office and volunteered for the city hall beat."

"Dull, boring and safe," Nick said.

"Yeah, I admit it," she said.

"And look what happened. An anonymous note with a cold-blooded threat."

She heard his muffled oath and felt the renewed motion of his fingers tangling in her hair. Somewhere inside her, fear and desire mingled strangely. Somehow she resisted the urge to close her eyes. "Can we stop this? I don't want to talk about it any more tonight." Even to her own ears, her voice sounded strangled. Like a cat, she rubbed her cheek against his knuckles. "I'm so glad you were there, Nick. I don't think—"

He made a sound, cutting her off, and got to his feet. "Why don't you just finish your wine while I get some gear together." In a few hurried strides, he was at the hallway. "I'll be done in a few minutes," he called over his shoulder. "The bathroom's upstairs. Make yourself at home."

Watching his hasty escape, Shannon was surprised at the sharp pain in her heart. She might have newly blossoming feelings for Nick, but if he felt anything, it was clear he wasn't going to act on it. He didn't plan to let her get any closer than any other witnesses on any other case.

Dejected, she got up from the sofa and began an idle survey of the house. Looking around again, the scrupulously neat, almost ascetic look of Nick's home suddenly bothered her for some reason. Nobody's home should be so...unhomelike. If it weren't for his ratty old cat...

Her eyes wandered to the stairs and she began to climb them in search of the bathroom. Coming out a few minutes later, she glanced inside another room and then stood staring in astonishment. The outside wall had been altered so that it was almost completely glass. The ceiling had been heightened and a skylight added. Hanging from various hooks all around the room were glass treasures. A workbench was strewn with tools, materials, thingamajigs that she didn't recognize. But one thing she did know. It was a studio.

Of course. The dragonfly lampshade.

Nick worked in stained glass.

Moving slowly, she realized the pieces suspended in the room were artistic creations in glass, nothing like the commercial stuff that could be bought by the truckload almost anywhere. These designs were painstakingly crafted in meticulous detail, all originals. The colors were vivid and sharp, or muted and ethereal, according to the whim of the artist.

And Nick was the artist.

With her hand on her heart, Shannon drifted over to look

at a wonderful fireplace screen depicting white cranes in flight over a landscape of water and cattails. It was breathtakingly beautiful. He was good. Better than good. And nobody knew. It was something he kept private. And yet, he had sent her up here. Surrounded by his artistry, her heart beating with joy and uncertainty, Shannon wondered why.

CHAPTER TEN

IT TOOK NICK THREE minutes to get his gear together and another thirty seconds to check his answering machine. In another minute he'd stripped off his shirt and pants, and in two more, he was dressed in worn jeans, a pullover and running shoes. Then he sat on the side of his bed reminding himself of his past, his future—if he did what he was thinking—and the cost of it all. He had never wanted a woman the way he wanted Shannon O'Connor.

Why the hell didn't he stay away from her, then? Let Cheryl watch over her. Or if that wasn't enough, he could detail Ed. Ed knew her, she liked him, trusted him. Nick swore softly. Shoving his fingers through his hair, he found himself on his feet. Ed was his partner and his friend, but he didn't want Shannon looking to Ed for protection or anything else. Nick wanted to be the one she relied on, and it wasn't just to watch over her like a good cop.

Against all his instincts, he wanted her. It didn't seem to matter that she was a carbon copy of his first wife, same blue-blood family, same wealthy upbringing, same exclusive schooling, same privileged life-style. Same inconstancy? No. He didn't want to think that Shannon's principles were as flexible as Leslie's. No reporter could write the kind of impassioned articles as Shannon, or hold such fierce opinions, and not be deeply principled. And loyal and brave and true. Why, then, since his lust for her was in danger of driving him crazy, didn't he let himself go and just begin an affair with her?—assuming she was willing.

He jerked his mind from the thought even as it formed. Lonely and jaded as he was, he shouldn't be engaging in fantasies about a woman like Shannon. She was young, fresh, vital, poised to taste the best there was to be had in life. The problems slowing her down right now were temporary, the result of a trauma that would have devastated a less courageous woman. She was getting herself together, and doing it like a trooper. Naturally she accepted the comfort and protection he offered. Any woman without a husband or a lover would. In a few months, her fear would be a distant memory. It was his duty to protect her from the bastard who was somewhere out there amusing himself taking cheap shots at her like that damned note.

Besides, his track record at sustaining relationships was not exactly good. If he took a chance with Shannon, how long could he keep her satisfied? He didn't doubt that they would be good together sexually, but women needed more, he'd learned. He'd failed to give that to Leslie and she'd turned to another man. And Tracey had simply settled for half a loaf. But with Shannon...Shannon would want everything. Would demand everything. She would tear his heart out by the roots. The truth was, he didn't know if he could stop at an affair with Shannon.

His gaze went warily to the door of his bedroom. He had heard her leaving the bathroom, then the sound of her footsteps stopping as she discovered his studio. Now he heard only silence. Tense as a sixteen-year-old on a first date, he left his bedroom and headed down the hall to her.

SHE WAS STANDING with her back to the door, studying a panel he'd nearly finished. It was a contemporary piece with the fiery colors of a sunburst at its center. Hearing him, she turned, looking up at him with a thousand questions in her eyes. "It's for a window in the geriatric ward at the hospital," he said, reaching to snap the light on underneath the glass work surface and illuminating the panel.

"It's beautiful…so…" She moved her hands, trying to find words. "So…uplifting."

"Old people in the hospital need a boost now and then."

"I know," she murmured, staring with fascination. "I did a feature about them once. They're often lonely and scared. So many are destitute and—"

"I know, I read it." He reached for a stray wisp of her auburn hair and rubbed it between his fingers. "I had a guilty conscience for days."

She smiled, turning to him, leaning her cheek into his hand. "I wish everyone who's touched by something I write would respond so handsomely." Her smile faded as she looked into his eyes again. "Your work is beautiful, Nick, inspired. That window looks exactly like the sun coming out after a storm. It…it takes my breath away. Why keep your art a secret?"

He shrugged, fighting the fierce joy he felt hearing her praise his work. "No reason."

She was watching him, her eyes searching, a little wary. "It's funny, just when I think I've got you figured out, Nick, I discover another facet of your character."

"I'm just a cop with a hobby."

"A cop with a gift." When he would have retreated, she captured his fingers, holding fast so that her face was cradled by his hand. "I can't believe you've been hiding this from the world. How would you have given it to the hospital without telling them who created it?"

He resisted the urge to bring her fully into his embrace. The smile he managed hiked up one corner of his mouth. "Well, the thought may have crossed my mind that you could deliver it for me. You're the logical choice since your fiery hair was my inspiration for the piece."

"Oh, Nick…" Turning her head, she kissed his palm softly.

"God, Shannon…"

Somehow, without either knowing who took the first step, they came together. A muffled sound escaped her as she buried her face in the side of his neck. It was too much for Nick.

The feel of her as his arms went around her was so good, so right. It was what he'd wanted for so long. He had no business holding her, but he couldn't have stopped himself now, no matter what.

"This is crazy," he said hoarsely. His hands swept over her shoulders, down to her waist, then flared out over the shape of her hips. She was small and slight, femininity itself. Everything about her seemed formed to fulfill his fantasies to perfection. Spreading his legs, he tilted her forward, pressing her softness against his arousal. A rising tide of desire rolled through him. God, it was heaven. It was—

"Nick, oh, Nick...please..."

He almost missed her whispered plea as the roar of his blood pounded in his ears. Not certain what she was asking, he reared back to look into her green eyes, and what he saw there sent his good intentions up in flames. With a groan that came from the depths of his soul, he caught her face in his hands and kissed her.

Like the feel of her body, her mouth was everything he'd fantasized. And more. She tasted sweet and erotic, like sun-warmed fruit on a summer day. Bunching his hands in her hair, he held her just where he wanted her. He sent his tongue deep, feasting on the sweetness of her while she clung to him with the kind of fervor that made him swell and ache with a pain he hadn't felt since he was a randy teenager.

He wanted to tear his jeans open and take her right then and there. She was like no other woman he'd ever desired. Touching her, holding her, *wanting* her, was unlike anything he'd ever experienced. The thought somehow found its way through the heat of his desire and reached his brain. Shannon truly wasn't like other women, at least, not at this time in her life. She had been hurt. She was vulnerable. She looked to him for protection. He had a job to do, and to seduce her now meant crossing a line that might have consequences he wasn't sure he could ever overcome if he wanted more than a brief moment in time with Shannon.

Denial formed in his chest, forging its way upward until it emerged as a deep, gut-wrenching groan. Tearing his mouth from hers, he shuddered, burying his face in her glorious hair. He loved her hair. It was like silky fire, fragrant with roses. While he brought his raging desire under control, he focused on that thought and not on the relentless ache throbbing between his legs.

"Why did you stop?"

She sounded uncertain and—God help him—close to tears. He pressed a soft kiss beneath her ear, unable to let her go completely. Not yet. "Whatever is happening here is...it's crazy, Shannon. I didn't count on it and I don't want it." The lie almost choked him. He wanted it so much, no amount of cold showers was going to make him forget just how much. "Things sort of got out of hand. I shouldn't have brought you up here. I should have taken you back to Wilderose House instead of—"

With both hands, Shannon shoved herself out of Nick's arms. "Don't say any more, Nick. I...you're right. Things got a little out of hand. I guess that stupid note unnerved me more than I realized. Besides, we're two adults, aren't we? There's no reason for you to take the blame for anything. There's nothing to blame yourself for."

She took a swipe at her hair, which had fallen forward, shielding her expression from him. "So, if you've got your stuff together, and your cat's fed, and you still plan to drive me home, then we should be getting on with it, don't you think?"

Shannon knew her tone was too bright, and she couldn't look at him while she spoke. When she finally looked up, he was watching her, his eyes dark and unreadable. She knew full well that she had returned his kiss with all the yearning that she had stored up since waking in the hospital and finding him at the foot of her bed. Actually, much longer, if she was being honest, but he didn't need to know that. Also, it had been easy to push the threat of that note out of her mind when she was being kissed by Nick. Now that he had kissed her—even though she had done the asking—she found she wanted much more than a few kisses. And yet...

She stole a look at the set line of his mouth as he ushered her out of his studio and down the stairs to the front door of his house. He looked like a man with his mind made up. She guessed it wasn't something like an affair with her.

THEY DROVE IN SILENCE out of Nick's neighborhood and headed for Wilderose House. As he drove through a well-lit intersection, Nick stole a glance at Shannon. The sweet-tasting temptress who'd taken him halfway to heaven ten minutes ago was gone. He couldn't blame her. He had been clumsy in trying to explain why he'd backed off after arousing them both to a heated frenzy. She had completely misunderstood.

"We haven't talked about your Dream Sight in a while," Nick said, trying for a neutral subject.

"It's Gran who has the Dream Sight, not me."

Nick didn't miss the tone of her reply. Coolly polite, she could be talking to a stranger. He ought to feel good that she was still speaking to him at all.

"You could've fooled me."

"Well, it's true. Besides, I didn't think you believed in psychics."

"I can't afford to dismiss anything that might shed some light on a murder case." With the green signal he downshifted, shooting the car forward before adding, "Or on your own case, as far as that goes."

"I'm not a psychic," Shannon said grumpily, her face turned from him in the dark. "I don't want to be. But if you want to talk about nightmares, now...well, I'm certainly into that."

He gave her a quick look. "Anything interesting?"

"Hardly. After the ninth or tenth time you dream something, it ceases to be interesting."

"You've had the same dream that often?" He was still a

skeptic about psychic phenomena, but after Shannon's strange insight into Becky Berenson's murder, he wasn't prepared to deny it completely, either. Any recurring dream of Shannon's interested him. "Tell me about it, anyway."

"It's nothing much. I'm in a courtroom with a judge and two lawyers arguing. A woman in the witness box is crying. I always get the feeling that I should go to her, as though she's reaching out to me for help."

"Do you recognize her?"

"No." Shannon frowned. "For some reason, her face is always veiled. And I never actually see the faces of the lawyers or the judge, either."

"How about the jury or others in the courtroom?"

"There's no jury and nobody else in the courtroom." She shifted restlessly in her seat. "It's the woman who's important, I'm sure of that." She gave a short, humorless laugh. "If she's looking to me for help, she's in big trouble, poor thing."

She bent her head suddenly, rubbing her temples wearily. "I'm so tired of all this, Nick. When will it end? That note tonight really scared me. If he can approach me out of the blue like that, then slip away scot-free, how can I ever feel safe?"

Stopping at a light, he looked over at her. "You are safe. Don't doubt it. Cheryl is backed up around the clock with a private security team headed by Jed Singer. I know him personally. He's good. Better than good. On top of that, your case is open at the Savannah Police Department. My own people patrol the road leading to Wilderose House regularly. We're going to find him, Shannon. Sending that note tonight was a mistake. It tells us definitely that you know something that threatens him."

She laughed bitterly again. "Oh, sure. And as soon as I remember it, he's dead meat, right?"

"I meant what I said earlier tonight. I'm not relying on your memory anymore. You must have left some evidence of what you were working on somewhere. I just have to find it."

For a moment, she stared through the side window into the night. "Did you thoroughly check my apartment?"

"Thoroughly, why?"

"I'm not sure...something Liza Westfall said."

"Who?"

She waved her hand in dismissal. "Just a co-worker at the paper. But she said something that clicked for me. I had a small hand-held recorder that uses those tiny cassette tapes. I always keep it in my purse. Did you find it when you sorted through the stuff I dropped when he...when I..." She drew in a breath. "Did you find it?"

"Yeah, and it had a tape in it, but it was new. It'd never been used. We checked."

She rubbed a spot between her eyes, thinking. "I could have taken it out. The used tape, I mean. I could have dropped it in my purse or something. It would have to be on my person or in my car." She looked at him. "You checked my car?"

"Yeah, nothing."

"Let's check again, the apartment, I mean." She sat up, suddenly energized. "Turn here, Nick." Tires squealed as he braked and took the turn at Oglethorpe and Whitaker. Her apartment was only two blocks away.

Nick stopped and got out. Shannon was on the sidewalk staring at her apartment building when he reached her. The front was landscaped to resemble a New Orleans courtyard. A fountain gurgled softly as they walked past, their footsteps loud on the shadowy brick-paved walkway.

"The bulb must be burned out on the carriage lamp in the courtyard," she murmured, frowning as they climbed the shallow steps up to the door. She laughed shakily. "I hate the dark, did I ever tell you that?"

"No, but it's not a problem. I'm not." Nick draped an arm around her shoulders and gently pulled her close. Inwardly he cursed the carelessness of the maintenance crew whose job it was to replace light bulbs and his own thoughtlessness in agreeing to stop here. Shannon hadn't been back to her apartment since the attack. With her admitted fear of the dark, her first visit should have been in the daylight.

"Here's my key. You open up." Her voice was breathless. Nick could feel the quiver that ran through her. Edging even closer to him, she closed her eyes and inhaled, then opened them as Nick turned the key and pushed the door open.

The stench hit them first. Swearing, Nick fumbled for the light switch. One look and Shannon gasped, then turned instinctively into Nick's arms.

His arms tight around Shannon, Nick surveyed the shambles that used to be her apartment and fought to keep his silence. If he let go, he would swear a blue streak, and it was no time to vent his own rage.

The original damage done during the attack weeks ago was nothing compared to the carnage spread before them now. Every item that Shannon owned was savaged, every book, every piece of glass, every thread of upholstery in her furniture was trashed, smashed, ripped apart, destroyed beyond salvaging. To add a particularly sick twist, something liquid had been poured over everything, then flour and sugar dumped over that. The carpet was stained beyond salvaging. The whole place reeked of spoiled food and evil intent.

"Oh, God, oh, God..." Shannon's fists curled into Nick's shirt, holding on desperately to keep from collapsing in sheer primal fear. Shudders racked her, beginning deep within and spreading throughout her whole body.

Nick held her tight, his mouth a thin, grim line. Who had done this? What miserable bastard was so obsessed with Shannon that he would devastate her house like this?

"C'mon, baby, we're getting out of here."

"Oh, Nick...what..."

"Not now, sweetheart. I need to call a unit."

"My...I have a phone..." She gestured vaguely toward the wrecked sofa where a small table leaned drunkenly. The telephone lay on the floor with the receiver off, dangling over the arm of the sofa.

"There may be prints," Nick said, stopping her when she made a move toward the phone. Privately, he doubted it. Whoever did this wouldn't leave anything forensics could pick up as evidence. With his hand on her waist, he urged her backward. "Let's use the radio."

SHANNON WAITED BESIDE Nick's car while the police converged on her apartment and began the painstaking job of sifting through the debris. With her arms wrapped around herself, she faced the fact that as long as the man who'd done this remained free, she was destined to be his victim. She could continue to function, in a manner of speaking, but having a bodyguard beside her forever wasn't the way she wanted to live her life. Cowering under the constant threat of evil wasn't acceptable, either.

If only she could remember.

Rubbing the dull ache between her eyes, she fought to penetrate the blank curtain of her mind. Every now and then, she had momentary flashes of something. She couldn't call it a complete memory, only a scrap of recollection. She had felt it as she stood waiting while Nick unlocked the door to her apartment. Then again, just before he turned on the lights. Before the vile smell and the dark specter of evil had overtaken everything.

She sent a wary look toward her apartment. The windows on both levels had been thrown open. Light poured from the rectangles. Men in uniform and street clothes drifted back and forth across her line of vision. She heard the sounds as they worked—low male voices, a burst of laughter, static from a police radio band, the clink of broken glass. Glass that had once been her china, or a cherished curio, or the remains of a framed picture. Which one? she wondered desolately. The one of Kathleen and Patrick O'Connor in the rose garden in 1932? The one of her brothers taken when they'd met up one summer day in London? Or the one of her father with *Maman* in Saigon, climbing the steps of the plane that took them out of

Vietnam? She wanted—no, needed—to know, but her fear
kept her from venturing closer to the scene of violence, knowing it was meant for her.

Inside, her emotions were in turmoil. Some deep inner compulsion had brought her back here tonight. Even now, something urged her to go up that walk again, to brave the fear, to
look—

Pain seared a white-hot arrow all the way through her brain,
and she almost turned to climb into the squad car. Running
away wasn't the answer, she thought. Cringing out here in
dubious safety wasn't the answer. She breathed deeply, eyes
closed, and waited for the pain to subside. When it did, the
rage came, warring with her fear. She glanced at the stern-
faced young rookie Nick had assigned to wait with her, realizing that he was speaking to her.

"Ma'am? Miss O'Connor?"

She looked at the young cop blankly. "Yes, what is it?"

"Detective Dalton wants me to drive you back to your
grandmother's place. Are you ready to go?"

"No."

"Beg pardon, ma'am, but Detective Dalton—"

His words trailed off as she turned abruptly and made her
way to her front door. She didn't want to go inside. It would
be a lot easier to climb into the car as Nick had suggested and
let him smooth over this particular ugliness, just as he and all
the other well-meaning people in her life had been doing since
her assault. But when was she going to say, Enough? When
was she going to be done with standing around gnashing her
teeth over all the awful things happening to her? She could
only end the tyranny of the man who was stalking her when
she took charge of her life again.

Wading through the shambles of her living room, she
homed in on the sound of Nick's voice coming from the vicinity of her bedroom. He looked up sharply when he saw her.
"I told Moynihan to take you home."

"Thanks, but I decided to stay." With her teeth clamped,

she looked around. It was the only room in the house that didn't smell bad. A mixture of face powder, liquid makeup and various bottles from her collection of toiletries had been poured over her beautiful white eyelet comforter and pillows, which had been slashed to ribbons.

Her expression bleak, she looked at Nick. "If anything's missing, or appears odd, how would you know?"

He shrugged. "We manage."

"I'm staying, Nick."

He moved closer, studying her intently. "Are you sure? It will be difficult to cope with something like this, Shannon."

"That's just the problem," she murmured. "I haven't been coping with much of anything lately. I've been too busy hiding from the horror of what happened or worrying about what might happen that I'm like a...a ship without a rudder. Sooner or later, I'm going to have to start living again. So—" with a lift of her shoulders, she gave him a weak smile "—now seems as good a time as later."

She went to work, heartened by the approval in his eyes.

CHERYL COULDN'T SLEEP. Word of the break-in at Shannon's town house apartment had reached her an hour ago, destroying any enjoyment she might have taken in having a night off. Shannon was safe under Nick's protection, but Cheryl had her own standards. She had spent the past hour checking the windows and entrances to Wilderose House. Then she'd personally walked the perimeter of the property. Which in itself was not exactly a chore, not for her. She loved the grounds of Wilderose House, and after satisfying herself that everything was secure, she headed for her favorite place—Miss Kathleen's rose garden.

With a sneakered toe to the ground, she gave the swing a shove and settled back, savoring the quiet and the fragrances, the sheer ambience of the old-fashioned garden. She liked to imagine Kathleen and Patrick here as young lovers—star-crossed lovers, to hear Shannon tell their story—but destined for happiness in the end. With the creak of the swing lulling her, she imagined Wilderose House as it looked then with Kathleen and Patrick finally reunited. It was easier to believe in happy endings for lovers in a bygone era than now. She herself couldn't think of a single contemporary one.

"Spotted the O'Connor ghost yet?"

Cheryl sprang up from the swing as Will O'Connor materialized out of the shadows. She swallowed the half-formed scream that had risen in her throat, her heart beating like a drum. It was from being taken by surprise, she told herself. Not because Will O'Connor made her heart beat faster. "Are you trying to get yourself shot?" she demanded, settling back on the swing.

"Why would a man get shot taking a walk in his own backyard?"

"By being mistaken for someone trying to harm his sister, that's why. Have you forgotten the reason I'm here?"

"I could never forget anything about you, Cheryl." Will sat down beside her, casually stretching his arm across the back of the swing. While she tried to figure out what he meant by that, he pushed the swing into gentle motion. "You didn't answer my question."

"I wasn't looking for O'Connor ghosts, but I guess I was thinking about them."

"Oh? Who?" She felt his gaze on her and kept her own straight ahead because…because the truth was, she didn't know what she would do if she turned and looked right into his eyes.

"Miss Kathleen and Patrick O'Connor."

He chuckled softly, and the sound stirred the hair at Cheryl's temples. "My grandmother would be surprised to learn that she is no longer among the living."

She began a halting explanation. "No, of course not. She…I didn't mean…that is, what I meant to say is that Patrick is the ghost I was thinking of…and—"

"I thought you didn't believe in ghosts."

"I don't!" Exasperated and rattled, she started up, but he caught her by the arm and gently urged her back down.

"Don't go. Stay awhile and talk to me." He sounded sincere, and she settled again, but warily.

Closing her eyes, she told herself he only wanted to pass the dark hours of an uneasy night. Anybody would do. Even Andy Welles's ex-wife.

"Why were you thinking of Patrick and Kathleen?"

She shrugged. "Shannon, of course. She's full of stories about your whole family. Sitting out here in Miss Kathleen's rose garden, I just seemed to—" She broke off, embarrassed.

"To feel the memories that must have been created in this place?"

"I guess you think that's silly. Or that I have no right."

"No." His denial was unequivocal.

"It must be the sense of history about this place," she said with a short, baffled laugh. "But I've never been very mystical before now. Does Wilderose House do that to other visitors?"

"Sometimes. For some people," he said, then went silent. Around them, the sounds of the night were familiar and soothing. The rose garden smelled sweet and evocative. Cheryl diligently kept her eyes on her hands, but she could almost taste the forbidden desire to turn to Will O'Connor, to touch him. To have him touch her. She had always—

"I've been wanting to ask you something for days," he said, and his brooding, intense look alone was enough to hold her captive. "When we talked, you said something about Andy that has bothered me ever since."

Andy. Of course, he wanted to talk about Andy. Why she had ever thought he might want to sit with her just for the sake of being with her, she couldn't imagine. It must be the roses, she thought desolately.

"I said something about a man needing to care for and protect his wife...if he loves her."

"In a perfect world, yes, I guess that's true."

"There, you're doing it again." When she looked at him blankly, he said, "Dancing away from a straight answer."

"I don't have to give you a straight answer about my relationship with Andy," she said stiffly. "Besides, you didn't ask a question."

"Here are two, then. Did he love you? Did you love him?"

She looked away. "That's none of your business, Will."

"Hell, I know that. I've always known that. It's just…" He seemed to come to some decision then. "Do you remember when we met for the first time?" he said.

She gave him a startled look, then nodded warily. "At the regatta on Sea Island. Andy brought me."

"You were in a skinny little top and white shorts that showed off your gorgeous long legs."

Cheryl's heart began a syncopated rhythm that nearly stole her breath away. "You wore a pair of khaki shorts and *no* top."

"Only until we cast off. Rules, you know. No shoes, no shirt, no sail."

"You came in second."

"I was distracted by a beautiful girl—" he touched her hair gently, then trailed the back of his hand along her cheek "—with topaz eyes and tawny hair. A sunshine girl."

Through her senses alone, she was suddenly aware of everything about him—the spiciness of his cologne, the width and power of his shoulders nudging hers, the strength of his thighs, the seduction of his voice. When she found her own, it was unsteady. "I was already committed to Andy."

"I know." He withdrew his hand, looking away from her. "But I didn't want to accept it. The next time I saw you, I engineered the whole thing."

"Will—"

His mouth twisted in a self-deprecating smile. "It was a retirement party for one of my managers."

"Jeff Barclay."

"It was at Huey's, a fun place. I thought I might get a

chance to talk to you, just…talk to you. Maybe share a dance.''

''And we did,'' she whispered, closing her eyes and recapturing the moment.

He picked up a tiny twig on the swing and sent it sailing. When he settled back, he looked at her. ''I never forgot that dance. You felt so right in my arms…so perfect.''

''Andy said you only asked to be polite.'' Her voice was barely audible.

''He was wrong.''

She managed to turn and look up at him then. She had always known that Will O'Connor was a threat to her carefully crafted defenses, but the impact when their eyes met nearly stilled her heartbeat. She wondered wildly what would happen if he ever learned the truth about her. Would he be repulsed? God, would he pity her? She didn't think she could bear that.

Will squinted off into the shadows, as though searching for words. ''He was always talking about you. He seemed to worship you. He was crazy with worry when you were on a case. He'd get so ticked off because you preferred working to being his wife. He told me—''

Something inside Cheryl snapped. She was suddenly sick and tired of Andy Welles getting a free ride, even in death. She sprang up from the swing, clearly startling Will. ''He told you a lot of garbage, Will. He set you up just like he set everybody else up, me included. He was a master at manipulating people and their emotions.''

With her hands on her waist, she faced him angrily. ''He wasn't crazy with worry because of my job. What worried him was far different. He was afraid I would tell somebody what a miserable slug he was and that it would get back to you or to somebody else in your social circle and screw up the nice, cushy life he'd made for himself.''

With a dark scowl, Will got up from the swing and advanced on her slowly. ''What the hell are you talking about?''

''I'm talking about the truth here, Will. I'm sick of keeping a dead man's secrets just so you won't be hurt or distressed or…or…whatever you feel about your precious cousin. Andy was a violent, abusive excuse for a man. Those vacations you think I took alone? I was hospitalized three times in the two rotten years I was married to him. And that house you say *I* demanded? He wanted it, not me. He wanted to be like his wealthy relatives, the O'Connors. He even planned some day to *own* the shipyard. *Your* shipyard, Will.''

She shook her head in remembered anguish. "No, he didn't love me," she said disgustedly, her eyes glinting with long-withheld tears. "He didn't love anybody but himself. And you want to know the real kicker in this farce? He didn't marry me for any of the traditional reasons a man marries a woman, Will. Not Andy. He married me because he thought *you* wanted me!''

With a choked cry, she turned and made a mad dash for the sanctuary of her room. Bitter tears scalded her eyes, nearly blinding her. Will had always rushed to Andy's defense, and tonight she really didn't think she could bear it. For so long, the dark, ugly secret of Andy's abuse had been buried inside her like poisonous waste. At first, she had told herself that she could build a good life in spite of it. That she could live and work and play just like other whole people and it wouldn't matter. But it did matter. It had stayed buried, yes, but leaking a little poison here and there, every now and then, contaminating the seeds of every new relationship as surely as though she was still married to Andy. Her remark to the encounter group seemed to mock her now. Free at last? Chained to the ghosts of her past, how could she ever be free?

CHAPTER ELEVEN

IT WAS AFTER 2:00 a.m. when Nick had finally persuaded Shannon to leave her apartment to forensics and let him drive her back to Wilderose House. It was raining, a soft, misting shower that was strangely comforting. He pulled to a stop and they sat for a moment in the silence after the swishing of the wipers ceased.

"Tired?" he asked, looking at her.

She smiled wearily. "That's putting it mildly. She reached down and gathered up some special things she'd managed to find in the wreckage of her apartment. He noticed they were nothing particularly expensive, mostly framed photographs, a few well-read books, and in one box, her collection of antique perfume bottles.

"Need some help?" he asked, his hand on the door handle.

"Please." She glanced up at the house, her eyes on her own bedroom windows on the second floor. "I wish I'd remembered to leave the light on in my bedroom," she said, hugging the framed pictures close to her chest.

Nick got out and went around to meet her. Rain clung to her hair, giving it a misty sheen. She was still a little too pale to suit him. With good reason. She'd had a hell of a day. "Why are you afraid of the dark?" he asked, taking a shopping bag full of books as she climbed out of the car.

She glanced at him sheepishly. "It's nothing really, no tragic event that could be expected to color my whole life. My brothers were fairly good-natured about letting me hang around them, but they were so much older that they often forgot about me. Which is what happened one day when I was about five years old. They went somewhere else to play and left me in an upstairs closet for several hours and I couldn't reach the doorknob. When I was finally discovered by my grandmother, I felt as though I'd been abandoned for days.'' She sent him an impish smile as they climbed the outside stairs to the upper gallery. ''Both Will and Ryan have always insisted it was an accident, but sometimes I wonder. To hear them tell it, I could be a real pain in the neck.''

At the French doors to her bedroom, he reached around her, allowing himself a quick moment of contact before pushing them open. Behind them, a brief streak of lightning lit the sky. He grinned at her. ''Were you a brat?''

''A hellion, so my family says.''

He nodded with a knowing look. ''In training even then to be a hard-nosed journalist, right?''

''I suppose so.''

It helped having Nick beside her, but she still tensed before stepping over the threshold into the dark room. Directly opposite the French doors stood the cheval glass mirror, the surface illuminated briefly in a flash of lightning. For a second, it seemed to Shannon that the people framed in the mirror were not her and Nick, but two other people.

Before she could touch the light switch, pain pierced her forehead, white-hot and agonizing. With a groan, she abruptly shoved the things in her hands over to Nick and rubbed at the spot.

''Shannon... Shannon, what is it?'' He tossed everything onto the chair beside the door, cursing because he didn't know the location of the light switch. In the shadows, he strained to see her face. She had had little color before; now she looked as pale as a ghost, her gaze riveted on the mirror.

''Look,'' she whispered.

He forgot the light. He stood transfixed while Shannon put out a hand, stilling whatever he meant to say. There was no need. His words died away unspoken. Just the look of her staring into the mirror stirred the hair on the back of his neck. Looking from her to the murky glass, he saw nothing, just the silvery sheen of it in a flash of lightning. He took a cautious step forward. The instant he moved, she gave a soft, plaintive moan and then sank down onto the bed.

Nick was beside her in an instant. He could feel the small shudders running through her body. She seemed caught up in whatever she'd seen in the mirror. The whole thing had taken only about half a minute. And it had been something, he decided, giving up the idea that her strange Dream Sight could be dismissed out of hand. Although he hadn't seen anything himself, there had been a...a presence in the room, a compelling force of some kind, whether he wanted to believe it or not. And its center had been in that damn mirror.

Shaking his head irritably, he sought to rid himself of the spooky feeling and reached around her to turn on the lamp beside her bed. Soft, rose-tinted light spilled forth, instantly dispelling the gloom. Nick took the first long, easy breath he'd had since entering those French doors.

What the hell was going on here?

"What was it, Shannon? What did you see?"

She stared straight ahead for a full ten seconds. "Will you believe me if I tell you?"

"Try me, damn it! I know something weird just went down here. I'm just not sure what it was."

Rubbing her forehead wearily, she said, "I saw the woman in my dream, only this time she wasn't in a courtroom. She was standing in her bedroom. And don't ask where it was because I don't know. Anyway, the door was locked, but whoever was trying to get in wasn't letting that stop him. He was hammering and kicking and yelling...."

"Do you recognize him?"

"No...no...he..."

"He what?"

"His voice. The threats..." She looked at him with a mixture of fear and helplessness. "He sounded exactly like the man who assaulted me."

"My God, Shannon." Acting out of his own need, Nick wrapped his arms around her. With his chin on her head, he rocked her gently until the trembling in her body ceased.

"You think it's my imagination," she told him.

"No. There was something there. I don't know what, but I felt it myself."

She lifted her head to look at him. "You saw them, too?"

He shook his head and felt her wilt with disappointment. "No, but for what it's worth, I'm less skeptical than I was a few weeks ago."

"Thanks a lot," she said dryly, but she settled back against him.

With his arms still wrapped around her, his chest to her back, he looked up and studied them as they appeared in the old-fashioned mirror. He was struck suddenly by how right they looked together. The irony of that thought was funny. It was only a few hours ago in his apartment that he'd convinced himself that Shannon was as wrong for him as any woman could be.

With a mixture of tenderness and possession, he noticed that her beautiful features looked pinched and pale with exhaustion. "You need to get some rest," he told her, even though leaving her alone tonight was the last thing he wanted to do.

"I guess you're right." But she made no move to let him up. Instead, she settled her body more fully into his. Desire rushed through him with the force of a freight train. It took all his willpower not to simply turn and strip her naked then and there. They could spend the rest of the night making love. It was what they both wanted. But she was tired. Needing rest. She needed rest, not sex.

"This has been a hell of a day for you, Shannon. The note was bad enough, and then your apartment. Now this. I've had seasoned cops collapse with less provocation."

She rubbed her cheek against his arm like a kitten, and he

felt heat and desire increase his already painful arousal. Catching sight of his own face in the mirror, he wondered that she didn't know what she was doing to him.

"If I feel like having a breakdown, I'll let you know," she said.

"You're not having a breakdown," he growled. "You proved it tonight going into that apartment right on the heels of receiving that ugly note." Their eyes met in the mirror.

"I'm trying to take charge of my life again, Nick."

"Good. But you didn't have to punish yourself sorting through your apartment tonight. I told Mike—"

"Mike Moynihan, the rookie cop? My baby-sitter?" Whether she realized it or not, she was caressing his forearm with her hand, slowly and sensuously. Sweet torture, Nick thought, forcing down the temptation to draw her close and tight between his sprawled thighs. He knew where that would lead.

"I decided that I'd had enough from this clown," she said. "It was my apartment he trashed, so it was my place to sift through the ruins."

His jaw set, as much against the sexual tension ready to explode inside him as for her defying his orders. "I just thought you'd be better off at Wilderose House."

Like Nick, Shannon had been watching their reflections in the mirror. "Then it would have been Mike and not you watching me have a psychic moment," she told him.

He ignored the remark about her clairvoyance. "Mike had better not be in your bedroom," he muttered, turning his face into her hair. The movement sent a thrill dancing down her spine. "Or anybody else, as far as that goes."

"Why?" she asked.

It was a moment before he realized she was waiting for an answer. Caution made him lift his head slowly to meet her eyes in the mirror. They exchanged a long, silent look.

"Why, Nick?" she repeated. "Why don't you want Mike or anybody else in my room?"

Because you're mine. The thought drilled through his mind with the force of a gunshot. He had the same feeling he got when he suddenly found the answer to a particularly rough problem. Or when he uncovered just the right thread that unraveled a baffling case. Who was he kidding? He'd been dancing around his feelings for Shannon for weeks now. The woman had turned him upside down. She had him coming and going. He was in love with her.

Still holding his gaze in the mirror, she whispered, "I heard that."

He looked alarmed. That damned mirror! Could she read his mind in the thing?

Shannon laughed softly. "Just teasing, Nick. Relax. I can't read your mind, or anybody else's." Her smile faded a bit. "Besides, I don't think I want to know what you were thinking just now. You didn't look especially pleased. Am I such a trial?"

"No." Tucking her head beneath his chin, he gave a soft, painful laugh. "Or at least, not in the way you're thinking." Without intending it, he began slowly stroking the line of her back. Even through her clothes, the feel of her enchanted him. Beneath his big hands, she seemed small and sleek and feminine. Savoring the softly giving curves of her body, he closed his eyes and imagined how she would look and feel naked. Just then, with a small sound, she wrapped her arms around his chest, and snuggled close.

With Shannon curling around him like a warm, loving kitten, Nick knew where this night would end if he didn't get up and leave right now. He took a few tortured seconds to try to persuade himself to do just that, but her warmth and weight were sweet torture. She felt so right in his arms. She smelled good, too. Like roses and rain. Helplessly, his mouth skimmed one side of her face, from her temple down the line of her cheek to the soft, seductive corner of her lips. They parted on a sigh and she whispered, "Don't stop, Nick. Don't stop this time."

From that moment, he was lost.

With a moan, Shannon opened to him joyfully. There was nothing halfway about the kiss. It was direct and purposeful, earthy and sexual. Shannon fell into it with wild abandon. Her breasts tingled. Her senses hummed. Her limbs went warm and pliant. She felt dazed and…claimed. Forgotten was his hurtful rejection of only a few hours ago. From the time that Nick had pulled her back from death, she had known that they were destined for this. And she wanted it. Craved it.

With her help, he got rid of his shirt hurriedly, then pushed the fabric of her denim skirt up high before finding her mouth for another deep, erotic kiss. His hands were restless and questing, sweeping down her back, clamping around her thighs, then the world tilted for a moment as he lifted her. With a gasp, she signaled her willingness by helping him settle her astride his lap. When he filled his hands with the softness of her buttocks, Shannon whimpered. Then they both groaned in mutual satisfaction as she rocked against the bulge in his jeans.

"You're sweet and pretty and…oh, so soft," he told her, giving up the kiss to explore the tantalizing line of her throat and shoulder and beyond. At the curve of her breast, he broke away with a harsh intake of breath and freed a hand from where it had slipped inside her panties to tear open the buttons on her blouse and toss it away. The clip of her bra deterred him another second or two and then he was at her breast, tasting, sucking, licking, his hot breath sending prickling sensations from her nipples all the way to the deepest part of her.

Shannon threw back her head, rocking with him in a sensual, age-old rhythm. Gasping with pleasure, she slid her fingers through his hair and clasped his head close, closer. From there, her hands drifted down along his strong neck, to his arms, then his shoulders. He shuddered as she explored his male nipples with her thumbs and caught her around her waist, squeezing her so tightly that it made her dizzy.

"We've got to slow down or it'll all be over," he breathed in her ear, the words sending shivers over her skin.

"We have all night," she whispered, closing her eyes when he flicked at a nipple with his tongue. *We have forever.* But she spoke those words silently, knowing he would not want to hear them. He would not want to be reminded of their linked destiny, not now. Not yet. Movement in the mirror caught her eye, and the fear that was always with her threatened, but it was only the two of them framed in the glass. She closed her eyes, shutting out everything except the near-painful pleasure of Nick's loving.

With his arms still around her, he found the button on her skirt. "This has got to go," he said, kissing her shoulder as he freed her of the skirt. "And these..." The panties followed, sailing a few feet further, landing on the frame of the mirror.

He leaned back to look his fill when she was finally naked. "You're so beautiful," he breathed, stroking the backs of two fingers over both breasts. "I knew you would be."

With a shiver, she realized that she liked Nick's eyes on her. When fantasizing about this—and she had, many times—she had thought she might be shy. She was not. She had also believed that she knew about sex. With amazement, she realized that she hadn't known the first thing.

"I don't want to be the only naked person in this bed," she said, moving both hands down his torso until she reached the waistband of his jeans. "Take these off."

His eyes, holding hers, were nearly black. Setting her aside gently, he nodded. Popping the snap, he shucked both jeans and shorts. And then he was beside her.

Gathering her close, he began kissing her again, nuzzling into the softness behind her ears, at her neck, at the curve of her shoulder. To her delight, he whispered to her, his words sweet or bold or darkly sensual. Enthralled, Shannon sighed and moaned, her pleasure mingling with the deeper, rougher sounds coming from Nick.

In the soft, rosy glow of the lamp, they were oblivious to

the storm, now whipped up into a frenzy of wind and rain. Nick kissed his way down her body, grazing her throat, her breasts, her tummy. When he sought and found the soft, moist core of her, she cried out in a swift, almost anguished sound. Instinctively her hips arched to him, moved restively against the rhythmic pressure of his hand.

Breathing like a man running a race, Nick pressed his open mouth against the giving softness of her belly. With Shannon so close to that moment, his control was nearly gone. Sensing it, he hauled himself up, swept her beneath him and spread her legs. Driven by a deep hunger to mate with the one woman who would ruin him for others forever, he probed her warm, wet softness. And then he gave a deep, shattering groan and buried himself to the hilt.

At that moment lightning, fierce and thunderous, pierced the night. The lamp by the bed flickered and went out, plunging the room into darkness.

Catching her face in the fingers of one hand, Nick forced her to look at him. There was only shadow and form, but he could *see* her. And he knew that Shannon saw him. "Don't be afraid, sweetheart," he murmured, his eyes as turbulent as the world outside.

Another crash shook the very foundation of Wilderose House, lighting the room with blue-white flame. For some reason, Nick and Shannon turned as one to look at the old-fashioned mirror by the bed. The image in the glass was a lovers' embrace caught for all time, eloquent without words. Erotic.

"I'll take care of you," Nick promised.

Shannon smiled. "I know."

Her hands on his buttocks wrung a groan from him and he bent his head, inhaling roses and rain and the sheer essence of Shannon, before gathering himself to thrust deeply again, and then again. They fell into a wild, natural rhythm, instinctively in tune with each other. In a burst of joy and passion, they were both suddenly at the threshold. Shannon climaxed sweetly, fiercely, passionately. As she breathed broken phrases and wild promises, Nick plunged deeply one last time, and with a shout found his own release.

THEIR BREATHING had slowed somewhat—finally. Nick still held her fast, nuzzling her ear, one hand fisted in her hair. Shannon wasn't sure about the etiquette of moments like this. But she was sure of one thing—her fear had melted in the fire of passion. The day, horrible as it was, seemed like a bad dream at the moment. And making love with Nick was as earth-shattering as she'd known it would be.

She hoped he was not already regretting it.

Her tone was soft in the darkness when she said, "You didn't mean for this to happen, did you?"

He eased his leg from between hers. Lifting his head, he looked at her, smiling crookedly. "Did I seem like a reluctant lover?"

"You seemed like every woman's fantasy lover, not that I've had all that much experience, but..." She turned her gaze to the flickering lightning signaling the end of the storm. "I think you would have been out of here and on your way back to your apartment if I hadn't been so...so...*willing*."

"Shannon—"

"It was partly the fear, Nick." Frowning, she looked at their reflection in the mirror. "First the note, then my apartment, then the scene in the mirror..."

"So you thought a little sex might be distracting, is that it?" His voice was quiet. Too quiet.

"No. No...it was more than that." She scooted up, pulling a corner of the sheet to cover her breasts. "I was afraid at first, yes...but soon I wasn't thinking at all. I just...just..." She waved a hand weakly. "I just *felt*. I was so caught up in what you...we... It felt good, so right...that there wasn't room for fear." She sneaked a look at him, then studied her hands clenching the sheet. "There wasn't room for anything except pleasure."

In the pale flicker of distant lightning, her distress could not be hidden. For a long moment, Nick simply studied her. Then his gaze shifted to the mirror. Lying back, he threw an arm over his eyes. "I'm as much to blame as you, Shannon. I'm a cop. I'm supposed to be working on flushing out the bastard who attacked you. Most of the time I stay focused on that, but the line between duty and what I want personally has become so blurred that…"

He turned his head and looked at her. "I crossed that line tonight. If one of my men had done this, I would have him up for disciplinary action in a heartbeat."

Shannon was instantly sorry that she'd brought it up. She should have accepted the fact that they were attracted to each other, enjoyed the moment, and let him get up and leave without subjecting them both to a sticky discussion of what had happened.

She watched him throw off the sheet and get out of bed. At least he'd admitted the compelling attraction between them. Instinct told her no two people could make love the way they had and feel only regret and confusion and guilt. She knew, too, that it wasn't the right time to try and figure out exactly what they did feel. It wasn't easy for a man like Nick to put his emotions into words. He was not a communicator; just the opposite, in fact. She would have to wait to learn his true feelings. She sighed. Maybe by then she'd know her own.

He had his jeans in his hands when she got up and went over to him. Somehow in the dimness, she could still see his extraordinary gray-green eyes. And the bleakness in his smile.

"I'm not apologizing," he told her.

"Me, either," she said.

"Good." He looked at the jeans he was holding, as though he wondered how they'd got in his hands, and then back to her. "Will you be all right?"

She nodded. "Cheryl's just a yell away and so is Will." It wasn't fear motivating her when she placed her hand flat on his chest. Beneath the muscled heat, she could feel the beat of his heart. It matched the runaway rhythm of her own. She looked up at him. "I'm not scared now, Nick."

He trapped her hand beneath his and hesitated only a second or two before swearing softly. Then he bent and kissed her, driving his tongue forcefully into her mouth. It was a kiss rife with conflict and hot with passion. He brought it to an abrupt end, then rested his chin against her forehead. "You're driving me crazy, do you know that?"

He was tense with desire and conflict; she could feel it. Rubbing her cheek against the prickly skin of his jaw, she thought how good it would be to make love with him again. But the next time should be Nick's choice. He must never be a reluctant lover again. Just then, a crack of thunder rocked the room and lightning flashed brilliantly. There would be another time, she thought, watching their reflections in the mirror. But not tonight.

CHERYL WATCHED Nick's car disappear around the curve in the drive. The outside gallery along the second floor was a good vantage point for checking the grounds. At the western boundary where Jed Singer was on guard, a tossed cigarette made a tiny red arc before landing on the crushed gravel of the path. Good. Jed on the job meant she could go to bed. The electricity wasn't yet restored, and until it was the security system worked off an emergency generator. Also, Singer was good. He'd come to the department from Special Forces in the army. Anything unusual on the grounds he would handle.

After a glance at her watch, Cheryl stretched wearily. Past two-thirty, but she didn't even hope to fall asleep quickly. Her own fault for losing it and blabbing her secrets to Will. She could just imagine his disgust. Why, oh, why had she said all that? And to Will, of all people. He had to be the last person she wanted to know the shameful truth about her marriage. Not that her revolting revelations seemed to be keeping him awake, she thought with a sigh. His windows had gone dark a good half-hour ago.

Moving quietly along the gallery, she checked the lock on Shannon's French doors then moved on toward her own room. Once inside, she closed and locked up, then took her weapon from its holster and put it on the bed while she undressed. Her hands were busy with the fastening on her jeans when she sensed someone else in the room. In a flash, she dived for her gun.

"It's only me, Cheryl."

"Will!" Pointing the weapon toward the floor, she leaned weakly against the tall posts at the foot of her bed and waited for her heart to start up again. When it did, she faced him furiously. "Are you trying to get yourself killed, or what?"

"Shhh…" He stood up, putting his finger to his lips. "You're going to wake everybody in the house."

She had a lot more to say, but she lowered her voice. "In case you didn't notice, Will O'Connor, this room is dark, and finding an intruder waiting for me is justification to draw my weapon. Haven't you got—"

"I'm sorry." Holding his hands up in front of him, he started toward her.

She turned hastily and reholstered the gun. Because her hands were shaking, she put the weapon down on the dresser top and then wrapped her arms around her waist. "What are you doing here?" she asked in a shaken voice, still not facing him.

"For one thing, making certain Shannon is settled."

"She is. Besides, that's my job."

"I saw Nick drive away."

"Yes."

"Hmmm."

Uncertain whether that meant he disapproved, Cheryl came quickly to their defense. "Whatever your sister and Nick do is between them. They're adults."

"I agree. Two lucky adults." He studied her expression. "You look surprised. I don't know why. Anybody can see that Nick's interest in my sister goes beyond looking for the man who attacked her. Way beyond. I think he's in love with her. As for Shannon, she's mixed up and vulnerable right now, but it's obvious she doesn't think of Nick just as the cop assigned to her case. He's clearly more than that to her.'' He chuckled softly, shaking his head. ''I seem to remember a couple of times since they met when there was little love lost between them.'' He was directly behind her now, keeping his tone low. ''They seem to have gotten beyond their differences tonight, whatever they are,'' he added.

''I know,'' she said. She longed to turn and look at him, but she didn't know what she'd see after spouting off like she had about Andy. ''I think they've always been aware of each other, from the moment they met. It was only a matter of time.''

Taking a breath, she turned. Without benefit of light, his face was in shadow, making it impossible to read his expression. He was so much taller than her dead husband. And bigger. But oddly enough, she felt no threat. Will wasn't the kind of man who would ever use his strength and size to intimidate a woman. The emotion rioting inside her wasn't fear.

''I didn't come in here to talk about Nick and Shannon,'' he told her.

''If it's what I told you about Andy and me—''

''Screw Andy!'' The words exploded from him. Startled, Cheryl backed a step. He sounded ferocious. He caught her hand, stopping her. ''Wait...wait...just...'' Drawing a deep breath, he turned her loose and forced a laugh. ''I'm messing this all up...barking at you, grabbing you.''

''Just tell me straight out, Will.''

With his hands at his sides, he looked at her, saying nothing for a few seconds. ''I'm trying to say I'm sorry for misjudging you. You threw me for a loop when you told me the truth about your marriage. I'm sorry for believing that bastard when he bad-mouthed you. I wish I hadn't been stupid enough to take him at his word just because I knew him—or thought I knew him. I suppose my excuse is that I didn't know you very well. But I do now. I wish I had followed my instincts from the very beginning when I..."

"When you what?"

He looked at her. And then, as though he couldn't help himself, he reached out and touched her cheek. "When I found it so hard to believe...after meeting you...that I'd been so wrong in my first impression of you. I thought you seemed a nice girl, a little shy, a little overwhelmed by all that crap at the regatta. And then later when I saw you at that party, I had the odd thought that you probably liked smaller, quieter gatherings."

"I did. I do. But Andy—"

Will put his finger on her lips to stop her. "Let's make a deal right here and now. Let's don't ever mention your ex-husband's name again. He hurt you and humiliated you. Any respect I felt for him is wiped out."

She searched his face through a film of tears. "Does this mean you believe me?"

Smiling gently, he took her face between his hands. "I believe you."

"I know how disgusting it must sound, that I tolerated his abuse all those—"

He stopped her with a kiss, his lips warm and firm, on hers. Then, still cradling her face, he deepened it. For a second or two, she was so amazed that she could only stand there. And then she was suddenly swamped with emotion so intense it was painful. With a sound wrenched from her heart, she tore herself free and stumbled back. "No!"

"Cheryl—"

She covered her mouth with the fingers of one hand. "No, don't...I can't. You don't understand."

"It was only a kiss, Cheryl. I wouldn't have taken it any further than that. I didn't come in here tonight with sex in mind." He stopped and raked a hand through his hair. "Well, maybe that's not quite true. The truth is, I've had sex on my mind since the day you came home with Shannon. Hell, longer than that. Since the day I first saw you. But tonight...well, I came because I want to set the record straight between us. I want us to start with a clean slate."

"Oh, God, you really don't understand," she cried. In a flood of tears, she looked hopelessly at the ceiling.

"Then explain it to me, love," Will said, speaking as gently as though she was a child.

When she saw that he meant to touch her again, she shied away until she was safely on the other side of the bed. Only then did she face him. "There's no such thing as a clean slate, Will. That's the legacy left to me by my ex-husband, or so I've learned from the encounter group. Erasing his name is a neat idea, but it won't erase what he did. Erasing his memory and what he did are fantasies. None of it erases how I feel. Nothing can do that."

For a few seconds, he just studied her. When he spoke, the certainty in his tone gave her pause. "You're wrong, sweetheart, although I can see you're in no shape tonight to believe that. Something *can* erase the past. Something I've been keeping right here inside me for years." He bumped his chest softly with his fist. "Waiting for the right lady to claim it. I know, I know...you say you don't want to hear it, but I have to say it, darlin'." His smile was a little off-center. "I love you, Cheryl Carpenter."

Oh, God, why is this happening to me? Cheryl thought wildly. He was saying all the things that could give her her heart's desire, but she was too confused to grab it. She could never have a normal relationship like other women. Why was he tormenting her, trying to make her think she could?

With his arms crossed over his chest, Will looked at her tenderly. "I'm thirty-seven years old. I've never had a wife, never even been engaged. You're the only woman I've ever met that I wanted to share my life with. I backed off when you belonged to my cousin, but all bets are off now."

"Oh, Will..."

"I mean it, lady. Get ready for me to come courtin'."

She stared at him, speechless and miserable and wildly tempted.

With his head to one side, he grinned again. "I guess a good-night kiss is out of the question, hmm?"

"I...I..."

His eyebrows went up. "Aye, aye? No problem." In four long strides, he was around the bed. Before she could think, he had her chin bracketed between his thumb and fingers. Then he was kissing her.

It was like the first time—a swift, intense rush of emotion. A tidal wave of pleasure. It caught in her throat. Stole her breath away. Swamped her heart. It was so wonderful that she swayed dizzily, forced to catch at his shirt to keep from falling. In fact, she wasn't sure she wouldn't just melt into a puddle right there on the floor. Oh, how she wished she was happy and whole.

How long they feasted on the kiss, she wasn't certain. Will was the one to come to his senses first. With a sound deep in his throat, he broke the kiss. He didn't seem able to say anything for a few moments. Beneath her hands clutching his shirt, his heart was beating a mile a minute. Just as hers was. Finally he let her go, and without another word, walked to her door, opened it and left.

In a state of stunned disbelief, she undressed and got into her bed. She would never get to sleep now, she thought, still a little dizzy.

Will O'Connor loved her!

Her eyes closed and she was out like a light.

CHAPTER TWELVE

IN THE MEN'S ROOM at the police station, Nick stood in front of the mirror over the sink. Not a pretty sight, he thought, noting the redness of his eyes and the five o'clock shadow on his chin. It wasn't five o'clock. It was ten in the morning and he was closing in on thirty hours without sleep. He'd come straight from Shannon's bed to his desk.

With a grunt, he stripped off his shirt and draped it over the electric hand dryer. When he turned the cold water on, the faucet gushed with pent-up pressure, splashing the front of his jeans. He bent and doused his face, hoping to soak away some of his fatigue. Using his hands, he scrubbed at the sweat and grime of the past several hours spent toiling over a list of Shannon's news stories and the file of Becky Berenson's murder, trying to tie them together. To be precise, trying to tie *all* the missing teenagers somehow to something Shannon was working on. It had to be. He knew it. *Felt* it. But how?

His face dripping, he looked up into the mirror. Without even trying, he was suddenly seeing another mirror, old-fashioned, free-standing, murky with age. The images there were nothing conjured from Outer Wherever, like Shannon's. They came from his own mind and featured him and Shannon and fierce lightning and even fiercer passion. For the first time, he found himself thinking Shannon might be right. Were they linked in some mystical way because he'd saved her life?

Ah, God!

A shake of his head served to clear the images, but it sent water droplets flying everywhere. He looked around, cursing as usual because they no longer had plain paper toweling to dry off with. He finally fished his handkerchief out of his jeans pocket and mopped himself dry. Then he pulled the shirt back over his head and resolved to get back to his apartment by lunchtime for a change of clothes.

He hadn't wanted to leave Shannon last night. They needed to talk, he supposed. But the sleaze who was stalking her was getting too close to ignore. Slipping her that damn note, then wrecking her apartment...who knew what else he might do? There was only one way to stop a crazy like that and it was with long hours, meticulous study of the facts, and maybe... just maybe he'd luck out on something.

Because if he didn't, the alternative was unthinkable. He had not let himself dwell too much on the way he'd felt making love to Shannon last night. He gave in now, with a shuddering release of his breath. It had been wonderful. Unbelievable. He'd never felt so powerful...almost rejuvenated when it was over. She made him feel things he'd never felt before, violently possessive...fiercely protective. Standing still in the middle of the men's room, he faced the one thing that scared the hell out of him. What if he failed? What if he didn't flush out her stalker before he struck again...successfully?

As he made his way back to his desk, he stopped to pour what had to be his tenth cup of coffee. Ed looked up from reading the typewritten sheets in front of him. "Looks like you and Shannon O'Connor had a very busy night," he said.

Nick gave him a sharp look. "What?"

Ed tapped a single page. "Your memo. From last night."

"Oh...yeah."

"The bastard sends her a threatening note with you sitting right beside her, then she finds her apartment trashed to a fare-thee-well." He shrugged. "I call that a busy night."

"Yeah."

"So, what do we have here?" Ed said. He picked up the plastic envelope containing the note. "No prints, letters cut from a magazine and pasted on, nothing from the apartment, again no prints, no clues, no screwups." He dropped the note and looked at Nick. "What we have here is nothing, boss."

Nick returned the look sourly.

"Shannon have any ideas?"

"She draws a blank, same as us."

"Literally," Ed said sagely, obviously referring to Shannon's amnesia. "I don't suppose she's remembered anything yet?"

"Nothing significant."

Ed picked up a thicker bunch of pages stapled together. "So, what about this other stuff I found waiting for me this fine morning?"

"Maybe nothing," Nick said, sitting down. "Those are the reports on the missing girls, and Becky Berenson's murder, and a list of the things Shannon was working on before she was attacked."

"I can see that."

"There's a connection, Ed."

"Now, I don't see *that*," his partner said, looking at Nick for an explanation.

Nick raked a hand through his hair. It was still damp. He couldn't tell Ed that his suspicion that the cases were linked came from Shannon's Dream Sight, so he settled for a half truth. "Call it a hunch," he said, thinking wryly that in some of the best detective stories, hunches played very well.

Call it what you would, there were just too many odd facts connecting the cases for him to dismiss. He stared hard out of the window and ran over the list in his mind. First of all, Shannon somehow knew the girl's name and "felt" Becky's feelings from the encounter at the bus station up until the moment she was killed in the bedroom. She knew *how* Becky was killed. And then, there was her strange reaction at the convenience store. Nick had run a make on the license from the pickup that had seemed to be the focus of her feelings, but had drawn a blank. It was registered to a deceased driver, and worse, out of state. A dead end.

Nick faced the window, blind to the traffic crisscrossing in his line of vision. And what about Shannon's recurring dream? He leaned back, deep in thought. Two lawyers. A distressed woman. A courtroom. And a judge. Those facts could fit a thousand scenarios. Most significant, however, was the thing last night in the mirror. She had recognized the voice of her attacker. While he was tormenting another woman. What the hell did it all mean?

"A hunch?" Ed was saying.

Nick looked at him. "Yeah, a hunch," he said. To hell with explaining why.

"You look like you had a hard night, boss. Why don't you—"

"I'm going." He stood up abruptly, the action sending his chair skidding backward. "Shannon has the encounter group today. I don't want to take any chances."

"You don't think Cheryl can handle it?"

Cheryl probably could handle it. To be on the safe side, he'd dispatched both Jacoby and Miller to Wilderose House an hour ago to accompany the women to the clinic. He wasn't taking any chances. Not with the woman he loved.

He wasn't fighting *that* anymore.

"HE'S GOING TO DO something crazy, I know it."

The encounter group—nine women and a teenage girl—looked at Francine. Her face was drawn, her eyes tired. In her lap, her hands twisted a tissue into shreds. "I'm not scared so much for myself as for Kelly."

Beside her, Francine's teenage daughter rolled her eyes. She was there only because her mother had insisted, she'd informed the group. *She* didn't need to tell the world their private life. What was the point? Bitching and complaining in front of a bunch of women and a shrink hadn't helped Mary Ellen Kirk, had it? "I'm not scared of him, Mom," she said, crossing both feet out in front of her. "He's all mouth."

Francine stared at her hands. "You should be scared. He

seems jumpy lately. Nervous. I don't know what to expect from one day to the next.''

The psychologist frowned. Since the death of Mary Ellen Kirk, nobody dismissed such statements from any member of the group anymore. "Have you thought further about taking some legal action now, Francine?'' Susan asked.

Francine darted a look around the group. "Oh, no. I don't think so. He would really go off the deep end if I did. Besides, it doesn't really help.''

The group members murmured among themselves. The system had certainly failed Mary Ellen.

Francine went on. "He came to the house last night. I wasn't home, but Kelly was.'' She glanced at the teenage girl. "She wouldn't open the door. She talked to him through it. She told him I wasn't home, but he didn't believe her. So he tried to kick it in. Kelly threatened to call the cops.''

"*That* really ticked him off,'' Kelly said, her mouth twisting. "But he left, didn't he? You just have to call his bluff— I told Mama that.''

"He left me a message,'' Francine said, her hands still restless in her lap. "Said to tell me the next time he wouldn't be so polite. He'd shoot the lock off and shoot me, too.''

With a toss of her head, Kelly flicked her long hair away from her shoulder. "He's a real jerk.''

"A dangerous jerk,'' Shannon said, unable to keep quiet.

Cheryl spoke for the first time. "Don't underestimate a guy like that. You could both be in serious trouble if he takes a notion to teach you a lesson.'' She looked at Francine. "Does he have a drinking problem?''

"Big time,'' said Kelly. "And he's mean when he drinks.''

Shannon made an impatient sound. "Susan, this situation has many similarities to the Mary Ellen Kirk thing. Surely this time, something can be done to prevent another tragedy.''

"What about it, Francine?'' Susan asked, looking at the woman. "You have options. We've talked about that. You can file a restraining order to keep him away from the premises.''

"'Premises.' Does that mean only her house?" Shannon asked, "or does it also include where she works, or where she goes to buy groceries, or her bank, or the mall where she shops?" She released a disgusted sigh. "It's ridiculous! The police can't be all those places at once. It means she'd have to have a bodyguard. The man himself needs to be arrested."

"Which they won't do," Kelly said contemptuously, "because he hasn't done anything yet."

Shannon turned to Francine, who seemed almost detached from the dialogue going on around her. "If you're not quite ready to trust the police, Francine, maybe it would be a good idea for you and Kelly to leave town for a while."

Francine smiled sadly. "And go where? That's if I could afford to go anywhere." She sighed deeply. "I have a brother here in Savannah. We've stayed there before when things got—" She shrugged. "It would be okay with him, I suppose. Temporarily, of course."

Shannon looked at Susan. "Would you just listen to this, Susan? Surely there's a better solution for endangered women than having to scurry around to a relative's house or bear the burden of an expensive stay somewhere out of town. What kind of system do we have that women can't put their faith and trust in it?"

But she knew Susan didn't have the answers. Options for women were somewhat better than they used to be, but so many people fell through the cracks, anyway. She didn't want that to happen to Francine. Or to anybody else in the room, she thought, looking around at the women she'd come to admire.

Her gaze fell on Cheryl, who had said very little since the meeting started. For her to be so distracted meant she had something serious on her mind. Which was strange, since she had seemed so different at breakfast this morning. Shannon didn't know what had happened between Cheryl and Will the night before, but something definitely had.

There was no established routine for breakfast at Wilderose

House. Gran was a very early riser and usually ate before Shannon was out of bed. Will mostly skipped it altogether. Since Cheryl was so conscientious about "guarding" her, she always waited for Shannon, and this morning was no exception. However, things had taken an interesting turn when they came downstairs together.

In the center of the breakfast table was a gorgeous arrangement of flowers, and lying across Cheryl's plate was a single, beautiful blush-pink calla lily. Cheryl had drawn in a startled breath and then turned the same shade as the lily. There had been a note, too, which she had unfolded with the kind of caution that she might have used in defusing a bomb. Then she'd looked at Shannon and shrugged, saying simply, "Will."

Shannon was thrilled. And delighted. She hadn't realized that her big brother had a romantic bone in his body. Now, if only Nick—

"I HAVE A CONFESSION to make."

The encounter group—all seven of them—looked at Cheryl. As always, some were keenly interested in the words of the others, but many were too mired in their own problems. They barely heard what anybody else said. To Cheryl, an audience of only one was one too many. But she had to do this. And she had to do it today.

Pulling her lips inward, she closed her eyes. She was through denying the truth. She was through running from her past. Most of all, she was through covering for the man who had abused her. Pouring it all out to Will had been the first hurdle. Like poison lanced from a wound, words were ready to gush out of her.

"I had my own reason for coming to this encounter group," she said, glancing around at the members. "It had nothing to do with the terrible memories of my marriage. The horror of that was past history, I told myself, and talking about it couldn't possibly do any good." She cleared her throat as the ghost of a smile came and went. "I hadn't counted on the persistence of this group and...others. I've been dancing around the truth. It can't be a secret to all of you that my ex-husband wasn't exactly picture-perfect. I thought I could tell just a little and let it go at that. Sort of like scratching at a scab when a wound is healed. The truth is, the wound wasn't healed. Not even close. The fact is that my ex-husband was a very violent man. And I was his victim."

There, it was said.

She gave Shannon a quick look and found only encouragement in her eyes. "For a long time, I wondered if his violence was something I'd brought on myself. I wondered if I was a disappointment as a wife. I wondered if I wasn't smart enough, or pretty enough, or was I too smart, or even too pretty. After a while I wondered if he guessed that I didn't love him. I know now that no reason gives a man license to assault a woman.

"The first time he hit me, we had been married for only five months. I came home from work after receiving a commendation I'd earned in the line of duty. As a rookie cop, I was so proud." Her voice dropped, as she added ruefully, "I went to bed that night with a cracked rib and bruised kidneys. Andy didn't like me acting like a man," she explained with bitterness. "That was the way he described my job as a policewoman.

"He apologized, of course, but it happened again a couple of months later, and so I resigned from my job." She glanced up knowing the women in the group would understand all too well. "Which made him happy for about a week. The next time was over the checkbook. I balanced the joint account and was thirty-seven cents off. I forget the reason why it happened next. Soon I simply lost count. He was usually drunk when he lost control, and his intoxication made a convenient excuse when he apologized. But as time passed, his ability to control himself seemed to be slipping. The night I left him, he wasn't drinking at all. He was just angry, enraged, actually. I had waited until he was sober to tell him. The truth is, there's no good time to tell an abusive husband that you're leaving him."

Her voice thick with tears, she drew in a shaky breath. "He was like a madman. If I hadn't managed to reach my service revolver, which I kept on a closet shelf, I honestly believe he would have killed me."

Shannon was looking at her incredulously. "Why didn't you tell somebody, Cheryl?"

"I was ashamed."

Beside Cheryl, Francine nodded. "I know the feeling."

"Speaking of feelings—" Susan looked at Cheryl "—would you like to put more of yours into words, Cheryl?"

Her eyes were dark and uncertain. "It's difficult. Until I started coming to these meetings, I thought I didn't have any feelings from that time. Which is ridiculous, as I know now. Listening to others, being encouraged to talk myself…well, it's like a cork has been pulled from a bottle that is nearly bursting with pressure. It was threatening at first to think about telling. I've been carrying this secret around for so long. Worse than that, I've been angry and defensive all this time. And of course there's the shame."

Her eyes fell to her hands. "I don't feel so ashamed anymore. That has to be one of the best things that the group has done for me."

"It's your ex-husband's shame, Cheryl," Susan said softly. "Not yours."

"Someone else said that to me just last night," Cheryl said, smiling softly. "For the first time, I think maybe I can start to believe it."

o

IT WAS NO SURPRISE to Shannon that Will was waiting for them when the meeting ended. She noticed with wry amusement that with Cheryl by her side, he barely gave his sister a glance. Her brother had eyes only for the pretty bodyguard. Will had finally taken the fall! About time, too, she thought, hiding a smile.

"I've been waiting for you."

At the sound of Nick's deep voice, her heart leapt. Before she caught her breath, he had slipped his hand beneath her arm and begun shepherding her aside, separating her from Cheryl. She sent a startled look over her shoulder at her body-guard, who was looking as surprised as Shannon.

Seeing Shannon's confusion, Will gave her a reassuring wave. "Don't worry, little sister, your bodyguard's taking a couple of days off." Ignoring Cheryl's surprised squeak, he nodded at Nick. "You're in good hands with Savannah's finest detective, right Nick?"

"Will!" Even to Shannon's ears, Cheryl's objection lacked conviction.

Will began hustling Cheryl toward the door. "So, we'll see you two when we see you."

Her mouth open, Shannon stared at them until they disappeared. She looked at Nick. "What was that all about?"

"You heard him, Cheryl has the rest of day off—the whole weekend if she wants it."

"She didn't mention anything to me earlier."

"She didn't know it," Nick said, pushing the door open and walking out beside her. "It's Will's idea." His mouth quirked in a smile. "I think he has plans to show her the town."

"Savannah?"

"No, guess again...New York."

"*New York!*"

"New York. I'll say this for your brother," Nick said, coming to a stop beside his car. "When he wants to impress a lady, he does it in style."

Now that they were outside, Shannon looked beyond Nick's shoulder, trying to find them. Spotting Will's Jeep, she saw the new lovers in deep conversation, Cheryl gesturing almost beseechingly at first, then with a little more heat. Will, crowding her a little, didn't give an inch. As Shannon watched, the exchange ended and they were suddenly quiet...and still. Then

Will swore and hauled Cheryl against him and kissed her. When he let her go, they were both breathless. And then they were laughing. After literally tossing Cheryl into his vehicle, Will climbed in beside her and they roared off.

The whole thing had happened in less than two minutes. Shannon sighed. "Well…"

"So…guess who's guarding your body this weekend," Nick drawled, tugging at a strand of auburn hair.

She looked into his gray-green eyes. "It obviously can't be Cheryl," she said dryly.

His chuckle was rich and soft as he hugged her. "No, not Cheryl."

"Hmm, I guess I have to settle for the big cheese himself, right?" she said, eyeing him from beneath her lashes. Then her eyes went wide as he grabbed her in a maneuver a lot like Will's and kissed her soundly. When she was pliant and breathless, he stepped back, calmly opened the car door and tucked her neatly inside. Neither noticed the amused looks from the crowd milling around the parking lot.

One man was not amused. He tossed an unread newspaper onto the seat of his Jaguar, cursing as the cop drove away with the bitch beside him. With both hands clenched on the steering wheel, he fought an impulse to slam his fist into something. He had a gut feeling that she was coming around. His snitch said no, that he was worried for nothing, but he knew better. He felt it. She could bring the whole thing down if she remembered. And she would.

He started the Jaguar. Timing was everything in life. He'd found that to be true from the moment he'd mapped out his plans and took the first step up the ladder to a position that would net him world-class power and prestige. What troubled him most right now was choosing the best moment to do what must be done. When she was with Dalton, it was too risky. The cop was good. Too good. Away from Dalton, now… Already he had had more than a couple of opportunities to do it, but he hadn't felt the timing was right. Not the time when in the clinic she had gone to the restroom alone. Or when she'd dashed to the public phones at the last council meeting. Several opportunities had presented themselves at the office of the *Sentinel,* too. Actually, she was a careless fool. Most of her time was spent in public places. A woman could be picked off easy as pie in a public restroom, in a parking garage, alone in a corridor. It was as though the bimbo didn't take him seriously. When he did it, he was going to chastise her for that. And it would be a pleasure.

Dalton was gone, he noted, heading west. When the man headed out of the clinic's parking lot, he drove off in the opposite direction.

CHAPTER THIRTEEN

"WHAT'S WRONG?"

Shannon's joy ended abruptly as Nick's car pulled away from the clinic. Flashes of light and images began, and her head pounded. She moaned softly and put her fingers to her temples.

Not now! Not now!

Marshaling all of her strength, she focused on shutting out the message. This was the last thing she wanted right now. She had finally accepted that something terrifying was behind the closed curtain of her mind. She knew she would have to deal with it eventually, but not now.

She had been so happy to see Nick, overjoyed to learn that Will and Cheryl would spend the weekend together, because it also meant that Nick, not Cheryl, would be her companion for the weekend. If it were up to Nick, she wasn't sure that he would choose to be with her again so soon after going to bed with her. She suspected that he still wanted to think of her as a case to be solved.

"What is it, Shannon?"

His voice seemed to come at her from a tunnel. She looked blankly into his face, all her energy taken up with resisting the Dream Sight. His eyes on her, Nick drifted dangerously into the lane of oncoming traffic, then swerved as a horn blared from an irate truck driver. Avoiding a collision by a scant inch, he blistered the air with choice oaths.

"I'm taking you home," he said grimly.

Shannon nodded, then leaned weakly against the seat, resigned. Wilderose House was more than ten miles distant. But then Nick passed the turn. As he slowed at an intersection, she recognized the neighborhood. Her own apartment was close. She didn't want to go there!

"No, Nick, I—"

"We're going to my place." He took another sharp turn, sped through a caution light, then turned into the quiet residential street where he lived.

Although she had been inside Nick's house only once before, she entered again without hesitation. The dragonfly lamp lent a warm, welcoming glow to the foyer, but better than that, Jake the tomcat sidled up to her ankles, purring a friendly greeting. She reached down and picked him up, burying her face in his soft fur. He felt warm and snuggly and...so ordinary. Nick went to fix him a bowl of Seafood Fest and she sank down on the sofa, still holding him, deliberately blanking everything from her mind except the pleasure of the cat's company.

Nick, of course, had other ideas.

When he came out of the kitchen, she noticed that he was no longer wearing his gun. But he was still all business. "Are you ready to tell me what that was all about?"

"There's nothing to tell. For once I don't have to tax your credibility. I didn't see anything."

"No memory flashes?"

"Not really."

"No details, huh?"

"Right."

"No Dream Sight?"

"No."

"That's odd, because as we pulled away from the clinic, you looked the way you do when it happens."

"Could I have a drink of water?" She gave a half laugh. "Interrogations make me thirsty."

He stared at her a long moment. "How about gin and tonic?" Without waiting for an answer, he headed back to the kitchen. Jake jumped down and followed him. After a few minutes, Nick was back. She took the drink, tasted it and then looked at him. "Haven't you forgotten something?" When he frowned, she explained, "Your trusty notebook."

His hand went automatically to his shirt pocket, but there wasn't one in his pullover. Instead, he fished the battered tablet out of his jeans, then cocked his eyebrow at her. "I'm ready when you are."

"Wait." Without expression, she hauled her handbag up from the floor where she'd dropped it and rummaged around in the depths of the thing. "Here." She handed him a small wrapped package.

He took it, looking puzzled. "What is it?"

"Open it."

After another glance at her, he tore it open. Then he simply stared at it, saying nothing.

"Happy birthday," she said, feeling suddenly self-conscious.

"It's not my birthday," Nick said, turning the small leather article over in his hands.

"I know." She gave him a challenging look. "If I waited for you to tell me something personal such as your birthday, or even where you were born, or if you have any family and where they might be…" She trailed off with a small shrug. "Well, it looks like I'd wait a long time."

"November 12."

"A Scorpio. I might have known."

Nick sat down abruptly. "Shannon—"

"Don't."

She silenced him, putting up a hand. "I don't want to know anything about you until you choose to tell me, Nick." Her smile came, and then faded. "Actually, I bought that as a joke."

He looked at the top-of-the-line pocket diary. Bound in expensive Moroccan leather, it was exactly the size of the cheap spiral notebook he carried. The thought that it was suited more to a corporate executive than an underpaid detective would never occur to Shannon.

"A joke?" he said.

"Well, you accused me of having a thing about your note-book."

"I don't think you have a thing about my notebook. I think you have a thing about being questioned."

"So now I'm making it easy for you." She noticed that he couldn't quite disguise his pleasure in the gift as he opened it, but she grimaced when he pulled out a cheap ballpoint pen to meticulously note the date. "Maybe for your real birthday, I'll get you a Montblanc to go with it."

He stopped writing, pinning her with a fierce look. "Don't get me a Montblanc," he said bluntly.

A few seconds passed while they dueled silently. It wasn't the expensive pen that was the issue here, she guessed; it was something else. Maybe when he got ready to tell her about something more than his birthday, he would tell her what it was.

"Well then," she said with another shrug, "let the inquisition begin."

With a grunt, he propped the notebook on his knee and began. "Something happened to trip your memory back there, Shannon. I've been with you before and I know the signs."

"Yes, that's odd, don't you think?"

"What's odd?"

"That nobody else has ever been with me when it happens. Only you. Do you think that means something?"

"Yeah, I do."

Surprise at his admission rendered her speechless.

With a gruff chuckle, Nick settled back in the corner of the couch and rested one arm along the back. "Don't look so surprised. I admit it. Finally." His amusement faded. "I can't explain this thing between us. Maybe it's the near-death thing, as you say. Maybe—"

"It wasn't *near* death," Shannon corrected him gently, "I really did die."

"Okay. You died. And I knew it when you did. I've never felt panic like that. Pure, unadulterated fear. Any vestige of professionalism went out the door, I can tell you. I don't know how I managed to figure out what was wrong, or how it could be fixed..."

"The answers don't matter, Nick. It was just meant to be."

"Maybe."

"Absolutely."

He wasn't in the mood to argue. "When your heart started beating again, I felt ...something." He shook his head, still mystified, then gave her a rueful smile. "It doesn't take a rocket scientist to see that nothing's been the same since, has it?"

"Not really," she said, returning the smile.

He shook his head. "It's a...lot to digest," he said.

"Uh-huh." What he meant was that it was a lot to accept. To believe.

"I don't like things I can't understand," he admitted.

"No."

As a detective, Nick dealt in logic and reason. He demanded rational explanations for the incredible things he witnessed around her. She should be relieved that he conceded as much as he did.

"How's your drink?" he asked.

She looked at it, then took another sip. "Fine."

"Want some chips or something?"

"No...but thanks."

"Everything under control?"

"Everything's under control."

"Then are you ready to tell me what happened back there?"

She sighed. "It wasn't much, truly."

"I know," he said, taking up his own drink. "You fought it off."

She flushed with guilt. It was true. Because of her terror in refusing to let the images come, she might have blocked something vital, a clue that would lead them to whoever wrote that note. And trashed her apartment. She might have learned who it was who wanted to kill her.

"I wonder if it's too late," Nick said, with a thoughtful look.

Instantly she tensed. Dread formed in her stomach, heavy and threatening. In the safety of Nick's house, protected by Nick himself, she had regained her composure. Now, in half a dozen words, the terror was back.

"Nick, please...I don't want—"

"I know, but you have to, baby." He reached over and took the drink from her, then set it aside with his own. He even abandoned his notebook. When she would have scrambled back into her corner of the couch, he reached for her hands. His grip was warm and firm. "Let's try something, okay? Let's try going back there to the parking lot at the clinic. To the moment when you felt something."

Although she was shaking her head, she knew it was no use. It was as though Nick's words had breached a barrier and it was too late to build it up again. Closing her eyes, Shannon shuddered, and like a curtain rising on a play, the flashes began. Images formed like pieces of photographs arranged into a collage that meant...nothing. No matter how she concentrated, she could make no rhyme nor reason out of the patterns. When Nick spoke she realized she was still shaking her head.

"What are you seeing?" he asked softly.

"Nothing," she moaned, rubbing at pain between her eyes that was excruciating.

"Yes, Shannon, you're seeing something. Let it come, honey. You're not in this alone. I'm right here. I'll stay right here. I love you."

At that, whatever blocked her memory was suddenly gone. Her body relaxed, as though trusting Nick for whatever came, and she forced herself back to the moments in the parking lot.

"We're at the clinic." The instant she verbalized the memory, the pain began to decrease dramatically. "We watch Will and Cheryl talk. They're across the parking lot from us. They're standing beside Will's—"

"Yes, beside Will's car," Nick said, almost seeing the scene with her.

"It's a Jaguar!" she said, blurting out the words, knowing that identifying the car was the first hard fact that might be of some use. Twisting her hands together, her eyes tightly closed, Shannon focused on the scrap of memory as fiercely as she'd rejected it earlier.

"Will was driving a Jeep." Nick said, baffled now.

"Not Will," she murmured, slipping into a near trance, "the man."

Nick's eyes narrowed. "What man?"

"He's reading a newspaper," she said, as though seeing from a distance. "He's wearing the watch...the Rolex."

"Do you know him?"

"No...yes..." She frowned, desperately trying to sort out what was reality from what wasn't. "I saw him before, at the clinic...the first day I went to the encounter group."

"When? How?"

"When we were walking out. He was pulling away in his car."

"The Jaguar again?"

"Yes. He has been watching me ever since."

"Do you think he's the one who passed you the threatening note in the council meeting?"

"Yes."

"The one who trashed your apartment?"

"Yes."

"How could you see enough detail to recognize the watch he's wearing?"

"Because I saw it up close when he...he..." Her eyes flew open. Jerking free, she pressed her fingers to her mouth.

"When he assaulted you? He's the one?"

Shuddering, she buried her face in her hands and burst into

tears. Nick swore and hauled her up into his arms. Holding her close, his face grim, he whispered reassurances and waited for the storm of weeping to pass. He would be happy just holding her for the rest of his days, he realized. Not for the first time, he thought how easily she could have been killed that night, how they never could have had this chance together. What kind of animal got off by brutalizing a woman like Shannon?

"I'm okay now," she said, sniffing a little, but she stayed burrowed into his solid warmth, her face nestled beneath his chin.

"Sure?" He pushed back to look at her.

"Yes." With her hand, she wiped her eyes.

"I've got a few more questions, sweetheart."

She laughed shakily. "Why doesn't that surprise me?"

He tucked her snugly against him. "Was all that pulled from your memory or your Dream Sight?"

"I guess a little of both." She frowned, unconsciously fiddling with the collar of his shirt. "I've been getting little glitches of memory for a long time now, although nothing really substantial. Nothing that would have identified the man who assaulted me."

"What about the watch? The car?"

"I don't know how I know, Nick. At the clinic, I was always a little jittery in the parking lot. Nothing really definite, just a feeling." She shrugged and gave him a rueful smile. "I didn't mention it because... Well, just... You see how you reacted? Can you blame me?"

"And the watch?"

"I definitely saw the watch when he was hitting me...." She shuddered again, but this time she forced her memory beyond the fear. "Seeing it now is Dream Sight and reality, a little of both, I guess. I couldn't actually see anything, could I? But I'm aware of the car and the man sitting in it. He's reading a newspaper and I can see his watch. How I know it's a Rolex, I can't explain. You'll just have to believe me."

She looked at him. "*Do* you believe me, Nick?"

"Yeah."

"You really mean that?"

"I mean it." With a soft chuckle, he leaned back into the corner of the couch, taking her with him. "I can't explain it and I don't understand it, but I believe it."

"All of the above goes for me, too. This isn't exactly easy for me to learn to live with."

For a few seconds, they were silent, both caught up in their own thoughts. Nick spoke first. "What we've got to do now is figure out who he is. I suppose this is a stretch, but do you think you could 'see' the license plate on that Jaguar?"

"No."

"How about his face?"

"Nothing."

They fell silent again. With Shannon cuddled next to him, Nick let his thoughts wander. This case had him baffled, not only because of the wild card that Shannon's psychic insight presented, but because there were so many unknowns. Usually he had a firm grip on most aspects of an investigation. The problem with this was that his own instincts told him the case was linked to others. Becky Berenson's murder, for example. Which related to the missing teen girls. The most vital question still remained. When would she conquer her fear enough to remember?

Until he found some answers, she was in real danger.

Instinct told him whoever was watching her was feeling the pressure. If her assailant knew she was suffering from amnesia, then he probably knew most amnesia was temporary. Because of that, he had to know she was a loose cannon as far as he was concerned. How long would he risk letting her walk around carrying information that would damn him?

"You're worried," she said suddenly.

She was too sharp to lie to. "A little." When she rolled her eyes, he owned up. "Okay, more than a little. But only when you're out of my sight.'' His tone grew colder than usual. And harder. ''He can't get to you as long as you're with me.''

''No.''

He stared beyond her, as though trying to see through a haze. ''It's frustrating as hell not being able to pin this guy down.''

''You will,'' she said softly.

He gave a short laugh. Now she was the one reassuring him. He raked a hand over his hair and drew in a resigned breath. ''Yeah, well, the sooner the better.''

''Speaking of police incompetence—'' She yelped, laughing as he caught her chin in his hand and gave her a fierce look. ''Just kidding, just kidding.'' Her expression sobered. ''You remember the woman in my encounter group who was being harassed by her ex-boyfriend, don't you?'' At his nod, she said, ''Well, he's still at it, only I think he's at the edge, Nick. I think this jerk is really going to hurt her or her teenage daughter if something isn't done.''

''Has she reported him?''

''No, can you believe it? She points to Mary Ellen Kirk and others like her that the system has failed so miserably, and she's scared to death of her ex-boyfriend. We're going to see two people hurt, Nick, Francine and her daughter, Kelly, who's only fourteen years old. Can't the police do something? Can't you?''

''We've been through this before, honey. She needs to file an official—''

''Can they keep him from punishing her for that?''

''If he violates—''

''If! If! Listen to yourself, Nick. It'll be too late by then. It could be another case like Mary Ellen Kirk's. The police were called and they arrived just in time to put her in a body bag.''

''Honey—''

She sprang up from the couch to pace the length of his living room. ''You know something, Nick? There's not much difference between what's happening to me and what's happening to Francine and Kelly. I just happen to know a cop. I just happen to have a family who can afford to pay for my protection. It's not fair. It's not right.''

She stopped abruptly. ''Why am I ranting and raving at you? You can't do anything.'' She paused a moment, looking thoughtful. ''But I can. You suggested it once yourself, but I just wasn't ready.'' She bent and picked up her drink. It tasted cold and tart. Over the rim of the glass, she met Nick's eyes. ''I can always write her story.''

''As a human interest thing or as an indictment of the system?'' Nick asked, afraid to hear her answer.

''I promise I'll be kind to Savannah's finest.''

''An indictment,'' he decided, then got to his feet and walked over to her. Reaching out, he took her drink and set it down on the coffee table, then pulled her toward him until they were touching from waist to knees. ''I guess this means no more council meetings, huh?''

She smiled. ''They were just too boring. Except that once.'' Neither of them could pretend amusement at the memory of the threatening note.

Nick nodded. ''So, what time frame are we talking here?''

''You mean when am I getting started?'' She looked suddenly mischievous. ''Why? Did you have something planned for the evening that's more interesting?''

''Damn right,'' he muttered, pulling her close enough to feel exactly what he had in mind.

''Hmmm.'' She went a little breathless when he bent and kissed the skin beneath her ear. ''I guess you mean dinner.''

With a growl, he squeezed her waist. ''Oh, you want to talk.'' She was sleek and pliant and laughing softly. He growled again and bit her on the neck.

''Hell, no.''

Sighing, she lifted her arms and wrapped them around his neck. Her voice dropped into a husky, loving caress. ''Does this mean you now see no problems in going to bed with me?''

"Making love with you. No." One hand found its way beneath her shirt and cupped her breast.

"What about duty and responsibility and the fact that I'm an active case you're working on and you'd crucify your people if they did such a thing? What about all that baloney?" she murmured, closing her eyes as she spoke, because he was nibbling his way up her throat, past her ear. She shivered from the things he was doing with his tongue.

Flicking at her nipple with his thumb, he came to a stop with his lips at the corner of her mouth. "I reconsidered, and my priorities are rearranged."

She rewarded him with a laugh and a kiss that nearly sank them both into the carpet. Instead, Nick suddenly broke the kiss to swing her up into his arms and then he headed for his bed.

"I WAS MARRIED once before."

She heard the caution in his voice. Beneath her hand, his heartbeat was steady and strong, but his decision to talk wasn't. She guessed how difficult it was for him to talk about his divorce. Nick would see that as failure.

"It didn't last long and there were no kids."

He seemed finished, so she said gently, "What happened?"

"It was because we were from two different worlds," he explained, his hand stroking her breast. "At the time, I was too young and arrogant to see the pitfalls."

"Was she of another nationality?" Shannon asked after another long pause.

"No, nothing like that. She was...she had been reared to expect a certain standard of living and I wasn't able to provide it when we were first married. I was in law school at the time."

"You're a lawyer?" Her astonishment was obvious.

"No, I quit before...actually I quit when she walked out."

"She left you because you couldn't afford to keep her in the style to which she was accustomed?" Incensed, Shannon flew instantly to his defense. "That's...that's...it's tacky, that's what it is. A lot of students have to struggle to make ends meet, but they manage. She could have, too. She—"

"She left me because our marriage was a mistake from the outset, Shannon."

"In what way was it a mistake?"

"I told you. We were from two different worlds."

Shannon turned slightly so that she could see him. "Let's have some details here, if it's not too much to ask."

"That's what I'm trying to tell you," he said.

"But it's like pulling teeth. I don't want you telling me anything reluctantly, Nick. It has to be something you want to share with me. If you don't understand that, then I don't want to know."

"I do understand it," he said, giving her a rueful smile. "Because I want to know everything about you, too."

She smiled. "Like what?"

"Where you went to school, who your first boyfriend was, your favorite food, your dog's name..."

"I don't have a dog."

"Well then, whether you like animals or not, and if you're one of those yuppies who doesn't eat red meat..."

"It's bad for you, but I confess to a weakness for a juicy steak."

"Thank God. So, do you vote Democrat or Republican, what's the best book you ever read, what's your favorite TV show, your favorite song, your favorite color? There's nothing about you I don't want to know," he told her, tipping her chin with his finger to get a better look into her eyes. "And that's why I'm trying to tell you where I come from, what made it so hard for me to admit that I was falling in love with a woman like Shannon O'Connor."

"A woman like me?"

"Yeah, beautiful, talented, classy, the darling of your family." He settled back and looked at the ceiling. "And *such* a family. It's like history repeating itself."

"What's so strange about my family?"

"Not strange, but...well, important, I guess. Definitely wealthy."

"That sounds like a criticism."

"Not a criticism, but it complicates things."

"How?"

"My ex-wife's family was a lot like yours. This time, I'm not looking at the future like some cockeyed optimist. I'm a cop, a detective in a smallish city. Savannah isn't the size of Atlanta, but I like it here. I like what I do. I will never reach the income level that comes to you just from your family's investments alone. You may not think differences like that make for complications, but I know from bitter experience that they do."

"Wait a minute. I hope you're not accusing me of being the same kind of snob as your first wife." She frowned at him. "What was her name, anyway?"

"Leslie. And don't put words in my mouth. Leslie tried, and then she looked around for somebody who had more in common with her."

"She left you for another man?"

"Yeah," he said briefly. "And it just happened to be a childhood friend, somebody her folks knew and approved of, somebody she should have married in the first place."

"She did that instead of staying with someone who was intense and sexy and ambitious and intelligent? She sounds very confused to me."

"Come on."

Seeing that he thought she was teasing him, Shannon shook her head helplessly. "Just for the record, I can already tell that I'm smarter than Leslie," she said dryly.

"Yeah, well, I'm smarter now than I was then, too. Anyway, the next time I didn't take any chances," he said. His tone took on a grim note. "And I still screwed up."

"You fell in love again?" In spite of her intense need to

know Nick's past, it wasn't easy to hear him tell about the women he'd loved.

"Not really." He was thoughtful for a moment, thinking back. "Tracey and I were both AFT agents. Unlike Leslie, we had a lot in common—family, education, income level. We lived together until—"

"You married her?"

"No. I didn't make that mistake again."

"You'd been burned once."

"I used to think that was it. I realize now that I didn't love her, or at least not in the way a man should love a woman. I should have. I wanted to, but the magic just wasn't there." He gave Shannon a slow, warm smile. "I know about magic now."

She reached up and kissed him lingeringly, and when he started to talk again, she sensed something coming. His voice dropped to a low key. "Tracey and I...well, we just sort of drifted along in this...relationship until..." He took a deep breath and wiped a hand down his face. "Until she was killed."

"Killed..." Shannon whispered the word.

"An ATF sting that went sour, thanks to the press."

"The press."

"Yeah, a reporter from one of the TV stations had been hot on the trail of the suspects. We learned later he had his own snitches in the organization. Tracey was undercover at the time. She was to get out at a certain signal. The whole thing blew sky-high when a TV van pulled up a few houses down the street. It was unmarked, but a two-year-old could tell what it was. Tracey was hit when the shooting began. She never had a chance."

"Oh, Nick..." Shannon touched his hand. "I'm sorry."

"I had to stand there and watch it." He raised his hand, pressing thumb and forefinger into his eyes, as if to crush the memory. "Cameras rolling, naturally," he said bitterly. "It made great stuff for the six o'clock news."

"You're still angry."

"Yeah, I guess I am."

Shannon lay quietly, understanding now why Nick had seemed so hostile when they first met. He drew no distinctions between a newspaper journalist and a TV reporter.

"You blame the press."

"Damn right. If they'd stayed the hell out of police business, she would be alive today."

"That reporter was just doing his job, Nick."

"Well, he made it impossible for me to do mine. And Tracey died."

It was true, no matter how you examined it, Shannon thought. She knew that serious consequences sometimes resulted when reporters acted irresponsibly. It was something all journalists were cautioned against. "Anybody can screw up, Nick," she said softly. "It happens." Was she feeling compelled to defend a nameless reporter, or herself? she wondered.

"This was a costly screwup," Nick snapped. Lying so close to him, Shannon felt the anger that still lingered in him. She wanted to stroke it away, to take some of it into herself, to share it. She did nothing, said nothing. Just waited for whatever he wanted to share with her.

When he spoke, his tone was thoughtful, not angry. "I keep wondering whether I could have done something differently," he said. "Maybe talked her out of the undercover stuff...but she liked it. The danger seemed to pump her up. We fought over it, to tell the truth. Still, I outranked her. I could have—"

"Stopped her? I don't think so. She sounds like a born risk-taker. She wouldn't have been happy doing the boring stuff."

"But she would be alive," he said plaintively.

"It's not just that reporter you blame," she said with sudden understanding. "You feel responsible, too."

He said nothing for a moment. "Not here," he said finally, thumping his forehead with the heel of his palm. "But in my gut, I do. Yeah, I do."

"In your heart."

"She wanted to get married, I think. Oh, she never said it, but after she died…it was tough. We should have talked. Maybe as a married woman, she would have been satisfied with routine assignments. Maybe she felt I didn't care enough about her, so she didn't take care of herself. Maybe she felt our relationship wasn't going anywhere, so why bother thinking about the future. I wish I had handled everything differently."

"It was her choice," Shannon said softly.

"It was a rotten choice."

"You say that only because she died. If she'd lived, the relationship would probably have run its course and she would be married to someone else now with a house in the suburbs and two point five kids."

A few seconds ticked by. Then he gave a humorless laugh. "Now I remember why I never liked this communicating business."

Shannon smiled, then said, "Getting back to Leslie…what did you mean when you said she tried?"

He shrugged. "You know how women are. She thought that we didn't talk enough, that I didn't share every little thing. Hell, I was up to my— Well, anyway, she worried that we didn't seem to have much in common except—"

"Except those times when you were in bed together?"

"Yeah, I guess so."

"And was that true?"

"That we only had sex and nothing else?"

"Yes, was that true?"

"No, I loved her. Or thought I did."

"But not enough to talk to her, to tell her how hard it was to keep your grades up and pay the bills and shoulder all the responsibility, plus keeping your little princess safe in her tower. I'll bet you didn't tell her all that stuff, did you?"

Nick was silent as he considered her question. "You're suggesting that my marriage failed because we didn't talk enough, aren't you? That I didn't share every little thing I felt or thought, so Leslie looked around and found someone who did do all that. Is that right?'' He leaned back to look at her.

"You tell me. Is it right?"

"And that if Tracey and I had talked more, she might be alive today. Is that what you're saying?"

She took a deep breath. "I'm not saying anything, Nick. And I'm not making any judgments, either. However, it makes sense, doesn't it? If you and Tracey had talked more, you might have understood her better. You might also feel less guilt about her death, Nick. It's okay to let yourself off the hook on that, don't you think?"

He settled back without answering. "I don't know about you," he said after a few minutes, "but I've had just about as much soul searching as I can stand for one night. How much longer do we have to keep this up?"

"No longer. This is not an endurance test." With a soft smile, Shannon turned on her side and gathered him lovingly into her embrace. He went, making a gruff satisfied sound as she kissed her way across his chest and up his neck to his chin. "You'll get a lot better at it as we go on," she promised.

"I'd rather make love," he said, nuzzling her sweet-scented skin.

"Mmm, sounds good to me," she told him, fitting her leg between his and rubbing sensuously against his hard warmth. "But first, just one more question."

He hesitated with a resigned sigh. "What is it?"

"Do you really think I'm beautiful?"

Chuckling softly, he replied, "Do you really think I'm sexy?"

Lifting her head to look at him, she asked, "Why do you always want the last word?"

"Because I'm bigger than you."

Her hand skimmed the muscled contours of his chest, past his waist to the heat and hardness beyond. "Hmm, you sure are," she murmured, cupping him gently. "Wow."

That was the last word.

CHAPTER FOURTEEN

SHANNON DIDN'T WAIT until Monday to write Francine's story. Hers, and too many other women's stories, begged to be told, and she was already mentally sorting through ideas about the best way to do it when she crawled out of Nick's bed the next morning. She would have been more than happy to stay there longer, but not without Nick. And he had bounded out like a man with a plan after treating her to an hour of fierce, uninhibited lovemaking.

A morning person, she had decided afterward, lying in a tangle of sheets, pliant and satisfied. With Nick for an alarm clock, rising early certainly had its moments.

They headed for the newspaper office as soon as they'd finished breakfast. She needed to grab her laptop plus some information she hoped to pull from the *Sentinel* files. Afterward, she and Nick planned to return to his place where she could put it all together, then write the story. It would take her most of the day, after which she would send it by modem to her editor. If she got it in early enough, Ernie could probably run it in the Sunday edition.

Liza Westfall drifted over just as Shannon pulled a fat file from a drawer. "Hmm, something really hot breaking on the political scene?" she asked. Openly curious, she looked at the labels of the files Shannon had already stacked on top of the cabinet.

"Oh, hi, Liza." Shannon grabbed for some papers that fell out of the file, then shoved them back in haphazardly. "I read your feature on high school dropouts last week. Nice work."

Liza dismissed the compliment with a grimace. "I wanted to focus on the number of guns that are finding their way into classrooms, but Ernie wanted the education thing."

"Didn't Chris Cullen just do a three-part series on teens and lethal weapons?" Shannon pulled another file.

"Yes, but it was my idea."

Glancing up, Shannon caught a glimpse of the other woman's anger and frustration. Liza wasn't the type to lightly accept an editorial decision that went against her. "We just have to roll with the flow sometimes," she said, not without sympathy.

"Ernie Patton is a world-class chauvinist," Liza said bitterly.

"Well..." True, Ernie was of the old school, but for the most part, Shannon had found him fair-minded.

"Not that you ever have any trouble getting anything you want out of him," Liza said, her jealousy surfacing.

Shannon sighed. "Look, Liza, I'm in a bit of a hurry here, if you don't mind."

"You never answered my question," Liza said, frowning at the stack of files. "Is something breaking at city hall? That *is* still your beat, isn't it? Although I swear it's beyond me why you want it."

"No, city hall's quiet. This is something else."

Bending down suddenly, Liza picked up a single sheet on the floor that Shannon had missed. "'New Hope House...'" Liza read, frowning as she studied it. "Hey, that's the place where they take in battered women, isn't it?"

"Yes, it is."

Liza looked at her shrewdly. "You're working on something new, aren't you. One of your famous exposés?" The last word was emphasized with sarcasm.

"It's nothing firm yet, just an idea."

"Uh-huh." Liza said, still thoughtful. After a second, she sent a sweeping glance over the newsroom, then back to Shannon. "Incidentally, where's your bodyguard?"

"Pardon me?"

"Oh, come on, Shannon. Everybody knows that Cheryl What's-her-name is here for your protection."

"What makes you think that?"

Liza shrugged. "Elementary, my dear. She arrives and leaves with you, she's not a journalist, has no other specific duties around the office and she sticks as close to you as a Siamese twin, except when that hunky detective Nick Dalton steps in. Not that I blame you. Until they find that guy who tried to…well, you know…until they get him, it's the least the police can do."

"Look, Liza—"

"Who's paying anyway? The newspaper, your family, or the taxpayers?"

Shannon closed the file drawer sharply. "Why, Liza? Thinking of doing an exposé yourself?"

"Hey, I didn't mean that the way it sounded, Shannon."

"Sure." Beyond the woman's shoulder, Shannon spotted Nick's tall silhouette at the end of the hall. "Excuse me, but it appears that the 'hunk' has arrived to protect me. It's been nice, but I've really got to run."

Following Shannon's gaze, Liza turned just as Nick walked through the door. Beside her, Shannon was in a flurry, gathering up files and her pad scribbled full of notes, dropping pens and extra paper clips into a tray on the nearest desk, and tossing an empty plastic cup with the cold dregs of her coffee into the trash. Nick took the files from Shannon with hardly a glance in Liza's direction, and together they headed for the double doors, immediately in deep conversation.

Her gaze speculative, Liza watched them until they disappeared.

THE WORDS TO WRITE Francine's story were already taking shape in Shannon's head as she and Nick made the drive back to his house. She felt a moment of regret that she had waited so long to use the resources of her profession to strike a blow for women like Francine. For everything there is a time, she reminded herself with a sigh. Her fear had held her captive until now, but she could not afford to be ruled by fear forever.

"You realize you're taking a risk when you let Ernie run your byline on this piece, don't you?" Nick said, flicking a glance her way as he turned into his neighborhood.

"Are you trying to talk me out of it?"

He glanced at her with a wry expression. "Would it matter if I did?"

She didn't answer that, but said instead, "Why do you think I've procrastinated so long? I'm scared to death I might inadvertently write something that pushes him over the edge."

"There's a simple solution for that one, honey."

She closed her eyes wearily. "I know, I know. Just regain my memory and identify him."

"Bingo."

"If only I could," she wailed. "But damn it, I just can't remember!"

As she'd done a thousand times in the past few months—without success—she concentrated in earnest, focusing mentally on the facts she'd been given about that night. When nothing came but the usual blankness, she groaned with frustration. Where had she gone that day in Atlanta? Why had she gone? Who had she seen there? What had she learned that had forced the intruder to try and kill her? With her head bent and her mind reeling with questions, she realized that her heart was pounding.

"Let it come, honey, don't fight it."

"I'm not fighting, I'm not...I'm..."

As always, when she tried to force her memory, the same thing happened. She had finally admitted in the encounter group that her amnesia was directly connected to her fear. Subconsciously she feared what her memory might reveal. Admitting it was one small step, according to Susan, who had praised her for taking that step. Now she needed to get beyond it. And she would. Soon. She had to. She just had to.

Nick pulled the car into his driveway. After stopping, he looked over at her. "No luck, huh?"

"I'm working on it," she muttered. She remembered nothing. As usual.

The panic had dissolved. All that was left was a nagging feeling of disappointment, in herself and the missed opportunity to finally clear up the mystery, once and for all. Heading up the sidewalk to Nick's front door, she said, "I'm certainly an unlikely champion for victimized women, don't you think?"

He put his key into the lock and opened the door. "Why do you say that?"

"What kind of person is it who doesn't hesitate to expose other women's demons, yet is too terrified to face her own?"

"A person who was nearly killed by an unknown assailant," Nick said, kicking the door shut and drawing her into a reassuring embrace. She snuggled into his warmth with a sigh, resting her head against his heart. His voice beneath her ear was a comforting rumble. "A person who, unlike Francine, doesn't yet know who her assailant is, and therefore cannot avoid him. And a person who's willing to take a personal risk to raise the awareness of the public at large." He dropped a kiss on her hair. "In short, a very special lady."

The mood that had dimmed some of her enthusiasm went away as Shannon hung on tight. "That's not the way you used to talk when you read my bylines," she said, smiling.

"The police department used to be your favorite target."

She grimaced, but he couldn't see it.

Nick laughed softly. "That long, loud silence I hear must mean that this time law enforcement won't quite get away unscathed, either."

"Don't panic yet. I still have to write it." She was quiet a second or two. "And wait for the fallout."

"Shannon—"

"Let's change the subject."

"Shannon."

Her eyes met his as he brought his hands up, cradling her face. "I'm not going to let anything happen to you. I don't care how far I have to go or what I have to do. I'm not going to let anything happen to you."

She stared at him intently, then managed a smile. "Okay."

Her eyes fluttered shut as he leaned down and touched his mouth to hers. She turned, soft and yielding, for the length of the kiss, then Nick felt the curve of her lips against his cheek.

"What's funny?" he asked, smelling her rose-scented hair with his usual deep pleasure while his hands savored the soft, giving curves of her bottom.

"Just thinking of something Liza Westfall said."

He bent a little at the knees so that he could look in her face. "Liza Westfall?"

"Yes, she thinks you're a hunk."

"Yeah?"

"But don't get any ideas, she's a barracuda in disguise."

He grunted, more familiar with Liza's personality than Shannon suspected. "She wants your job."

"I know, but how did you know?"

"Cheryl mentioned it."

Shannon frowned. "She knows why Cheryl is with me. Does it matter?"

Nick moved, urging her toward the room where his personal computer was set up. "Not really. With Cheryl a constant presence, people were bound to notice sooner or later. What matters is to avoid any opportunity for the scum-bag to get at you."

"Well, that is certainly not a possibility this weekend," she told him, setting her laptop and the files on a table. Like everything else in Nick's house, the room he used as an office was neat and orderly. She hid a smile, wondering what his reaction would be after she finished her article. Her own work habits were not neat and orderly.

He was at the door when he turned and said, "I'll be upstairs if you need…anything."

She looked up and said, straight-faced, "Pizza and beer, I guess...later, okay?"

He grinned. "That, too."

SHE WAS STILL SMILING as she switched on the laptop and paused, waiting for the signal to call up her files. She hadn't worked on the briefcase-sized computer since the accident, she realized. It was new equipment for the reporters at the *Sentinel* and she wasn't quite as comfortable using it as the larger stationary computers. There might be something in her notes that she could include in this article from some preliminary work she had done on abused women a few weeks before her assault.

After the blips and beeps ceased, she began idly scanning the list displayed on the small screen. At a word, suddenly she faltered. Pain, quick and sharp, blinded her for a few seconds. With her eyes closed, she waited, knowing that the moment would pass if she did nothing. After a few seconds, she drew a deep breath and forced herself to study the highlighted file.

"Suicide."

She remembered discussing the suicide of a woman in the Victorian District with Nick. Marion Chaney. The name came easily to her, the reason, she guessed, because she and Nick had discussed it while she was still in the hospital. She had never finished the article. Looking at it, she remembered thinking sympathetically about the loneliness and despair that must have consumed Marion Chaney to drive her to suicide. She couldn't afford the time to get sidetracked on that tragedy today. Maybe next week, she thought, quickly scrolling past "Suicide" and highlighting "Abuse." In a few minutes, the pain that had struck momentarily had subsided and with her usual absorption, she settled in to finish the task at hand.

Francine's story.

Much later, the article had shaped up nicely. She wouldn't be able to use Francine's name, of course. That would put her in more jeopardy than she already faced with that jerk—to use

Kelly's word. At the thought of the teenage girl, she hesitated, glancing at the phone, then when nothing happened, dismissed the feeling that it had been about to ring. Or that she needed to make a call.

She sat for a while sifting through the pages of the files she'd pulled to write the story. On the floor directly above her, she could hear the soft hum of small machinery. Nick, the artist, was working, she thought. The machine sound was the polisher. After cutting glass, the edge was polished before being fitted into whatever pattern he was creating. The floor creaked slightly. He was moving around.

Why was she distracted? She looked at the phone again and picked it up. But then she put it back again and reached instead for her bag on the floor beside her where she'd dropped it when she sat down. Fishing around inside, she searched for her small address book. Suddenly as she searched, for no reason that she could explain, she was bombarded with strange mental flashes. Bits and pieces with no meaning. Disjointed parts of a collage that had yet to arrange themselves into a coherent whole.

The strange moment ended as she pulled her hand from her bag, holding the address book. But her unease did not end. She paged through the book until she found Francine's name and then she picked up the phone again and punched out the number.

After a full ten rings, she was about to hang up when Kelly answered. "Hello?"

"Hi, Kelly, this is Shannon. Is your mom there?"

"No, she's out. It's just me."

Shannon studied the jumble of papers in front of her without really seeing it. It worried her that Kelly was alone and unprotected at home. Was that why she had felt compelled to call?

"You shouldn't be there alone, Kelly. Keep the doors and windows locked until your mom returns, okay?"

"Yeah, sure. Okay." Gum popped. A muffled sound came through the phone. Maybe Kelly wasn't alone.

Shannon drummed her fingers on the desk. With that lunatic harassing them, you'd think Francine would be more careful about leaving her daughter. But of course, Kelly wasn't your average fourteen-year-old.

"Hey, I gotta go, Shannon. I'll tell my mom you called, how's that?"

"No need, Kelly. I just wanted to chat. You take care, right?"

More popped gum. A definite snicker in the background. "Right. See ya."

Shannon replaced the receiver and sat back thoughtfully, still unsure why she had felt compelled to make the call. Kelly was tough and streetwise, but she was just a kid. What was to prevent the guy harassing Francine from turning his attention to Kelly? Buck, that was his name. Although Francine had been careful not to mention it, Kelly had said it a time or two. What was needed with Buck and men like him, she decided, picking up the papers and cramming them back into the file jackets, was a taste of his own medicine. Somebody ought to slap him around a little, see how he liked it. Trouble was, people like Buck stayed away from anybody who might turn the tables.

Nick came into the room and lifted his brows at the expression on her face. "You look ready to punch somebody's lights out."

"Francine's ex," she muttered.

"What's he done now?"

"Nothing, I hope. I was just thinking about him."

"Thinking about him?"

"Yes, I looked at the phone and—" She glanced at the telephone again and frowned. "I thought it was going to ring, and when it didn't, I thought of calling Francine and then... Kelly answered..." She trailed off, still frowning.

"What is it? Getting messages from computer screens

now?'' He moved in close, stopping just behind her. "Sorry I don't have any antique mirrors.''

"It's not that... At least, I didn't think so until just now.'' She was suddenly energized. "Nick, I know you're going to think I'm paranoid, or overreacting or something, but could you just call the dispatcher at the police department and ask them to check Francine's address? Just have a black-and-white cruise down her street and make sure everything seems okay? Maybe even ring the doorbell?'' She gave him a beseeching look. "Is that possible?''

"No problem.''

She looked startled. "Really? Just like that?''

"Yeah, just like that.'' He reached past her for the phone. "When you get one of your communications from beyond, I've learned not to question it.'' Punching in the numbers, he grinned at her. "Still, I'd like to keep it just between us for the sake of my professional reputation.''

She laughed and rubbed her cheek against his arm. "Thanks, I think.''

With the phone cradled between his shoulder and chin, he gave the dispatcher the name and address and asked for a follow-up report. While he spoke, his hands went to her neck and shoulders and began gently kneading. With a sigh, Shannon closed her eyes, tuning out his conversation with the dispatcher, and letting him work his magic. Oddly, the anxiety she'd felt after talking to Kelly was gone now.

"They'll get back to us,'' he told her after replacing the receiver. Using both thumbs, he worked his way down her spine.

"Hmm.''

"Feel good?''

"Uh-huh.''

"You about finished here?''

"Just about. I need to transmit it to the *Sentinel*. After that, it's just you and me.''

"Hmm.'' He glanced casually at the list of files displayed

on the screen. As he scanned, his fingers moved skillfully, erasing the tension in her muscles. He was halfway down the list when his hands suddenly stopped moving.

"What is it?"

"This isn't the same list of files that's on your computer at your office."

"No, but it's almost the same. The laptops are new at the *Sentinel,* and I had duplicated most of my files when the assault happened. I wasn't quite accustomed to using it, which is the reason I didn't take it with me to Atlanta."

"How do you know that?" he asked sharply.

"I...I don't know. It just...came to me. But it makes sense, doesn't it?"

"Yeah, it makes sense. So you have work on this laptop that isn't on your computer at your desk?"

"And vice versa. To tell the truth, I'm not sure what's on it."

"What did you take with you to Atlanta?"

"The tape recorder, don't you remember? The night we found my apartment trashed, I was looking for the taped notes."

As he scanned the screen, he noticed the file entitled "Suicide." "This is Marion Chaney, I assume."

Beneath his hands, Nick felt her tense up. He looked first at the word, then at her. "What's wrong? Have you remembered something?"

She dropped her head into her hand, shaking it with a soft laugh. "Don't you ever give it a rest, Dalton?"

The glow of the monitor on his face lent a hard, determined look to his features. "Only when I close a case," he said.

The phone rang and Shannon snatched it up. "Hello." She paused, listening, nodding, then passed the receiver to Nick, who listened intently for a few moments before snapping out a couple of questions.

"You can relax," he told her as he hung up. "Francine and Kelly are okay."

"Was it a false alarm?"

"Not really. A pickup pulled away from the address just as the SPD unit turned the corner."

"I knew it! Was it Buck?"

"Is he the boyfriend?"

"Yes."

"Then it was Buck. Seems Francine got back moments after your call. According to the officers, she was extremely upset to find him alone with her fourteen-year-old daughter."

"Oh, my God."

"Relax. Apparently, everything's okay. Francine made arrangements to take Kelly and stay with her brother for a few days. They took off with our guys following, so at least you can rest easy that they got safely to the relatives."

"I'm not sure Francine ever rests easy, Nick."

"It's probably a good thing that Buck knows he's under surveillance. It just might be that he'll think twice before throwing his next punch if he has to serve time for doing it."

"Oh, when is Francine going to wake up! She has to call his bluff before he hurts her or her daughter."

With her head resting against his midriff, Nick sank his hand into her hair. "You can't force these things, honey. She'll come around when she's ready."

"I just hope it's not too late when it happens."

For a few seconds, they were quiet, studying the problem, each coming at it from different directions, but each equally frustrated. Every atom of Shannon's being rejected sitting idly by until Francine or Kelly became another statistic like Mary Ellen Kirk. Nick knew from experience that nothing pushed an abused individual into taking action until he or she was ready.

The computer made a beeping sound, drawing their attention to the files listed on the screen. As before, just looking at the word "Suicide" made Shannon's heart beat with dread. But with Nick standing behind her, the fear that lodged itself in her throat was manageable. Barely. Swallowing hard, Shannon told herself to get a grip and opened the file.

They both started reading, and three minutes later, Nick gave her shoulders a quick, hard squeeze. "Hey, we may be on to something here," he murmured.

"We could be," Shannon said more cautiously, her eyes glued to the words in front of her.

"An Atlanta judge who's been quietly divorced for several years comes up for a prestigious appointment. His ex, living in Atlanta, who incidentally got a huge financial settlement at the time of the divorce, suddenly commits suicide. You, however, dig around and find that the judge was here in Savannah that day." Nick looked swiftly around, snagged a stool with his foot, and sat down where it was easier to read the monitor. "If I had found this earlier, I would already have paid the good judge a visit."

Shannon said nothing. What she was reading reminded her that her recurring dream had a judge in it. And a weeping woman.

Nick hit a key to scroll a page down, still reading intently. "How did you get on to this? I remember when we got the call. It was an apparent suicide. A woman was found dead in her apartment from an overdose of drugs. Prescription stuff found right in her bathroom. The investigating officers took the whole thing at face value. An aging woman, living alone, few friends..." He shrugged. "There was no trail to follow, nothing to link her to anything like this."

With a shake of his head, he turned and looked at her. "What tipped you off that there might be more to it?"

"I have no idea."

Nick frowned. "What?"

"I'm telling you, I don't know any more about this than you do." She glanced at the monitor. "Not one bit of that is familiar to me, Nick."

He dropped his head, sighing.

"I'm sorry," Shannon said in a small voice.

With a half laugh, he looked at her. "This is a hell of a note, isn't it? We finally find what could be the missing link and you still draw a blank." With a rap of the table, he came to his feet. "*Damn it,* Shannon!"

Shannon got up, too, her eyes following him as he paced. "Do you think I like this, Nick? I don't. I hate having a hole in my memory. I hate losing a week out of my life. And to make it worse, whatever it is that I can't—or won't—remember scares the living hell out of me."

Gritting his teeth, Nick raked both hands through his hair. His frustration was so great, he almost growled with it.

"I wonder how you would feel if you had to deal with all that," she said quietly. "It's terrifying—not just the fear, but the loss. The blankness. The void."

"You've got to get beyond it, Shannon."

With her arms crossed around herself, she swung away, turning her back on him. "Do you honestly think I've been playing games here, Nick? Well, think again. I don't remember what happened that night, but worse than that, I worry that I never will. And if I don't, I'll never be a whole person again." She drew in her breath with a little hitch. "He... he...w-will have taken more than a week of my life, Nick, he will have taken a piece of me. A piece of *me!*"

Feeling mean as a snake, Nick swore liberally. He put his arms around her from behind and enveloped her in a close embrace. "I'm sorry, sweetheart. I know you can't remember. I know it's not like flipping a switch in a dark room and suddenly everything's clear and bright."

"Then why are you so angry with me?" she demanded, stiff and unyielding. "Why are you yelling at me?" She pulled free and looked at him.

"Because I'm a bastard," he said shortly. "Didn't I tell you before that I'm not good with relationships? Well, now you see it firsthand."

"Don't start with me on that, Nick," she warned, a dangerous light in her eye. "We're talking about something else altogether here and you know it. This has nothing to do with us as lovers.''

He was still for a few seconds, his gaze locked with hers. Suddenly, he was shaking his head. "Come here," he said, reaching for her. She fought him for a second, but before she had a chance to escape, he had both arms wrapped around her and his face buried in her glorious hair. "I want you to tell me just this one thing," he said, locking her firmly beneath his chin.

"What?" she said, resisting the urge to melt into his heat.

"How is it that some other lucky bastard hasn't already grabbed you?"

She smiled against the hollow in his throat. "Many have tried, but I was holding out for a handsome, hard-working, slightly dumb detective."

With a finger beneath her chin, he drew her mouth up to meet his and kissed her gently, then a little more seriously. She responded with a heat that in seconds was scorching in its intensity. He tore his mouth away, breathing hard. "And sexy," he groaned, rocking against her softness. "Don't forget sexy."

With a low laugh, she slipped her arms around his waist. "It goes without saying." Lifting her face, she invited him into another long and lingering kiss. Then, taking him by the hand, she headed for his bedroom.

THEY WERE FINISHING a pepperoni pizza with beer when he brought up the subject of Marion Chaney again. Shannon had faxed her finished article to the *Sentinel* and Ernie had called an hour later praising it. A feature about the rights of adoptive parents written by Liza Westfall had been bumped to make room for Shannon's story. Liza would not be happy.

Stretched out on the carpet, resting on one elbow, Nick was studying Shannon's notes as printed out by the computer. He put the paper down and looked at her. "Can we talk about this again, sweetheart?"

She sighed. "If you insist."

He put the papers aside and started to rise. "No," she said, reaching to touch him. He settled back, waiting. "It's okay. I want to do it, Nick."

Reluctantly, his gaze left her face and he looked at the print-out. "Marion Chaney's ex-husband is Judge Franklin Henderson. After being married for thirteen years, they were divorced on the grounds of irreconcilable differences. It was immediately after the divorce that she moved to Savannah, dropped her ex's surname and moved into a neighborhood where she kept to herself. She was almost reclusive, according to your notes."

He looked questioningly at Shannon, who shrugged. "You mentioned that when I was in the hospital, but I don't really remember anything more."

He went back to the printout. "You've written several questions here, but haven't answered any of them. 'Does irreconcilable differences hide something sinister? Autopsy shows several broken bones, old injuries. Accident(s) or abuse? What was the judge really like? Why did M.C. revert to her maiden name? Why was she so reclusive? Friends (few and far between in Savannah) say she wasn't always. Something very fishy about M.C.'s suicide.'"

He put down the printout and looked at her. "Do you always add those little side notes?"

She shrugged. "Sometimes."

"You're good. But you know that."

She smiled. "It's in the genes."

"Yeah, really."

She picked up the printout of her own notes and studied it curiously. "I must have been temporarily insane to even think of giving up journalism."

Nick reached over and raked his knuckles gently down her cheek. "No, just temporarily spooked."

Her smile faded. "Fear is a terrible thing, Nick. Whatever the reason for it, it paralyzes. It steals your soul." She searched his face, intent on making him understand. "The women in the encounter group are a good example. Every one of them has been victimized in some way or other, and as a result, their fears have caused them to close themselves off. They're like flowers that fold up with the setting sun, only they've withdrawn from life. They miss all the sunshine."

She frowned, seeing the group clearly in her mind. "Francine, Mary Ellen Kirk, a rape victim named Sissy...even Cheryl."

His look narrowed. "Cheryl?"

"Her marriage to Andy Welles wasn't happy, and she carried the scars inside for a long time. She's finally gotten beyond it, I think. Now maybe she can be truly happy with Will."

"You're saying love is the key."

"Not exactly. Although it's a powerful incentive, I can tell you." She tried to explain. "Falling in love with Will probably helped, but what really happened is that Cheryl finally found the courage to face what was buried inside her. We can't pick up the pieces and put ourselves back together until that's done."

Nick lifted her chin and looked deeply into her eyes. "What was buried inside you, Shannon?"

"Anger—I was so angry at the man who did this to me—frustration, anxiety. I wondered if I'd ever be a whole person again. But the biggest thing was the fear."

"You're too strong to let fear rule your life for long," he told her, brushing his thumb across her lips.

"All I wanted to do was hide. To withdraw from anything the least bit provocative. I went back to my job, but I was too afraid to take on the substantive stuff. Hard news was a reminder of my personal experience with violence, so I avoided it."

She curled her fingers around his wrist, trapping his hand between her neck and shoulder. "The assault affected me in a more personal way, too. It was so...so big that I had no room for anything else. I would have recognized that I loved you long before I did if I hadn't been so paralyzed emotionally.''

She glanced up to find a storm of emotion in his eyes. "I do love you, you know," she said.

"No," he said, suddenly moving close and tumbling her down on the floor. With her hair spread wide around her like dark fire and her smoldering eyes, she looked like a Gypsy. "I didn't know. Show me, Shannon."

She opened her mouth to say something, but he silenced her with a kiss. "Don't tell me," he said against her lips as his hands found their way beneath her shirt to her breasts. "Show me. I need to feel it here—" one of his hands went to the cleft between her breasts "—and here." Another found the silky nest at the apex of her thighs, pressing in a place that drew a small gasp from her.

"I love you," she whispered. "I knew it from the minute you took my hand and brought me back to life."

"God," he groaned, kissing her eyes, her cheek, the corner of her mouth. "I love you, too."

"Then *you* show *me*." Her mouth opened beneath his and they fell headlong into pleasure.

THEY TACKLED THE PIZZA with renewed appetites after making love. Nick separated the last two pieces and passed one over to Shannon. "You know that I'll have to make a trip to Atlanta right away," he told her, biting into cold pepperoni with every appearance of enjoyment.

"Checking on the judge, you mean?"

"Uh-huh."

"*We* need to make a trip to Atlanta," Shannon replied firmly.

With pizza halfway to his mouth, Nick stopped and gave her a patient look. "We're not going to argue over this one, Shannon. If you make a trip to Atlanta and Henderson is the man who's stalking you, he'll guess that you've regained your memory. He'll be forced to try and silence you once and for all.''

"Have you forgotten that Cheryl is in New York and won't be back until late Sunday night? What'll I do for a bodyguard? The backup man, you'll recall, just happens to be with her.''

"I'll go Monday morning, then. Cheryl and Will should be back, and you'll also have Jed Singer's protection," Nick said implacably. "He's good. He's a pro. You'll be perfectly safe."

She gave him a long, measuring look. "I want to go, Nick."

"This one isn't up for discussion, Shannon," he said, matching her expression with an equally stubborn scowl.

She finished her beer and reached to take his empty can out of his hand. "We'll discuss it later."

He opened his mouth to discuss it now, but she slid her arms around his neck and began kissing him. Later, he said to himself, losing the thread of the argument as pleasure and passion dragged him under. We can discuss it later.

CHAPTER FIFTEEN

CHERYL CALLED SUNDAY from the interstate using Will's car phone to tell Nick that she was back in Savannah and that she could resume her duties guarding Shannon anytime. Shannon and Nick were in his king-size bed with the Sunday papers spread all over when the call came. They hadn't gotten around to breakfast yet.

With his hand over the receiver, he looked at Shannon. "Cheryl and Will just left the airport and are on their way home, so there's no excuse left for you to go to Atlanta."

Shannon reached for the phone, smiling cryptically into Nick's eyes. Tipping the receiver so that Nick could hear the conversation, she said, "Hi, Cheryl. How was New York?"

"Wonderful. I've never seen so much crime."

Nick chuckled and Shannon laughed. "What's this? A romantic weekend with my brother and you're still thinking like a PI?"

"I'm not sure I'm thinking at all," Cheryl said, her tone going husky and low. "It wasn't New York that was wonderful, it was your brother."

"Ah. You sound very happy."

"It was just…incredible, Shannon. Thanks to Will."

"Hmmm, I always liked him well enough," Shannon said dryly.

"I have always loved him," Cheryl said.

Always? Shannon met Nick's eyes. "This sounds very promising," she mouthed silently to him. Then to Cheryl, "I guess you two have worked out your differences."

"Yes. I can hardly even remember what I thought they were."

Shannon snuggled into Nick's embrace. "My brother always was a lucky guy."

"Thank you," Cheryl said, and Shannon could hear the smile in her voice. "So, how was your weekend?"

"Good," Shannon said, shivering a little as Nick kissed his way up her throat to her ear. "It was good. Detective Dalton made a very adequate bodyguard in your absence. Ouch!"

"Shannon? What's the matter?"

"Uhhmmm, nothing, nothing," Shannon said on a sigh. Nick was now soothing the spot on her ear where he'd nipped her. "Detective Dalton was also wonderful."

"I see."

Nick reached up suddenly and took the phone. "No need to hurry for Shannon's sake, Cheryl," he drawled. "You're off-duty for what's left of the weekend. Just be on hand at Wilderose House by eight in the morning. I'm booked on a flight to Atlanta at nine."

"We're *both* booked on that flight," Shannon said, ignoring Nick's fierce look. She was determined to go with him to check on Marion Chaney's past and Nick was just as determined to keep her safe behind the walls of Wilderose House. Between bouts of intense loving, they'd argued just as intensely over it. They'd reached a stalemate.

"Just be here at eight, Cheryl," Nick said firmly.

"Hey…" Cheryl sounded concerned. "Is everything okay there? I can head directly home if—"

"No."

"No!"

"Well, if you're sure…"

"We're sure," Shannon said, her gaze locked with Nick's.

"Will wants to give me a tour of the family cottage out on Sea Island," Cheryl said, not quite able to disguise her pleasure. "It's a good hour's drive, so we won't be back until morning."

"Go," Nick said. "Have a good time."

"I have never known Will to take any woman to Wilderose Cottage," Shannon said after Nick hung up the phone. "Things are really serious with those two. I couldn't be happier. Cheryl is perfect for Will." She gave him a meaningful look. "Even though she's an ex-cop and he's an O'Connor."

Nick studied her thoughtfully. "You really mean that, don't you?"

"How can they fail? They're crazy about each other."

Nick pushed the papers off the bed and pulled her over until she was sprawled on top of him. She went, laughing. He buried his hands in her thick, auburn mane and pushed his arousal against her softness like a randy teenager. She made him *feel* like a randy teenager. "Come here," he growled. "I'll show you crazy."

IT WAS LATE AFTERNOON. Shannon was in the bathroom soaking away the aftereffects of truly amazing sex when the phone rang again. Nick picked it up. Even before his partner spoke, he heard the pulsing sound of an ambulance.

"Sorry, Nick, I know you left word that you were taking the whole weekend off," Ed said. "But I think you're gonna want to come down here for this one."

In the act of drying off, Nick lowered the towel slowly. "What's up?"

"It's another girl, Nick. A fourteen-year-old."

Nick swore. "Is she—"

"Not yet, but it's touch and go. The paramedics are with her." Averting the receiver, Ed called out an order to someone nearby. "She's been beaten up, Nick. And there are marks on her throat where he tried to choke the life out of her."

Nick went still, his eyes cold and hard.

"Sound familiar?"

"Yeah, very."

"It's the same MO as Shannon's assault."

"Did anybody see anything?"

"You're going to like this," Ed said. "We've got the perp. We're running a make on him right now. Should hear something by the time you get here."

Nick frowned. "Who is he?"

"Says his name is James Buckley."

Looking toward the bathroom Nick caught a glimpse of Shannon's leg extended in the tub as she sponged it off, her skin glistening with water. Little clumps of bubbles clung here and there. She had very slim, almost delicate ankles. Suddenly he recalled the scene of her assault when he'd walked in the door of her town home. His first look at Shannon's ankles had been in that moment when she lay near death on the floor behind her bar.

He bent his head, squeezing his eyes tight to block the memory. "How did you get the call?"

"Motel manager," Ed said briefly. "Fed up with trouble-makers, he says. It's one of those flophouse places that opens right on the street. Had a drive-by shooting about three months ago, remember?"

"Yeah."

"Same motel, same room. Could very well be the same suspect."

"Uh-huh."

"Guy says he heard the ruckus and called 911. We got the stupid ape in the act of choking the life out of this…this kid, Nick." Ed's voice was full of disbelief. "Jeez, she's no bigger than a minute. Then he began to bluster when the two uniforms made the arrest, something about the kid holding out on him. Claims he bought her clothes and was letting her live rent-free for a month, and she was supposed to pay him back. Claims he's her *uncle*." Ed made a disgusted sound. "In his dreams, I say."

"Pay him back? His fourteen-year-old niece?" Nick shook his head. "Right."

"He's drunk or high. Maybe both. We're thinking his rap sheet will show him with priors in dealing and possession and who knows what else. Guy's flush with a couple of thousand in his wallet and credit cards up the kazoo, plus he's driving a white Mercedes and wearing a Rolex. Apparently business is good.''

Nick's gaze was fixed on Shannon climbing out of the tub. "A Rolex, you say? You're sure it was a Mercedes and not a Jaguar?'' Shannon looked up sharply.

"Yeah. With the expensive car and wristwatch, plus the MO similarity, I've already questioned him about Shannon's assault. He knew about it, was dumb enough to say she brought it on herself. Claims her journalism is what ticked him off.''

Nick frowned. "How's that?''

"Today's article in the *Sentinel*. The little girl read it and I guess she identified with the victims, whether with the women in the piece, or the kids, I don't know. Anyway, that little burst of rebellion might have cost her her life.''

"Do we have an ID on her yet?''

"Not yet. There's no way he's her uncle, but he claims her name is Tammy Rainbow. Can you believe that?''

Rainbow. Nick shook his head at the sound of it. A futile effort by a young girl to bring hope into her life. And now she might have no life at all.

He rubbed wearily at the stubble on his chin. He needed another shave. After his shower, he'd planned to share a huge steak with Shannon—they worked well together in the kitchen—then maybe a movie on his VCR and after that, they would make love. Again. He'd lost count of the times they'd made love over the weekend. What he hadn't planned to end a leisurely weekend with was reality in the form of another teenage murder.

"I think he's our man, Nick. I think he's the one who assaulted Shannon.''

"Sounds like it.'' Nick tossed the towel aside and stood up. "Give me fifteen minutes. I'm on my way.''

SHANNON WATCHED WIDE-EYED as Nick pulled a drawer open and took out clean underwear. "What's going on, Nick?'' she asked, her hands holding the towel against her chest. "A four-teen-year-old girl, is that right? Is she— Did he say she was—?"

"He's not sure. The paramedics are there." He hesitated, then said, "They're holding the suspect."

"Incredible," she murmured, watching him shrug into a shirt, then tuck it into his khaki pants. Her eyes followed him as he moved to the armoire where he'd emptied his pockets the night before. Back into them went his money clip, his loose change and his badge. When he was done, he reached for his weapon.

"It gets even more incredible," he told her, tucking his notebook into his shirt pocket. "We think he's the animal who assaulted you, Shannon."

She brought her hand to her mouth. "Are you sure?"

"Yeah, the way he—" He broke off, his look angry and as hard as flint. "Let's just say the damage done to this little girl was a lot like what he did to you. He mentioned you, can you believe that? He's mad as hell at you."

"Why!"

"Your journalism, at least that's what Ed said he told him. He's high on something and talking his rear off." Nick swept up his dirty towel and hurled it at a clothes hamper. "I can't wait to get my hands on the dumb bastard!"

Shannon was still trying to take it in. For the past few months she'd lived in fear that he would find her. Now, on a lazy Sunday in May, suddenly it was all over. But not before he'd claimed another victim. A smaller, more vulnerable victim.

Shaking her head, she said, "Who is he? What's his name?"

"Buckley."

She stared at him. A moment of sudden realization was followed by alarm. She heard Kelly's voice in the encounter group complaining about the man harassing her mother. His name was Buck. Could it be? Dear God, could it be?

"Buck," she whispered.

He caught her arm and gave it a little shake. "You know him, Shannon?"

"My God." Closing her eyes, she swallowed once, hard.

"What is it, damn it!"

"Kelly," she said, shaken. "The victim, the young girl, is it Kelly?"

"Kelly? Why would you think—"

"Nick! Is it Kelly?"

He looked blank. "I don't think so. The name doesn't fit. Buckley said her name was Tammy Rainbow."

"Nobody is named Rainbow, Nick. It's obviously something she made up."

"Would Kelly make up a name like Rainbow?"

"I don't know. Maybe." She stood a second, thinking of Kelly's cynicism. Her disbelief in a brighter future. Did she fantasize about a better life to escape one that was too often ugly and violent? Turning abruptly, she went back into the bathroom to put on her clothes. "I'll only be a minute," she told him, slipping a shirt off the hook on the back of the door. "Wait for me."

She had only one sleeve on when Nick pushed the door open. "You're not going anywhere, Shannon," he told her flatly. "You're staying here."

She stared. "You've got to be kidding. Of course I'm going. What if it's Kelly?"

"It's a long shot. Her name is Tammy, not Kelly."

"Kids pretend, Nick. Especially troubled ones. And if James Buckley is the man who's threatening her mother—"

"You don't know that."

"But if Kelly—"

"Even if it is Kelly," he said evenly, "you can't leave this house. You're safe here. You'd be at risk traipsing around a crime scene. You can't go, Shannon." His broad frame filled the doorway. She almost backed up a step at the look of him. He was not her lover, but a hardened, street-tough cop. She hadn't seen that side of him in a long time.

"In the first place, she will probably have been taken to the hospital by the time you get there," he said, softening his tone. "The paramedics were working on her when Ed called. Second, even unarmed and in restraints, the man who assaulted you is a vicious animal. We don't know what his reaction would be on seeing you. We don't know what *your* reaction would be on seeing him, Shannon."

"I want to see him," she cried. "I want to confront him!"

"Have you forgotten the beating you got from this creep? No doctor in his right mind would allow you to rush over and confront the man who put you in the hospital...if you'd even consent to ask a doctor."

He was making good sense, and Shannon knew it. Still, she hated backing away from a challenge. "I could handle it," she said, scowling.

"Maybe. Probably." The last was spoken sincerely. He reached out and pulled her close. "But we'll never know because you're not getting the chance." He kissed her hair.

He was right, of course. With a sigh, she rested her head against his chest. "Just because I'm giving in, don't think that you're going to win all our arguments so easily."

He tipped her head back and let his gaze rove lovingly over her face. "I'll keep that in mind."

Both of her eyebrows rose suddenly. "Just do me a favor, okay?"

"What is it?" He held her gaze warily.

She tapped his shirt pocket where he kept the notebook she'd given him. "Remember to keep notes," she told him. "*Lots* of notes. If nothing else, I want a good story out of this."

He kissed her hard then, cautioned her not to answer the door under any circumstances until they had the suspect locked up, and left.

DEEP IN THOUGHT, Shannon wandered aimlessly through Nick's house. With the capture of the man who'd hurt her, she should be feeling enormous relief. The fear that lurked just beneath her every thought should be gone. She jumped suddenly as Jake the tomcat moved out of the shadows and curled around her ankles. She was feeling neither relieved nor free of fear. She didn't feel any different from the way she had been feeling since the assault.

Was it because Nick wasn't in the house with her?

Or was it because everything was a little too pat? Why couldn't she simply accept that James Buckley was the right man? Why this nagging feeling that something wasn't quite the way it looked?

Jake meowed plaintively. Realizing he wanted something, Shannon followed him obediently as he led her through the kitchen to the back door. Of course. He'd just eaten. He wanted out. Thankful for that small, mundane moment, she fumbled only a little opening the door, waited as he scooted out, then watched him disappear into the shadows. A keen look around Nick's backyard revealed nothing. She closed the door and headed back to the living room.

Another thing she'd hoped for hadn't come to pass. She had thought with the capture of the man who'd assaulted her, that her amnesia would vanish. Maybe it was naive thinking anything so complex could be resolved so simply, but she'd hoped it would. Her mind was as blank as ever about that night. And what about her recurring dream and the woman in the courtroom? Did that have nothing to do with her assault? What about Marion Chaney's suicide? And her own anxiety about it? Did that mean nothing?

Too many unanswered questions.

With her arms wrapped around herself, she looked through the window where sundown had cast the world into sudden shadow. A huge magnolia in Nick's front yard stretched dark, leafy limbs into a near-black sky. Two squirrels scurried across the lawn, then climbed the tree, home safe. A woman walked

by on the sidewalk urging her youngster ahead of her, the little
boy whining and reluctant to call it a day. Nick's neighbor
was killing the motor of his lawnmower. His lawn was richly
green and as smooth as velvet. Two doors down, a pizza delivery van had stopped. Shannon remembered reading somewhere that more people ordered pizza on Sunday than any
other day.

Still uneasy, she left the living room and went to Nick's
study where the computer screen threw out eerie green light.
Please, God, don't let it be Kelly.

Unwilling to wait for Nick's call, she went to her handbag
to get her address book. She would call Kelly's mother herself.
Maybe somebody would be at Francine's house to answer the
phone. The minute she plunged her hand inside, she felt the
same sensation of terror she'd had yesterday. This time she
didn't try to block it. She was safe now, wasn't she? Her
tormentor was in custody. Drawing a deep breath, her heart
pounding, she pulled the sides of the purse open and began
withdrawing the contents.

Out came her keys, her wallet and checkbook, her press
badge, two pens, a small mirror, a lipstick, a tiny notepad, a
comb, a brush, a pack of gum, opened, a roll of breath mints,
unopened, a small bottle of spray perfume, Paris, another notebook, an address book and calendar, a coin purse, a tiny aero-
sol hair spray...and that was it. Her hands were still shaking
and her heart was still pounding.

Why? Why? Why?

With a furious cry, she turned the handbag upside down and
shook it violently. Nothing came out, but she heard a sound.
Something trapped inside the lining? Loose coins? Extra keys?
Putting her hand inside, she felt all around. Nothing, unless...

Moving more carefully, she felt along the seams of the canvas. She touched something small tucked into the crease of
one corner. Fumbling with the purse, she tried to figure how
to get at it. There must be a tear somewhere. Without wasting
any more time, she took a letter opener from Nick's desk and

slashed a hole in the lining big enough to get her hand into, then reached inside.

A minicassette tape.

She stared at it, dumfounded. Instantly, she recalled what it was. And how it got there. And what it contained. Her mind whirled dizzily with returning memory. She looked around wildly for something in Nick's things to play it back.

Dear God, it wasn't James Buckley. It was the judge, and Marion Chaney *was* the key. Shannon didn't know how Buckley was involved in her assault—or even if he was involved. The man who wanted Shannon dead was Judge Henderson.

And he was still out there.

She sent a fearful glance to the window, the street utterly dark now, and wondered if he was actually out there. In Nick's neighborhood. Did he know that she was alone? Had he just been waiting for his chance? She put a hand on her chest as a thought struck. Had she remembered to lock the back door when she let Jake out? Her heart racing, she took a step to go and check.

The doorbell rang, stopping her short.

For a full minute, she stood frozen. Jangled nerves fed her runaway thoughts. It was ridiculous to think the judge could know that Nick was gone. What had he been doing, for heaven's sake, watching the house the whole weekend? Unlikely. He didn't have anything to do with James Buckley, so he wouldn't expect Nick to leave her unguarded. He wouldn't even know about Buckley. And he certainly wouldn't ring the doorbell if he had come to kill her.

Her throat dry, legs unsteady, she walked to the door, rising cautiously on tiptoe so that she could see into the peephole. The face looking back at her wasn't a crazed judge, it was a teenage girl. With a glad cry and a rushing sense of relief, she pulled the door open.

"Kelly!"

"Hi, Shannon." The girl stood there in jeans and a T-shirt looking uncertain. Behind her, the neighborhood was quiet and peaceful. And dark. Up and down the street every one hundred feet or so were little oases of brightness where the lights had activated automatically. The mother and her little boy were safely inside, the lawn-conscious neighbor had disappeared after turning on his sprinkler system, the squirrels were quiet and the pizza man was still there.

All's well. Then why was her mouth dry and her nerves screaming?

Without a word, she reached for Kelly, tugging her inside by the arm and then closing the door hurriedly.

"I gotta talk to you, Shannon," the girl blurted out. "I need to tell somebody."

"What's wrong? Is it your mother?"

"My mom? No, it's— At least, not yet. He hasn't done anything yet, but that's why I wanted to talk to you." She studied her feet a second or two before meeting Shannon's eyes. "I hope it's okay, me coming over here like this, but knowing your job and all, and you and Detective Dalton being friends, well…I just figured you'd be the best person to talk to."

"How did you know where to find me?" Dear God, if Kelly could find her, then *he* could find her.

She shrugged. "Like I said, you and Detective Dalton being friends, I thought I'd check here before making that long haul out into the country to your family's place and all." She glanced around, then met Shannon's eyes and shrugged. "Looks like I got lucky, huh?"

"Here, let's sit down." Shannon motioned her to a sofa and sat down with her. She wondered briefly what Nick would think if he knew the rest of the world could find her as easily as this teenager.

"Is he around? Detective Dalton, I mean?"

"No, he's…he had to respond to a call." She thought about trying to reach him via the police dispatcher, but there was open fear on Kelly's face as her eyes darted to the shadowy corners of the room, then to the darkened stairwell just off the foyer, and then to the windows. In her lap, her fingers were never still, twisting and flexing. Shannon winced as the girl cracked her knuckles, the sound magnified in her anxiety.

"What's wrong, Kelly?"

"I'm not staying long." She studied a mobile made of stained-glass hummingbirds hanging in the window. "Detective Dalton has some really cool stuff in here," she observed, but she was again looking down at her own hands.

Shannon reached over and touched her knee gently. "You can tell me, Kelly."

"It was your article," she said suddenly. "You didn't mention my mom's name, but I know it was about her." She darted a quick look into Shannon's eyes. "Wasn't it?"

"In a way it was," Shannon said, hoping she had not inadvertently catapulted this child into something she would regret forever. "I used the circumstances of your mother's problems to illustrate the problems of victimized women everywhere, Kelly. Why? Did it cause trouble for your mother? Did Buck get mad? I never meant—"

"Well, I don't know. You see, I didn't stay with my mom last night. I was with a friend. A couple of friends, actually." She stopped, closed her eyes and gave a small, hopeless little shudder, and when she looked again at Shannon, her eyes were brimming with tears. "We talked it over and we, like, decided I should come and tell you everything. Now that I'm here, though, it's so bad I don't know whether I can...or not." She darted another glance at Shannon. "You know?"

"It takes a lot to shock me, Kelly," Shannon said in a tone that she hoped sounded calm and reassuring, when she felt anything but.

"It *is* about Buck, although I haven't seen him today."

"Yes. What about Buck?"

"He's not really interested in my mom anymore." Her tone changed then. "He's really chasing me and my friends," she said, disgust and bitterness twisting her young features. "I didn't tell the truth that day about him threatening my mom when he came to the house. It was really *me* he was threatening."

"What do you mean, chasing you? In what way, Kelly?"

"This is hard," Kelly said, looking to the ceiling.

Concern became suspicion. Shannon searched her mind for a way to ask the all-important question. Kelly was only fourteen. Even if she'd been to some of the encounter group sessions, there was still her extreme youth to consider. Sadly, her innocence had been violated long ago. "Has Buck said or done anything to violate you in any way?"

Kelly gave a half laugh. The tears falling down her cheeks caught at Shannon's heart. "Yeah, Shannon. I guess Buck has done a few things to *violate* me. My friends, too, if you want to know the truth."

"What things, Kelly?"

The girl hesitated for a moment. Her gaze was fixed on her hands, unmoving now. Shannon could almost hear her thinking, weighing what to say, whether or not to say it. Thinking of consequences. It had taken a lot of courage for Kelly to decide to talk to a reporter.

"He has a friend," Kelly said, speaking softly, almost inaudibly. "This guy wants girls, like, you know, *young* girls. He treats them really nice, giving them clothes and makeup and stuff, then he takes them on trips."

"Trips?" Shannon fought to breathe calmly. If she showed her agitation, her outrage, Kelly might stop talking. She needed to hear everything, and if it turned out that James Buckley was the one, she vowed not to rest until she saw him brought to trial. For his brutality to Tammy Rainbow alone, he deserved the maximum sentence.

"Yeah, and they meet friends of his there." She was still looking at her hands.

"What happens with his friends, Kelly?"

A tear fell with a plop onto Kelly's linked fingers. "Uh, ummm..."

"Kelly? It's okay, honey. Tell me."

"Sex. They have sex."

It didn't take much longer to get the details from Kelly. It seemed that once she'd gotten past the major hurdle—revealing the fact that the abuse was sexual—then she had quickly and thoroughly told everything. She was in possession of a dirty secret that had been destroying her life—and that of other young teenagers. Some, Kelly knew. Others were not from Savannah.

"Did you know Becky Berenson?" Shannon asked. She saw instantly that Kelly recognized Becky's name.

"No." Using a paper towel she had just taken from the kitchen, she wiped her cheeks dry and blew her nose. "When I read about her in the paper, I wondered. But I didn't say anything." She looked directly at Shannon. "I was scared to say anything, Shannon. I'm still scared. Buck's going to kill me."

"No, he—"

"Really, yes, he is. And maybe my mom, too. When he finds out what I've done…" She shuddered, managing to draw herself into a small, tight bundle on the sofa. "That's why I took so long about telling," she explained. "He kept saying he would kill my mother." She looked over at Shannon, her eyes mirroring emotion that made her look too much like Francine. No young girl should know such depths of hopelessness, Shannon thought, scooting closer until she could slip an arm around her. Kelly resisted momentarily, then with a small whimper, she turned into Shannon's embrace.

"He can't hurt you anymore, Kelly. Buck was arrested this morning. That's where Nick is right now."

Kelly's sobs ceased as she took it in. "He's in jail? The cops know what he's done?"

"Not everything." Shannon stroked her hair, feeling the trembling of the small frame quieting. "But when you're feeling a little better, we'll get freshened up and both of us—you and I—will call a police unit and they'll drive us to the police department. Nick will meet us there and you can tell him exactly what you told me." She looked into the girl's tear-washed eyes. "You'll be a genuine hero. They've been searching for the people who've been victimizing young girls in this area for a long time now."

"I can't believe it was so easy," Kelly said in a tone of wonderment. "Maybe I could have done this before. Maybe that girl..." Her voice hitched as a sob caught in her throat. "Maybe she would be alive today if I had."

"Becky's fate was not in your hands, Kelly," Shannon told her, praying the child could accept that. "There is plenty of blame to go around for unfortunate children like Becky. You've done a courageous thing today." She tipped Kelly's face up and looked at her. "You've saved lives today, Kelly. Think of it that way."

Kelly settled back after a moment. "I can't go with you to the police station right now. I have to do one more thing first."

"What's that, Kelly?"

"There's somebody who is waiting for me, somebody I promised I would get back to after I talked to you. I promised you would help and now I need to go tell her everything's going to be okay." She sniffed and wiped at her nose with the heel of her hand, the gesture so childlike that for a second Shannon felt almost amused. But with another thought, amusement vanished.

Dear Lord, don't let Kelly's friend be Tammy Rainbow.

She stood up. "Who is your friend, Kelly?"

"Oh, just somebody I met when she came into town a few weeks ago. Wow, like, she's gonna be relieved big-time that Buck's out of commission."

"What's her name, Kelly?"

Kelly rolled her eyes. "I know it sounds dumb, but she calls herself by a made-up name. I think she's running from her folks, you know?"

"Kelly. What is her name?"

"Tammy Rainbow."

STANDING AT THE WINDOW, Shannon watched Kelly climb into a car that had pulled up in front of Nick's house. The driver appeared barely old enough for a license, but the extreme youth of Kelly's friends no longer surprised her. They were headed for the hospital to check on Tammy. Her testimony about Buck and his link to teenage prostitution could wait, Kelly had stated adamantly. Tammy came first.

Her small chin had wobbled as she said it, but her backbone hadn't. Nothing Shannon said had persuaded her to wait for the squad car to take them. That way, Shannon could have gone, too. Resting her forehead on the cool pane, she breathed a silent prayer.

Please, please, let Tammy survive.

Hadn't Kelly and her friends suffered enough at the hands of James Buckley and his evil associates?

She must call Nick. Kelly's revelations would solve one problem, but there was still the matter of Shannon's recovered memory. She was still at risk as long as the judge's involvement was known only to herself. With a sense of unease, she surveyed the front lawn and the street from the window. Nothing appeared at all sinister in the scene. A car cruised quietly by, then disappeared around the corner. The lawn sprinkler across the street was still going, the pizza man was still there.

"Meo-o-ow."

She nearly jumped out of her skin. Jake, unaware that he'd nearly given her cardiac arrest, wound himself around her ankles again. Except for two things—food and the call of nature, the cat required little attention, but when it was time for either one, she was learning, it was time.

"Ready for your dinner, huh, fella?" she murmured, reaching down and giving him a few strokes with hands that weren't quite steady. Only as she massaged his ears did she wonder how he'd gotten back inside. Had he slipped by her unnoticed when Kelly went out? Must have. She would feed him right after she called Nick. Straightening, she glanced one last time to the quiet, dark street. And frowned.

The van bearing the familiar logo of the local pizza place was still there.

And Jake, who should be outside, wasn't.

Her fragile sense of security vanished, whipped away like a rug snatched from beneath her. Her eyes wide and frightened, she turned from the window. Fear was suddenly all-consuming, suffocating. With her heart threatening to burst out of her chest, she looked into the hushed, dark shadows of the hall leading to the back of the house.

And that was when she saw him.

CHAPTER SIXTEEN

TAMMY RAINBOW would survive. She was bruised and broken and terrified, but she would survive. Looking at the small, defenseless figure as the paramedics worked over her, Nick was reminded of another dark night only a few months before when Shannon had been the victim. He could only wonder at the twisted demon inside James Buckley that drove him to inflict such violence on women. Shannon was bad enough, but a fourteen-year-old girl… God, it defied all understanding.

Tammy stirred weakly as they transferred her from the floor of the squalid motel room to the gurney and began wheeling her toward the ambulance. Nick closed his eyes, shaking his head as she called piteously for her mother.

Buckley had been flying high, watching indifferently through a haze of drugs and alcohol as the paramedics fought desperately to save Tammy, but he had sobered fast enough once he spotted Nick on the scene. Then, when he realized that Nick suspected him of the attempted murder of Shannon O'Connor, he had instantly clammed up and demanded a lawyer.

Brooding and thoughtful, Nick watched from the seamy motel room while Buckley was hustled, handcuffed, to the nearest squad car. He should be feeling relieved at finally nailing Buckley, but for some reason, he was bothered by a sense of unease. He'd been unable to shake it ever since leaving Shannon at his house. The cop in him was bothered by that. He didn't like unsolved puzzles.

James Buckley had motive and opportunity. He had talked

freely of his hatred for Shannon and her journalism in general. But he denied he had assaulted her, and something about his vehement denial had rung true. Nick almost believed him. A touch of Shannon's clairvoyance would come in handy right about now.

His hand went to the notebook that she'd given him tucked in his shirt pocket. Maybe the judge in Atlanta—Franklin Henderson—was the one, after all. The thought made the hair suddenly rise on the back of his neck. He went as still as death. Suddenly he *knew,* without doubt. Call it Shannon's clairvoyance rubbing off on him, call it a cop's intuition. Hell, call it magic, he didn't care. He just knew with heavy, terrifying certainty that the judge was the one and Shannon was in peril.

He tossed the glassine bag containing vital evidence and slammed out of the room. What the hell had he been thinking of to leave her alone? What the *hell* had made him jump to the conclusion that Buckley was the one?

"Call the station and have them dispatch a unit to my place!" he shouted to Ed, who looked startled. "Now, goddamn it!" He felt for his weapon, gave it a sure, confidence-inspiring pat. By the time he hit the sidewalk, he was running.

FEAR WAS A POWERFUL FORCE, Shannon found, her gaze locked on the shadowy figure standing so still in Nick's dining room. It kept her motionless and wary when every atom of her being urged her to run screaming. It sharpened her senses. She saw everything in keen detail. Judge Henderson was shorter than she remembered. Thicker through the belly. His arms were heavy and longer than his torso. His hands looked lethal. He hadn't bothered with a mask. Was he that confident? A dozen ideas came pell-mell into her brain as she calculated her chances of getting away alive this time. She wondered if she could make it to the phone in the next room before he caught her. Or if she was fast enough to sprint through the hall to the kitchen and out the back door.

"I wouldn't try anything if I were you," he said softly,

moving in closer. "I haven't had this thing very long. It would be a pity if it should go off before we've...talked." She saw the gun in his hand then. And the glint of his Rolex.

"What do we have to talk about?" Shannon asked, hoping that he would believe she didn't recognize him. "I don't even know you."

He smiled, looking like a shark circling a pond minnow. "Surely you're not going to keep up this ridiculous pretense, Ms. O'Connor. You know who I am. It would surely have been better for you if you'd never heard of me, but...you reporters. You're never satisfied, are you?"

"I've never written anything about you."

"No, but you would have...you would have." The silky note disappeared. "Where is it?" he demanded coldly.

"Where is what?"

"The minicassette tape. My source tells me you use a hand-held recorder to get every little thought when you're digging into other people's business." The last phrase was sneered.

"Source?" she murmured.

"Yes, source. I thought you'd appreciate the irony of that. Where would you worshippers of the fourth estate be without your goddamn sources?" His smile was a travesty. "You have yours, I have mine."

She could not waste time trying to guess who might have betrayed her to this madman. He was insane. Shannon could see it in his eyes. He had somehow discovered that she was investigating the apparent suicide of his ex-wife and he had tried to silence her. Forever. She drew a deep, cleansing breath and vowed that he would not find her the easy victim she'd been that first time.

"I don't have the tape with me," she told him calmly, even though her heart raced. "Why would I? I'm a guest in this house. I don't take my work with me when I spend a weekend with a friend."

He brushed her reply aside with a wave of the gun. "Maybe

not, but before I'm finished with you, I think you'll probably tell me where it is.''

The hall led to the kitchen and possible freedom. She edged a little closer in that direction. He was a short, fat man. Maybe she could outrun him. The important thing now was to keep him talking. Maybe Nick would come in time.

Please, Nick, I need you.

"Even if I turned it over to you, there's still my computer," she said. "You can't destroy that. It's linked to the mainframe at the *Sentinel.*''

He smiled, shaking his head almost pityingly. "If there was anything on your computer, Dalton would have found it. And I wouldn't be here. It's as simple as that. So, you see, I must have that tape.''

"What do you think I learned about you that is important enough to threaten me like this, Judge Henderson?''

"Ah,'' he murmured upon hearing his name. "I see that your memory has indeed returned.''

"More or less,'' she said.

"Well then.'' He sounded brisk, all business. "My ex-wife, of course. And I don't just think you found out. I know you did.'' He chuckled and Shannon felt a chill run up her spine. "Oh, you might be interested to know that my law clerk, the one who was so forthcoming to you that day, is no longer with me. Above all else, I value loyalty and discretion in my employees.''

The gloves were off. So be it. "Did you kill him, too?'' His law clerk had been a frazzled, overworked man named Tim something. She had the name as well as everything he'd revealed about the judge on the tape.

"A drive-by shooting,'' Henderson stated coolly. "You know how the streets are in cities these days. No one's safe.''

She put out a hand. "Judge Henderson—''

"Don't move.''

Shannon froze. All semblance of cordiality left him. The man's moods changed with mercurial swiftness. The thought alarmed her. He could as easily decide to shoot her quickly and be done with it as to draw her out with this kind of sick torture.

If only Nick would come.

But no, she couldn't afford to indulge in wishful thinking. She couldn't wait for Nick to deal with the judge. To get out of this alive, she would have to conquer the fear that had her brain panicked and careering in ten directions at once.

Think, Shannon!

"You've been watching me in the pizza van, haven't you?"

He gave an exaggerated sigh. "I've had to move the thing half a dozen times. The air conditioner isn't working well, either. You've been a lot of trouble to me, Ms. O'Connor."

"Judge Henderson, you can't possibly expect to get away with this."

"Of course I will. I've gotten away with everything else." He looked at her slyly. "Actually, I couldn't have planned things better if I'd tried. After reading today's paper, I figure they'll think one of the violent types you castigated in your article got to you."

"I didn't name anyone in that article, Judge."

"So much the better. The men in the lives of any one of the women in that stupid encounter group are suspects."

"How did you know I was in an encounter group?"

"My source, dear girl, my source." He gave an exaggerated shrug of one shoulder. "Oh, what the hell—it's too good to keep. I'll bet you didn't know your friend and colleague Liza Westfall was eager to sell you out, did you?"

Liza. No surprise there. "What about loyalty and integrity, Judge? If Liza betrayed me, she can hardly be trusted not to betray you."

"I plan to take care of that, don't you worry."

God, the man was a lunatic. "Judge Henderson, this is crazy. Let me—"

"I'm not crazy!" His eyes blazed suddenly and Shannon's nerves skittered in alarm. "She drove me to it, that stupid bitch. It's all her fault. Marion! Plaguing me from the grave even now. You're all alike. Always demanding. Always nagging. Sucking a man dry. Pushing us to the limit, then when we're forced to commit the final act, you come back to haunt us. If she'd stayed silent—''

He shook his head, waving the gun. "And *you!*" he said suddenly. Shannon's breath caught in her throat. "You're just as bad. Why did you have to drag it all up again? Why didn't you mind your own goddamn business!"

Henderson was too caught up in his own delusions to notice that she had scooted a little closer to the hallway. "Your wife didn't commit suicide, did she, Judge Henderson?"

He was suddenly sly again. "I like to think that she did," he said, smiling affably.

"Because she divorced you?"

"She was a fool."

"She divorced you because you abused her."

"She was stupid and weak. She sniveled about every little thing." He aimed the gun straight at Shannon, then turned it away with a chuckle. "She had a dozen lovers."

"Did she really?"

"She denied it, but I knew better." With his free hand, he suddenly rubbed at his temple.

"Do you have a headache, Judge Henderson?"

"No!"

"You were afraid she was going to tell the world the real reason she divorced you, weren't you?"

"She denied that, too, but I couldn't take the chance."

"If it got out that she'd been a battered wife, it would have ruined your chances for that appointment, wouldn't it?"

"I wanted that federal judgeship," he said fiercely. "I worked for it, planned for it. I deserved it. It's mine." Frowning, he shook his head as though trying to shake the headache. "It still will be. I just have to take care of a few loose ends." He looked at her. "I never leave loose ends. You remember me telling you that?"

She nodded. "I remember, Judge. Ah…do you have any medication for that headache?" She waved a hand toward the kitchen. "Why don't you let me get you some water and you can just—"

"Do you take me for a fool, Ms. O'Connor? That's another thing about you females. Always trying to play up a man's weaknesses. Marion was always trying to push a pill of some kind on me. I don't need any of that." He gave a short cackle of laughter. "That's how I did it, you know. Gave her a bottle full of those damn pills. Poetic justice, I called it."

"How did you get her to take them?"

He shrugged. "Told her I'd beat the hell out of her if she didn't."

Shannon felt the sickness of it, the sheer hopelessness of Marion Chaney's last hour. The judge was mentally ill, but she had no sympathy for him. He had certainly shown no sympathy for his victims.

As for herself, she wouldn't be another one.

She had eased another step toward the kitchen door. He shifted suddenly, and she noticed that his hand was unsteady holding the gun. Was this her chance?

Catching sight of Jake perched on the bookcase behind Henderson, calmly cleaning a paw, she realized suddenly that she must not have locked the back door when she'd ushered him out. Then Kelly at the front door had distracted her when she'd thought to check. She felt a crazy urge to drop to her haunches and call the cat over. Not that he would come to her unless it suited him. Nothing moved him except the call to eat.

"Hello, Jake," she said impulsively. "How about some Seafood Fest?"

On cue, the cat jumped down and darted between the startled judge's legs toward Shannon. She lunged for the kitchen door as Henderson leapt at her, her scream echoing high and wild in the night.

NICK ROARED UP THE STREET toward his house and stopped his car with a loud screech of brakes. He could not recall ever having felt fear like this—overwhelming, blind, panic-inducing fear. On the frenzied ride from the motel, he had used techniques that he'd perfected over the years to stay calm. But that had been when it was only his own skin he was worried about. This time—this night—he was scared for Shannon. That made it a whole different ball game.

From his peripheral vision, he was aware of the pulsating blue flash of a squad car turning the corner. Good. He might need backup, but he could not wait for them. Pushing the car door open, he was out and running for his house—his weapon drawn—when he heard the explosive pop of gunfire and Shannon's heart-stopping scream. The sound tore through him with the ferocity of hot lead. For an instant, he actually wondered if he had taken a bullet through the heart himself. On her second scream, he reacted like a wild animal whose mate had been taken.

"*Shaaa—nnon!*" The cry, wrenched from his soul, echoed in the night sky and beyond. Propelled by fear and adrenaline, he pounded up the sidewalk, took the four steps in a bound and crashed the door open with one kick.

It slammed against itself and toppled the dragonfly lamp to the floor. When it shattered, the foyer was plunged into shadowy darkness.

Nick went as still and cautious as a jungle cat stalking prey. Behind him, he heard the two cops who'd answered his call for backup. Hoping they could see him in the dark, he signaled to them and slipped through the door, instantly stepping sideways. Then, plastered against the wall, he waited.

His chest felt ready to burst. Was Shannon okay? Where was the bastard? Nick knew he was there. Although nothing moved that he could see, he knew he was there.

He wanted to call Shannon's name. Just wanted to say it. To hear the sound of it. But it would be just like her to answer, to give away her position because she sensed his need. He clamped his jaw and squinted fiercely, trying to pierce the dead, dark denseness around him.

She was afraid of the dark.

Hold on, baby. I'll get you out of this and you'll never have to fear the dark again.

Suddenly he felt something. Just a whisper of motion. New fear spiraled through him. Shaking sweat from his eyes, he searched the shadows. And there it was. Behind the entrance to the dining room, he heard the quick flutter. A figure moved, stepped forth, a gun pointed in his direction—all in a split second. Then fire exploded out of the barrel. Simultaneously, Nick, too, was firing. Bullets slammed into the wall beside him. Above him. At him.

He never heard the one that struck him.

IMPRESSIONS. Disconnected thought. Urgency. A sense of detachment. And no feeling. He could feel nothing. Below him, an intense, frantic tableau unfolded on the floor of his foyer. Watching it, Nick was weightless, indifferent, a spectator viewing a scene of life-and-death activity.

It was his life in the balance.

His death.

Shannon crouched beside his body on her knees. She seemed oblivious of the paramedics, of the tense cops looking on, of the curious neighbors milling around the front door. From where he watched, Nick saw her tears. She wept softly, desperately, but with no sound. She held his hand between her breasts, as though in pressing it against the frantic beat of her heart, his own might somehow miraculously transcend reality and begin again.

The words of the two paramedics were an irritant. He resented the intrusion into the soft, quiet peacefulness where he hovered.

"Come on, Nick...give me a *break!* Get with it, man."

"Can you hear me, Nick? Breathe, damn you! Breathe..."

They faded again and Nick knew the enveloping sense of peace again.

Except for Shannon's tears.

Don't cry, Shannon. It doesn't hurt. There's no pain, sweetheart.

A sudden explosion gave the lie to that. His body arched with the jolt of electricity. Shannon wasn't there anymore. His connection to her was gone. Her heart was not beating for his. His need for her was suddenly frantic, overpowering. More desperate than this fleeting, ephemeral moment out of time.

And then she was back. Her hand slipped into his and held on fiercely while her whispered endearments fell into his consciousness like soft spring rain. Joy flooded his soul.

"Shannon..." Somehow he found the strength to hold on tight.

"I'm here."

THE AMBULANCE HURTLED through the streets, its siren pulsing high and shrill in the warm Savannah night. Nick lay quietly while two technicians worked urgently over him, one checking his vital signs, the other speaking directly on a portable phone to an attending physician at the hospital while he swabbed something on the back of Nick's hand, readying it for an IV. The medics worked with a sense of urgency, as though not daring to believe the evidence of their eyes. Barely half an hour had passed since a bullet from a madman's gun had struck Nick squarely in the chest and he'd suffered cardiac arrest. They had both just witnessed something they could only call a miracle.

Nick squeezed Shannon's hand reassuringly, wishing he could erase the bruised, fearful look from her green eyes. He, of all people, could sympathize with what she was feeling. Hadn't he felt the same thing when she lay lifeless and still to his touch on that cold night all those weeks ago?

He was still trying to make sense out of what had just happened to him, but he had the most important fact. The bullet with his name on it had struck the notebook that had been tucked in his shirt pocket. The sturdy leather notebook Shannon had given him.

Reading upside down, Nick made out the name stenciled on the nametag of the medic taking his blood pressure. Jerry. "Don't I know you?" he asked, settling back. He was sure that Jerry was the EMT who'd been on the scene when Shannon had been hurt.

"Yeah," Jerry replied, winking at Shannon. "I just told your lady...we're all gonna have to stop meeting like this."

"Speaking for myself," Nick said, managing a weak chuckle, "I never want to see your ugly mug again."

"Put that oxygen back over your face," Jerry ordered. It was the third time Nick had shoved it aside to talk around it.

"I don't need it," Nick complained. "I'm fine now."

Shannon leaned over and kissed him. "Humor us, okay?" she said, caressing his jaw. Her mouth was soft and warm. He relaxed as though he'd been given a tranquilizer and allowed her to fix the oxygen in place again.

He felt the ambulance slowing and guessed they were at the hospital. He focused on Shannon's face, squeezing her hand again. Somehow he couldn't seem to let it go. "Give me a minute to get rid of these two, sweetheart, and we'll go get married."

Her face dissolved into tears. "Oh, Nick, you came so close. So close." She shuddered. "Never again. I don't ever want to go through that again."

He was fuzzy on the details, but he knew he didn't want to go through that again, either. "What about the judge? Did I get him?"

"He's dead."

"No notebook to save him, hmm?"

"I'll never say another word about that notebook," she said fiercely. "I *love* that notebook."

"I'm feeling pretty fond of it myself, considering," Nick said dryly.

The truth was, he didn't think it was the notebook that had
saved him. Like Shannon all those weeks before, he had died
from the impact of that bullet. He had actually bought the
farm. His option had been a compelling one: peace, joy, a
place without violence and crime, a place where no atrocities
to children ever happened.

But it had meant leaving Shannon.

He wasn't ready to give her up. They had just discovered
each other. For now, and for a long time in the future, they
belonged together here on earth. He nuzzled against the
warmth of her palm cupping his face. They'd talk about that
later. Just now, he needed to touch her. To be close to her. To
have her hold him. Forever wouldn't be long enough.

EPILOGUE

June 16—Wilderose House

TODAY I MARRIED *Nicholas Edward Dalton. Nick. It was a huge, lavish affair, suitable in every way for the granddaughter of Patrick and Kathleen O'Connor. Nick's words, not mine. The truth is, a small wedding with just a few friends and family would have satisfied me, but Nick insisted. He says we start as we intend to go on. The differences in our backgrounds that troubled him for so long no longer matter. They never mattered to me. Perhaps Nick had to experience that same moment out of time that I did to truly accept that we are meant to be together.*

And, of course, we are meant to be together. It was reaffirmed to me tonight. I was deeply asleep when something woke me. Beside me, Nick stirred as though he, too, heard or felt something. He turned and put his arms around me, pulling me close until we lay spoon-fashion, and then he settled again. Leaving me looking at the mirror.

There was no storm. No lightning, no thunder. The glass in the mirror was shimmery and very bright, not like the murkiness of other Dream Sights. Odd, I thought, because there was no nightlight anywhere, no full moon. Images began shifting and turning. I was aware of color, a rainbow of color. From the strange iridescence, two figures materialized. Nick and me. I had the impression that I was watching time-lapse photography, or something like it. There were houses and places and people, children and old folks. And always, the two of us, Nick and me. It was a Dream Sight of our life-to-be, Nick's and mine. It was good. It was enduring. It was beautiful.

SHADOWS IN THE MIST

PROLOGUE

SOMETHING EVIL was happening.

He knew it was a dream. That happened sometimes. Caught halfway between sleep and waking, some part of his brain was aware that the events unfolding in his mind were only a dream. None of it was real. He would wake up in a few minutes and find himself in his own bed and the incredible goings-on would be revealed as a fantasy from wherever dreams are born. But still, there was that odd feeling as he dreamed that it just *might* be real. It just *might* be that he was with Joanna again. That he was a part of her life and that he was meant to be a part of what was happening.

Ryan shifted restlessly, and moonlight fell across his face. As though at a signal, a light came on in a closed garage and two men entered from an interior door. Between them, they supported a third man, who could not walk. Drunk, Ryan realized. And consequently helpless. With a low moan, Ryan resisted. What the two intended was dark and deadly.

Wake up, Ryan told himself. Enough. The dreams he dreamed lately were sufficiently dark and deadly to haunt even his waking hours. He didn't need to experience someone else's nightmares, too. No matter. His need to distance himself was futile. The scene continued inexorably toward a grisly end. One man opened the door of a low-slung luxury car and shoved the drunk inside. Then, bending forward, he reached around the now unconscious figure behind the wheel and started the engine. Touching the appropriate buttons, he lowered all four windows, then straightened and closed the door.

Exhaust from the engine began to cloud the interior of the garage. Moving briskly now, the two men stepped back from the car and turned to go back into the house. The bang of the garage door as they closed it echoed in Ryan's head like a shot in a barrel. Behind them, white smoke billowed from beneath the car.

Stop. Come back. Don't leave him.

From the prison of sleep, he pleaded with them as the deadly carbon monoxide spewed out of the car's exhaust pipe. He could barely see the car now for the fumes. But he could see the victim. Clearly.

With a groan, Ryan flung his arm over his face, hoping to block what he knew was coming next. But, of course, he couldn't. Somehow Joanna was suddenly in the house. Not a house, he realized now, but a place of business. An art gallery? With an attached garage.

He sensed her fright. His heart pounding, Ryan wanted to warn her away as she pulled desperately at the door and then she was standing there. Trapped in his dream, he was forced to watch her engulfed in a cloud of acrid-smelling white smoke. He watched as, horror-struck, she covered her mouth and nose with one hand and fumbled for the switch on the wall beside the doorway and slowly, mechanically, the automatic garage door opener activated and cold, fresh air rushed in.

It was her scream that awakened him.

He came to himself sitting straight up on the couch. Wet with sweat and breathing hard, he waited for his heart to slow down. It was just a dream. Thank God. One of those particularly intense ones. The kind that scared the hell out of you, no matter how old you were.

Joanna. Good God.

His mind skittered quickly over the image of his ex-wife. He got up and stumbled through the open door to the screen porch. For a few blank moments, he just stared at the ghostly look of the neglected landscape. Palm trees swayed in the quickening ocean breeze. The hushed roar of the surf calmed him.

Understandable that Joanna would be in his mind, he told himself. He was at the cottage on Sea Island where they had honeymooned.

How long ago, O'Connor?

Fourteen...no, fifteen years ago.

When you were an ambitious, arrogant, hotshot of a fool.

And now you're a washed-up, middle-aged has-been. Who says you never get what you deserve?

He turned on his heel with a snarl and headed back inside the cottage. He wasn't about to get caught up in ancient history. Muttering a curse, he yanked on his pants and went in search of a drink. Something sharp and strong and with enough of a bite to banish the aftermath of a helluva nightmare. Staring into the black Georgia night, he hefted the glass, then downed it all in one gulp.

Helluva nightmare.

CHAPTER ONE

"FIRST CALL FOR FLIGHT 664 to Montreal. All handicapped passengers and unaccompanied children may board now."

"That's you, Daniel. You'd better get in line."

"I'm not boarding with a bunch of little kids, Mom. I've done this by myself since I was seven, for Pete's sake. I've got seat number 27A. When they call that number, I'll get in line."

Joanna Stanton rolled her eyes. What had happened to the little boy who had never questioned authority? This insistence on "being a man" was wearing.

She watched him shrug his battered carry-on over his shoulder, the only baggage he'd packed. "Do you have everything? Are you sure you have enough underwear? You know how it was the last time you went to see Grampa Jem. You forgot to take any socks."

"Seats 50 through 84 may now begin boarding."

"It didn't matter because it was summer," Daniel said, dismissing an old, worn-out argument. "I'm gonna be okay, Mom. I just wish I felt the same about you. For the last time, will you level with me on this? Why am I being hustled off to Montreal?"

Joanna closed her eyes. Who was the kid here, Daniel or her? "I've told you, Daniel, I have no ulterior motives in sending you to visit your grandfather. You know you like Montreal."

"Don't try to snow me, Mom. You have some reason for

getting rid of me and I just haven't figured it out yet. But I will.''

"Daniel—''

"And when I do, if I think there's something going on and you need me, I'm outta there and back here to Chicago so fast your head'll swim.''

"You're fourteen years old, Daniel,'' Joanna said. "Don't even think it.'' Pushing her hair back from her face impatiently, she eyed the line of ticket holders. She'd never been a very good liar, and with Daniel it was nearly impossible. He saw through her in a way that bordered on the uncanny. In fact—

"I'm calling you every day, I just want you to know that,'' her son said, wearing his famous stubborn expression.

Where did he get that? she wondered. "We've discussed this, Daniel. Grampa Jem's phone bill will skyrocket if you do that. I'll check in with you every few days, cross my heart.''

"Uh-huh.''

Joanna breathed in patiently. "I will, Daniel. Have you ever known me to lie?''

"No, Mom, and that's what's got me worried. I've got a feeling—''

"Ignore it, Daniel. Ignore anything except a real live distress signal from me. If I need help, you'll be the first person to know.''

"Yeah, I will.'' He gave her a look she couldn't quite read, then flashed her a lopsided grin. "So...behave yourself, okay?''

She punched him playfully. "That's my line, kid.''

He reached for her and hugged her hard. A lump came to her throat as she returned the embrace. He was so precious to her. He was everything that was right and good in her life. She was truly doing the best thing sending him to Jem Stanton.

"Seats 25 to 49 now boarding.''

He stepped back, still looking reluctant. "Don't forget me, okay?"

"With my grocery bill cut in half, the TV all to myself, the radio down to a reasonable level, how could I forget you, Daniel?"

"And call me," he admonished, backing toward the exit. "Often."

She propped her hands on her hips. "Will you put a lid on it?"

He stopped, came back in three long-legged strides and hugged her again, fiercely. "Take care, Mom. I love you."

"I love you, too."

PLEASE, GOD, TAKE CARE of my son. Keep him safe until we can be together again.

With both her hands resting on the wheel, Joanna lifted her head and released a shuddering breath. Okay, that was behind her. Daniel was off to Jem Stanton and presumably safe. Upon leaving the airport, she'd been too shaken to drive, so she'd pulled over into the parking area of a fast-food restaurant until she had herself under control again. She couldn't sit here for the rest of the day, even though the idea sounded a lot better than what she did have planned. With a sigh, she started her car and pulled out into traffic.

It was Sunday, not a regular workday, but she headed for the interstate, which would take her to her destination, a posh, upscale suburb of Chicago, and a small art gallery called Rico's. Although Joanna was an illustrator of children's books, for the past six months she'd been managing the gallery in which she was a part owner with a man named Enrico Fellini, thanks to David Stanton.

Seven years ago, when her husband, David, had died of a sudden heart attack, she had been grateful for the income derived from Rico's. At the time, she had been content to let Rico himself manage the business while she continued her own career. But then, about a year ago, Rico had developed a serious disease and the treatment had eventually rendered him temporarily unable to work. Joanna had readily agreed to manage the business for the duration of his chemotherapy with the help of his friend Sammy Feldstein.

Six months had passed. An artist herself, she was familiar with the business and had actually enjoyed the undemanding duties of a merchant. She liked negotiating with suppliers and chatting with customers. There was little creativity required, just a talent for management and a rudimentary knowledge of bookkeeping. In fact, an accountant did most of that. But not all. And that was where the trouble had started.

Her suspicions had begun when there seemed to be more paperwork from the imports—which constituted a good bit of Rico's stock—than there seemed to be stock to sell. One afternoon when a new shipment arrived, instead of waiting for the employee who usually uncrated and catalogued the stock, Joanna began the job herself. Halfway through the chore, she opened a collection from an obscure artist, wondering what Rico had seen in the work. While she was examining a particularly ugly Egyptian fertility goddess, the statue slipped from her hands and crashed to the floor, sending a king's ransom of diamonds cascading over her feet.

Within the hour she had been at Rico's house demanding an explanation. Perhaps it was his illness, or perhaps he was simply caught by surprise, but Rico immediately admitted everything. Tearful and emotional, he explained that his medical bills had mounted beyond his ability to pay. An associate, whom he refused to name to Joanna, had suggested a way out. Rico would receive the art shipments and simply pass along specific merchandise tagged by his associate.

"You've got to forget what you saw today," Rico had warned her. "These people are not the type to rest easy if they suspect you've discovered how they're getting the ice into the States."

"Ice?" Joanna had stared at him incredulously. "Listen to

yourself, Rico. What's happened to you? This is crime on a grand scale. You're not a criminal, for heaven's sake."

Fellini sighed and dropped his head back against his chair. "What difference does it make, Jo? I'm living on borrowed time, anyway. I don't want to leave Sammy destitute, trying to pay the bills after I'm gone."

Sammy was his longtime friend. "Does Sammy know about this?" she'd asked.

"No." Rico straightened and managed a stern look. "And you won't tell him. Promise me, Jo."

"It's not my place to tell him, Rico. It's between the two of you, but the business itself is another thing entirely. You can't continue, you know that."

He nodded wearily. "Right. I'll tell them."

"When, Rico?"

He shrugged, rubbing a hand over his bald head. Before his illness, he'd had thick, dark hair. Now, only a little peach fuzz covered the high, round dome of his skull.

"Rico?"

"I hear you, Jo. Give me a little time to negotiate with them, will you?"

"Negotiate?"

"I have a feeling a man doesn't just walk away from a situation like this. Let me feel them out and I'll get back to you."

Joanna didn't like it, but had little choice. Rico was probably right in his assessment of the delicacy of extricating himself from the partnership. "No more shipments, agreed?"

"Yeah, it's over."

She frowned, taking in his utter dejection. "You'll be careful, won't you, Rico? People who would do this...well, I don't think they play by the same rules as we do."

"I'll be careful," he said, getting slowly to his feet. "And I want you to take precautions, too. How about taking a few days off? Just until I get this cleared up."

"Do you think that's necessary?"

"I do. Don't forget, you have Daniel to think of."

The risks to Rico and herself were one thing. It was another matter entirely when Daniel was brought into the mix. "Daniel is at risk only if they discover that I know something. Maybe they won't."

"What did you do with the diamonds when you broke the statue?"

"I put them into another statue and repacked everything to look just the way I found it. I was afraid to do anything else until I talked to you."

"Hmm."

"Not good enough?"

"I don't know, Jo. I just don't want anything happening to you or Daniel because of my stupidity. To be on the safe side, why don't you send him up to Dave's father in Montreal?"

"Yes, I will."

"And you go with him."

"We'll see."

He'd leaned forward suddenly, forcing her to look at him. "This is heavy stuff, Jo. I won't lie to you. I'm in deep. Really deep. I don't care for myself, but I don't want harm coming to you or Daniel or Sammy. So promise me you won't do anything foolish."

"I won't."

"Good. Joanna?"

She turned to look at him. "Yes?"

"I'm sorry."

That had been late yesterday afternoon. She had immediately made the arrangements to send Daniel to Montreal. Telling him had been the problem. It was no wonder that he had suspected something. She was no good at fooling Daniel. He had always been able to pick up on her moods with laserlike accuracy. Only one other person had ever been able to see through her like that.

Lord, where had that thought come from? She hadn't thought of Ryan O'Connor in eons. She hadn't *allowed* herself to think of Ryan. As she approached the elite little shopping village where Rico's had been established nineteen years ago, she couldn't imagine what had put her in mind of him today. Shaking her head, she drove to the end of the street to the gallery, a Victorian house that Fellini, with the help of his friend Sammy, had lovingly renovated. The only deviation from the original structure of the house was the attached garage, a necessity for Rico's precious vintage Cadillac. As the original owner, he cherished it nearly as much as a priceless piece of art.

No enclosed garage for any other employee, however, Joanna included. As she had done for the past six months, she pulled into one of the parking spaces reserved for the art gallery. Once out of the car, she noticed the smell. Frowning, she looked toward the closed garage.

Fear flared when she saw the white fumes curling upward from the bottom of the door. And then panic.

"SUICIDE, YOU ASK ME."

"Yeah, but from the looks of the guy, if he'd waited a little while, he'd have kicked off, anyway."

"I had a cousin died of cancer. Looked like that."

"Walkin' skeleton, you can tell 'em a mile away."

"Uh-huh, suicide, pure and simple."

There was nothing pure or simple about death, whether suicide or otherwise, Joanna thought, hearing the cynicism of the policemen as they went about the business of collecting forensic evidence. Unfeeling, uncaring cretins, to speak their thoughts out loud, but maybe that's how they dealt with the more grisly aspects of their job. Huddled in Rico's small, cluttered office in the back of the gallery, she tried to shut out the words, but only succeeded in calling up private thoughts that were more painful. Would she ever forget the feeling as she fought her way through the deadly cloud of carbon monoxide to shut off the engine? Or her anguish when she saw Rico's limp, lifeless body slumped over the wheel of his beloved Coupe De Ville?

"Ms. Stanton..."

Joanna blinked up into the sharp eyes of a detective. "Yes."

"Detective Forrester, Gus Forrester, Ms. Stanton. I just need to ask a few questions."

"Yes. All right."

"Mr. Fellini was your employer, is that correct?"

"Friend. He was my friend." She sighed. "And business partner. I own a third of the gallery."

"And the balance?"

"Rico has two-thirds."

"I see. You say you've been managing the shop since he took sick."

"Yes. Six months, more or less."

"Has he seemed...despondent to you lately?"

"Yes, I suppose so. The chemotherapy was very hard on him. Some people manage it without too much difficulty, but Rico... well, he didn't."

"His friend, Mr. Feldstein—"

"Sammy, yes."

"Mr. Feldstein says Fellini hasn't been himself for several months. Would you agree with that?"

"No, he hasn't been himself." *He's been a criminal.*

"Do you think his mental condition might have been serious enough to make him contemplate taking his own life?"

No. However, his fear of his new "business associates" might.

"Ms. Stanton?"

"I'm sorry..." She rubbed at her forehead. "I'm no psychologist, Detective Forrester. How can I make a judgment like that?"

"I apologize if my questions upset you, but—" he gave her a brief, dispassionate smile "—I'm only doing my job, Ms. Stanton."

"I understand."

"It's necessary."

"Yes."

"Can you think of anything pertinent to Mr. Fellini's business or personal life that might shed a different light on what's happened here today?"

He was smuggling diamonds for some sleazy people. You could ask them. "No, not really." Joanna stared at her hands. Steady as a rock. She was getting better and better at lying lately.

Detective Forrester made an official sound, something between a grunt and a harrumph of approval and straightened up. "Then, in that case, it looks like the coroner's probably right on this one. Suicide, pure and simple."

Turning her face away, Joanna said nothing.

NOT SUICIDE, BUT MURDER. Pure and simple. Joanna had no doubt about that. Rico was sick, but he'd already got through the worst of the chemotherapy. The prognosis from his doctor on his last visit had been positive. Men with his condition could look forward to another seven to ten years of life. He had a successful business and a friend he cherished. Rico would not commit suicide.

She had been afraid to tell Detective Forrester that. A murder was a major complication. Now that she knew about the diamonds, her first priority had to be Daniel. For his sake, she had to keep her knowledge to herself. Thank God Daniel was safe in Montreal.

Pray God he stayed safe in Montreal.

With a loud snap of the locks on her luggage, Joanna lifted the black-and-tan suitcase off the bed and set it on the carpet. She was doing the only thing she could, getting out of town, she told herself. It would mean missing Rico's funeral, but it had been Rico's idea for her to get away and although nothing had happened to make her think otherwise, she couldn't quite shake the feeling that it was only a matter of time until the people who'd murdered him would wonder whether they had succeeded in getting rid of everyone who knew about the diamonds.

But where was she to go? What would she say to explain to Daniel that she was leaving Chicago? Where would she be safe? Groaning, she sank down onto the bed and stared at the telephone.

There was one place. It was halfway across the country, which made it even more appealing. It had been fifteen years since she'd been there, but there were people there that she could count on. It was worth a try.

But first things first. She picked up the receiver and dialed Jem Stanton's number in Montreal. Daniel answered.

"Hi, sweetheart."

"Mom, I thought it would be you."

"Thinking about me, are you?"

"Yeah, a lot."

"How're things with your grandfather?"

"Oh, fine. Grampa Jem's fine. I'm fine. The weather's fine. Spike the dog's fine. When will the coast be clear and I can come home?"

Joanna raised her eyes to the ceiling. "Not just yet, Danny. In fact—"

"What now, Mom?"

"Well, actually, I'm leaving for a little while, dear. A buying tour for the gallery that will probably take me a few weeks. I—"

"A few weeks!"

"I'm afraid so."

"Like where, Mom?"

She cleared her throat. "Well, Boston first, then New York."

"Where will you be staying in Boston?" her son asked. "I've got a pen. Give it to me."

With her fingers crossed, her eyes closed and her heart aching, Joanna lied smoothly, "The Sheraton, of course. Isn't that where I always stay in Boston?"

Daniel grumbled a reply. "And in New York, you usually stay at the Four Seasons, right?"

"Uh-huh."

"Of course, silly me."

Ignoring his sarcasm, Joanna forced a cheerful tone. "But I'll be calling you, honey. Keep in mind that you don't need to run up Grampa Jem's phone bill."

"Right, Mom," he said dryly. "So, when do you think you'll be heading back home? I'm getting a little antsy here."

"Not for a while, Danny." With tears blurring her vision, Joanna squeezed the receiver tightly. He wasn't buying a word of this stupid conversation and she might as well give up trying. But, dear Lord, she couldn't tell him the truth! "You be good and look after your grandfather, Daniel. Just remember I love you. Bye, now."

Before getting in any deeper, she hung up. There was a limit to how much deception she was willing to engage in. Knowing Daniel, she was going to have a ton of explaining to do once they were together again. Until then...

Holding down the disconnect button with a trembling finger, she stared at the phone, still uncertain about her next step. If there was any other option...

"There isn't," she murmured, sniffing away tears and releasing the button. Then, taking a deep breath, she punched out the area code and the number for information in Savannah, Georgia.

CHAPTER TWO

SHE RANG THE DOORBELL.

Waited.

Rang again.

Dear God in heaven, she couldn't believe she was standing at the door of Wilderose Cottage again after fifteen years. If there were any other option, any other remote possi—

The door was jerked open and she was face-to-face with Ryan.

Neither of them said a word for the first few seconds. He looked stunned, Joanna thought, as well he might considering the circumstances. He also looked...worn, she decided, taking in the five o'clock shadow darkening his cheeks, his long hair, still damp from a recent shower, by the look of it. But his gaze was the same, as sharp and penetrating as ever, his eyes as blue as heaven's skies. He was shirtless and lean as a hungry wolf.

In fact, a wolf might have looked friendlier.

"Hello, Ryan."

"Joanna? Jo?"

"I guess you're surprised to see me."

"Yeah. You might say that."

She shrugged. "It's been a while."

"Fifteen years."

She sent a quick look over her shoulder, finding only wide, velvety green lawn shaded by a dozen lush palm trees. It still wasn't too late to simply stammer an apology, climb back into her rented car and go...where?

She turned back to find Ryan looking beyond her with a scowl. Okay, she'd hardly expected a warm welcome. "I know you don't want company," she said. "But…Shannon and Nick sent me."

"Shannon."

She sighed. "Look, could I come inside for a few minutes? I know you're no happier to see me than I am to be here, but I'd like to explain."

Without a word, he stepped back and let her in.

As she walked into Wilderose Cottage, the past rose up like a phoenix from ashes. The house was an oceanfront "light-house keeper's" cottage, and probably worth more than half a million on today's real estate market. Sea Island had at one time been known as Millionaire's Island, the elite of Boston and New York having discovered the Georgia coast during the early part of the century. But to Joanna, it was the summer place of the O'Connors, her almost relatives.

And it just happened to be the place where she and Ryan O'Connor had spent their honeymoon more than fifteen years ago.

"We tried to phone, but your line is out of order."

"It's not out of order, it's not connected. Shannon knows that."

She stared at him. "You choose not to have a phone?"

"It's possible to survive without one," he said, crossing his arms over his chest. "It's not like I'm doing without food and water."

"Oh, of course. It's just that—"

What about Daniel? How was she going to ease his fears if she didn't keep in touch by phone? She wrapped her arms around herself. Oh, this was a crazy idea. She shouldn't have let Shannon talk her into it. She should have insisted—

"What are you doing here, Jo?"

"I don't know. I was just asking myself that question." She looked around blankly, at a loss. The sound of the sea was strangely soothing. She stood, conscious of the familiar smell of salt air and marsh. She'd been living in the Midwest forever now, but the sea and this cottage, even Ryan himself, seemed so right somehow. And she was so tired. The rushing sound of the ocean intensified. Or was it inside her head?

She looked at Ryan, saw his lips move as he spoke to her, but with the roaring in her ears, she could only stare at him. Then everything went black and she knew nothing.

WITH A MUFFLED SOUND, Ryan swooped to catch her. She was a featherweight in his arms, slightly built, delicately colored, totally unconscious. His heart hammered as he carried her over to a deep, wide couch and gently lowered her onto it.

God, she was as pale as a ghost! He tried to think. Help. He probably needed to call some— With a fierce curse, he realized he couldn't call anybody. He didn't have a telephone. Stupid, stupid. It was one thing to disconnect the phone for his own personal reasons, but when it might mean disaster for Joanna, it seemed an incredibly stupid thing to do.

He conducted a frantic search of her face, willing some sign of life to appear. But she was so still. Lifeless. He picked up her hand and rubbed it. "Wake up, Jo, wake up. Please, Jo, don't do this. *Damn!*"

Dropping her hand, he felt for a pulse in her neck, but the collar of her shirt got in the way. Quickly, he fumbled at the buttons, pushed the material aside and felt again for a pulse. Whether it was his anxiety or not, he couldn't tell, but he felt nothing. New fear streaked through him. Visibly trying to calm himself, he closed his eyes for a few seconds and then looked down at her. Her chest barely rose and fell, she breathed so shallowly. What could be wrong?

Damn! Joanna in his house after so many years. And unconscious. His mind crossed from anxiety into full panic. He had to do something. But what? What!

Beneath the tailored shirt, she wore a flimsy pink bra. He could see her nipples through the lace. Now, along with panic, he battled a rush of desire. God, she was beautiful. He closed his eyes against memories of just how beautiful she was.

He began working at the belt cinched at her waist. As he loosened it, his eyes moved frantically over her, taking in the purity of her features. He frowned over the dark circles beneath her eyes. And her color! God, she had no color whatsoever. Whatever was going on in her life was taking a toll.

Abruptly he gathered her up and held her in a fast, intense embrace as though he could infuse life and warmth back into her by the sheer force of his will. Her perfume was flowery and feminine. And familiar. Oddly—crazily!—it was a step back in time. Fifteen years fell away like they were nothing. This was Joanna he held—*Joanna!*

For a few seconds, it didn't seem the least bit strange that he'd opened his door to find his first love standing there. Even after all this time, she looked just as lovely. More lovely. She felt good and right in his arms. The size and shape of her fit as naturally as ever. He buried his face in her hair, pulled the scent of her deep into his lungs and closed his eyes, as blacked out in his own way as Joanna was.

She whimpered suddenly, and the feelings coursing through him were so profound that for a moment he didn't release her, but just held on, rocking her gently. "You'll be okay, Jo. Just relax."

She stirred, just the faintest flutter of her eyelashes. It reminded him that she probably would not appreciate waking up to find herself half dressed and in a clinch with her ex-husband. The man she'd walked away from. As far as he knew, she'd never looked back. Never felt a minute's regret.

"Stay here," he said, pressing her back against an oversize pillow in the corner of the couch. "I'm going to get something to—" He didn't bother finishing the statement. He just headed for the bar. Fumbling with the bottles, he located what he wanted and splashed a hefty amount of brandy into a glass. Then, noticing his own unsteady hands, he poured another one for himself. She was still looking dazed when he got back to her, but he noticed she had managed to rebutton her blouse.

"Here, drink this and just stay quiet for a while. What in hell happened, Jo? You walk in here, say about ten words and fall on the floor in a dead faint."

She didn't take the glass or reply. She just seemed to retreat deeper into the cushion. With a grunt, Ryan tossed his own drink back, then sat on the edge beside her. With one hand behind her neck, he held the glass to her lips, nodding as she drank it. "That's the way. All of it, now...good girl, good girl. Just a drop or two and—"

"Enough! Y-y-you're...chok-king me!" She fell into a fit of coughing and took the glass from him.

"Sorry."

Catching her breath, she leaned back against the big pillow.

"Better now?"

"I'm fine. I'm sorry. I don't know what happened. I was looking—"

"You fainted is what happened." With his head cocked, he stared at her intently. "What I want to know is why? What's going on?"

"Why? I guess because I haven't had lunch."

He sent a quick look at the clock on the wall. "It's nearly 8:00 p.m. When did you last eat?"

"What day is this?"

"It's Monday, for God's sake!"

"Then that's probably the reason." She gave him a rueful look. "Actually, I haven't eaten since sometime yesterday, Ryan." She watched him straighten up, getting ready to explode again. "Please, please..." She put the glass to her forehead, closing her eyes. "I can explain. I will if you'll just give me a chance to get myself together."

With his arms crossed over his chest again, he settled back on the edge of the couch, facing her, his thigh against hers. "You look like hell, Jo. Why don't I open a can of soup or something? You'll probably make more sense if you eat something.''

"I don't want to put you to any trouble. I—"

"It's no trouble." He got to his feet, his eyes still on her. "Stay," he said when she attempted to get up. "And drink that," he added sternly. "I'll just be a minute."

GREAT. YOU PLAYED that scene with real finesse, Joanna. First you appear out of the blue on the man's doorstep, you intrude even though he's made no secret of the fact that he wants to be left alone, then you fall in a faint at his feet. So get out of this one if you can, and then...then what? You have no other option.

With both hands cupping the snifter, Joanna thought longingly of blacking out again, which, unfortunately, was not an option. She had never fainted in her whole life. Never. Until now. Of course she'd never experienced a period of prolonged, intense stress to compare with the past forty-eight hours, either. But to pass out within ten minutes of seeing Ryan again...well, he must be thinking that in the time since their divorce she had become even more of a shrinking violet than she'd ever been.

Looking around at the familiar interior of Wilderose Cottage, she found it hard to believe she was here again. How she had loved this place! Her earliest childhood was filled with memories of longing to live here. But although her mother had been an O'Connor, she was related only through adoption and consequently Joanna had always felt just outside the magic circle.

Magic. That was what she had expected upon her marriage to Ryan. What a naive little fool she had been.

"Here it is, chicken noodle. Time-tested panacea for invalids." Ryan set a TV tray in front of her with a bowl of soup, a spoon and a glass of milk on it.

"I'm not an invalid, Ryan. I just...lost it for a moment."

"Eat," he commanded. "You can explain why you 'lost it' after you get a little color back."

She knew that tone. Fifteen years apparently hadn't changed Ryan or his tendency to boss her around. Because she was feeling weak and wilted, she picked up the spoon and began eating.

She managed half of it and some of the milk only after Ryan insisted. "I hope brandy and milk go together well," she muttered, sipping without enthusiasm. Even before she had tasted the soup, the effects of the brandy on her stressed-out system were telling on her. Now heat curled in her stomach, spreading lazy, sleepy tentacles through her from tip to toe.

"Think of it as a brandy Alexander," Ryan said dryly.

She darted him a quick look, but nothing showed in his eyes. He had made a brandy Alexander for her on the morning after their marriage. The memory streaked through her, a blend of pain and regret. As she shoved the TV tray aside, she did the same with the renegade recollection. She wasn't here to reminisce about the past they'd shared. She was here because she was desperate.

"What's going on, Joanna?"

She leaned back. "It's going to sound crazy. All the way here, I felt as though a stranger had taken over my body, my life. I can't believe this is happening to me."

"Explain it to me, then."

She looked at him. "I guess the bottom line is that I'm running away, Ryan. Something happened…I mean…I stumbled on something I wasn't supposed to know and I was told…or rather, I felt it might not be safe for me to stay and answer any more questions. And once I decided to run, I realized I didn't have too many options about where to go." She shrugged. "So, here I am."

"Your only option was to seek out your ex-husband?" There was a wealth of skepticism in his tone. "Tell me another one, Jo. We haven't given a thought to each other in fifteen years."

Speak for yourself, she thought, staring at her hands. "I didn't seek you out, Ryan. I told you, it was Shannon's idea for me to come here to Sea Island."

"My little sister has been known to meddle where she shouldn't, but even for Shannon, this is going too far. I'm not here enjoying a holiday. I want privacy. I need it. She knows that. I'm not running a bed and breakfast, damn it!"

Mortified, Joanna shoved the tray aside and stumbled to her feet. "That's exactly what I told her," she said in a stifled voice. She had never felt so humiliated. She put a hand to her cheek. "I'm sorry. I don't know how I let her talk me into— Oh, this is embarrassing. *She* didn't talk me into anything. I knew it was a crazy idea and I went along with it because I couldn't think of anything else."

Fumbling for her bag, which had fallen to the floor beside the couch, she caught it up and began digging into it for the keys to the rental car.

"Oh, can it for God's sake." Reaching out, he pulled her bag out of her hands and tossed it onto the cushions. "You're here now. It's late and you say you haven't got anyplace else to go. I can put you up for the night. Tomorrow we'll work something out."

She stared at him. "I can't stay here knowing I'm not welcome, Ryan."

"Why not? Shannon must have told you I've been holed up here for nearly a year now, shunning every overture she's made to 'bring me out of myself.'" His tone rang with sarcasm. "You didn't let that stop you then. So why now?"

"I don't know, Ryan." She bent her head, rubbing the spot between her eyes wearily. She was truly so tired she could hardly think. She *couldn't* think, or else she wouldn't be here sparring with a man who made no secret of the fact that she was unwelcome. "I really don't know."

"Sit down."

She looked at him. "What?"

"You heard me, Jo, sit down. Before you fall down," he

added, rolling his eyes. He nudged her then—his touch was more gentle than she expected—and she sank without objection back into the corner of the couch. For a few moments, he stood over her, studying her intently.

"I'm sorry," he said quietly.

The last thing she'd expected was an apology, and it provoked the tears that she'd ruthlessly withheld since this whole fiasco had begun. She blinked fiercely. "It's not necessary. You have a right to your privacy. I'm intruding. I know it. I—"

"Enough, for God's sake!" He waved both hands in the manner of a football referee calling time. "Let's both agree that we're not having a tea party here and get down to business. Now...what's this 'something' that has you freaked out? Have you been fooling around with unsavory types?"

She laughed suddenly, but the sound was far from mirthful. "You think you're making a joke, but that's exactly what I've been doing."

His eyes narrowed. "You surprise me, Jo."

"I haven't committed a crime if that's what you're thinking...at least, not knowingly. But someone I know has, and I may be dragged into it." She looked at him. "It seemed the smart thing to do to—"

"Get out of Dodge?" he drawled, one eyebrow raised.

"Something like that." She was again studying her hands.

"Who is this character? Seems to me you've been careful not to name names."

Not for the first time, Joanna worried that telling everything to Ryan, of all people, might not be the most discreet thing to do. He was a journalist. An investigative reporter whose byline had appeared over some of the most controversial journalism of the past ten years. Her little intrigue probably wouldn't qualify as a world-class drama, but it was big enough to scare her out of her wits. It was big enough to send her flying halfway across the country seeking the dubious protection of a man who'd turned his back and walked away after only eighteen months of marriage to her. Should she trust him now?

"Got it all sorted out?"

"What?" She frowned up at him and found him shaking his head.

"You're as transparent as you always were, Joanna. I can just hear the argument going on inside your head. 'Will I? Won't I? Should I? Shouldn't I?' You can't come in here expecting my protection without telling me what I'm letting myself in for, lady. You'll have to level with me on this one whether you want to or not." His mouth twisted. "Whether you trust me or not. Emphasis on the trust, my dear ex. Spill it, Jo, and then we'll take it from there."

Suddenly her anger outweighed her exhaustion and humiliation. She stood up, facing him over the coffee table. "I don't *have* to do anything, Ryan. I'll admit it was a brazen thing to do, barging in on you the way I did, but I can leave the same way I came. As for trust, I don't think either one of us is qualified to make judgments there." When she finished, he had his arms crossed over his chest, watching her keenly.

"Well, that accomplished one good thing," he said with a flash of amusement.

She sniffed and pushed her hair back behind her ears. "What?"

"I made you mad as hell—as usual—and it dried up those tears." He reached over and rubbed his thumb beneath one of her eyes. Again his touch was surprisingly gentle. "Truce?" he suggested, both eyebrows lifted.

Do I have any other choice?

"I suppose."

"So, who is this character who is terrorizing you and what did you see that you shouldn't have?"

The idea of Ryan being untrustworthy was ludicrous. He was short on commitment and staying power, but not integrity. "I don't know his name and what I saw was about a cupful of loose diamonds. They were smuggled into the country through a business that I own in partnership with a man named Enrico Fellini, whose body I discovered yesterday in the garage attached to the shop.''

A beat or two of silence passed and then Ryan whistled softly.

She looked at him. ''Did I do the right thing in 'getting out of Dodge'?''

''I'd say so.''

''I came to Savannah because I knew Shannon's husband, Nick, was a detective here. I had to trust somebody.'' She rubbed her forehead again. ''When I told him what happened, he said he'd start his own inquiries, then suggested Sea Island as a good place to wait it out.''

''Nick's good.''

This time it was Joanna who crossed her arms over her chest and looked Ryan straight in the eye. ''Believe me, nothing short of this bizarre situation could have induced me to appear on your doorstep, Ryan O'Connor.''

He grinned. ''Is that a fact?''

''It most certainly is.''

He looked beyond her to the view through the windows of the cottage. So dark was the night that the line separating the sea from the horizon was invisible. ''Well, you *have* appeared, and I think it makes good sense for you to stay. At least for the time being.'' He glanced down at her. ''I've got questions, a lot of them. You've probably guessed that, but they can wait until morning.''

Joanna nodded, feeling relief and...she wasn't sure what else. There were things she didn't want to talk about...ever. He left to get her luggage, and she watched him go with troubled eyes. Murder and diamond smuggling, even crime on an international scale, seemed uncomplicated compared to the things she didn't want to talk about with Ryan O'Connor.

DANIEL TOSSED FITFULLY in the grip of the dream. His mother was in the airport at a bank of telephones. She looked shaken

and scared. She could hardly put the money in the slot to make
the call. Then she began talking. She was pleading with whoever it was. Drawing back abruptly, she dropped the receiver.
As it dangled, swinging back and forth, a voice, threatening
and vicious, came out of it. His mother seemed frozen, unable
to run away. Daniel knew she wanted to and he urged her on
silently, desperately.

Run, Mom, run.

But it was no use. Even knowing her to be in danger, he
was helpless, forced to watch her terror. To suffer. To do nothing. Voicing his torment in a long, anguished cry, he finally
awoke.

He found himself sitting bolt upright in his bed. Looking
blankly around, he couldn't remember at first where he was.
Then Spike, Grampa Jem's dog, whined, pulling him back to
the present.

Elbows on his knees, Daniel wiped at his face, trying to
erase the horror of the nightmare. His mother was into something deep, he knew it. Felt it. She had sent him here to
Grampa Jem's to get him out of the way—out of danger. At
least, that was what she was telling herself, he guessed, rubbing Spike's warm, floppy ears.

Daniel didn't know how it happened that he could sometimes tap into what other people were thinking. Or feeling.
He'd read about déjà vu, but he didn't think it was that. He
thought it was something more...special than that. Whatever
it was, it was telling him his mother was in trouble, big time.
It had something to do with Rico's suicide. Daniel had figured
that out right away, from the dream, of course. He had seen
his mother in a smoky garage and Rico dead in a car, but for
some reason that dream hadn't scared him as much as he
thought it would. Someone else had been there, he wasn't sure
who. He couldn't see him, even though in his dream he'd tried
and tried to see a face.

But now none of this excused the fact that he was stuck
here in Canada when he was supposed to be taking care of

her. He had been the man of the house since he was seven, and he was responsible.

Moving quietly, he tossed the covers aside and got out of bed. Pleased at the prospect of a late-night escapade, Spike wagged his tail enthusiastically, but Daniel calmed him with a firm command. He waited at the door of his room, listening. He didn't want to disturb Grampa Jem. His grandfather was old and a little deaf, but he wasn't senile. Not by a long shot. He was sharp as a tack. Couldn't fool *him* much. Besides, he didn't like sneaking around trying to fool Grampa Jem. When he explained his plan, he hoped to talk Grampa Jem into going along with it.

The telephone was in the kitchen. Daniel knew the house well and didn't need to turn on a light to find his way there. He called Spike away from the door and, moving very quietly, took the receiver off the hook. With the dog flopped at his feet, he dialed the number of the hotel in Boston where his mother was supposed to be. He'd memorized it earlier before going to bed, knowing he was going to make this call after Grampa Jem was asleep. He hadn't planned on falling asleep himself. Or on having a nightmare. Jeez, he *hoped* it was only a nightmare.

The switchboard at the hotel picked up after half a dozen rings. Daniel took a deep breath. "Hello, would you please ring Mrs. Joanna Stanton's room? She should have checked in earlier today."

"Sorry, sir, you'll have to speak up. I can't hear you."

"Stanton." Eyes closed, Daniel repeated patiently, "Please ring Mrs. Joanna Stanton's room."

"Stanton, you say? How do you spell that?"

"S-t-a-n-t-o-n."

"I'm sorry, we have no one registered under that name."

"Maybe she was registered earlier and has already checked out." With his forehead resting against the cabinet, he held his breath.

"Yes, that's possible."

His lungs gave way. "Well, could you check it, please?"

"Just a moment."

With his foot, he rubbed along the ridge of Spike's backbone. The warmth of the dog soothed him somehow. On the other hand, the feeling he was getting from the hotel was bad.

"Sorry, sir. No Joanna Stanton registered within the last forty-eight hours."

"Thank you." Daniel hung up, leaving his hand on the receiver. His head hung low, he thought about what to do next. He wasn't surprised that his mother wasn't in Boston. If only he knew what was going on. If only—

He lifted the receiver again and dialed his home number in Chicago. It dawned on him that any incoming messages might give him a clue. He could pick up the messages by remote control. After two rings, the answering machine kicked in.

The first couple were routine stuff. A reminder from his dentist that he was due for a checkup. A call from the bookstore that something his mother had ordered could be picked up. One of his friends had called. He'd forgotten Daniel was going to Montreal. Then a crackling, staticky call—like something from a cellular phone that was breaking up—telling his mother that they needed to talk. A strange man's voice. No name. No number. It didn't sound friendly to Daniel.

He hung up, then stood staring thoughtfully at Spike, still sprawled at his feet.

"What's the matter, boy?"

Daniel squinted blindly as his grandfather snapped the kitchen light on and shuffled toward him. The old man's white hair was messed up on one side where he'd been sleeping on it. He'd put his glasses on in a hurry, Daniel guessed, because they were a little skewed. As he crossed the kitchen floor, eyeing Daniel shrewdly, his hands worked at the belt of an old striped robe. Daniel recognized it as one he'd given to his Grampa a long time ago for Christmas.

"I'm sorry for waking you up, Grampa," he said with an apologetic look. "I just needed to use the phone."

"At 2:00 a.m.? Want to tell me why, Dan?"

His grandfather was the only one who ever called him Dan. He liked it. Grampa had never treated him as though he was a little kid, even when he'd *been* a little kid. "It's sort of complicated, Grampa."

The old man didn't move. "I got time, boy."

"Well..."

"Why don't we go back to your room?" Jem Stanton suggested. He gave a command to the dog, who stood up instantly and trotted beside them. "It's chilly out here, even if it's June. My blood's thinner than cheap gin now. Got a nice rockin' chair in that room. I'll sit there, you climb back in bed, and we'll just talk this out. Does that suit you?"

"Yes, sir."

When they were back in his room, Daniel waited until his grandfather was comfortable in the rocking chair that he'd been rocked in as a baby, according to his mom. He'd pulled the quilt off his bed and draped it around the old man before crawling back into bed and propping himself up against the headboard. Spike jumped up, too, and settled on Daniel's feet. "I woke up because I had a dream."

"Hmm, sometimes a dream can grab a man right in the gut, all right."

"Yes, sir, that's the kind this one was."

"A doozy, was it?"

"Yes, sir. It was about my mother."

Stanton nodded. "That'll sure get your attention. Bad dream featurin' your mother."

Daniel swallowed hard. "I think my mom's in trouble, Grampa."

The old man's eyes narrowed. "What makes you think such a thing?"

"Mostly, it's just a...feeling I have. But there's other stuff, too." He stared off into space for a while, wondering how much to reveal.

"What other stuff?"

"I just called the hotel in Boston where she's supposed to be and she isn't even registered."

"Didn't she call you this morning from there?"

"She called me and told me she was in Boston, but I didn't really believe her, so I just called the hotel myself and I was right. She hasn't been there."

"Now, Dan, knowing your mother, I don't think she would be doin' anything that might put her in jeopardy. It's hard to tell with women sometimes. Maybe there's something goin' on that she isn't quite ready to let you in on, have you thought of that?"

"Yes, sir, but I don't believe that's it."

"Hmm."

He looked directly at his grandfather. "Grampa, I need to ask you something and I need you to tell me the truth, straight out."

"I'm not in the habit of lying to you, boy."

"No, I know that, but neither is my mom and she's been telling me one whopper after another for the past week. So I need your word that you'll tell me the truth."

"You got it, boy. Shoot."

"Do you know where my mother is, for sure?"

Stanton shook his head. "Fact is, I don't, Dan. She assured me she would keep in close touch and if there was any problem, to leave her a message on her answer phone at your place in Chicago."

"Doesn't that strike you as strange, Grampa?"

"Well, now you mention it—and in light of the fact that she's not at the hotel in Boston, I reckon it does, Dan."

"I think I know where she is."

"You do?"

"Yes, sir. I think she's in Georgia. In Savannah."

"Well, heck-fire, son, she's taking a little time to visit her mother there. Nothing peculiar about her wantin' to be with Jessica that I can see. Is there?"

"I don't think she's with Granny Jess."

Stanton studied the boy for a moment. "Don't tell me, let me guess. You've already checked it out."

"Yes, sir, I called. I didn't exactly ask for my mom, I just chatted with Granny Jess as though I was making a regular phone call. We shot the breeze a little—I like to talk to her, even though I've never visited her in Savannah. She always comes here or we go places together, her and mom and me...to Disney World or Washington, D.C., or the Rocky Mountains. Places like that, you know." He shifted suddenly, leaning forward to make his point. "But she didn't mention my mom, and if Mom had been there visiting her, don't you think she would have? She'd have said something like, 'Oh, by the way, Danny—she calls me Danny—by the way, your mother and I are having a lovely visit.' Don't you think that sounds like the way it would have gone? *If* my mom is there, which she isn't."

Jem Stanton rested his hands on his knees. "Well, I have to say you make a good case for the way you see it."

"So, do you see it some other way, Grampa? Can you tell me where my mom is?"

He couldn't and they both knew it. Jem Stanton studied the pattern on the quilt wrapped around his knees and wished he were twenty years younger. No, maybe just ten years younger. He wished he weren't half crippled with arthritis and half blind from cataracts and with a bad ticker to boot. Then he could shoulder all this worry and anxiety for the boy he loved more than anybody else in the whole wide world. But he was old. Worn out.

"What's on your mind, Dan?" he asked, knowing this conversation wasn't just idle talk on the part of his grandson. Like Dave, Daniel's father, he would have thought it all out and already charted his course. It was just courtesy on the boy's part to tell it to him in advance. "What do you plan to do to locate your mother?"

"I think I know where she is, Grampa," Daniel said. "Even

though she's not with Granny Jess, I think she's in Savannah. And I need to go there and check it out.''

''You're sayin' you want to catch an airplane to Georgia?''

''Yes, sir, that's what I'm saying.''

''I don't reckon you're the least bit scared of an undertakin' like that, eh?''

''No, sir. I've been flying on my own to see you here in Montreal since I was seven. I can handle it.''

''Won't do me any good to try and talk you out of this, will it, boy?''

''No, sir. No disrespect intended, Grampa, but this is something I have to do.''

So young and full of piss and vinegar, Jem thought, his eyes a little misty. He was thankful suddenly that they were in a dark room, that Daniel couldn't see the way his hands trembled or see on his face how scared *he* was. The boy had spunk all right, but…well, escapades like this were for the young and fearless.

''You've got a good head on your shoulders, Dan. Just like your dad, did I ever tell you that?''

With a smile, Daniel nodded. ''Yes, sir. Mostly everything I know about my dad I learned from you.''

Stanton studied him with a faraway look in his eyes. ''You never looked much like Dave, but you think like him, boy. You think like him, and that's the important thing. That's the thing that will take you through an adventure like you're contemplating here.''

''I'll be okay,'' Daniel promised confidently.

''You'll call me the minute you land there in Savannah, won't you? I'll want to know you got there safe and sound.''

''Yes, sir, I will.''

''And you'll keep me posted even if things don't go as you figure them to.''

''Yes, sir.''

The old gentleman threw off the quilt with a brisk movement and got to his feet with a lot more energy than he felt.

No sense cryin' and whinin' to the boy. His mind was made up. A blind man could see that. "Then I'd better let you get some sleep, because you're probably goin' to hit the floor pretty early tomorrow mornin'. Am I right?"

"Yes, sir, I guess so."

"Well, good night then."

"Good night, Grampa Jem. And…thanks."

"You're welcome, boy."

"And don't worry. I'll be careful."

CHAPTER THREE

THE SEA WAS HYPNOTIZING. Almost. Considering the situation
she was in, nothing could completely ease Joanna's anxiety.
With her hands curled around a coffee cup, she watched
broodingly as huge waves rolled onto the beach. Every now
and then, a streak of lightning flickered on the gray, dreary
horizon. A storm was brewing.

"Sleep late," Ryan had suggested last night. Fat chance.
Knowing his style, she knew he was going to expect answers
to his questions. She'd worried all night long, her eyes popping open every hour or so. At dawn, she had finally given
up and crawled bleary-eyed out of bed.

She sighed, rubbing her forehead. To leave or to stay. That
was the question that plagued her now. She hadn't figured out
how she was going to tell him what he wanted to know without bringing up Daniel. She simply didn't want to talk to Ryan
about Daniel.

And speaking of her son...she was going to catch it from
him, as well. But that would be delayed until she managed to
figure out a way to call him. Sometime during the course of
the next couple of days, she would have to. Once she managed
to locate a phone, of course. Knowing her son as she did, she
could get away without calling him only for so long. A couple
of days and he would be one unhappy camper in Montreal.
She sighed, closing her eyes. Who would have thought Ryan
would choose to live without a telephone? As for Daniel, she
would just have to trust his grandfather to keep him calmed
down.

"And if you manage that, Jem Stanton," she muttered, "you're a miracle worker."

"Talking to yourself?"

Ryan's voice slashed through her thoughts. With the cup halfway to her mouth, Joanna started, splashing coffee on the front of her sweatshirt. "Aaahh..."

"Here, give me that." He reached to take the cup from her as she got up, brushing sand from the seat of her jeans, swiping at the coffee stains on the front of her sweatshirt with disgust. "Did you scald yourself?"

"No, it was lukewarm, anyway."

"Sorry."

She took the cup from him and tossed away the dregs.

"You're up early, aren't you?" he asked.

"Yes. I'm not used to lying around in the mornings."

"That's not the way I remember it."

"A lot of years have passed since then. These days, I'm a complete nineties woman. I have to juggle a lot of things in the course of a day, and lying around doesn't get it done."

She looked at him then and had to catch her breath at the sight of him. He was fresh from a shower, unshaven, his dark hair still uncombed, but slicked away from his face so that he looked like something from the pages of *GQ*. No, not *GQ*. His features were too rugged, too world-weary, stamped with too much experience to liken him to a male model. Joanna realized again that Ryan's incredible blue eyes remained unchanged.

She turned, intending to head back to the cottage when he stopped her. "Walk with me?" he invited, lifting his brows. "I'd like to clear the cobwebs, start with a fresh outlook, as they say. We've got a while before the rain comes, I think."

Joanna hesitated, then setting her cup down on a log half buried in the sand, she fell into step beside him.

Ryan looked at her. "Are you feeling better this morning?"

"Yes." With her eyes on her feet, she matched her strides to his. "I'm sure it was because I was so stressed out over…everything, you know. I never faint. Never. I'm fine now."

"I'm glad to hear it." Ryan crammed his hands deep in the pockets of his Windbreaker. "I went to your room a few minutes ago and found it empty. I thought you had left."

She laughed shortly. "Where would I go?"

"Anywhere away from here. I don't know—your mother's house, Shannon's place?"

"I didn't feel I should worry my mother with this. Shannon agreed. She and Nick decided that I would be safer here. Wilderose Cottage is isolated, it has a security system—"

"Which I haven't bothered to activate," Ryan said dryly.

"Well…" Joanna shrugged. "You asked, and that's the reason I'm here. That, and the fact that Shannon is nine months pregnant and due to deliver any minute. Which is the reason that she couldn't drive me out here. Nick and I refused to let her make the trip just to present my case. If you had a problem letting me stay, I told them I would deal with it."

"By picking up your purse and hauling your cute little ass out of here as fast as you could if I proved inhospitable."

If he was trying to provoke her, he was nearly succeeding. "There was always that option," she said evenly.

"Good thing I'm such a sucker for a cute little—"

She whirled to face him. "Look, you've made it perfectly clear that having me here is a pain. Subjecting me to that kind of insult is overkill. You were right thinking I might have left when you found my room empty this morning. It was the first thought I had. What woman in her right mind would want to stay under those circumstances?"

"A desperate woman?"

She held his look doggedly. "Exactly. But this morning I was wondering if I was *that* desperate."

"Ah, hell, Jo…"

With the wind whipping at her hair, she had to hold the tangled strands that had escaped her French braid. "You know the funny part, Ryan? I was waiting until you woke up, thinking of asking your advice. Crazy, isn't it? I know you must have run into some pretty dicey situations in your career. I figured you might have some advice for me on…on precautions to take, or something. I don't know. I just…'' Still holding on to her hair, she looked out to sea, where the waves were kicking up with a fury. ''I just thought…oh, darn, I don't know what I thought.''

''Never did learn how to swear, did you?''

She closed her eyes without answering, and sighed. Both had stopped. Side by side, they faced the open sea.

''I didn't realize Shannon's baby was due,'' he murmured, watching the fury of the whitecaps. ''Doesn't seem like she could be that far along.''

''She is. You've just lost touch——'' she waved a hand, frowning ''——out here, cut off from your family. From the world. When Shannon told me how long it's been…well, I just found it hard to believe.''

''Why?'' he asked, hurling a flat stone into the churning surf. ''For fifteen years I never took an honest-to-God vacation. Don't you think I deserve one now?''

''Is it a vacation?''

''What else would it be?''

She lifted a shoulder. ''Escape. Denial. Sanctuary. It could be any number of things.''

''Jeez, another shrink. Just what I need.'' He threw another stone with more force.

''Don't worry, I'm not here to bug you. You've heard it all before. On top of that, to hear Shannon tell it, it's like preaching to the hearing impaired.''

''My little sister managed to tell you quite a lot in the time you spent with her yesterday,'' he drawled sarcastically.

''She told me only what she believed I ought to know, considering that I was about to force my company on you for an unlimited stay.''

In the distance, the horizon had disappeared. Sea and sky blended in a vast, gray landscape. Frequent lightning pierced the bleak canvas. "It's okay, Jo," he said quietly. "You can stay as long as you need to. At least, as long as you can put up with my foul temper."

She gave him a quick look, still uncertain. He turned and their eyes met. For a second, a heartbeat, she glimpsed something there that reminded her of the old Ryan. But in a moment, as quick as a flash of lightning, it was gone and he was a brooding, oddly restless stranger again.

Looking toward the horizon, she considered her options, severely limited as they were. She could not afford to refuse his offer to put her up even if she really wanted to. Wilderose Cottage was the nearest thing to a safe haven that she was likely to find. Putting up with her ex-husband would simply be the price she had to pay, she told herself. They were adults. They'd parted amicably all those years ago. More or less. Surely they could coexist peaceably for a couple of weeks— or however long it took.

Dear Lord, don't let it be too long.

Wilderose Cottage. She repeated the name, pictured the inviting coziness of the place, its welcoming warmth. The summer house of the O'Connors was to be her safe haven for the duration of this bizarre time in her life. The dream place of her lonely childhood was to be her sanctuary. The irony of it struck her with a blend of pain and pleasure.

How many of her childhood memories—happy and otherwise—had their beginnings at Wilderose Cottage? She was not a blood relation of the O'Connors, even though Jessica, her mother, had been reared by Patrick and Kathleen O'Connor, Ryan's grandparents. Patrick had given Jessica his name, but from early childhood, Joanna had sensed her mother's deep yearning to be a *real* O'Connor. It seemed a natural thing that Joanna, too, longed for the same connection. So even though she was a welcome guest at the many O'Connor family outings, she had always felt just outside the magic circle. That was why her marriage to Ryan when she was just out of college had been so miraculous. That Ryan, five years her senior, should have noticed her—fallen in love with her!—had been nothing short of a miracle.

It had turned out to be a very short miracle.

With a fierce show of electricity and a loud crack of thunder, the storm moved closer.

"We'd better be heading back," Ryan said, hunching into his Windbreaker. They turned together and, picking up the pace, retraced their footsteps in the sand.

They walked in silence all the way back to the cottage. The large, wraparound porch on the back side faced the ocean. Together, they climbed the stairs. Ryan reached around Joanna for the screen door, then allowed her to enter the porch first. Once they were out of the weather, both seemed reluctant to go inside. The interior of the cottage invited intimacy. Both were wary of that.

"I think I'll get a refill of my coffee," Joanna said, already stepping into the living room. "Can I bring you one?"

"Yeah, that'd be good."

"Black, no sugar, right?"

In the act of shrugging out of his Windbreaker, he gave her a quick look. It had been many years since she'd fixed him a cup of coffee, yet she had remembered how he liked it. He wasn't sure why that pleased him. He nodded. "Black and no sugar."

Tossing the Windbreaker on a chaise longue, he dropped down into a cushioned chair and rubbed a hand over his face. Except for the woman who cleaned the cottage twice a week and the occasional stranger he encountered on his lonely walks along the beach, he hadn't seen or spoken to anybody except the closest members of his family—and them only rarely—since moving into the cottage. After what he'd been through, he wasn't ready to deal with people, certainly not with Joanna. But what the hell choice did he have?

"Here you go," she said quietly, shoving a mug into his line of vision.

"Thanks." He accepted it and took the first taste. Over the

rim, he watched Joanna move across to the chaise and sit down. Her hair was a tangled tawny mess, but on her it looked good. Just as those tight jeans did. She was almost as trim as she'd been at twenty-two, he decided, watching her settle in the corner of the chaise and tuck one leg beneath her. On closer inspection, he realized just what the differences were. The breasts in the oversize sweatshirt were more lushly rounded than before, the curve of her hips ripe rather than sleek. He remembered how beautiful her body had been when he'd first seen her naked. She had been—

He choked on the scalding coffee.

"You okay?" she asked, poised to get up.

"Hot...went down the wrong way," he croaked, waving her away.

She watched him a few seconds, chewing on her lip. "Ryan—"

"Joanna—"

They spoke at once. With a sweep of his hand, Ryan motioned for her to go ahead.

She breathed deeply, looking as though she was about to face a hostile jury. "I know you've got a lot of questions, Ryan."

"To put it mildly."

She shook her head helplessly. "I can't believe I'm mixed up in something like this."

He leaned forward and set his mug on a low glass table. "Let's talk about the dead body first."

"Please—" She rubbed her forehead. "Don't...the person who died, Rico Fellini, was a very dear friend. He—"

"Even though he was smuggling diamonds without your knowledge and consent in a business he owned jointly with you?"

"He did it for the money. He—"

"Don't they all?" Ryan interjected cynically.

"He did it so Sammy wouldn't be saddled with a crushing debt after he died."

Ryan looked confused. "He knew he was going to die?"

"Yes. No, he was sick. He had cancer. He also had a lot of medical bills, and Sammy, his friend, was going to have to pay them," she explained patiently. "He didn't intend to drag anybody else into this."

"They never do."

"He simply got into something that turned out to be more than he bargained for."

Ryan frowned and looked at her narrowly. "You said he didn't intend to drag anybody else into his little sideline," he said as sudden suspicion struck him. "I have that right, don't I, Joanna? It was without your knowledge and consent?"

"Of course," she snapped. "The moment I found the diamonds, I went straight to his house and demanded an explanation."

"And was told he did it for love." At her expression, he shrugged. "Or whatever."

"I'm not judging Rico and you shouldn't, either," she told him stonily. "But whatever his reasons, I think he was murdered because he tried to stop. At least, that's what he promised me he intended to do. He was going to tell them the shipment that I opened by mistake was the last one, but I don't think they were willing to go along with that."

"Maybe he tried to help himself to some of the ice."

She looked at him. "I don't expect you to believe this, but he wouldn't do that."

"Let me reserve judgment on that one," he said dryly.

She set her coffee aside carefully. "The police think Rico's death was a suicide...because he was sick...but I think he was murdered."

Inside, his stomach was in a knot. From the moment Joanna had mentioned a body, he had been preparing himself for a rerun of his nightmare. He'd spent the night trying to recall exactly what he'd dreamed, but as he did with all his nighttime visions, he had buried this one deep in his subconscious. Especially this one, because Joanna had played a starring role.

"How did he die?" he asked. He made his tone casual, almost indifferent, but inside he was a mass of screaming nerves. Because he knew. *He knew.*

"In his garage. The car exhaust, you know? Carbon mon—"

"Yeah, yeah. Carbon monoxide poisoning." He got up abruptly and walked the length of the screen porch until he reached the corner. Standing with his palms flat in his back pockets, he stared out at the storm, now in full-fledged fury. Rain came down in torrents. The force of the wind had bent the palm trees into bowlike shapes, their long, green branches lashing wildly in the rain.

"You'd better go inside," he told Joanna as she came up to him. She looked anxiously at the havoc being visited on the landscape.

"Yes, we'll be soaked if we stay out here." She started back to the door. "You're coming, too, aren't you?" she asked, looking at him over her shoulder.

"In a minute."

"Ryan—" She flinched at a flash of lightning followed by a mighty boom. When he didn't move, she faced him, her hands on her hips. "Come inside, this is ridiculous!"

With an impatient grimace, he swung away from the screen, swept up his Windbreaker and followed her into the house. The moment the door closed behind them, she lit into him. "What is it with you?" she demanded angrily. "Standing there with no protection, you're a prime target to be struck by lightning. Do you know how many people are killed that way each year? It's not a rare thing, whether you know it or not, Ryan."

"Is this what I've got to look forward to while you're staying here?" he countered, stepping toward her so that she backed hastily up against the edge of the bar. "I've managed to survive without a nanny for this long. I don't need anybody telling me to get in out of the rain."

"That was not just rain. It was lightning."

"Whatever," he muttered, turning away as he caught the familiar scent of her.

"That's it, isn't it?" she said suddenly, moving up beside him. "You don't care if you put yourself in harm's way, do you, Ryan?"

She waited a few minutes, hoping he would talk to her, but if his stony expression was any clue, she would wait a long time. So far, they had been tiptoeing all around the reason why he was holed up on the island, his career on hold, his door closed to family and friends. Sighing, she decided they might as well clear the air now. If they were going to coexist for the next few weeks, she didn't see how they could keep up the charade that he was here for a vacation.

"I was sorry to hear about Pete Mann, Ryan," she said quietly.

"Yeah. Me, too."

"He was a nice person," she said, glancing at him. "A gentleman, very kind. I liked him."

She sensed his tension, yet there was nothing to be read in his expression that she could see. "Everybody liked him," Ryan said.

"He had a great sense of humor. He always said it was a good thing, because—"

"Because he was so ugly, yeah."

"He wasn't ugly," she said softly. "Far from it. He used to call when he was in Chicago. We'd have dinner."

"Yeah," he said, rigid with repressed emotion.

"We missed him after—"

"We? Who's we?" He turned then and looked at her, shifting the focus of their conversation from Pete. "I just assumed you never remarried after Stanton died. Stupid, I guess, since you're a beautiful woman."

"I didn't. I'm not married."

"Then who's we?"

She took a deep breath. "Rico, Sammy, friends, family." *Daniel.* The wind seemed to turn chilly suddenly. Only after she wrapped her arms around herself did she notice that Ryan was positioned the same way. If body language meant anything, she thought, they were each armored against the other. Or braced for something they might hear from the other that would...hurt?

Not that. Never that.

Joanna knew Ryan was aware that she and David had had a child. She didn't know whether it meant anything that he still hadn't mentioned Daniel. Perhaps it was logical, since she had wanted a child more than anything when she'd been married to Ryan and he hadn't been interested. The last thing on his agenda had been a child. Especially her child.

"How about breakfast?" he asked suddenly. "Are you hungry?"

So much for any meaningful dialogue about Pete Mann or anything else. "It's late," she said, glancing at the clock on the wall. "It's past noon. Why don't I fix us a sandwich or something? You do have food on hand, don't you?"

"Yeah, the woman who cleans twice a week brings stuff in." He shrugged, then pushed his hands into his pockets. "I leave her a list and some cash and she does the rest."

Because she'd done nothing but criticize him since getting here, Joanna bit off the response she could have made about a man who didn't even leave his house to buy food. Or a newspaper to keep up with the goings-on in a world that had once meant everything to him. Until now, she hadn't really believed that Ryan could have become so reclusive. But if he relied on hired help to buy his groceries...

"Convenient," she murmured, heading into the kitchen. This was going to take some getting used to. She didn't realize he had followed her until he spoke.

"Everything's on hand," he told her, taking a seat at the bar to watch her work. "Just help yourself."

"Anything you'd like especially?" she asked dryly.

"Surprise me," he said, a smile playing around his mouth. He had a beautiful mouth, wide with a full bottom lip, teeth white and even. It was a sensual mouth. She had seen it in her dreams for a long, long time after—

"Ham and swiss on rye," she said, closing the door to the refrigerator with her hip. She tossed the two bags from a supermarket deli onto the counter and reached for a knife. "Not very original, but quick. Heavy on the mustard, no lettuce, pickle on the side, right?"

"Right," he murmured, his eyes on her every move.

Quickly Joanna put the sandwiches together. In the pantry where the bread was stored, she found some tortilla chips. She poured some into a big bowl and rooted around in the refrigerator until she found piquanté sauce. "How's this?" she asked, pushing the plate toward him.

Ryan thanked her and bit into the sandwich. "Some things haven't changed," he said after a moment, then popped a crisp chip into his mouth. "You still know your way around a kitchen."

With her own sandwich still untouched, she shrugged. "There's nothing very challenging about putting together a sandwich and dumping chips into a bowl. But if you mean I do it efficiently, then I suppose I haven't changed much. I'm still as domesticated as ever."

"You were always more comfortable around the house than me," Ryan said, biting into a dill pickle spear.

"What can I say?"

"That was a compliment."

She made a small, derisive sound. "You never used to consider my domesticity so attractive."

He put his sandwich down and looked directly at her. "I considered everything about you attractive, Joanna."

"Funny how different my memories are from yours," she said with a touch of long-buried bitterness. "What about my tiresome habit of nagging you to spend more time at home and less time jaunting around the globe?"

"You had a right to demand more time with me. I shouldn't have—"

"Married me at all?"

"Don't put words in my mouth, Jo," he said quietly, both hands resting beside his plate. "I started to say that I shouldn't have expected my wife to be satisfied with a part-time marriage. I should have thought of that before asking you to marry me."

"Why did you?" Joanna asked quietly, looking at him. "I've always wondered about that." She pushed her plate aside. Her appetite had vanished.

"Come on, Jo. You know why we got married."

"No, I thought I did at the time, but I'd like to hear it from you now."

"We got married because we were crazy about each other." Sliding off the stool, he picked up his plate and walked to the sink, dumping it with a loud clatter. "At least, I thought the feeling was mutual. Later on when you were so eager to call it quits, I did wonder if I'd imagined what we had together."

"I wasn't eager to end our marriage," Joanna said, stung that he would accuse her of having no staying power when it had been Ryan who'd jumped at the chance to have his freedom. "I tried everything I knew to save it. Which was pretty difficult when most of our communicating was done long distance."

He made a tense movement with his shoulders. "As I said, a lot of the problems we had were my fault. I admit that. I should have considered how hard it would be to keep love alive when I had to be gone so much of the time."

"That *was* the problem, Ryan," she told him flatly. "Your career came before our marriage. You needed that more than you needed what we had together."

He turned and looked at her. "You're wrong about that, Jo. But it was too late when I figured it out."

Joanna's heart was beating hard. She wasn't certain she knew what he was saying, but she did know that she wasn't ready to examine the problems they'd faced when they were married. She'd come here because she had no other place to go. She hadn't reckoned on rehashing who and what went wrong so long ago. Too long ago. She had honestly thought she would die when she knew for certain that she would not grow old with Ryan O'Connor. That she wouldn't have his children. Live in a house they'd built together. Share in the "for better or worse, in sickness and health...until death," as they'd vowed. No, God, no, she hadn't come here to get pulled into that misery again.

She busied herself gathering up her own dirty dishes and carried them to the sink. She was very careful to steer a wide path around Ryan. Clearing her throat, she spoke nervously. "Just as I'm not used to sleeping late, I'm also not used to doing nothing. I wish I'd brought my art supplies with me, then at least I could paint."

"Paint." Ryan had wandered back to the windows, watching broodingly as the storm unleashed its full fury. He turned with an odd softness in his expression. "Remember how you used to fill a sketch pad a week with those funny-looking little sketches?"

"For the past twelve years, I've made a decent living with those 'funny-looking little sketches,'" she told him, turning her back on him to clear away the things from their lunch.

"Hey, I didn't mean that the way it sounded," Ryan said, walking quickly to her side. He touched her arm, and she immediately shrugged him off. "Jo...Jo, look at me." When she refused, he sighed. "That came out wrong, Jo. Your talent was never in question. It was your belief in yourself."

"Well, I believe in myself now." He was right, of course. She hadn't believed in herself in those days. She pulled open the dishwasher and began loading plates, cups and utensils inside, intensely aware of him and the uncanny way he had of looking deep inside her.

"Do you remember how mad you got when I sent some of your sketches to a guy I knew who had a connection?" Propped against the counter, Ryan looked at his feet and shook his head. "Holy Hannah, you were so mad I thought you were going to set fire to my bed with me in it."

"You had no right," she said, recalling the incident with searing clarity. Her art was hers. Hers alone. Ryan had had his job as a featured journalist for a national news magazine. He was well respected, his successes in those days coming fast and furious. She herself had felt almost dazzled by Ryan, strangely disconnected from him in spite of the fact that they were married. But she did have her art and she had jealously guarded it. When she had learned what Ryan had done, she had felt almost violated. It had only been after their divorce that she had actively—fiercely—pursued a career as an illustrator of children's books. So insecure had she been in those years that she had been surprised by her success.

"I know how well you're selling now," he said, watching her scour a spot of mustard from the countertop. "I have all your books."

She stared at him, astonished.

"So you didn't need me after all, did you?" He was smiling slightly.

When she managed to find her voice, she said, "Not for that."

A moment of time passed. His smile faded. "What did you need me for, Joanna?"

Love, laughter, warmth, a connection with another person to make me feel I really did have a special place, that I wasn't just a shadow in the mist. Since Ryan was the last person she wanted to know the secrets of her heart, she decided it was time to end this discussion. "Look, Ryan, all of this is so much water under the bridge, isn't it? I don't see much purpose in dissecting what happened fifteen years ago. It's over and done with. We both made mistakes, we agree on that. So..." She gave him a bright look. "Since I won't be able to while away the hours painting, I'd like to explore the attic if you don't mind."

"The attic?" he repeated, confused.

She nodded. "You don't remember those long, rainy afternoons spent clumping around in the attic when we were kids?"

He thought for a moment, then gave a short laugh. "I do, now that you mention it. But I don't have any particular inclination to do it again." He shook his head. "There's nothing of any value up there...is there?"

"Only memories," she said softly.

He pushed away from the counter, half smiling, his gaze fixed on her. It was clear to Joanna that his own memories were nothing he cared to revisit. With a lift of his eyebrows and a casual wave of his hand, he motioned her toward the stairs. "Be my guest."

CHAPTER FOUR

JOANNA ESCAPED to the attic with relief. So far, every encounter with Ryan had left her shaken. She had not expected to be talking so frankly about their shared past. Most of the memories of her marriage to Ryan had been buried and forgotten. Well, almost forgotten. It was disturbing to have them dragged out like so many dusty keepsakes.

Her eye fell on a box of sailing trophies marked with the names of both Ryan and his brother, Will. Sailing had been their passion, she recalled, and hers as well. But the times were rare when they had allowed her to sail with them. There were some privileges a mere girl was allowed only occasionally.

She held up a silver cup, squinting through the tarnish to read the inscription. Sea Island Regatta. She remembered that day well. Ryan and Will had beaten out the competition handily. They had sailed through the finish line smiling, tanned, rumpled and triumphant. And so handsome that it had stolen Joanna's breath away just to look at them. But of course her attention had been focused on Ryan. It had been in a shower of celebratory champagne that he had caught her up and kissed her soundly. Until that moment, her love had been her own well-guarded secret, the stuff of fantasies. She replaced the cup and shoved the box back where she found it. Fantasies, she had learned, died hard.

She turned swiftly and her elbow caught on a stack of books, sending them crashing to the floor. Journals, she realized, studying the faded covers. Curious, she opened one and stared at the scrawled signature on the first page. Cameron

O'Connor. Seoul, Korea. 1953. Sinking slowly to the floor, she scanned the first few lines. She was well aware of Ryan's father's reputation, but she hadn't realized he had documented his experiences in a journal. In several journals, she thought, glancing at the bookcase.

Dust flew as she picked up the fallen volumes and stacked them back into the old bookcase. Obviously no one had handled the journals lately. Holed up here for months, how had Ryan managed to resist reading his father's memoirs?

Her own fascination for Ryan's family was as strong as ever. She had been fifteen years old when Cameron O'Connor was killed in an airplane crash while doing a feature on Hawaii's volcanoes, but her memories of him were vivid. He was that kind of man. When he did join the O'Connors for one of their get-togethers, more often than not he would have just returned from some far-off destination. He had covered the wars in Korea and in Vietnam, as well as other trouble spots in the cold-war world. His observations were as familiar to Americans as the editorials from their own local journalists. Joanna still shivered with memories of the fall of Saigon as told by Ryan's father. He had barely escaped with his life when he had gone back to get his wife Michelle, Shannon's beautiful French-Vietnamese mother and Ryan's stepmother.

Smiling faintly, Joanna settled back, crossing her legs Indian-fashion, and opened the last of the journals.

SHE MET RYAN COMING UP as she was descending the stairs nearly three hours later. "I was just getting ready to send out a search party," he said. As she drew closer, he reached out and brushed something from her shoulder.

"What is it?" she said, shaking her head with alarm.

"Just a cobweb." He grinned when she shivered and made a face. "Relax, the spider is long gone."

"Ugh!"

"Still scared of creepy-crawlies, huh?"

"Are you still scared of snakes?" she shot back.

He laughed. "Damn right."

She sniffed and started past him.

He eyed the stuff she had in her arms. "What's that?"

"Treasure," she said, letting him see the children's books she had discovered in an old trunk.

He looked them over. "Haven't you already read them?"

Joanna punched him on the arm. "Cute. Yes, I've read them, but I'm going to read them again. For research."

"Research?"

"Yes, I have a contract to illustrate a series of books, and the author asked for something old-fashioned." She showed him the top one. "Some of these are copyrighted in the thirties. I already have some ideas, but I want the books to have an authentic look. These will help a lot."

"Do you think you can concentrate on something like that right now?"

"Yes, oddly enough I usually lose myself in my work, no matter what's going on in my personal life." She thumbed through one of the books. "I just wish I had the materials I need to do some preliminary color sketches. Still, pencil sketches are a start. I can do that."

"Come with me." He was three strides ahead of her when he realized she hadn't moved.

"Come where?"

"To my workshop," he said with exaggerated patience. "What did you think? If I had something more romantic in mind, I would have been more subtle."

She stepped off the bottom stair and began walking with him. "I don't blindly follow anybody anymore until I know where we're heading." She chose to ignore the crack about romance.

"I'll remember that, Miss Care and Caution."

"If I were truly careful and cautious, I wouldn't be in the mess I'm in now."

"You won't get an argument from me on that one." With his hand lightly touching her, Ryan guided her through the house, onto the porch and down the steps to a brick-paved path that led around to the side of the cottage and beyond to the separate buildings that comprised the O'Connor summer place. The rainstorm was spent, leaving everything soaked and glistening in the midday sun. Joanna was transported back in time by the rain-sweet scent of the landscaped grounds. Blossoms on honeysuckle and wild rose were bedraggled, but the heat of the sun released their fragrance. The air was thick with it. Birds had forsaken their shelters; their sounds were a raucous assault on her ears. She wished suddenly that Daniel could be here, that he could see this place, that she could share with him the memories of her own childhood shared with—

She put a brake on her thoughts. Daniel couldn't be here, and there was no point in daydreaming about it.

"Brings back memories, doesn't it?"

She should not be surprised that Ryan had tapped right into her thoughts. Hadn't he always done that? She shrugged and said nothing.

"Damn, the winds must have kicked up more than I thought." Dropping her arm, Ryan strode over to a boathouse, where the door had somehow blown open, exposing a sailboat inside. Through the door, Joanna could see the sleek, trim lines of the boat. Her heart skipped a beat as her eyes fell on the name.

"The *Lady O*," Joanna murmured in disbelief. They'd bought the boat on their honeymoon and named it after her. She remembered her joy in at last becoming an O'Connor, Ryan's lady. His Lady O. That day, she had tasted true happiness.

"I told Will to sell all this stuff off," Ryan muttered, glancing around at the collection of expensive gear required for sailors. His face stern, he bent over and tugged the tarpaulin back into place and retied the rope that had come undone. Then, with the flat of his hand, he slammed the door and gave it a hard tug to be sure it had caught.

"It was a top-of-the-line sailboat," Joanna pointed out coolly. "Maybe Will uses it."

"He hasn't used it or anything else around here since I've been here."

"Which has been six months, not six years," she said dryly. "Did you ever think that maybe he didn't want to intrude on your privacy? Maybe he took you at your word that you didn't want company."

"I told him to sell that damn boat fifteen years ago."

With her fists propped on her hips, Joanna demanded, "Why?"

"For the same reason that I got rid of everything else that reminded me of the stupidest mistake I ever made," he told her savagely. "Now, you made me say it. Are you happy?"

"Why wouldn't I be happy?" she asked of no one in particular. "Old family friend, honored guest, respected ex-wife that I am, how could I not be happy?"

He was silent a long minute or two, then, with a groan, he raked a hand through his hair. "What the hell am I doing?" He dropped his head back, closed his eyes then opened them to look at the sky. "Jo, what the hell are *we* doing?"

"Playing with fire?" She held his eyes only a second or two before her gaze slid away to fix on the stretch of sea that could be seen through the trees.

"I didn't realize there was so much anger bottled up in me, Jo."

"About us, you mean?"

"Yeah. Hell, it's been fifteen years. You'd think—"

"We never worked it out, Ryan. We parted abruptly. You went to Afghanistan and I filed for divorce. It was six months later when you came back. Then, that night—"

"I'll never forget that night." His tone was deep and low and intense, so intense. She darted an uncertain look at him, and her breath stopped at the expression on his face. "I thought we had patched it up," he said. "I thought you'd come to your senses. I thought the divorce was off and our marriage was on again.''

She felt a rush of fury so consuming that for a second she could not speak. "Then why did you get up the next morning and announce you were going to leave again?" she cried.

"It was my job!" Ryan said, his own fury surfacing. "You knew that before you married me, damn it. Besides, as it turned out, you had good ol' Dave Stanton to keep you company!"

"David was my friend, nothing more!"

"Not for long, baby," Ryan said, sneering. "You were married to your 'friend' within three months."

To her horror, she felt tears gathering behind her eyes. She wouldn't cry over this. She couldn't. Pressing a hand to her stomach, she headed blindly away from him. Back to the house. She wouldn't stay here and listen to him turn it all around to make the death of their marriage her fault. She would leave, goddamn him! He thought she hadn't learned to swear? She had. Along with a lot of other things she had been forced to learn when he'd shown her that their marriage would always take second place to his precious career. That *she* would always take second place.

"Jo! Wait up, Jo...please." He caught up with her, reached for her arm, then backed off slightly when she shook free of him. "Look, let's save this talk for another time," he suggested. When she kept on walking, he swore softly. Keeping pace with her, he studied her profile. "I...we..." With a curse, he stopped, and for some reason Joanna couldn't fathom, she did, too. "I don't know what's going down here, Jo. I mean it. You show up on my doorstep and I let you in and it's like I opened more than just the front door. It's like a trunk that's been shoved in a dark room and locked. You lift the lid and wham...all these feelings and pain and resentment are suddenly...exposed." He gazed intently at her. "You know what I mean?"

She shrugged. "Maybe." He had to strain to catch her reply.

He looked away, then back again. "So, how about turning around and heading back to my workshop? There's something there you'll like, I promise you."

"What is it?"

"It's a surprise."

"I need to get some sketching done," she said, not looking at him. She was afraid to look at him.

"First we check out my surprise."

She turned, raising her eyes to his face. "I've been on the receiving end of your surprises before," she said dryly, "and I remember a couple of times both of us would probably like to forget."

"This is not like that overnight camping trip when a lizard got in your sleeping bag."

A spark of humor warmed her eyes. "Or the wine-tasting weekend where you never quite sobered up?"

He raised his eyebrows. "I seem to remember a very giggly partner that weekend."

She laughed reluctantly. "Okay, we were both equally dumb that time." She sighed and turned back toward his workshop. "Oh, what the heck…but just keep in mind that I'm not falling in with every scheme you come up with like I used to."

"Understood."

They had reached the door of his workshop. Pushing it wide, Ryan urged her inside and through the cluttered interior without giving her much of a chance to take in the changes. She was familiar with his hobby, of course. He liked working with wood and he was good at it. She had observed early in their marriage that it was more to Ryan than a creative outlet. While working with his hands, his mind was usually caught up in his next assignment, sorting through his thoughts, exploring facts, examining evidence. During those times, he had had a tendency to shut out everything else, Joanna included.

Looking back, she realized that it had been Ryan's way, nothing more. Every creative individual had his own methods. But as a young bride, she had felt excluded by Ryan's complete immersion in the creative process. Success and some growing up had taught her much. Now she had her own creative process. She guessed she wouldn't feel nearly as neglected and insecure if she were married to a man like Ryan today.

"Come this way," he said, nudging her through his work space to the stairs. "It's up here."

Joanna looked at the winding metal stairs uncertainly. "Michelle's studio?" Michelle O'Connor was an artist. The daughter of a French diplomat in Vietnam and his French-Vietnamese wife, she had married Cameron after a whirlwind courtship just as the war was winding down in Vietnam. She was a gifted painter, trained in Paris. Joanna had been in awe of Michelle all her life.

"My stepmother hasn't been around in a long time," Ryan replied. Curling a hand around her wrist, he pulled her along as he started to climb the stairs.

"Are you suggesting that I should use Michelle's studio while I'm here?" she squeaked.

"Yeah. It's got everything you need, I think." He seemed oblivious to her dismay. At the top of the stairs, he surveyed the room which stretched the whole length of the workshop below. Dropping her wrist, he went around throwing open cabinets, pulling at drawers, raising blinds. A huge drawing board dominated the center of the space. Situated to catch the best natural light from the skylight above, it was an artist's dream. Eyeing the whole layout with her heart in her eyes, Joanna's fingers itched to grab her brushes, to break open tubes of paint and begin right that minute to create the series she'd been commissioned to do. She glanced at Ryan, knowing her eagerness must be written all over her face.

"I wouldn't want to intrude," she murmured.

"My house is your house," Ryan said, propped against a

cabinet that contained more supplies than she could use in a year.

"I don't have any supplies."

"Michelle would be the first to offer what's on hand."

"Are you sure?"

He crossed his arms over his chest. "Michelle lives for art. You're an artist. Ergo, this studio is yours for the duration. She would insist on it."

She smiled at him. "Thanks."

They stood looking at each other for a few seconds. From the open windows, the muted roar of the tide made a peaceful sound. The smell of the sea was salty and nostalgic. There were a lot of things unresolved between them, but just now nothing seemed particularly relevant. It was a moment of perfect communication.

Pushing away from the cabinet, Ryan walked to the stairwell. With a faint smile, he disappeared down the winding steps and left her to her own devices.

JOANNA WORKED with intense concentration until the natural light began to fade. With daylight savings time, she figured it must be late, possibly 8:00 p.m. As she swished paintbrushes in warm soapy water at a small sink, her thoughts turned naturally to Daniel. She was going to have to figure out a way to call him somehow. She also needed to pick up the messages from her answering machine at home. Leaving as abruptly as she had done was bound to make some of her friends curious, others concerned. Really, Ryan should have a phone.

"So, was it a productive day, or what?"

Before turning to answer Ryan, she dropped the washed brushes into a jar and set them beside the sink. "I think so. I've got several sketches started. It helps considerably to be able to add color." She gave him a smile.

He was standing in the stairwell three steps from the top, visible only from the waist up. However he'd occupied his time, it had been dirty work. The sleeves of his denim shirt were rolled up, exposing brown smudges on his hands. Paint, she guessed. Or shellac. He was probably putting the finish on something he'd made. She was curious suddenly.

"How about you? Did you get much done?"

"Come and see."

She followed, descending the metal stairs with a little more caution than Ryan. At the bottom, she saw that he'd made an attempt to straighten some of the clutter. Still, Ryan would never be compulsively neat. The only orderly area was the pegboard where his tools were arranged. She knew how impatient he could be when he was deep into a journalistic endeavor. Woodworking must be the same. If he needed a tool, it would be maddening not to be able to put his hands on it.

Her eyes went directly to the baby cradle in the middle of his worktable. Joanna recognized it instantly. She had spent many hours as a child soaking up Ryan's family heritage. The cradle was copied from a picture in an old family photograph album Kathleen O'Connor had brought from Ireland. It was beautifully crafted, the spindles meticulously turned, sanded as smooth as silk, then stained the color of pale pecans.

"It's beautiful," she murmured, tilting her head to see from another angle. "Just beautiful."

"Careful," he told her, his eyes also on the cradle. "I rubbed the finish on, but it's still tacky in places."

"I recognize it."

He looked at her. "You do?"

"Yes. There's one just like it in an album that used to be in the glass case in Miss Kathleen's study at the big house in Savannah."

"Yeah, I thought Shannon might get a kick out of it. That is, if I can get it to her in time." He gently nudged the cradle with his finger. "From what you tell me, I'm cutting it close."

"Actually, when I saw Shannon two days ago, she told me she'd been experiencing false labor for a couple of weeks and that's usually a pretty good sign. If I'm any judge, the birth of the first O'Connor of this generation is imminent."

"Nick Dalton would probably take exception to calling his firstborn an O'Connor," Ryan said, his eyes on the gently rocking cradle.

"You may be right," Joanna said with a smile. "But any offspring of Patrick and Kathleen will always be an O'Connor to my way of thinking."

"My grandmother would probably agree with you," Ryan said dryly. In the act of wiping stain from his fingers, he paused and looked at her. "You know about these things," he said, studying her face. "After all, you've been there."

"False labor and all," she said.

"You always wanted a baby."

"And you didn't."

"I didn't think the time was right."

"So here you are fifteen years later. Has the time never seemed right?"

"A man needs a wife to be a father."

"Then we agree on something."

"Gee, I'd better make a note of this," Ryan said with heavy sarcasm. "It has to be a milestone."

She turned and faced him squarely. "This is beginning to feel familiar, Ryan. Anytime the conversation turned to babies, I could always count on you getting defensive."

"You mean getting reasonable."

"I mean defensive, negative, as in, no-way, not interested," she said, looking him in the eye.

"Considering the way things turned out, I guess I was right, huh?"

They were squared off again. As she looked at him, the two of them exchanged sudden rueful smiles. Was this the way it was destined to be between them forever? she wondered. Could they never discuss the failure of their marriage without nearly coming to blows? And why did they even need to discuss it? It was over and done with, a part of their past that neither wanted to think about ever again.

"Tell me about your son, Daniel," Ryan said after a moment.

They were the words she had hoped he wouldn't speak. She glanced down at one of the children's books she'd brought with her, then set it down carefully. "What do you want to know?"

"He would be...let's see now...fourteen years old, right?"

"Yes."

"Where is he?"

"He's with his grandfather in Canada—Montreal."

"David's people?"

"Actually, there's just one person. Emily Stanton died about two years ago. David had no other relatives." With her eyes on the old-fashioned book, she turned a page idly. "I wasn't aware that you even knew Daniel's name."

"Pete and my mother kept me informed," he said. "And I used to kill a lot of time at the office of the *Sentinel* when I was in Savannah. Your mother's office there was practically papered in pictures of you and her grandson."

Joanna shrugged. "She's a doting grandmother, what can I say?"

"I don't know what you could say, but I've often wondered why you don't visit."

"We see my mother at least four times a year."

"But never here in Savannah."

"My memories of Savannah aren't particularly happy."

"That's not the impression I got from your reaction to the junk in the attic."

"I was just passing the time, Ryan," she said quietly.

He leaned against his worktable, arms crossed against his chest. "It didn't seem that casual."

"I can't deny that I've always thought of Wilderose Cottage as a special place." She turned another fragile page of the little book. "You knew that when we married."

"Yeah. Sometimes I wondered if you married me just to become an O'Connor."

"The only way to become an O'Connor is to be born into the family," she said stiffly. "From the outset, I was outside the magic circle."

He frowned. "There was no magic circle, Jo."

"I know that now," she said with a slight smile, "but most of my childhood and during the time we were together, I believed that there was something special and wonderful about being an O'Connor. I wanted to be part of that. I *longed* to be part of that."

"You make it sound like some sort of dynasty," he said with a perplexed laugh.

"To me, at the time, I suppose it was."

"That's ridiculous, Jo."

She shook her head. "I know. At least, now I know. But back then it didn't seem ridiculous. If you remember, I lost my father when I was eight years old. From that time, it seemed natural to turn to the O'Connors to satisfy my yearning for a family and…oh, a sense of belonging, of continuity, I guess. After all, my mother had been reared by Patrick and Kathleen. Patrick was her stepfather before he married Kathleen, you know. Maybe I picked up on some unspoken needs of hers."

She looked up and found Ryan studying her with an odd expression. "Not having a clue about all this 'way back when,' I must have seemed pretty insensitive," he said slowly.

"Not really. You were all caught up in your own insecurities. I can see that now."

"My own— How so?"

"Well, I think you were obsessed with trying to make a name for yourself as a journalist separate and apart from your father's. It's pretty common for the children of famous people to seek their own success. I recall that it got a little irritating for your name always to be linked with Cameron's."

"It was frustrating being constantly compared to him, too," Ryan agreed, "no matter what I did or how good I was. Seems I could never measure up in the eyes of his adoring public."

Joanna smiled. "That's the same thing Cameron said when he was a young journalist and the public compared him to his famous mother."

Ryan gave her a surprised look. "How do you know that?"

"From Cameron himself. His journals are in a cabinet in the attic."

"I knew they were up there," Ryan said, rubbing the back of his neck. "I've just never felt...compelled to read them."

"You should sometime. They make fascinating reading. You both have a lot in common."

"I've definitely heard that before."

"I'm not talking about the fact that you share the same profession," she told him. "You might learn some things that surprise you. Your father's experiences weren't all guts-and-glory successes. In fact—"

She hesitated and Ryan looked at her curiously. "In fact, what?"

"I think your father's secrets are something you should discover for yourself," she told him. Gathering up the book, she turned away and started toward the door. She stopped suddenly and looked back at him. "I just realized that I probably should have asked permission to read Cameron's journals. Do you mind?"

"Of course not. He would be the first to offer. He liked you." Ryan lifted the cradle from the worktable and set it on a shelf near the window to dry. With a turpentine rag, he removed most of the stain from his hands, then tossed the rag into a bin beside the door before opening it and going out with Joanna.

"Want to hear something funny?" he asked as they walked toward the house.

"What?"

"He once told me that as soon as you grew up, I should marry you."

It gave her a warm glow to think that Ryan's father had liked her that much, but her joy was dimmed when she thought how disappointed he would have been if he had lived to see the disaster they had made of marriage to each other.

"No comment?" he asked, bending a little as they walked along so that he could see her face.

"Only that perhaps you should have taken his advice and waited until I grew up."

It was a second before he laughed out loud. The sound was infectious, and Joanna laughed with him. She caught the scent of him, mixed with the smell of the sea. The moment was sweet. It made her heart ache a little for what might have been. With a sigh, she realized that there was something about Ryan that still made her heart beat a little faster.

"You never used to have much of a sense of humor about yourself," he said, still chuckling.

"Look who's talking."

"Yeah, I'm still pretty touchy when I think somebody's pulling my strings."

She sent him a quick, almost flirtatious look. "Some things never change, huh?"

"They do, actually, no matter how we resist." His smile faded. "I've had to grow a tougher skin in the past year or so."

"Are you talking about Pete's death?"

"Yeah."

"You never cared much what anybody said about you in the past," she said, casting him a thoughtful look. "A tough shell is something reporters have to have right along with a gift for words."

"A tough shell," he repeated with a short laugh. "Funny thing is, I discovered it was just that—a shell. Underneath I wasn't as tough as I thought I was."

"Nobody is when they lose someone they love."

"Yeah." Ryan pushed his hands deep into his pockets and squinted toward the sea, where a magnificent sunset had turned the sky into a wild burst of scarlet and gold.

After a moment, Joanna said hesitantly, "If you want to talk about it, Ryan—"

His breath left him in a rush. "God, how did we get on this!" he exclaimed suddenly. "I came here to forget that day, and I was doing pretty good until—"

Stopped in the middle of the walk, she speared him with a look. "Until I showed up?"

"You want the truth? Yeah, until you showed up."

"You were doing pretty good, huh?"

"I think so."

"Turning into a recluse, shunning your family, worrying the people who love you to death, trashing your career. Yeah, right. Heavens, I don't know why anybody would think otherwise."

"You know, that's always been one of your problems, Jo. You're one sarcastic female." He conjured up a condescending smile. "You may not see this, but you aren't in much of a position to lecture me about how to live. Your own circumstances leave a lot to be desired, if you ask me."

"My circumstances are a result of things beyond my control," she returned hotly, her angry eyes locked with his. "Whereas *you* can walk out of here any time the spirit moves you and not have a worry in the world."

"Yeah, sure," he muttered, looking beyond her at the sunset. Oddly, its beauty now seemed to mock him. What was he doing, fighting with Joanna? He was a bastard. She hadn't chosen her circumstances.

And you have.

The sneaky little voice that sometimes plagued him was clearly audible now. In moments of bleak honesty, he admitted that holing up on an island and rejecting the rest of the world, friends and enemies alike, was the coward's way out. But it didn't help in the midnight hours. It was then that demons came out to taunt him and ghosts appeared to haunt him. How could he find the words to confide something like that to Jo? To anybody?

"Dinner's in the oven," he said, almost mumbling the words. "Frozen something."

"Fine," she snapped, turning on her heel to get away from him. "I'm not picky."

"It's timed," he said, watching her take the steps with a fury that he'd stirred in her. "I'm going for a jog on the beach. You don't have to wait."

"Don't worry, I won't."

CHAPTER FIVE

WHEN HE GOT UP the next morning, she was gone.

With the exception of maid service and a rare appearance from his grandmother, whom he dared not offend, Ryan had spent the past six months living his life answering to no one. Until Joanna showed up, he'd risen when he pleased. At night, when he finally fell into an exhausted sleep—or occasionally, one induced by too much alcohol—it was at a time that *he* chose, no one else. He ate when and if he got hungry. He showered only if it suited him. There was no one to please but himself.

But all that was before Joanna came.

Half awake, surrounded by deafening silence, he reflected on the fact that only two days had passed since she'd shattered his solitude. But he knew she was gone. The house was more than silent; it was empty. Something stirred deep in his gut, then spread through him with the speed of quicksilver. Concern, disbelief, panic.

She couldn't have left. They didn't know who was mixed up in that mess back in Chicago, and until they found out, she was a woman in jeopardy. They'd already killed her business partner. If she was headed back there, didn't she know they wouldn't hesitate to kill her, too?

In the doorway of her empty bedroom, Ryan anxiously rubbed a hand over his face. It was his fault, damn his big mouth. His vicious temper. He shouldn't have said half of what he did last night. Wouldn't have said it if she hadn't hit a nerve by bringing up Pete's death. When he realized where the conversation was going, he had felt a rising sense of panic. He'd grabbed randomly at a topic, any topic, just to veer away from the carnage their dialogue might unearth.

Pushing away from the door, he strode through the house—noticeably lonely and still without her. Without the signs he now associated with her. In the bathroom the fragrance of her special soap and feminine froufrous was conspicuously absent. The kitchen was sterile without the smell of coffee brewing, as it had been the mornings since she'd arrived. He shoved the door open to scan the empty yard and beyond to the wide stretch of deserted beachfront. Nothing moved.

How had she managed it? Yesterday, while she was in the studio, he had driven her rental car to the 7-Eleven and called to have it picked up. Muttering a string of curses, he went back to his bedroom, peeling off his shorts and tossing them aside. Without wheels, she couldn't be off the island yet. She hadn't been gone long enough to get much farther than—

Damn it! He didn't know how far she could have gone. What if she'd left in the middle of the night? He yanked out clean underwear and had it on within seconds, and his jeans, too. He reached blindly for a shirt, pulled it over his head, then thrust his feet into moccasins. He was searching for his wallet—and cursing—when he heard the sound of the front door.

He met her in the hall. One look at him and she stopped dead in her tracks.

"Where the hell have you been?" By some miracle of self-control, the words came out softly. Very softly.

"I needed to make a phone call."

"You needed to make a phone call."

"That's what I said, isn't it?" She pulled her T-shirt away from her midriff, where it clung, and blew a strand of her untidy hair out of her eyes. She was flushed and winded and, to Ryan, sexy as hell. "You don't have a telephone, so I jogged to the convenience store about a mile from here."

"You jogged—"

She released a gusty sigh. "Are you going to repeat everything I say, Ryan? I jogged a mile to make a phone call. Is there some law against that?"

"Only one rooted in common sense."

Her hands went to her hips. "What is that supposed to mean?"

"I can't believe you're naive enough to just sashay out of here in broad daylight, inviting anybody who might have followed you—"

"Followed me? I flew in from Chicago, Ryan."

"Oh? And how did you buy your ticket?"

Her expression changed. "With a credit card."

He turned from her, rolling his eyes. "Don't tell me, let me guess. The credit card was in your name."

"Of course, who else—"

"Making it almost too easy for anybody who might be interested to know your destination."

She was silent for a few seconds. "I guess I should have thought of that."

His heartbeat had slowed to almost normal. "Damn right you should have. You don't know for sure what you're dealing with here. You felt scared enough to look for a safe hiding place, but it won't be safe for long if you dart out to make phone calls in plain sight of the whole world."

"I'll remember that."

Now that he had himself under control, he contemplated her for a moment in silence. Once again, her tawny hair was confined in a French braid that had worked loose enough to free the baby-soft curls around her face. Even sweaty and disheveled, she was as pretty as the June morning. He thought suddenly of the petal softness of the wild roses on the cottage grounds. Joanna had the same air of delicacy, yet there was a hint of strength in the line of her jaw, in the directness of her gaze. At the base of her throat a small pulse beat. He had the insane urge to lean forward and put his mouth to it.

"Who did you call?" he asked after clearing his throat loudly.

Hesitant, she chewed her lower lip. "Friends," she said after a moment, then added, "my son."

He frowned, wondering about the friends. One special friend? A man? Was there a man in Joanna's life?

"I just needed to touch base," she said. "I left abruptly, you know."

"You didn't even tell Daniel where you were going?"

She glanced at him quickly. "Not exactly."

"And now you're worried about him?"

"I...maybe...I'm not sure." She left him to head into the kitchen and start brewing coffee. When she finished, she turned from the gurgling sounds of the percolator and leaned against the counter. "I wasn't able to reach him. I got Jem's answering machine instead, so I had to leave a message."

Ryan's expression narrowed. "I assume you didn't say where you were."

"No, just that I was between stops and as soon as I reached my hotel, I would call again. I neglected to say which hotel."

"It bothers you that there was no answer?"

"Yes, although it's possible that they're fishing or something like that." She paused, looking troubled. "It bothers me more to lie to my son."

"It's for his own good."

She gave a short laugh. "It's obvious you aren't a parent. No kid in the world accepts that excuse, no matter how compelling the reason might be."

With a grunt, he shifted position, his eyes following her as she went to the sink for a drink of water. She was in good shape, he thought. Her skin glowed from the run and her eyes were bright and clear. He liked looking at her. "He likes to fish?"

"Daniel? He loves to fish." She smiled, and the concern that had etched a little line between her brows cleared. "He's a nut about fishing."

"Canada has some prime spots, that's for sure."

An electronic timer signaled that the coffee was ready. Still smiling, Joanna reached for the decanter and poured two cups. "Sounds like you're still as avid a fisherman as ever."

Ryan took the coffee. "It's the best sport in the world, bar none."

"Then you and Daniel would get along just fine."

He grunted, noncommittal. He hadn't figured out yet why he shied away from talking about her son. Maybe he didn't like the idea of David Stanton giving her the child that he'd denied her when they'd been married.

Joanna had wandered to the breakfast nook nestled in a deep bay window and curled up, nursing her coffee between both hands. She sat watching the surf, her amber eyes clouding up again with worry. Ryan went over and dropped down close behind her on the cushioned bench. Spreading his legs wide, he rested his own coffee mug on one thigh. With his eyes on her profile, he said, "It scared the hell out of me when I woke up and found you gone, Jo."

"I'm sorry, I didn't think. Like I said, I'll be more careful from now on."

"I've got a foul temper, or so I've been told. My first thought was that you'd decided you'd rather take your chances elsewhere than put up with me."

From where he was sitting, Ryan could just see a tiny movement of her cheek as she smiled. "I considered it."

The feeling that rose in him was pure, unadulterated relief. He was relieved that she wasn't going to leave him.

Leave him?

That was an odd way to put it. He studied the swirls in his coffee for a moment. Even if Joanna chose some other option to cope with this crazy situation she'd found herself in, it wouldn't be like *leaving* him, for Pete's sake. You had to *be* with somebody before you could leave them. And they were nothing to each other anymore. Just friends, uneasy ones at that. If she did leave, there would be nothing personal in it.

This time. And if she was going to stay, they should have an understanding about her boundaries. He set his coffee down.

"We need to set some ground rules, Jo."

After a brief hesitation, she turned to look at him. "What kind of ground rules?"

"I've been thinking about your situation. We can only guess about what really happened to your friend Rico. Maybe he was murdered, maybe not, but to be on the safe side, let's say he was. You can't know whether or not he told the killer that you know about the smuggling operation. Again, let's assume he did, which means you've got to stay close. If you need to leave for anything, I'll go with you."

The significance of his offer made her blink. "I don't expect you to alter your life-style on my account, Ryan. I never intended to draw you into this mess. You don't—"

"I don't have any choice now," he told her bluntly. "I *am* involved. What kind of jackass would sit back and watch you walk straight into danger and do nothing? If you need to leave for any reason again, just tell me."

After a moment, Joanna nodded and murmured, "Okay, if you think—"

"I do think." He stood up, holding her gaze. "After today there won't be any reason to leave here to make a phone call. I've already arranged for the line to be reconnected."

She looked surprised. "When did you do that?"

"Yesterday when you were busy sketching."

She made an exasperated sound. "Well, if you'd bothered to tell me, it would have saved us both some bother."

"If you had mentioned you needed a phone, I would have told you."

"This is ridiculous, Ryan. Without a referee, we could trade barbs until we're both blue in the face. I get the message. I won't leave again without telling you."

He shoved a hand through his hair. "Hell, Jo, I...it's just that when I...I mean, when you—"

"It's okay."

He held her gaze for a moment, then gave a short laugh. "Yeah, well. Anyway, I would have known when you left if the security system had been up and running, but when I tried to reactivate it, I found a problem."

"It doesn't work?"

"No, but it's been off for several months. Don't worry, I've taken care of that, too. Somebody's coming to check it out. Within a day or two it ought to be up and running."

"When will we have a phone?"

"Not today. I pushed, but they wouldn't budge. We'll have to wait another couple of days on that, too."

She got up, her eyes on his face. "Are you sure you're okay with this, Ryan? Stopping for a few days is one thing, but disrupting your life, possibly putting you in harm's way when you have absolutely no reason to get involved..." She shook her head. "I've been thinking that Nick Dalton could probably arrange some kind of protection for me until this is all cleared up. He—"

"He has, Joanna. He did. He sent you here." He reached for his coffee again. "It's settled. That is, if we can manage to get along for the duration."

Joanna thought about that for a few minutes. "It's funny, you know? I don't remember us fighting so much when we were together."

"I don't remember you being so opinionated."

"I was. I just didn't express my opinions. Maybe I should have."

"Yeah, then I would at least have known what you were thinking. A good fight can clear the air."

"When would we have found the time?"

She hit a nerve on that one. "Did we have so little time together?" His expression was thoughtful as he sank onto a stool and hooked one foot on the lowest rung. "When it was over...when you were gone...I was haunted by my memories of all that we'd done together. It was years before I could go to the restaurants we'd liked best." He squinted, thinking back. "Remember that little Italian café on Mulberry Street where they made mouthwatering veal scaloppine?"

"Tony Baccho's."

"Yeah. And the marinara." He kissed his fingers. "Nobody made marinara sauce to compare with Tony's."

"I know what you mean." Joanna gazed beyond him for a moment. "I was in New York a couple of years ago and dropped by." She laughed, without much humor. "I don't know why I went, maybe just to see if the food was as good as I remembered."

The moments ticked softly by as their thoughts took private turns. It had been years since Ryan had allowed himself to remember Joanna with anything except bitterness and anger. It dawned on him suddenly that as long as he hung on to those feelings, he had been in no danger of experiencing anything more painful. Such as the emptiness in his life when he knew she wouldn't be waiting at the end of an assignment. Or the despair he felt knowing someone else had taken his place.

He looked at his ex-wife. "What went wrong, Jo?" he asked quietly.

"I'm not sure. Everything that could go wrong, I suppose." Her smile was soft and tinged with regret. "Maybe we're asking the right questions now, only we're fifteen years too late."

THEY SPENT THE REST of the day working. Joanna gladly climbed the stairs to Michelle's studio and immediately lost herself in the whimsy of her art. From time to time, she heard the whine of Ryan's saw directly below her. She wondered what he was making. While his hands were busy shaping wood, was he planning his next assignment or had he truly given up journalism? Or was he, like her, recalling bits and pieces of their lives together? Wondering what they could have done to change things. Wondering about the "road not traveled." Would her life have been better? Would Ryan's?

She sighed, swishing her brushes in warm, soapy water. No, Ryan had known excitement and travel and a dozen different cultures. He'd seen the wonders of the world and then some. Perhaps he had thought of her from time to time, but she couldn't imagine that he felt too much regret for a failed marriage and the times they might have shared.

Or the child they might have shared.

She veered away from that thought cat-quick. Fumbling a little, she began sorting through the paint tubes she'd used, wiping them so that they could be returned to Michelle's stock. At the sound of voices below, she froze as her stomach clenched in instinctive fear. The only human voices she'd heard since arriving at the cottage were Ryan's and her own. Who was he talking to? Should she hide? Run?

"Jo!" Her heart stumbled as Ryan called up the stairs to her. "We've got company."

She approached the winding stairs cautiously, peeking around the curved steel banister long before she reached bottom. Relief poured through her at the sight of Nick Dalton wearing a grin a yard wide. He looked rumpled and unshaven and very happy.

"Joanna. How ya doin'?"

"Okay, Nick. And you?"

"Fantastic. Couldn't be better."

With a quick look at Ryan, she took the bottom step with less caution and began to smile. "I don't have to ask what brings you here, do I, Daddy?"

Still grinning, Nick self-consciously wrapped a hand around the back of his neck, glancing from Ryan to Joanna. "I guess it shows."

"A little," she teased, sharing a smile with Ryan.

"It's a boy," Ryan told her. "Nicholas O'Connor Dalton."

"Seven pounds, six ounces, all his fingers and toes and red hair to boot," Nick said proudly. "Can you imagine that? He's perfect, fantastic!"

"Congratulations," she said, giving him a warm hug. "How's Shannon?"

"Fine, great," Nick enthused, his joy encompassing everything and everyone. "She did it the old-fashioned way, too. No drugs, nothing. She was incredible. She...she's..."

"Fantastic?" Ryan put in dryly.

Joanna chided him with a look. "And how about you?" she asked Nick. "Giving birth can be...well, an experience."

"Me? Hell, I almost passed out just from watching. Fortunately, it was quick. In fact, we almost had it in the car. The pains—"

"We?" Ryan said, one eyebrow raised.

Nick gave a self-deprecating laugh. "I guess you had to be there, man." He shook his head at the memory and his voice got a little gruff. "It was something. Shannon and I...well, we..." He shrugged, looking sheepishly at both of them. "I guess you had to be there."

"I know the feeling," Joanna told him softly.

"Yeah, I guess you do," Nick said, still smiling. "What do you hear from your son? Is he okay? Montreal, isn't it?"

"I hope he's okay," Joanna said. "I called this morning, but he and his grandpa were out. I'll try again tomorrow." She glanced at Ryan. "Will we have a phone by then?"

"Possibly," Ryan said. "If not, there's always the 7-Eleven."

"You should never have had the phone cut off, Ryan," Nick said. He glanced at Joanna. "Shannon's been after him ever since—"

"Yeah, well, you can tell her I've seen the error of my ways when you give her my felicitations on the birth of my nephew. She can stop nagging me now." The look he sent Joanna was mocking. "Jo's taken over that job."

Joanna opened her mouth to argue, but changed her mind when she saw the interested way Nick was watching them. She began talking before he could put whatever it was he was thinking into words. "Ryan has something for the baby. Wait'll you see it."

From the look in his eye, Nick knew she was steering the conversation away from the two of them. Possibly because of his mellow mood, he let the moment pass and let himself be ushered over to see the gift Ryan had made for his newborn son.

He was pleased and touched when he saw the cradle. Shannon would love the idea that her brother had set aside his depression long enough to make it. Nick left after thanking Ryan, firmly shaking his hand and then giving Joanna a big hug. She watched him go, marveling at the emotion that he seemed unable to hide. As a detective, Nick was hard as nails. She'd recognized that instantly when Shannon had taken her into the police station and introduced her. He didn't look hard today. He looked dazed and happy, just the way a new father should look. She felt a pang somewhere deep inside. Nicholas O'Connor Dalton was a very lucky baby boy.

"WHAT'S THIS?"

"Chicken corn chowder." Joanna turned from the cabinet with her hands full of dishes to find Ryan lifting the lid off the soup pot and sniffing curiously at the contents. "The ingredients to make it were in the freezer. The *bottom* of the freezer."

He grunted and replaced the lid.

"What's the matter? You don't like corn chowder?"

"I like it fine," he said. "I just didn't know there was anything in the freezer except steak."

"That doesn't surprise me." She tossed napkins and silverware on the table. "I had to root beyond a side of beef before I found one skinny chicken and a few frozen veggies. Do you eat anything except steak and eggs?"

"Spaghetti and meatballs occasionally."

"Prepared by the deli and delivered by your housekeeper, no doubt."

He shrugged.

Two spoons hit the table with a clink. "Ryan, do you know how much cholesterol there is in a twelve-ounce steak?"

"Eleven ounces?"

"Cute."

Ryan stood eyeing her silently as she went about readying the table for the meal. After a moment, she huffed out a sigh and stopped, looking at him. "What?"

"You tell me."

"What is that supposed to mean?"

"You're ticked off about something. Ever since Nick left this morning, you've been bitchy as hell." He leaned a little closer, studying her. "Is it a woman thing? I remember—"

"It's not PMS! You know I never—" She stopped, unwilling for the conversation to get personal.

"Then you *are* ticked off."

She rolled her eyes before resuming the task of setting the table.

"I thought you might work it off in your studio, but—"

"Michelle's studio."

"*Your* studio," he repeated firmly. "While you're here, it's yours."

"I wasn't in the studio."

"No?"

"No. I was in the attic."

"Again?"

"You said it was okay."

"It is okay, Jo, but—" He gave her a mystified look. "What's so interesting up there?"

"Just…things." Finished with the table, she went to the stove to check the chowder.

"What things?"

"Old stuff, keepsakes, mementos, books—"

"My father's journals? What's up? You thinking of writing his memoirs?"

"No, but it's a good idea. Why don't you do it?"

"Because I've got some—" He broke off abruptly. "Because it doesn't interest me, that's why. So what other junk did you discover?"

"No junk, although that's apparently the way you think of it."

He was silent for a moment, obviously picking up something in her tone. "You want to fill me in on what you mean by that or do we play twenty questions?"

"I found your things, Ryan."

He was suddenly wary. Joanna thought he looked ready to turn on his heel and walk off. "What things?" he asked.

"Your awards, commendations, photographs, things you collected on your travels, copies of special articles and so on." She stopped and looked at him. "Possessions you once prized, Ryan. I found everything tossed haphazardly in a couple of cardboard boxes like it really was junk."

"You know the old saying, 'One man's junk—'"

"'Is another man's treasure,'" she finished quietly. "I think I understand that old saying better than I ever did before. It upset me when I found all your wonderful things just…just shoved in a corner like so much rubbish, Ryan."

"You don't seem upset," he retorted. "You seem mad."

"Well, maybe I am. The more I see—" She shrugged and sighed. "I guess it just gets to me."

"Nobody asked you to hang around," he said, his tone suddenly cold and hard. "If you don't like what you see, you can always pick out a hotel. There are plenty between here and Chicago."

Deliberately, Joanna replaced the lid on the chowder and looked him in the face. "It won't work this time, Ryan," she said quietly. He simply stared at her. "I'm suddenly recalling why I never had the guts to fight with you. Whenever you felt pushed into a corner, you'd always try to turn the tables on me. As I mentioned before, I've matured somewhat from those days. While I'm here, if you become aggressive and rude I'm not going to fold up and go sulk all by myself. Not that the idea doesn't have some appeal. As much as I'd like to haul out of here and find a nice, safe hotel, there aren't any nice, safe ones. I'm stuck and you're stuck with me."

His blue eyes were cold as glass. "So you're going to spend the days sniping at me over stuff that's none of your business?"

She gave that some thought, then leaned against the table, nodding. "It must seem that way to you, and you're absolutely right. I have no business poking and prying. If you want to reject everything you've achieved, it should be nothing to me."

Even before she stopped talking, he was shaking his head. "You can't even make an apology without sounding judgmental."

"I wasn't apologizing, I was explaining."

"And we're arguing again."

"I wonder why."

"Yeah. Good question." He picked up a cracker and munched on it thoughtfully, studying her the whole time. "I've got an idea."

Joanna was instantly wary. "What kind of an idea?"

"Let's go back to this morning. Even after scaring the hell out of me by disappearing, we managed to get along the rest of the day. What happened?"

"Nick came and told us about the baby."

"Yeah."

"You were surly as a bear after he left."

He shot her a look of instant denial. "Come on."

"It's true. The minute he drove off, you were spoiling for a fight. I can't imagine why. Maybe it's cabin fever or something. Heaven knows, it's about time."

"It's not cabin fever."

"You're admitting his visit made you grouchy?"

"It wasn't his visit."

She frowned. "Then what? Weren't you happy to hear about their baby?"

He walked to the window and stood looking out, his back to her. "It was the way the two of you acted."

"What?"

He turned and looked at her. "You want to know something funny? I was jealous."

"Jealous? Of what?"

"It was as though the baby...his birth...the experience... one you'd both shared...linked you in some way. And I felt excluded. Outside the magic circle, to use your own words."

"There's no magic circle, Ryan, as you told me just yesterday. But having a baby is a special experience, one that changes you forever. One moment you're an individual, and the next, your life is forever linked to another. As Nick said, maybe you have to be there."

"Maybe."

Joanna fell silent, sorting through a jumble of thoughts. The irony of what Ryan was saying hit her hard. When they were married, her need to have a child was one of the problems that had driven a wedge between them. That he should be feeling he'd somehow missed out because of his fatherless state was almost ludicrous.

"It was your choice that we not have a child," she reminded him quietly.

"I know that."

"Your career was more important then."

He was staring through the window again. "I know that, too."

Joanna walked over to stand beside him. "That's why I find it so incredible that you've rejected everything now."

"You don't understand."

She waited a few seconds, wondering whether to speak her thoughts. Ryan had drawn the boundaries clearly with everyone, his family, his editors, his professional associates. By simply being here, she had intruded on his privacy. She studied him from beneath her lashes. His mouth was tight, his jaw clamped. But there was such a look about him. Pain, regret, guilt—she could only guess at it. And all of it sat so heavily upon him. Maybe she would just test the water, then, if he went off like a rocket, she would voluntarily haul herself up to "her studio" and give him the privacy he so valued.

She cleared her throat softly. "This is about Pete, isn't it?"

His face, stern before, was now fierce. "Mind your own business, Jo," he growled, looking straight ahead.

"He wouldn't want you obsessing over this forever, Ryan."

He turned then and looked at her. Joanna gasped a little at the ferocity of his expression. "He—I—I knew him, R-Ryan. He would die if he thought you gave up like this be-because of him."

"Die?" Spoken quietly, the word was even more deadly. "Die, you say? He's already dead, Jo. I can only kill him once."

"You didn't kill him!"

"I killed him!" It was a shout. It cut through her like the lash of a whip. "Can't you get that through your head? It was me. My fault. It wasn't a...a...tragic accident." His mouth twisted. "I orchestrated everything. It was a plan I conceived." He hit his chest with his forefinger. "Me. Nobody else. So when it ended in disaster...in death, Joanna, death— do you hear? When it ended in death, it was my fault."

"I'm sorry." Her apology was almost inaudible.

He turned away. "I need some air."

"Ryan—" But he was already across the floor, wrenching the door wide. She winced as it slammed shut behind him.

So much for testing the water. He hadn't gone up like a rocket exactly. He was more like a time bomb. His feelings about Pete and Pete's death were coiled inside him, ticking away. She shouldn't have intruded. The lines were drawn and she would honor them from now on. Her appetite gone, she turned the burner off under the chowder and left the kitchen. She only hoped Ryan found some peace before he shattered into a thousand pieces.

CHAPTER SIX

FOOL. JERK. Bad-tempered bastard.

Breathing hard, Ryan ran flat-out along the edge of the shore, his thoughts locked in an unceasing internal dialogue. His own words echoed and reechoed in his head, a recording going on and on forever. With every thud of his Reeboks on the wet sand, he cursed himself.

He had no excuse for his rotten reaction to Jo when she mentioned Pete. She wasn't trying to hurt him. Joanna never intentionally set out to hurt anyone. Not even her bastard of an ex-husband. She might have changed in some ways from the time when they were married, but she hadn't changed that much. The clincher was that she was right on target. Pete would hate it if he could see Ryan obsessing over something that could not be undone.

Feeling that his very survival depended upon it, Ryan poured everything he had into a new spurt of energy. But it was as though Pete ran with him.

"Get a life, Ryan. Put it behind you, you big, dumb Irishman."

With his dead partner's voice in his head, he ran as though pursued by Pete's ghost. His heart was beating out of his chest. The muscles in his strained thighs screamed for relief. He slowed down, staggered to a stop, then, with a muffled, anguished cry, fell to the ground.

Rubbing his hands over his face, he ached for oblivion. Or for the healing power of tears. But nothing came. His eyes

were as arid as his spirit. As bleak as the desert where Pete
had died.

God, I'm sorry, Pete. I didn't know—

But of course he had known. He'd known, and in his arrogance he had ignored the knowledge. In his lust to be the
first, the best, the most daring, he had persuaded his partner
to his way of thinking for the sake of a story, and now Pete
was dead.

Drawing in a shuddering breath, he looked around blankly.
He had no idea how far he'd come. The night was moonless
and overcast, as dark as pitch. Fog rolling in from the sea
obscured the distant lights of other islanders. He could see
nothing in the stretch of beach in front of him. His life was
like that, he thought. No matter how he tried, he couldn't see
where to go from here.

JOANNA CAME AWAKE SLOWLY. Frowning, she listened hard
for a moment or two trying to identify the sound that had
disturbed her. On the bedside table, the clock read 2:38. Like
any mother, she thought first of Daniel. But Daniel wasn't
here. The realization brought no comfort. If her son did need
her, how would she know? Rising halfway to her elbows, she
looked around the bedroom.

Catching another sound, she sat all the way up. It could
only be Ryan. With no telephone in the house, who was he
talking to? Concerned without really knowing why, she threw
the bedclothes aside and went to investigate.

Like hers, the door to Ryan's bedroom was ajar. They had
discussed not closing each other off for safety's sake. Her
heart thumped in sudden fear. They had assumed the threat
would be to her, not Ryan. She knew next to nothing about
self-defense. What would she do if—

The sound that Ryan made sent a chill all the way down to
her toes. It wasn't a cry for help, at least not for help from an
intruder. It was a cry wrenched from his soul. From the look
of him, he was in the throes of a nightmare. A terrible night-

mare. Without thinking, she hurried to his bed and reached out to touch him.

He was shaking all over. His skin was cold to the touch and clammy. In the pale light that came from the open door, she could see that he was caught in whatever horror was unfolding in his dream. His face glistened with sweat. Tossing his head restlessly on the pillow, he moaned and muttered broken phrases, unintelligible words, anguished sounds. He cried out suddenly, thrashing wildly as though fending off demons.

"God, it's blood, it's blood! No, Pete, no, no-o-o-o…ah, God, Pete…"

"It's okay, Ryan, it's okay." Shattered by his pain, Joanna murmured soothing, meaningless words, her hands firm on his shoulders. "Wake up, it's just a dream, Ryan."

Fighting off her hands, he sat up abruptly, his gaze wild and unfocused. "Medic!" he cried. "We need a medic here!"

With her hand on his shoulder, Joanna gently shook him. "Wake up, Ryan! It's Joanna. You're at home, at Wilderose Cottage."

He did not hear her. From the look in his eyes, he was thousands of miles away. And what he saw destroyed him. "Pete! No, don't…don't…don't die, please…" Drawing in a shuddering breath, he released it in a long wail of grief and despair that tore through Joanna like a hot knife.

"Ah, Ryan, Ryan, don't…" Helplessly she reached for him, and he turned blindly into her embrace, burying his face in her hair, holding on to her desperately. His chest rose and fell like bellows. His whole body shuddered. To see him like this touched something in Joanna that brought tears to her eyes.

"It's okay, it's okay." Joanna tenderly stroked his hair as he calmed. Compassion and some other emotion swirled through her like warm honey. She sensed when he finally realized that he had been dreaming and her touch was not a part of his fantasies. He made a sound, a heartfelt utterance that was at once relief and pain and pleasure. He moved his head and nuzzled the soft curve of her breast through the silky film of her nightgown, then drew in a deep breath.

She was so warm and soft. That was his first coherent thought. Until that moment he'd been at the mercy of his nightmare and had only sensed the deliverance that had come with her to drive away his demons.

She smelled...womanly. Captivating. Like the sea in the morning. It was heaven to feel her softness, to luxuriate in the compassion that flowed from her heart to his. It was torture to know that there was sweet oblivion to be found in her body if he could just abandon the last shred of his principles. But, God, he wanted to. Needed to. He rubbed his cheek slowly and sensually against her breast and heard the soft rush of her breath as the nipple peaked. Deep in his groin, his own body stirred, tightened, hardened.

Just one kiss. How could that hurt? He pulled the nightgown off her shoulder, baring her breast. His blood heating, his mouth moved to the peaked nub and he kissed it. God, she was sweet. His tongue swirled languidly over smooth, marbled flesh. The fingers of his hand curled around her other breast, plucked gently at the nipple. When he heard her smothered cry, he lifted his head and sought her mouth with his.

The kiss was deep and carnal, and he lost himself in it, loving the taste of her, the feel of her. She was like no one else, no other woman. The response that rose inside him was like nothing else. With both hands tangled in her hair, he held her just where he wanted her, drunk with the feel of her body, the softness of her hair, the erotic pleasure of her mouth.

He thought she might have made a momentary movement of resistance, but everything in him screamed for more, not less. He *couldn't* quit now. It had been—he didn't know, for-ever—since he had even thought of wanting a woman. Had he *ever* wanted a woman the way he wanted Joanna? Pulling her closer, he ground the aching hardness between his legs against that place between hers that was made for him. That belonged to him. As naturally as though the years had never been, Joanna's body fell into the rhythm he set for them. And he knew then that she was not going to stop him.

"God, Joanna, it's good." His breath hot, his lips frantic, he kissed her face, her eyes, her nose, the soft skin at the hollow of her throat.

"Ryan—"

"Let me—" With a swift, decisively masculine movement, he swept the covers to the floor and drew her beneath him. Her nightgown caught and he fumbled with it, shoved it up impatiently, baring her long legs. And then he was at her lips again, kissing her open-mouthed, hungrily, urgently.

He was naked. The thought came distantly to Joanna. She moaned, moving her hands restlessly all over him, delighting in the feel of his skin, his shoulders, his long, rugged torso. But she had always loved touching Ryan. No other man had ever come close to giving her the same thrill, the same deep, sensual satisfaction.

"Ryan..." With his mouth fastened to her breast, his name came out in a rush. Every tug drew from her a soft, pained whimper. The throbbing ache in her womb became more and more urgent. She moved restlessly, thrashing her head and her legs. She cried out when his hand closed over her, then arched to receive him when he delved deeply into her soft woman's flesh. His thumb went unerringly to the tiny kernel of her passion and stroked...stroked. Flushed and panting, she gave herself up to the moment. Then suddenly she was catapulted over the threshold. With a rush of heat and light, her whole body shuddered into a bright, splintering climax.

She came down with Ryan kissing her, showering her with endearments, holding her close, promising her the moon and the stars. She laughed shakily as tears flooded her eyes and overflowed.

"What's funny?" he asked gruffly, nuzzling her ear with his mouth while his other hand was still clenched in her hair.

"I can't believe this."

He smiled against her cheek. "What? That I gave you a climax or that you cried?"

"Both!"

He lifted his head, still smiling, and looked at her. "It's nice to know some things don't change."

"What things?"

"You still burst into tears when you come."

"Ryan—"

"And you're still shy about it." He relaxed, shifting so that his weight was no longer on her, and rested his head beside hers. When he didn't say anything or seem to want to move, she began threading her fingers through his hair. She liked the feel of it. And his skin. And his body close to hers.

"Ryan?"

"Hmm…"

"Are you…I mean, you didn't… Ah, don't you want to…"

He answered with a pained chuckle. "I *do* want. I want like hell, but I don't think you meant for this to happen when you came in here."

"No, but—"

"I'll be okay. Just having you here beside me is…I don't know. I guess I never thought I'd be lucky enough to have you in my bed again."

"It scared me when I heard you cry out. I've never seen anybody in the throes of a horrible nightmare."

With his thumb and forefinger, he rubbed his eyes. "Not a pretty sight, huh?"

"Did I bring it on?" she asked anxiously. "When I brought up Pete's name tonight, your reaction was so—"

"I overreacted, you mean. I was rude and overbearing. I meant to apologize when I got in from running on the beach, but you were already in bed. I'm sorry. You happened to say just the right thing. If he could see me now, Pete would be the first to give me hell."

She heard him out, then drew in a deep breath. "I don't know, Ryan. We're all different. We have to handle things in our own way. Maybe somebody else would have bounced right back, maybe not. But when it comes right down to it, we do finally have to put the bad stuff behind us. We just have to get up and carry on.''

''Somehow.''

''Yes…somehow.'' She turned and gave him a soft smile. Actually, she wanted to give him a kiss, something loving, not sexual. But considering his aroused, unsatisfied state, she didn't. ''You'll get beyond it, Ryan. I know you will.''

With his hand softly stroking the side of her breast, he lay quietly for a few moments. ''I usually have to ride out my nightmares alone.''

She was very still. ''If you want to talk about it…''

''I'd like to forget it.''

''Yes.''

''I *wish* I could forget it.''

What could she say? she wondered, feeling his pain. ''Do you dream about it often?''

He squeezed his eyes shut. ''Only when I sleep.''

''Oh, Ryan…''

''It was my fault, Jo. His blood is on my hands and I can't forget it.'' He brushed idly against the side of her breast, then cupped it as though the feel of her gave him comfort. ''If I hadn't been such an ambitious, arrogant bastard, Pete would be alive today.''

''You can't know that.''

''Yeah, I can. I do.''

Her hand stopped. ''How do you know it?''

''It's a long story.''

Tell me, Ryan. Let me share it. She closed her eyes, waiting. It surprised her how much she wanted him to open up to her.

He shifted then, pulling himself up so that he was above her, propped on the pillows stacked against the headboard. But he didn't let her move away from him when she tried. He tucked her in the curve of his shoulder before settling back. It felt familiar and right somehow, lying in bed in Ryan's arms after making love. Once their best times together had been like this. Ryan was usually mellow after sex. Flushed and tingling, high in the afterglow of a climax, she had been mellow, too. In that mood had come their rare moments of true intimacy.

"We were in the Middle East," Ryan began suddenly. "The country was a disaster. You wouldn't believe the atrocities—a chaotic government, homeless families, hungry children, adolescents, who still should have been playing soccer, recruited to be soldiers. Instead, their childhoods were interrupted, stolen almost before they began so that they could learn to kill and maim."

"It must have been terrible," Joanna murmured.

"*Terrible* is too nice a word. We…Pete and I…had been told by our editor in New York to do whatever it took to highlight the reality of the war, to show what was actually happening to the American public. Shake their apathy. Wake them up, Ed Penrose told us."

"Your editor?"

"Yeah. He's a ruthless tyrant, but he upped circulation of the magazine about twenty percent. Nobody argues with success, right? I wish I could blame Pete's death on him, but—" He shrugged, breathed in deep and slow, then exhaled hard. "No, Ed gave us the assignment, and it was up to Pete and me to make it happen."

Through the open window, the sound of the sea was suddenly melancholy, but Joanna didn't even think of getting up and going back to her own bed. She was exactly where she wanted to be.

"We made it happen all right. I got a message from one of the rebel leaders that he wanted to talk to 'the world.' He needed a TV camera for that, naturally. The news team of O'Connor and Mann definitely had access to TV cameras. He demanded an exclusive interview. Needless to say, he didn't have to twist my arm. The last thing I wanted was other journalists butting in on a scoop like this. I also didn't want any diplomatic red tape to complicate things, so I didn't bother to let the military or the embassy people know that I'd been contacted.''

Joanna felt him tense and lean over, reaching for something on the bedside table. Even in the dark, his hand found the drink he'd been nursing before he fell asleep. Had he been drunk? she wondered. Did he drink every night to ward off the terrors that invaded his dreams?

Ryan replaced the empty glass on the table. "Pete tried to talk me out of it," he said.

"Why? I don't see—"

"It was risky. He knew it and I did, too. Pete was always more cautious than I. He kept my feet on the ground."

"Maybe," Joanna said thoughtfully. "But you were the lightning rod, Ryan. Between the two of you, you were a dynamite team."

He shrugged, unimpressed. "The countryside was infested with rebels. It was hard to tell who was friendly and who wasn't. Some of them hated everything about the United States. About the whole Western world, for that matter. The general—and I use the term loosely—who wanted the interview demanded total secrecy. He claimed he needed the forum to announce something of major importance. If he was just another delusional two-bit rebel, then no harm was done by letting him blow off steam. If he wasn't full of crap, then it could have turned out to be Pulitzer material." He pulled a hand over his face wearily. "I never got the answer to that."

"What happened?"

"It was a setup. They wanted world-class hostages, anybody would do—Americans, Canadians, United Nations peacekeepers—anybody. It just happened that I took the bait."

"If they wanted hostages, why did they kill Pete?"

"They didn't intend to. The whole thing was like a bad movie. I had a bad feeling from the outset. When we reached the rendezvous point, my instincts were screaming. Even before we stopped, the general's flunkies began to converge on the jeep. I yelled at Pete to hold on and turned the jeep around on the spot.

"They began shooting at us." His voice changed, dropped to a soft, almost detached tone. "That's the trouble with unseasoned soldiers. Some of them—the kids mostly—just pointed those damn Uzis at us and let fly. They weren't concerned with taking hostages. If they didn't get us, there were plenty more hungry journalists out there."

"It sounds...horrible," Joanna whispered.

"Yeah, horrible."

"So...so Pete was hit by Uzi fire?"

"I didn't realize it at first. We were a good three miles from the action when my adrenaline settled enough to take a good look at him. When I did, I lost it. God, he was bleeding all over his shirt. He was shot in the leg, too. And he hadn't said a damn word."

"Ryan..." She looked at him through a haze of tears, but he didn't pause. He was back in the desert of a godforsaken country somewhere in the Middle East.

"When it rains, it pours," Ryan said bitterly. "The jeep's radiator had been hit. It had been spewing steam almost from the moment we hauled out of there. The motor finally quit. Pete was bleeding—" He stopped, then went on, his voice shaking a little. "I used everything I could get my hands on to stanch the blood pouring from Pete."

He cleared his throat roughly. "I went a little crazy, I guess." Joanna didn't think he was aware how tightly he held her against him. "I don't know how far we were from the campsite, but I carried him there, anyway. It was too little too late. He was gone long before we made it back."

She rubbed her hand over his chest. Her throat ached with the desire to do more, to say something—anything—that might comfort him. "I'm so sorry," she whispered, knowing how inadequate it must sound.

"You haven't heard the worst."

What could be worse than having your best friend die in your arms?

"I knew it was going to happen."

She frowned. "What?"

"I...had this...premonition."

"Oh, Ryan, don't torture yourself like that. You didn't know anything of the sort. No one could."

"I did."

"You're telling me you knew before it happened that Pete was going to die?"

"Not exactly. I didn't know he would be killed. I didn't know anybody would be killed, but I had a bad feeling. I...it came to me in the middle of the night. Like a dream. I saw blood and violence. The jeep was in my dream. There was smoke, or at least I thought it was smoke, but now I know it was steam...from the radiator. You know how you sometimes dream that you need to run, but your legs won't work? They're mired in quicksand or something? Well, that was part of my dream, too. It was a warning and I ignored it."

"It was coincidence, not a warning."

Ryan shifted again so that he was turned on his side. With his face close to hers, he looked into her eyes. "It wasn't coincidence, Jo, no more than it was coincidence that I dreamed about you."

Her eyes were wide. "You dreamed about me? When?"

"The day you came back."

She stared at him wordlessly.

With his fingers, he brushed the hair away from her cheek and then cupped her face in his hand. "Just like the dream about Pete, I dismissed it. And then morning came and there you were, standing on my doorstep looking scared."

Still speechless, she shook her head.

He gave a soft laugh. "Yeah, I know. Spooky, isn't it?"

"Well—"

"Right."

It was incredible, unbelievable. It couldn't be true, not really. She strained to see the expression on his face, but with the light from the hall behind him, his features were cast in shadow. All she could really see was the shape of him silhouetted in the backlight, broad shoulders, muscled biceps, tapering waist. And she still found him as appealing as the first time she'd seen him naked.

"Did you dream about my son as well?" she asked quietly.

"Daniel?" As always when she mentioned Daniel, there was a subtle tension about him. "No."

Joanna didn't miss his reaction. Just as well, she thought. Things were complicated enough between them. Throwing Daniel into the mix would be playing with fire.

"Jo…" As his thumb feathered over her lips, he looked into her eyes. "Don't go back to your room tonight. Stay here with me, will you?"

For a second, she couldn't speak. Stay with him? She was shocked by how much she longed to do just that.

"Not for sex," he said. Resting his forehead against hers momentarily, he gave a gruff laugh. "Not that I wouldn't like it…love it…but it feels good just having you next to me, just knowing you're close. Not being so goddamn alone. I'd forgotten—" He stopped, pulled away to look at her. "Do you understand what I'm saying?"

Did she understand loneliness? The empty feeling that came in the midnight hours with the knowledge that no one, absolutely no one, was thinking of her in that special way?

"Jo?"

"Yes." Her voice was a whisper.

He cupped her cheek more firmly in his palm. "Which is it? You understand, or you'll stay?"

She closed her eyes the way she used to as a child when she finally found the courage to jump into the deep end of the swimming pool. "Both. Yes to both."

JOANNA RELUCTANTLY SWAM up from the depths of sleep the next morning. Feeling warm and safe, she lay for a moment suspended somewhere in that gray area between wakefulness and slumber. Then when Ryan stirred beside her and pulled her snugly into the warm curve of his body, she remembered everything.

"Don't move," he growled into the nape of her neck. "I'm having a dream and it's too good to quit."

She made a sleepy sound, then stretched so that her legs tangled with his. Ryan groaned, pushing his morning arousal against the softness of her derriere. For a few delicious moments, neither one moved.

Caressing the sleek skin of her midriff beneath her nightgown, he slid his hand up to her breast. She sighed and shivered with pleasure.

He filled both hands with the lush softness of her breasts. "God, this feels good, doesn't it?"

"Uh-huh." To lie would have been ludicrous. With his open mouth at her ear, she couldn't think, anyway. His tongue explored the sensitive skin inside, and she shuddered, moving in restless search of...something.

"Do I have to honor my promise?" It was a hoarse, barely intelligible question. With his hand at her breast sending fierce, sweet sensations swirling all the way through her body, and his arousal thrusting in tantalizing rhythm behind her, Joanna wanted more.

"What promise?" she gasped.

It was all the encouragement Ryan needed. Somehow her nightgown was stripped away and he was up on one elbow, pulling her beneath him with no thought for anything except to quench their thirst for each other.

Joanna had the vague thought that Ryan would take her instantly, and she was ready—more than ready—but he slowed down suddenly.

Taut with control, his eyes hot and hungry, he paused just to look at her. "I've been dreaming of this," he said, his voice low and husky, "since you came back. You're beautiful, Jo, even more beautiful than when we—I'm still crazy about you, did you know that?''

"Ryan..." She put out a hand and touched his cheek. They smiled into each other's eyes. Her hand fell to his chest, where she sifted languidly through the crisp, curly hair. He was broad and heavy, utterly masculine and beautiful in his masculinity. She'd always loved—

With my body, I thee worship.

Her hands went still. When she'd taken that vow, she had meant it with her whole heart and soul. Her infatuation with his youthful handsomeness had blinded her to his recklessness. Now that recklessness had aged into a more dangerous kind of sexuality. The wildness that had both fascinated and repelled her was still irresistible. She closed her eyes and pushed away that momentary brush with the past.

She found his nipples, caressed them, then paused at a strange ridge along his ribs. A scar. She put her lips to it and felt pleasure when he groaned. She moved to kiss his nipples and he swore fervently, growling a string of broken phrases and erotic promises. Then he clamped her face in his hands and drew her up, seeking her mouth. When their lips finally met in a wild, passion-driven kiss, they were lost.

She was swept into the familiar as Ryan's hands moved everywhere. His mouth was intimate and clever and arousing. She was weak with wanting when he gathered her close and thrust into her, hard and deep. Her body knew and fell effortlessly into the rhythm he set. The years of separation might never have been. He pushed her higher and she went willingly until ecstasy claimed them both.

THEY LAY PANTING, luxuriating in the afterglow. Joanna kissed the side of his neck. Ryan kissed her temple. Her hands wandered over his shoulders, stroked the skin at the small of his back. He breathed in the fragrance of her hair and savored the feel of her softness beneath him. After a few minutes, he shifted his weight to turn onto his back.

I've just had sex with my ex-husband! she thought incredulously. *How on earth did it happen? What came over me? Have I lost my mind?*

Joanna didn't want to think—but there it was. She stole a quick look at Ryan. He was staring at the ceiling. Maybe he was feeling a little dazed, too. The sudden peal of the doorbell brought him straight up in the bed. They stared at each other in shock for a moment.

Ryan frowned ferociously. "Who the *hell* can that be?"

As he left the bed, Joanna looked around self-consciously for her nightgown. She really didn't want to walk in front of Ryan without a stitch on. Ryan, of course, felt no such reluctance. Stark naked, he walked out of the bedroom to the hall to see who was pounding on the door. Wearing the sheet like a toga, she was searching for her nightgown when he reappeared.

"It's some kid," he said, thrusting his legs into his jeans. "He'd better have a damn good excuse ready." Wordlessly, he picked up her nightgown from the floor on his side of the bed and handed it to her.

"Thank you," she murmured.

"Hey…" He tilted her face up with a finger beneath her chin and said, "We have some things to talk about. Let me get rid of this kid and I'll be right back."

She nodded. "I'll make the coffee."

One eyebrow arched. "Can we have it in bed?"

The pounding at the front door got louder. He looked impatiently in that direction. "Hold on, damn it!" he roared.

"Go," she said, waving him off.

Back in her own bedroom, Joanna snatched up the robe that lay across the foot of the bed and put it on. Apparently whoever was pounding wasn't intimidated by the ban on visitors to Wilderose Cottage. She made it to the archway separating the kitchen from the family room just as Ryan opened the door. She froze in shock.

"Daniel!"

CHAPTER SEVEN

"HI, MOM." With a cheeky grin, Daniel threw his arms around his mother and gave her a big hug. "Surprised you, huh?"

"Daniel—"

Stepping back, he turned to Ryan. "You must be Ryan O'Connor." He stuck out his hand. "Thanks for taking care of my mom. She gets the idea sometimes that I'm just a kid and tries to read me out of what's happening. It never works. I don't know when she's gonna wise up."

Ryan shook the boy's hand, willing his expression to reveal nothing. He felt as though he'd just been kicked by a mule. He wasn't sure how he'd expected Joanna's son to look. But he hadn't expected—what? A strange sense of kinship? A feeling that he would have known Daniel if he'd walked up to him on the streets of Beirut?

The boy was sandy-haired, tall and lanky. He wore jeans and a faded 49ers T-shirt. His running shoes would never be respectable again. Ditto for the battered duffel bag at his feet. But it was Daniel's shrewd blue eyes that caught and held Ryan. It was as if the kid could look right into him and see everything. Fourteen years old? Yeah, going on forty.

"So..." Daniel transferred that look to his mother. "How's it going, Mom?"

Joanna pulled her robe a little tighter. "How did you find me, Daniel?"

"Elementary, my dear, it was—"

"Daniel!"

"Sorry, Mom." Daniel shoved his hands deep into his pockets and shrugged. He gave Ryan a conspiratorial look. "Mom hates it when I do Sherlock."

"Where is your grandfather?" Ryan asked sternly.

"Well, it's a long story." Daniel screwed up one corner of his mouth. "Actually, he's still in Montreal."

Joanna gasped. "How on earth did you get here?"

"I flew. Remember we had those frequent flyer miles accumulated on USAir? This seemed like a good time to cash 'em in."

Tearing her gaze from her son's, Joanna looked at Ryan. "I can't imagine what Jem was thinking, to let him do this," she said helplessly.

"Yeah, I definitely owe Grampa Jem, Mom," Daniel explained. "He wasn't too hot on the idea when I first put it to him, but he came around. That reminds me, I need to call him and check in. That's what I've been doing at every stop along the way. He'll be relieved to hear that I made it okay."

"I'll bet," Ryan said.

"Uh-huh," Daniel said. "I couldn't have done it without him."

Looking beyond him, Ryan asked, "How did you get to Sea Island? A taxi?"

"You didn't hitchhike?" Joanna said in a threatening tone.

"You know I never hitch, Mom. You'd have a seizure." He glanced at Ryan. "And a taxi out here from the airport would cost big bucks, man. I just took a taxi to a used bike shop in Savannah—the cab driver recommended it—and negotiated the price of that baby over there." With a hitch of his chin, he indicated a much-used bike that was propped against a palm tree. He grinned cockily. "I got it cheap, and heck, it got me here."

"Come inside, Daniel." Gathering her wits, Joanna caught his arm and dragged him toward the kitchen. "You have some big explaining to do, young man. When I sent you to Montreal, I meant for you to stay there. You had no right to leave."

Daniel stopped and looked into her eyes. "You had no right to lie to me, Mom." His tone was matter-of-fact.

"I had a good reason for doing what I did," she responded.

Wearing a stubborn expression that looked oddly familiar to Ryan, Daniel said, "I had a good reason for doing what *I* did."

"You had a good reason for disobeying me, Daniel?"

"I didn't disobey, Mom. You never told me that I couldn't come to you if I needed to."

Ryan, watching the exchange, decided to step in. The kid was arguing like a seasoned lawyer. "Why did you think your mother needed you?" he asked.

Daniel turned to him, not saying anything for a moment. He gazed deliberately at Ryan's bare chest, then lower to his unsnapped jeans. Decidedly uncomfortable, Ryan suddenly wished that he'd put on a shirt. He folded his arms over his chest.

"My mom needed me because she's in danger."

With a frown, Ryan lowered his arms slowly. "What gave you that idea?"

Joanna hovered in the background as some subtle shift in polarity had both males focused on each other.

"I...I just..." For the first time, Daniel's remarkable aplomb slipped. "I just had a feeling."

"You had a feeling." Ryan felt a strange *knowing* settle somewhere inside him. He rejected it ruthlessly. "What kind of feeling?"

Daniel shrugged. "Just a weird kind of feeling. Haven't you ever had a *feeling?*"

Dodging the too-savvy look coming from the kid, Ryan turned to Joanna. "Does he do this a lot?"

"He's never done anything like this," Joanna replied, still looking shaken. "Daniel—"

"I mean," Ryan interrupted patiently, "does he get these *feelings* a lot?"

"What?" Confused, Joanna clutched a handful of her robe at her neck.

"Mom doesn't know. I never told her."

Everything in Ryan resisted what he was hearing. He wanted to crush the suspicion that was born with his first look at the boy. He wanted to demolish the kid's easy self-confidence, his nonchalance in relying on nothing more than *feelings* to strike out in a risky, foolhardy search for his mother.

For his mother and who else?

But he pushed that thought deep inside. On one level, he knew his reaction was out of place. Joanna's son wasn't a public figure with a secret to be exposed in Ryan's next feature article. Nor was he a young hoodlum with a yard-long rap sheet. Nevertheless, he pinned the boy with a hostile look.

"Danger, you said. What kind of danger to your mother did you sense? Her plane would crash? She'd get mugged on the street? What?"

"No, it had to do with Mr. Fellini." Beside him, Joanna made a startled sound. "Mr. Fellini is, or was, her business partner in the art gallery. He's dead. He—"

"I know about Fellini."

"I think he was murdered," the boy said candidly.

"Daniel!" Joanna whispered.

Ryan made a gesture with his hand to quiet her. "Just a minute, Joanna."

"And if he was murdered," Daniel continued, still focused on Ryan, "then that would explain why Mom hustled me out of the way, made up that goofy story about going on a business trip and not being in the hotel where she said she'd be." He chewed the inside of his cheek, thinking. "The thing I couldn't figure is why she stopped calling." At that thought, he turned to her. "Why is that, Mom? You knew I'd be worried."

"Ryan doesn't have a phone yet," she murmured.

Daniel looked skeptical. "Hasn't got a phone? Jeez."

"It's ordered," Ryan said abruptly.

Wearing an interested expression, Daniel gazed around the interior of the cottage. "A nice place like this, you'd think a person would have a phone," he commented. "And a fax machine and a PC—across-the-board communications equipment, the whole nine yards, you know? You being a big-time reporter and all."

"How did you know I was a reporter?"

"You're famous, Mr. O'Connor," Daniel said simply.

"You never explained how you found me, Daniel," his mother said hastily.

"It was pretty easy. You've talked enough about Georgia and how when you were a kid you hung out here on Sea Island with the O'Connors. I had a feeling you were here."

"Another feeling," Ryan said softly.

Meeting Ryan's eyes, Daniel cocked his head as though coming to a decision. "The truth is, my feelings aren't exactly…ordinary feelings, if you know what I mean."

"You want to explain that?" Ryan said.

"What are you talking about, Daniel?" Anxiety sharpened Joanna's voice. She sensed something between Ryan and Daniel that excluded her.

"I sort of…know things sometimes," Daniel explained, his eyes locked with Ryan's. "Sometimes I know them before they happen."

Ryan turned abruptly and walked to the bank of windows that faced the sea. Midmorning sun glistened off the surface of the water. Because it was a calm day, the glare was blinding. Inside him, nothing was calm. Inside, he churned. He burned. He didn't know if he could contain the emotions roiling through him. The incredible thought that had come to him could not be. Joanna would never—

"I didn't figure you'd believe me," Daniel said, coming to stand beside him. "I know it's weird."

Ryan didn't answer. What could he say? But Joanna made further discussion unnecessary.

"Come, Daniel," she said, her voice shaky. She caught her son by the arm and once again turned him toward the arched entrance to the kitchen. "I'll fix you some breakfast, then we'll have to go to the convenience store and call your grandfather. He'll be worried."

"You're not going to pull his chain over this, are you, Mom?" Now that the moment was upon him, Daniel was suddenly anxious over the consequences of his escapade. "It was all my idea. Grampa Jem was just trying to help."

Joanna propelled him firmly through the door. "I know very well whose idea it was, Daniel, and this time you're going to pay dearly for doing something so reckless and dangerous."

"I had to do it, Mom."

From his position in front of the window, Ryan spoke. "Don't argue with your mother, Daniel," he said firmly. Ignoring their surprised looks, he added, "Get him something to eat, Joanna. I'll ride down to the convenience store and call Jem Stanton. You have his number, right?"

"Yes, I— In my address book." She found her purse and handed him the book. "You're going to use that bicycle?" She eyed the sorry vehicle skeptically.

"I have a Land Rover in the garage."

Her mouth fell open. "You have a—"

"Take care of Daniel," Ryan said coldly. "I'll see you later. We'll talk." He brushed past both of them, heading for the rear of the cottage.

"Jeez," breathed Daniel. "He's something else, Mom."

Joanna, watching Ryan stride off, said nothing.

WITH HER ARMS WRAPPED around her drawn-up knees, Joanna sat on the sand, lost in the beauty of the sunset. The sky was a panorama of glorious color, vivid pink, crimson and deep purple. The spectacle always delighted her, sunset at Sea Island. In Chicago, trapped in the frenetic pace of urban life, she had often fantasized about Sea Island.

At this moment, Chicago seemed a lifetime away.

"I called Stanton."

Ryan. He'd kept her waiting all day. The hours had been difficult and long. Daniel had been full of questions about Ryan, and she'd fielded them as best she could. For some reason, Ryan had made an impression on her son unlike any other man. His questions about his own father had never contained such intense curiosity. Apparently Ryan felt no such compulsion to know Daniel. Why else would he stay away all day, especially after the night they'd spent together?

Or—and this thought made her quake with fear—was something far more disturbing bothering Ryan?

She glanced up and found him staring far out to sea. Wind whipped at his shirt, threatening to tear it from his jeans. "It took you long enough," she said, pent-up anxiety making her irritable. "Where have you been?"

"Driving. Thinking."

With a sigh, she held her hair away from her face in the wind. "I know Daniel's a major complication, but I simply had no idea he would show up here. It's incredible, really. He—"

"There's plenty of room here for the boy."

"Are you sure? Because—"

"I haven't spent the day thinking about that. I've been thinking about us."

"Oh." Well, she shouldn't be surprised to hear that. She knew he hadn't planned on starting an affair with her. No more than she had planned to get involved with *him*. In the hours since waking up in his bed, when she wasn't occupied with Daniel, she'd tried desperately to sort out her feelings for Ryan. But it had been no use. What happened had been too sudden, too incredible.

"I hope you've had more luck finding answers than I have," she said quietly.

"I'm not talking about what happened last night."

She wished he'd look at her. She couldn't tell anything from where she sat. All she saw was his profile, and it looked pretty grim. "What then?" she asked.

He stood another minute with his hands in his back pockets. Then he came over and sat down beside her on the sand. "I was talking about what happened after we separated."

"No wonder you look so grim."

"Yeah, I'm just beginning to realize what a major screwup that was."

"We've talked about this, Ryan. What's the point in dragging it up today? If you're afraid that I'll assume something because we slept together last night, then I'll tell you straight out: you have nothing to fear. I'll never try to tie you down again. Or drag commitments from you. I'm not the person I was then, and you're not—"

"Hush, Jo." The look in his eyes stopped her. "That's not what I wanted to talk about. I've been thinking about the last time we were together."

She fixed her gaze on the horizon. The sky was already darkening. It would be night soon. She shivered a little in the cooling breeze.

"Jo?"

"That was fifteen years ago, Ryan."

"Yeah. We were separated. That seemed to be what you wanted, and I gave in. I—" He stopped when she whirled to face him.

"It was what *you* wanted, Ryan."

"If you really believed that, then I really screwed up. I didn't want the separation *or* the divorce."

"We talked about this then, Ryan. You can't have marriage without the compromises that come with it. I needed a permanent home, not an apartment in a high rise where you dropped in every time you finished a tour to rest up and have a little sex. I could live with a part-time husband a few months of the year, but not most of the year."

"I know it was tough. I've admitted that. I wish—"

"Do you know how many months you actually spent in that apartment after we were married?"

He lifted a shoulder with a sigh, not looking at her.

"Three months...almost."

"It wasn't going to be like that forever, I told you that. The foreign assignments were stepping stones to something better in the States."

"Maybe." She wrapped her arms around her legs and put her chin on her knees. "Maybe we gave up too soon. We'll never know."

"You had your job, too," he reminded her.

"A good thing. I'd have gone crazy without something."

"David Stanton was there to hold your hand."

She turned and gave him a long, hard stare. "David wasn't holding my hand in those days."

Ryan's expression was equally hard. "Maybe not, but after the separation, he was right there, Johnny-on-the-spot."

The wind was kicking up strongly now. She swiped at a long strand of hair that whipped across her face. "What is the point of this conversation, Ryan?"

"I think you know."

With her heart hammering, she held his gaze. "Know what?"

He dropped his head, staring at his feet for a full minute. Then looked at her again. "When I came home from Afghanistan, we spent the night together."

She nodded mutely.

"That's what I wanted to talk about. We used protection, right?"

"Yes."

"We argued the next morning when I got that call to go to Northern Ireland."

"Your memory is as good as mine, Ryan. It was the same thing over again. Even with the threat of divorce, your job came first."

"We've hashed and rehashed this, Jo. It isn't—" She

started to say more, but he held up a hand. "It's okay. I understand. But what I don't understand—have never understood—is that you must have gone directly to David Stanton."

"He'd invited me to a ski weekend," Joanna said softly, wearily, "and I had declined. But with you on the way to Ireland, the divorce proceedings firm again, I decided to go."

"What else did you decide that weekend?"

She didn't duck the question. "Your career was more important to you than I was. Your leaving for Ireland proved that. With David I knew it was different." She rubbed her cheek against her knee. "The weekend in Vermont was an opportunity for me to know if I could ever be with another man."

She glanced at him and her heart stopped. He was facing straight ahead looking fierce, so fierce. "And you found you could." The words were said without expression. He didn't turn to look at her.

"Think what you want," she said coldly. "I've explained."

"And three months later, you married him."

"My marriage to David doesn't concern you."

"Oh?" He did look at her then. "I think it does, Joanna."

"What do you mean?"

"Were you ever going to tell me that you married David Stanton knowing you were pregnant with my child?"

Joanna scrambled to her feet. Wrapping her arms around her waist, she turned away from the accusation in his eyes. She had known that some day she might be forced to have this conversation with Ryan. But she hadn't known it would be just hours after spending a night of love with him. Or that she would be living in the same house with him, dependent on his goodwill for her safety.

She closed her eyes, opened them again and saw the sky. It was definitely night now. There were no stars.

"I wasn't sure about that," she said quietly.

"You knew that you were pregnant, didn't you?"

"Yes, but—"

"And he was such a great guy that he agreed to marry you, anyway," he said, struggling to keep himself under control.

"He wanted to give the child his name," she countered. "Oh, it's so...I don't expect you to—"

His breath came out in a rush and he swore bitterly. Then he wheeled away from her, striding toward the edge of the water as though he couldn't trust himself to look at her another second. She watched as he tipped his head back, eyes wide, and struggled to bring himself under control. "I can't believe it, Joanna. I don't *want* to believe it. How could you do something so...so..." He shook his head.

"You don't understand. It was—"

"Reprehensible...that's what it is. Criminal." As though he couldn't think straight, he paced restlessly, rubbing the back of his neck. "I swear to God, you're not getting away with this."

"I wasn't trying to get away with anything. I—"

"Did you think you could keep it a secret forever? He's *my* son," Ryan declared, hitting his chest with a fist. "You made a major mistake ever getting within a thousand miles of me with a secret like this. If you think those thugs running diamonds are mean, just wait'll you get a taste of a fight with me. And I'll do it all nice and legal. You'll—"

"Stop it!" she cried. "Just...stop for a minute, damn you!"

His laugh was short, contemptuous. "When I get ready, lady, and not a minute—"

With a broken cry, she stumbled away from him, intending to go back to the cottage. She had taken no more than six steps before he caught her by the arm. She whirled, jerking free. "Keep your hands off me, Ryan! If you won't give me a chance to try to explain, then so be it. But keep away from me. When you calm down, then we'll talk about this. Maybe."

"We'll talk now, damn you!"

"No." She caught at her hair to hold it away from her face. "You may be able to bully other people into doing whatever you want, but I don't have to tolerate your ill temper. You've had everything your own way most of your life. Not this. Threaten me all you like about Daniel, I couldn't care less. He's mine and always will be. You couldn't take him away from me if you tried.''

Walking with dignity through deep sand wasn't easy, but she managed it for a few more yards. Then he grabbed her again, but this time with less aggression. ''Just a minute, Jo...wait, damn it!''

She stopped, but didn't look at him until he released her.

''Where's Daniel right now?'' he asked.

''Playing a video game in the family room.''

''Then we can talk on the porch, okay?''

''Talk, yes,'' she said coolly. ''Scream and insult each other, no.''

He rubbed a hand over his mouth, then met her eyes steadily. ''This has...knocked me for a loop, Jo. Maybe I overreacted. If so, it's because...hell, isn't it to be expected when a man discovers he's got a kid who's fourteen years old and he never even knew it?''

''Come on,'' Joanna said, heading again toward the cottage. ''I'll try to explain.''

RYAN COULDN'T STAY in his chair. He kept lunging up, pacing, his eyes restless, hands fisted at his thighs.

''When is his birthday? Was he...okay? Was your pregnancy normal? How much did he weigh?''

Details. Naturally, being Ryan, he'd want details. Joanna sighed, clasping her hands together in her lap.

''December 12,'' she said quietly. ''He weighed six pounds and fourteen ounces. My pregnancy was normal. He was... is...never sick.''

After one long look at her, he thrust a hand through his hair and flung himself into the chair beside her. Could the closeness they'd shared in the night really have happened? she wondered. Would that brief renewed taste of passion be something that she was destined to relive like all the other memories of moments shared with Ryan? The truth lay inside her like broken glass. But then, she had known what it would mean if he ever found out.

"Why did you do it?"

"I don't expect you to believe me, but I didn't know." He was instantly ready to argue, but she put up a hand. "You promised I could explain. Now listen."

He gave her one brief nod. Joanna sighed, fixed her eyes on the dark, restless sea beyond him and prayed for the right words to explain the inexplicable.

"When you came home after being in Afghanistan, I was so glad to see you, so happy that the separation seemed as wrong to you as it did to me. I thought you understood my reasons for suggesting the divorce. When you came to me that night, I thought it meant things would be different. Then, the very next morning, you didn't even hesitate when the call came to go to Northern Ireland. I was crushed, confused and heartsick. One day at home and you left without a backward glance. I wanted a real marriage, not a part-time affair. I wanted children. I wanted a house, friends, a church to go to regularly. In my misery, I realized you would never share my desire for any of that."

She paused, looking at Ryan. With his head bent, he stared at the floor.

"David Stanton was more than my employer. He was my friend and mentor. He was also in love with me, and during the separation from you, he had made no secret that he wanted to marry me. But I...I wasn't sure that what I felt for David was enough to build a life together."

"You got over that fast enough," he said coldly.

"I didn't, to tell the truth. Even after spending the weekend with David, I was still very uncertain. But I discovered I was pregnant and my whole world seemed turned upside down. I did not have unprotected sex with either you or David. I—"

"Maybe not, but you had sex. And with both of us."

She rubbed her forehead wearily. "Yes. I...it..." She

stopped, gazed a moment or two at the ceiling to gather herself, then swallowed hard. "I know it must seem so irresponsible, so...wrong. When I think back now, that time is like a black void, a bad dream I thought would never end. But it did. And the only good thing to come of it was Daniel. He's the best of me and his father, whichever one of you that may be."

It took a second or two for her words to register. He stared at her in shock. "What the hell does that mean?"

"Exactly what I said. I've never been certain if Daniel is your child or David's."

Disbelief, suspicion, incredulity—all showed on his face. And finally, scorn. "Do you really expect me to believe that, Jo? Try again."

"It's true." With a sigh, she stood up suddenly, unable to sit there and bear his ridicule. For fifteen years, she'd tried to find some measure of peace in the mess she'd made of her life. Nobody knew how she'd tried to simply get beyond it.

With her hands tightly laced in front of her, she stood where Ryan had been moments before, looking out at the night. "I could have been impregnated by either one of you. I've never known for sure."

"Didn't you think *I* might want to know for sure?" Ryan asked sarcastically.

She glanced at him over her shoulder, then gave a mirthless laugh. "Not really. Why would I? I knew your feelings about having a child. Especially an unplanned baby. To you, he would have been a nuisance. I knew you would never settle down to help me raise him. Oh, I think I knew that you'd reject the divorce, under the circumstances, but I didn't really want a reluctant husband any more than I wanted a reluctant father for my son.

"David, on the other hand, could not have been more supportive. He was a proud, indulgent father-to-be, and when Daniel was born, he loved him unconditionally. He taught him to ride his trike and then his bike. He took him fishing with him, he taught him to play catch. He told him stories and encouraged Daniel in whatever endeavor he thought of.'' Joanna's smile was a little crooked. "And he thought of lots of things. My son was—is—a handful.''

Ryan was dumbfounded. For the longest time, he simply looked at her. "I don't believe what I'm hearing," he said slowly. "You had no right to keep this a secret from me. You had no right to decide I wouldn't make a good father. You don't have a crystal ball. You're not clairvoyant. You didn't know any of that stuff, Joanna. You assumed too much.''

"I did what I thought was best for my child," she told him with a lift of her chin.

"He's my child, too," Ryan said fiercely.

"I've told you—"

"I don't give a flip what you've told me. Daniel is my son. I suspected it when I first saw him and after hearing the details surrounding his conception, I *know* it. He's mine." He thumped his chest with his fist as though to settle the argument once and for all.

Joanna's brow furrowed. "You can't possibly know that, Ryan.''

"I do.''

She lifted her shoulders in bewilderment. "How?''

"Because I have something that David Stanton couldn't possibly have and I've bequeathed it to Daniel."

"What? How can you—" Utterly bewildered, Joanna shook her head. "What is it?''

"Second sight," Ryan said flatly. "He's psychic, Joanna, and he got it from me.''

CHAPTER EIGHT

IT TOOK DANIEL ONLY fifteen minutes at Wilderose Cottage to pick up on the heavy vibrations. Lying in bed that night with his hands folded beneath his head, he thought over the situation. He had never seen his mother so stressed out. Yeah, she was troubled over those guys back in Chicago and all the stuff that was going on over Rico's death and all, but he had a feeling that something else was going on here. And for some reason, his arrival on the scene had complicated things.

He turned his head and studied the view from the window of his bedroom. He was sorry about that, because he liked this place. Truth was, he liked it here on Sea Island better than any place he'd ever been. All that travel with his mother and his grandmother and Grampa Jem was nice and all, but Sea Island—boy oh boy it was just about paradise. He felt...right here. It was just a feeling he had, but he always went with his feelings.

That was another thing, he thought, watching the slow revolutions of the ceiling fan in the dark. Ryan O'Connor had known instantly what his feelings meant. He had picked up right away that Daniel hadn't just deduced where his mom was by studying facts and stuff like a detective. Ryan had cottoned to it in no time. It was weird. He had never known anybody else who tapped right into his psychic ability. Not that he'd ever explained his, well...gift to anybody. That was just it. He hadn't *had* to explain to Ryan O'Connor. The man had *known*. And Daniel knew he knew.

He threw the sheet aside and got up. Walking to the window, he checked the stretch of beach to see if he could spot Ryan. Nope. Not yet. Something was bugging the guy big time. It might be Daniel's sudden appearance, of course. That would make sense. Here was this sweet set up: a beautiful woman in jeopardy. And his mom was beautiful, no doubt about that. Yeah, romance could blossom. Ryan might have designs along those lines. But Daniel didn't want his mother compromised or anything. Not that she had expressed any interest in men for as long as he could remember. She hadn't. So it might be interesting to see whether his mom and Ryan had eyes for each other. He had a feeling they matched pretty well.

But even if nothing came of that, he knew his mom had come to Sea Island because she felt safe here. He really needed to talk to Ryan, to get a fix on just how suitable the guy was. His mom was going to need somebody tough and smart and…well, cool…because this thing wasn't going to end without a showdown. Daniel was prepared to do whatever was necessary to protect her, but when it came right down to it, he was a kid. He didn't have anything to use as a weapon except his intelligence.

And, of course, his psychic powers.

IT WAS THE MIDDLE of the night when Ryan got back to the cottage. After leaving Joanna, he had run along the beach until the stitch in his side became unbearable and his punished lungs had screamed for relief. He could hardly contain his fury. Almost fevered in his rage, he'd pushed his body to the limit, but his imagination wouldn't quit. The years he'd missed watching Daniel grow up! He felt cheated, deprived. Vivid scenes flashed in his mind of David Stanton teaching his son— *his* son—to ride a bike, to fish, to throw a ball. As he'd stared at the black, restless sea, he'd felt deeply, bitterly betrayed.

Letting himself in to the cottage, he stopped in the kitchen and opened the cabinet where he kept the extra booze. With a bottle of bourbon in one hand and a glass in the other, he headed down the hall toward his bedroom.

Passing the room where Daniel slept, he slowed, and then, drawn by some irresistible force, he stopped. The glow from the outside security light fell across the boy as he lay sprawled on his back, sleeping. Unable to stop himself, Ryan walked closer. Holding his breath, he studied the half-formed perfection of his son as he slept in adolescent abandon.

The sheet was slung over the edge of the bed. He wore only a pair of jockey shorts, and in the pale light, he seemed all arms and legs. The O'Connor men were tall. If he ever grew into his limbs, he'd be as tall as—Ryan closed his eyes, the hurt mushrooming inside him again.

He'd be as tall as me.

He realized suddenly why he'd felt so stunned at the first sight of Daniel. It was because of his resemblance to Will, Ryan's brother. He had the same loose-gaited, gangly stride. He had Will's slow, lazy smile. His blue eyes, now…they were straight from Patrick O'Connor, Ryan's grandfather, and Cameron, his old man.

And me.

Looking down at his son, Ryan thought of his father. He hadn't been around much when Ryan was a kid. Cameron O'Connor had belonged to his public. Ryan had known from earliest childhood that a whole nation admired and respected his father, thanks to radio and television. At the first sign of trouble around the world, Cameron O'Connor was up and gone.

Not much time to be a father.

Was it so shocking that Joanna had assumed Ryan would be much the same?

Moving silently to the chair beside Daniel's bed, Ryan sat down. Uncapping the bourbon, he poured a hefty measure into the glass and leaned back. Early on in his courtship of Joanna, he had talked about his boyhood and how he'd longed for more time with his father. He had resented the fact that Cameron seemed to place the demands of his career before his obligations as a father. If you got right down to it, he and Will had been practically fatherless, Ryan thought. If it hadn't been for their grandfather, neither would have had much in the way of a male role model at all.

Will had subsequently taken up Patrick's first love, the shipyard. And Ryan had taken up journalism, in the family tradition.

He wondered suddenly if he'd been influenced by his absentee father so much, or if it had been his grandmother, Kathleen. She, not Cameron, had been the one to nurture his interest in writing. She had put him to work at the *Sentinel* in Savannah when he was fourteen. Kathleen had been his mentor because Cameron was never around.

Or had he sought a career similar to his father's to get Cameron's attention?

"Hi."

With a start, Ryan realized that Daniel was awake and watching him. He started to rise.

"You don't have to go, do you?" the boy said, his voice husky from sleep. He propped himself up on one elbow. "I waited up, but I guess I finally fell asleep. I wanted to talk to you."

"What about?"

"My mom, for one thing."

Ryan set his bourbon down beside him on the floor and rested his ankle on his knee. "And what's the other thing?"

"I wanted to explain some things."

"Such as?"

"Can we talk about my mom first?"

"Sure." Ryan leaned back. "I'm listening."

Daniel scooted up in bed and hooked both his arms around his knees. "What have you done to make sure nobody can just walk in here and do something to hurt her?"

"There's a security system. It—"

"It isn't worth a sh—worth a plugged nickel, if you'll par-

don my French. I came right up to the front door this morning.
Anybody could. Have you considered a first-class guard dog?
Grampa Jem's got a springer spaniel, and he's nice and all,
but I don't think a springer spaniel's got enough...authority,
if you know what I mean. A German shepherd's what we
should get, I think. I had a friend in Chicago, Ben Eckstein?
He had this awesome shepherd named Buddy. I'm telling you,
Mr. O'Connor, you couldn't get within shouting distance of
their place.''

"The reason you walked right up is because the security
system isn't in place yet," Ryan explained patiently. "I expect
someone no later than tomorrow afternoon to fix it. It's taken
care of.''

"What about a guard dog?"

Ryan smiled. "Do you know any?"

"No, but I bet you could call the police station in Savannah—" He stopped suddenly. "Do you happen to know anybody on the force? That's the best way to get reliable information. They may have a K-9 corps here. If so, they'll know
where to get a good dog. Maybe a reject, you know? I had
this friend—''

Ryan held up a hand, trying to discipline his smile. He was
enjoying himself. Daniel was— He suddenly recalled Nick
Dalton's words. Daniel was fantastic.

"My sister happens to be married to the chief of detectives
at SPD," he said.

Daniel gave him a delighted look. "No sh—uh, no joke?
Man, this is great. Hey..." Another thought struck him.
"Since this guy is your brother-in-law, you think we could
maybe take him into our confidence, I mean, regarding my
mom's situation? First, can he be trusted?"

"Yes," Ryan said dryly.

"Then what do you think? Should we fill him in?"

"He knows.''

"Oh. Good, very good," Daniel said, nodding sagely.

"He's already working on the problem," Ryan said, his lips

twitching. For a few moments in the shadowed intimacy of the room, they were in perfect accord. Ryan suddenly realized that it was impossible to fight the urge to smile and at the same time hang on to the dark emotion that had driven him out onto the beach. He tried to remember a time when he and his father might have talked like this, might have spent an hour in such total harmony. No moment came to him. No memory surfaced.

Daniel got back to business. "So, you think the security system will be on-line sometime tomorrow, huh?"

"Yeah. And if the professionals I called don't show, I think I know enough to make do on my own."

"Yeah, yeah. That's cool."

"You can rest easy, Daniel," Ryan said, seeking to reassure the boy. "I won't let anything happen to your mother."

"Okay. Thanks."

They exchanged smiles. The sight of him hunched there, with his elbows crooked over his knees—his bony, adolescent knees—sent a feeling through Ryan that was new, but...good.

My God, Joanna, how can I ever forgive you?

"Now, about those other things I wanted to mention." Clearing his throat, Daniel prepared to address a subject that was a little more delicate than his mother's safety.

Ryan crossed his arms over his chest. "Shoot."

"I noticed that you didn't seem to have a problem with my explanation of how I got here."

"I don't think you explained in much detail," Ryan countered.

"Well..." Daniel studied him as though still a little uncertain about coming totally clean.

Ryan raised both brows, waiting.

"I had this dream," Daniel said.

"Not a feeling?"

"Well, the dream and the feelings sort of...dovetail, if you know what I mean."

"Uh-huh."

"My mom was in the airport and she was talking on the phone. Just from the way she looked...ah, the way I saw her in my dream, I mean, well, it was plain that she was scared. She felt...in danger. Now, you don't have to believe that if you don't want to, but I know it's true. And I think it has to do with something Rico was involved in." Daniel hesitated for a few seconds, looking up at the ceiling, down at his knees, out the window, and finally at Ryan. "Crazy as it sounds, I think someone really bad is looking for my mom. She really is in danger. I don't know why—I wish I did. But I used every bit of my...ah...special talent to find her so I could be here to protect her...if she needs it."

"Special talent?" Ryan repeated.

Dropping his gaze, Daniel studied his two thumbs pressed together on top of his knees. "Like I said before, sometimes I know things, I sense things. I've never put it to the test before like I did this time, but I got here, didn't I? Maybe I can figure out where the danger to my mom is coming from." Stopping, he gave Ryan a straight look. "Unless you can come up with a better idea."

"Probably nothing so innovative," Ryan said.

For a second, Daniel looked disappointed. "Yeah, well, I knew you'd think I was full of crap," he said philosophically. "I guess it's a lot to lay on a person and expect them to just swallow it, no questions asked."

"Hmm," Ryan said, deciding to let it slide. For now.

Daniel was looking at him again. "But if you're thinking I'm just a kid imagining big, bad guys chasing after my mother or trying to come up with a reason for leaving Montreal so she won't ground me till doomsday or something like that, then you're wrong, man. I'm as serious as a heart attack here," he said, leaning forward in his intensity.

"I don't think your concern for your mother is a figment of your imagination," Ryan said quietly.

Daniel waited a second or two before nodding as though satisfied. "Now...one other thing..."

What now? Ryan thought.

"I know you and my mom are old friends," Daniel began cautiously.

"We knew each other as children," Ryan said.

And, of course, as man and wife.

"Uh-huh. I know about Sea Island and the sailing and big family gatherings and all."

"It was a long time ago."

"Yeah, like they say, that was then and this is now."

"Uh-huh." Ryan cleared his throat.

"You aren't kids anymore."

Was he about to get a lecture on sexual morality from his own son, as incredible as that seemed? Ryan felt an odd compulsion to reach down and pick up his drink. Instead, he uncrossed his legs and braced both feet firmly on the floor. A man ought to be prepared at a time like this.

"I guess you and my mom here alone together will just have to be okay, under the circumstances," Daniel conceded. "After all, she's in danger and this is sort of a...safe house. You know, one of those places where they put witnesses to protect them when they—"

"Daniel," Ryan broke in, "I know what a safe house is."

"Okay. I just wanted you to know that my mom's reputation means a lot. She's not exactly a feminist, you know? At least, I don't see her that way. Not like those women you see who're always upset about injustice and equal pay and everything. She earns enough, if you want to know, because she's really good at what she does—she's an artist, did you know that?—and she was practically running Rico's, the art gallery, while Rico was sick and all. But when it comes to men, well, she isn't very experienced, you know what I mean? She might *look* like a woman who knows her way around, but actually—"

"Say no more." Ryan stood up. "I get the picture."

"It's not that I don't think you're a gentleman, Mr. O'Connor, but—"

"Ryan. Why don't you call me Ryan?"

"Ryan. Yeah, okay."

"Your mother is a guest in my house, Daniel. I've promised her that she will be safe here," Ryan said in a quiet tone. He waited as the boy absorbed that, then nodded. "Here's my promise to you: nothing will ever happen between your mother and me that will hurt her or make you unhappy or cause her to regret her decision to come to Wilderose Cottage after all these years."

"Okay. That's good. I just wanted to clear that up." With a smile, Daniel lay back, getting comfortable again. Stretching out flat, he punched his pillow, making it right. "I hope you don't mind."

"I don't mind." Moving to the bedside, Ryan reached for the sheet dragging the floor and handed it over, then watched as Daniel settled down again. "Mission accomplished?" Ryan asked, smiling into eyes as blue as his own.

"Yeah, thanks, Ryan."

Ryan wanted to touch him. Maybe even hug him. The feeling was so unexpected, so powerful, that he was shaken. Instead, he backed away, somehow retrieving his drink and the bottle of bourbon. Then he headed blindly for the door. In the hall, something—a sound, the soft rustle of a nightgown, something—made him glance across at Joanna's bedroom door.

She was silent and still, watching him. In the glow of the nightlight, her features were ghostly pale, unsmiling. Had she been listening? Their eyes met, and hers glinted with tears. But he didn't speak. With the emotion triggered in the scene with Daniel still swirling in his mind and senses, the magnitude of his loss overwhelmed him.

To Joanna, he had nothing to say.

RYAN WASN'T TALKING. For two days, Joanna had made coffee early, hoping to catch him, but he hadn't appeared. Amazing how much time he could spend in his workshop or on the beach—with Daniel tagging along, yet!—when he really put his mind to it.

She had questions, darn it. She had explanations to offer. She had a conscience that badly needed cleansing. Two whole days was long enough to wait. At a sound, she turned expectantly, but it was only Daniel emerging, sleepy-eyed and amiable, from his room. Right behind him, she realized with a catch in her breath, was Ryan.

The two of them—father and son!—seemed in perfect accord. Male bonding, it seemed, had cemented their friendship. Not that it needed cementing. Daniel had taken to Ryan as naturally as if he'd known him all of his life. My God, how was it that Ryan had known instantly about Daniel when *she* hadn't known in fourteen years?

Why, why had she never mentioned Ryan to her son?

She wished now that she could go back and change that. In all the stories she'd told Daniel about her childhood, about Wilderose House and Savannah, about Wilderose Cottage and Sea Island, about the people who had made her lonely childhood special, how could she have conveyed the essence of it without telling him how very special Ryan had been to her? How could she have portrayed Ryan as just another O'Connor?

And how was she going to fix it?

Breakfast was bearable only because of Daniel.

"Hmm, Mom, these pancakes are awesome," her son told her, slathering butter over his second stack, then drowning them in maple syrup. She had never succeeded in discouraging that. He glanced at Ryan. "Mom makes the world's best pancakes."

"How would you know?" Ryan asked, eyeing the mess on Daniel's plate doubtfully. "You've drowned the taste in butter and syrup."

"That's the secret," Daniel said, attacking his second helping with undiminished zeal. "Mom's recipe is just right to soak up the butter and syrup. Some pancakes, the syrup rolls right off, see? Like they're plastic or something. Not my mom's.'' He paused, stuck out his fork and pointed at Ryan's unfinished plate. ''You're not done, are you?''

Ryan gazed at his plate. ''I think so.''

''I'll bet you're not in the habit of eating breakfast,'' Daniel observed, showing the uncanny insight that never quite failed to surprise Joanna.

''What makes you say that?'' Ryan asked.

''Well, a lot of times you've been in places where three square meals a day wouldn't be possible, am I right?''

With a short laugh, Ryan nodded. ''Pretty close, I guess.''

Daniel chewed thoughtfully before asking, ''Were you ever just plain scared? I mean, you've reported from South America, Northern Ireland, Kuwait, Bosnia—just to name a few. Those places aren't exactly Central Park.''

After a quick look exchanged with Joanna, Ryan seemed to withdraw again. ''Central Park can be pretty risky,'' Joanna said, drawing Daniel's attention. ''You enter the grounds after dark at the risk of your life.''

''Well, sure, but—'' Daniel turned back to Ryan. ''Wasn't it somewhere in the Middle East that Pete was killed?''

Ryan stood up, shoving his chair back.

His pancakes forgotten, Daniel looked from Joanna to Ryan. ''Did I say something wrong?''

Joanna spoke. ''Daniel—''

''I'm going to see if I can figure out what's wrong with the security system,'' Ryan said.

Daniel stood instantly to go with him. ''Great. I was hoping we wouldn't just wait around for those guys to fix it. There's no telling how long that'll be.''

''I'll need some help with the dishes,'' Joanna reminded Daniel.

''Aw, Mom.''

''You know the rules, Daniel,'' Joanna said firmly. ''We're Ryan's guests. There's no maid service. The kitchen doesn't tidy itself after a meal.''

"But the security sys—"

"Give your mother a hand with the dishes, Daniel," Ryan ordered curtly. "I'll be outside when you finish."

Daniel's face fell, but he didn't argue. Joanna knew how much he'd prefer to follow Ryan—he was insatiably curious. Once he scented a mystery of any kind, he was like…like his father. The truth was, Daniel had inherited more than a natural curiosity from Ryan. He was tenacious, single-minded, intrepid, a born risk-taker. David Stanton had been none of those things. He'd been a dreamer, a collector, intuitive and sweet-natured. How had she closed her eyes to the signs that Daniel was Ryan's son for so many years?

Daniel's questions began the instant the door closed behind Ryan.

"Mom, what was that all about? What did I say? What's wrong with asking about Ryan's experience overseas? Jeez, he's been everywhere, he's seen everything. I think it's great. Why isn't he working now?" Daniel paused in the act of stacking the plates at the table and looked narrowly at his mother. "He *isn't* working now, is he? He's on some sort of leave of absence, isn't he?"

Joanna inhaled slowly. "Daniel, listen to yourself."

"Huh?"

"Only Ryan can answer those questions. Some of them are intrusive. You can't invade a person's privacy just for the sake of satisfying your curiosity."

Daniel paused, looking stricken. "I didn't mean—"

"I know you didn't mean anything except to satisfy a natural curiosity about Ryan's career. You're right. He's been everywhere and he's seen more places on the globe than anybody I've ever known."

She took the plates from her son and set them down on the counter. "Since we're his guests here, I'll tell you this and ask you to put yourself in Ryan's place. Pete's death hit him very hard. He hasn't gotten beyond it yet. Sometimes that happens."

"It's been over a year, Mom."

"Sometimes it takes a long time."

"Like when my father died," Daniel said, watching her intently. "You didn't smile for a long time. To me, it seemed like forever."

Her smile was soft and sad, as though to acknowledge the truth of his memory. "It seemed like forever to me, too. And I think Ryan believes it will be forever. But you and I know that the pain of death fades eventually."

"And we're left with the good stuff."

She smiled fully then. "Yeah, we're left with the good stuff." Reaching out, she put her arm around his skinny middle and gave him a quick hug. "Did I ever tell you what a great kid I think you are?"

Daniel grinned, hugging her back. "Nah, tell me now."

"You're a great kid and I'm a lucky mom."

"Well, hey, in that case…" He gazed around at the dirty dishes. "Do I have to finish this stuff?"

With a laugh, she shoved him back and flipped down the door of the dishwasher. "Absolutely," she told him. "Start loading!"

IT TOOK ALL OF FIFTEEN minutes for Ryan to get himself sufficiently under control to concentrate on the electronic panel in front of him. Standing at the side of the house where the box was mounted, he got the door open and stood looking at the maze of wires and electrical gadgetry. He didn't know enough about security systems to fix anything except the most elementary problems, but he—

Stopping, he rubbed a hand across his face. Why the hell had he stalked out of the kitchen like that? His response had probably stifled any interest Daniel might have had in his professional life. He didn't want that. He wanted Daniel to know who he was, what he was about. He'd spent the past two days working on it. He wanted Daniel to know all the things about his dad that Ryan had never known about Cameron.

"So, you got it figured out yet?"

"Hey, Daniel…" Ryan straightened, slammed the door of the panel box and met his son's eyes. "I've got a confession to make."

Daniel eyed him cautiously. "Yeah?"

"The security system may as well be a Chinese puzzle as far as I'm concerned. There are hundreds of wires in there and no less than six colors. Like it or not, we're going to have to wait for the experts."

"Uh-huh." Daniel chewed at his inside cheek, studying the ugly gray box. "A lot of people have trouble with electronics."

Ryan nodded. "You can definitely count me as one of them."

"But not me."

There was a moment or two of silence as Ryan studied him. "You know your way around, do you?"

"I've monkeyed around some, computers and CDs, sound systems, stuff like that." He reached out and pulled the door of the panel box open. "Yeah, I see one thing right away."

Ryan stepped back, waiting.

"The salt air is probably the culprit," Daniel said, pulling a cluster of wires out and examining them. "Deteriorates steel if it's not properly treated. That's why ships have to have such sophisticated paint, you know? Makes sense that anything that's exposed to excessive conditions right here on the beach is gonna suffer." He turned to Ryan. "You got any wire cutters?"

Wordlessly, Ryan reached for the toolbox at his feet, found the wire cutters and handed them over.

"Thanks." Daniel pulled a black wire free from the cluster, and using the wire cutters, stripped some of the deteriorated plastic away. "Got any electrical tape?" he asked Ryan.

Ryan, having anticipated that, handed it over.

In another ten minutes, Daniel had stripped and rewrapped several of the wires. Then bundling the cluster back into the space where he'd found it, he nodded briefly. Stepping back, he gave the whole panel another critical look before slamming the panel door and flipping the small lock that secured it.

"This is not a very dependable system," he informed an impressed Ryan. "Any determined intruder could break the lock with a good blow. You need something more sophisticated."

"Like a German shepherd?" Ryan returned dryly.

Daniel laughed. "Actually, that would be my first choice."

Folding his arms across his chest, Ryan gave him an affectionate once-over. "I'm impressed, Daniel. Where did you learn all that?"

Daniel shrugged, but he was pleased. "Here and there."

"You must have a sound system at home in Chicago that won't wait."

"Pretty much."

"Is music a hobby of yours?"

"I like music, but then I like lots of things." He looked at Ryan, but his thoughts were introspective. "It's like I have this deep curiosity about everything...anything, you know? It can be about people, or about things and how they work, about events, sports, stuff in the news...." He shook his head. "I wonder sometimes if I could ever settle down to one subject, like you have to do in college, you know? I can't think of any particular *job* I'd like to do. I mean, forever."

"I know the feeling."

"Really?"

"Yeah." Ryan slipped his hands into his back pockets, gazing beyond Daniel toward the sea. "So I took up reporting."

"I can understand that," Daniel said, his gaze following Ryan's to the water and beyond.

The moment was golden. Staring at the reflection of morning sun on the sea, Ryan knew he might never again have so perfect an opportunity to offer Daniel a glimpse of himself. As a reporter and as a man. All it would take was ripping away the shell that had protected him. He had done it with Joanna. Could he do it now with his son?

"You asked about Pete...." he began in a husky tone.

"Uh-huh," Daniel said, giving him a curious look.

Again Ryan gazed out to sea, then drew in a deep breath. "Do you know how to sail?"

"Uh...a little. Lake Michigan, you know. I've never owned a boat. Mostly I sailed with friends." He added hastily, "but I like it a lot."

Ryan nodded, then gestured for Daniel to follow. "Come on, then. Now that you've fixed the alarm, we'll set it and take the *Lady O* for her first sail in a long, long time."

"Hey, radical!" Happily, Daniel fell into step beside Ryan. And together they headed toward Wilderose Cottage to tell Joanna.

CHAPTER NINE

THE SAILS OF THE *Lady O* snapped smartly in the wind as the slim, twenty-foot boat tilted on a forty-five-degree turn. Ryan was deft and sure at the helm, his body leaning into the wind, eyes alert and gazing straight ahead. Daniel watched admiringly. Although he'd jumped at the chance to sail with Ryan, he had been slightly anxious. His experience as a sailor left a lot to be desired, but Ryan clearly was an expert. He might not have taken the *Lady O* out lately, but he'd been sailing somewhere, Daniel guessed, fascinated by all the possibilities. The Caribbean? Acapulco? California? Martha's Vineyard? Or was it somewhere a lot more interesting? Like the Persian Gulf. Or the Adriatic. Or off the coast of Africa.

As the *Lady O* knifed through water as green as glass, Ryan swayed easily with the movement of the boat. Daniel had been clumsy at first, but Ryan was patient while he adjusted. He'd actually laughed when they'd nearly capsized while making a turn when they'd first left the dock. Daniel was getting the feel of it now, though, and he relaxed a little.

They would have taken Joanna with them, but two things had happened within a few minutes of making their sailing plans. The security people had come by and blessed Daniel's repair of the system, which was now up and working fine. Then, just before they left, the phone people had arrived to reinstate phone service. So all the measures that were available to safeguard his mom were in place. The fence around the grounds of Wilderose Cottage was wired, windows and doors were secured. With the added protection of a telephone,

Joanna had urged them to sail without her. For added security, they had a cellular phone with them in the boat.

"Let's stop for a while," Ryan said suddenly, reaching for the mainsail.

Making sure they had a good view of the dock and the back of Wilderose Cottage, Daniel turned in his seat and surveyed the area. There were other sailboats in the vicinity, bright spots of color against the vivid blue of the sky. A few speed hulls trailed white wakes, but they were far enough away that they posed no problem. "Sounds good," Daniel responded, hefting the anchor overboard while Ryan secured the mainsail.

With the flap of the sails quieted, a sense of peace descended. Leaning back on his elbows, Daniel tracked the flight of gulls circling overhead. The slap of water against the hull of the *Lady O* blended with the cries of the birds. Without a word, Ryan passed Daniel a bottle of water and then both relaxed, drinking it. The view of Wilderose Cottage was unobstructed. Palms swayed in the foreground near the house. Ever mindful of his mother's safety, Daniel's gaze moved to the building that housed a studio where she'd told him she'd been working ever since she'd arrived at the cottage. He could see her through the windows and calculated that it would take them about ten minutes to get to the dock if they needed to.

"This is great," he said, turning his gaze to Ryan. "I could really get into this if I hung around here very long."

With his eyes on Daniel, Ryan tipped up the bottle and drank. "Yeah, there's nothing quite like Sea Island."

"That's what my mom always said."

"Yet you never wanted to visit?"

Daniel shrugged. "It just never seemed to work out that way. We took lots of vacations, but never here." He leaned forward with the bottle between his hands and rotated it back and forth. "To tell the truth, I've always wanted to know more about this whole area, Sea Island and Savannah and all. That's pretty logical, don't you think? My mom did grow up here, but she seemed...well, I'm not sure how to describe her when the subject of Sea Island and the O'Connors and stuff came up. She'd just sort of...close up, you know?''

"All childhood memories aren't happy," Ryan responded. "You're old enough to understand that."

"Sure, but she was more than a kid when she left here. She had already graduated from college." He looked at Ryan. "She went to New York right after graduation, did you know that?"

"Yeah."

"I guess you were at the *Sentinel* here in Savannah, huh?''

Ryan stared at a gull that had perched on the end of the *Lady O*. "I started there, yes."

"My grandmother was the managing editor then, right?"

"Jessica Howell, yes."

"She's neat, don't you think?"

"One of the best."

Daniel smiled. "I guess you think Miss Kathleen is pretty neat, too, huh?"

Ryan smiled faintly. "You know much about Miss Kathleen?"

"I know she's your grandmother and the owner and publisher of the *Savannah Sentinel*, that she came from Ireland in the Roaring Twenties on a ship that capsized and sank in a storm in New York harbor. She married Patrick O'Connor and they had a son, Cameron, who was your father. My grandmother, Jessica, was their stepdaughter somehow or other, and they raised her as their own."

"For someone who never visited Savannah," Ryan said dryly, "you know a lot about the O'Connors."

"They're sort of family," Daniel said simply.

The remark seemed to catch Ryan off guard. A few seconds passed. "Yeah," he said then, looking away and studying the horizon.

A lone craft off to their left was cruising more slowly now, closer to shore. "You asked about Pete," he said finally.

"I didn't mean to butt into something that's none of my business," Daniel said earnestly.

Shaking his head, Ryan replied, "I know that Pete was friends with you and your mother. I can understand why you're curious about what happened. And I—"

"Not curious exactly," Daniel said, studying the bottle of water in his hand. "That makes me sound like some kind of weirdo geek or something. I just liked him a lot and I'd like to know that he was doing something…you know, worthwhile when he was killed. I don't want to think that he died for nothing…for no reason." He transferred his gaze back to Ryan.

Staring into those earnest blue eyes, Ryan wished he was anywhere but where he was. Why had he marooned himself in a boat a mile from the nearest dock to explain to this boy his role in the death of a friend?

"He wasn't killed for no reason," Ryan began quietly. "He was killed doing his job. He was a photographer, one of the best in the business—maybe *the* best in the business. You've heard about the country where it happened. Pete chose to go there. He believed—and I agreed—that there were things going on in that country that should be reported. Things the world should see, and he was uniquely qualified to make that happen."

"Not very many Americans were killed there," Daniel observed, surprising Ryan with his knowledge. "Why did Pete have to be one of them?"

Aching somewhere in his chest, Ryan tried to find the words. "I don't know the answer to that," he said quietly, gazing beyond Daniel toward the horizon. "People die before their time. It happens a lot, Daniel—in car accidents, or with a fatal disease, or in earthquakes and fires…even suicides. Wiser men than I have puzzled over that question since time began. As for Pete…" Ryan drew a deep breath. "The truth is, Daniel, he would be alive today if it weren't for me."

"How?" the boy asked simply.

He forced himself to look into Daniel's eyes. "I persuaded Pete to go that night. We had been contacted by the leader of a group of rebels who wanted media exposure. Warlord, the media had dubbed him. Pete was reluctant, but I talked him into it. Instead of talking, they began shooting almost before we stopped the jeep." He frowned, remembering. "I could see the general shouting, waving his arms. But his men were out of control." His mouth twisted. "They missed me, but Pete was hit twice."

Daniel was studying him intently. "Why did you believe a crazy rebel?"

"He wasn't crazy. He was the commander of a significant band of soldiers—ragtag and ill trained, poorly outfitted, but there were a lot of them."

"So you thought hearing his point of view might help somehow."

"Well, yes...but—"

"And it might have if somebody hadn't started shooting."

"I'll never know." Ryan blew out a long breath, shaking his head over a question he'd pondered a thousand times. "His men were inexperienced. Or scared. Or stupid. Who knows? I didn't stick around to ask for an explanation."

Daniel nodded, chewing on his lip for a moment or two as he sorted out his thoughts. Taking his time, he screwed the cap on the empty bottle, then tucked it away. "You and Pete were a team, he told me that before. I don't think you could have hustled him into something he really didn't want to do."

"I didn't exactly hustle him." That much at least was true, Ryan thought, though the knowledge brought no real relief. What he'd done was to keep to himself his own misgivings about the venture.

"Then what?" Daniel asked, puzzled.

Ryan forced himself to look into those innocent eyes. "I had a bad feeling about the whole thing, Daniel. I should have heeded it. At the very least, I should have told Pete that I felt bad vibes. But I didn't."

Even before he finished, Daniel was nodding. "I know what you mean. Boy, do I!" He leaned forward, his hands on his bony knees. "You're out in the middle of a desert in some godforsaken country. You get a message from a nutty warlord. Let's forget what a sensational story it'll be. You get this feeling—you don't have to describe *that* to me, man. Not hardly. You think, should I say we don't do this gig, Pete, because I've got a feeling? Or do you ignore the feeling because you aren't even sure yourself that it means anything?"

With a rapt expression, Ryan found himself nodding, slowly. He was fascinated with Daniel's uncanny insight into the way he'd felt that day.

"So you get to the site and all hell's breaking loose… pardon my French…and you realize—too late—you should've listened." He stopped and looked at Ryan. "Is that how it was, sort of?"

"It's close…yeah, it's pretty close."

Daniel leaned back in the boat, stretching both arms out straight along the side. "Pete wouldn't blame you, man, you can count on that. You said yourself, he chose to go. If you'd succeeded, it would have been another amazing moment for your résumés."

A brief smile crossed Ryan's face. "Are you sure you're only fourteen years old?"

Daniel grinned. "Mom says fourteen going on forty."

"Mom's got it right, I think."

They spent a few seconds of shared camaraderie. Above them, gulls circled lazily. They looked when one zeroed in on a target, executed a plunging dive, then rose smoothly with the wriggling fish in its bill. Farther out, other sailboats skimmed before the wind. With his thoughts on the incredible conversation he'd just shared with Daniel, Ryan was barely conscious of the speed hull in the distance.

Daniel's next question caught him by surprise.

"So, what about Joey?"

Ryan's head whipped around. "Joey?"

"Yeah, Pete's little girl. Joey. I think she's about nine years old, but I'm not sure. You must know her, you and Pete being so close and all."

How was it this kid could turn him inside out so easily? "I know her," he murmured.

"Did you go and see her and her mother when it happened?"

"I saw them. At the funeral and then...afterward."

"Is Joey okay?" There was a note of concern in Daniel's voice. "I know how I felt when my dad died suddenly like that. I was seven, but I still remember it. If it hadn't been for my mom and Grampa Jem and some friends..." He shrugged, a little self-conscious. "Well, they made a big difference."

Of all the things he hated about Pete's death, robbing Joey of a father topped the list. Pete's wife, Judith, was a sleek, ambitious New Yorker with a demanding job as an editor in a major publishing house. Ryan had been chilled by her composed acceptance of Pete's death. He'd written it off to her intense involvement in her career. After all, Pete had been absent almost as much as he'd been around. He recalled thinking Judith wouldn't have too much difficulty adjusting to a life where Pete wasn't around at all. But Joey was something else. Shy and sensitive, she had adored her daddy, and the feeling had been mutual.

Ryan's guilt had been a great motivator. He had spent several days in New York after the funeral just to satisfy himself that Pete's family would be okay, especially Joey. Her nanny proved to be warm and affectionate, young enough to cope with Joey's energy, caring enough to be a surrogate mother. Satisfied that the child was in good hands, he had retreated to Sea Island.

"I haven't been back to New York to see Joey and Judith for a while," he told Daniel. "But I've called several times."

"How? I thought you didn't have a phone."

"There's one at the 7-Eleven where I get bread and milk."

Daniel scrambled up suddenly with a surprised sound, nearly capsizing them. "Ryan, look at that boat!"

"Watch it!" Ryan ordered, positioning himself to counteract the thrashing of the boat while he looked where Daniel pointed. He caught his breath. It was the cruising speed hull. The situation hit him like a fist to the gut. Two powerful inboards could eat up the distance to Wilderose Cottage in seconds.

"I don't think those guys are just pleasure riding," Daniel said urgently. "They're headed toward our dock."

"Let's get the sails up," Ryan said, his hands already on the rigging.

"My mom's there alone!" Daniel cried, launching himself toward the lines that released the mainsail. Moving frantically, they unfurled the sheets and secured them, then set a course directly toward the speed hull. The boat had cut its engines back to a near crawl.

"It's two men and they've got binoculars!" In his fear for his mother, Daniel fumbled with the rigging, then lunged to his feet to grab at the boom that shot beyond his reach.

"Daniel, be careful!" Ryan's tone was sharp. "We want to get to the dock without capsizing."

"But my mom—"

"Try to see their registration numbers," Ryan told him. "Or a name—anything to identify them."

"There's nothing. It's blank where the numbers should be."

"Be calm now. We're heading straight for them. They'll either explain their interest in Wilderose Cottage or they'll take off as soon as they realize we've noticed them."

"What if it gets worse than that?" Daniel asked, pale with worry.

"It won't," Ryan said curtly. Glancing up, he nodded with satisfaction as the sails billowed in a blessedly favorable wind. "Get out the phone," he told Daniel.

"Jeez, I forgot we had it." Scrambling forward, he fumbled

in a hatch compartment and pulled out the phone. Then he frantically punched out the number at Wilderose Cottage.

Before she had time to answer, Ryan calmed him with one look. "Panic won't help your mother, Daniel. Tell her we've spotted a boat that appears to be watching the house. Be sure she locks the doors and stays inside. Tell her not to open for anyone. We'll be at the dock in less than eight minutes."

"Yes s-sir." Daniel swallowed once, hard. "Hello, Mom?"

He waited as she spoke, then meeting Ryan's eyes as she talked, he gave a short, surprised laugh. "No kidding? Well, tell him a couple of jokers are out here in the water in a speed hull watching the house with binoculars. No, wait..." Daniel stretched as far as he could without actually standing, craning to see beyond Ryan. "They've spotted us, Mom. They're turning! Jeez, holy-moly, they are *outta* here, goosing those two inboards to the max!" He listened another moment, nodding. "Okay, I'll tell him. We're on our way in right now!"

"Tell who what?" Ryan demanded.

"You're not gonna believe this, Ryan," he said excitedly. "Talk about perfect timing."

"What!" Ryan roared.

"Right." Daniel winced. "No sweat. Mom's in safe hands."

Ryan scowled darkly. "Whose hands?"

"Savannah's finest, man. Nick Dalton just dropped in."

AS THE *LADY O* BUMPED gently into the dock, Ryan's gaze went directly to Joanna. She was pale, and her eyes were anxious as they met his. He thought of sweeping her up and holding her close, but he wasn't sure she would welcome any reassurance from him. Beside her, Nick looked stern. Ryan knew from his expression that he hadn't driven all the way out to Wilderose Cottage for a social call.

"What's happened?" he asked without preamble.

"In a minute," Nick said, catching the rope and securing

it at the dock. Daniel scrambled out of the boat and went directly to his mother.

"Are you okay, Mom?"

"I'm fine," Joanna told him, giving him a hug. "What were you talking about on the phone?" She looked at Ryan. "Someone in a boat was spying on us?"

"Someone was looking at Wilderose Cottage," Ryan said calmly. "It could be someone interested in the property. This is prime real estate, after all."

Daniel stared at him. "Those guys weren't shopping for a summer place, Ryan. Get real."

"Daniel..." Joanna rebuked him.

"Well, it's true. They were in a boat with no markings, no name or numbers."

"I'll have it checked out," Nick put in quietly, studying Daniel with interest. "We haven't met," he said, putting out his hand. "I'm Nick Dalton."

Daniel grinned, taking his hand. "I'm Daniel. This is my mom."

"I gathered that," Nick said, smiling. He glanced at Ryan before looking back at the boy. "I think your mom told me you were visiting your grandpa in Montreal. What happened? Tired of fishing in that cold water?"

"Nah, I just thought my mom might be missing me." He flashed Joanna a mischievous look. "So I decided to surprise her."

A seasoned sailor, Nick bent to give Ryan a hand securing the boat while Joanna and Daniel collected the empty bottles. "I'll bet she wasn't the only one surprised," he murmured for Ryan's ears only. "How in hell did he get to the island?"

"Don't ask," Ryan snapped, turning to head toward the house. In front of them, Joanna and Daniel were beyond earshot. "Daniel is...something else," he said, watching his adolescent amble with something like bemusement. He was already taller than his mother.

"He seems a nice kid," Nick said, watching them go.

"Yeah."

Nick was silent, his gaze on Daniel thoughtful. There was speculation and something else in his perusal. At his side, Ryan walked with controlled urgency. Nick was trained to observe in his line of work. Had he noticed Daniel's uncanny resemblance to Will O'Connor? God, his life had become more complicated in the past three days than he'd ever dreamed it could be.

He pulled his sunglasses off and wiped the sweat from his face. The last thing he wanted was a discussion with his brother-in-law about his newfound paternity. At least, not just yet. What he wanted to know right now was the reason for Nick's visit.

For a long moment, he looked down at the dark lenses in his hand, then he put them back on his face. "Let's have it," he said tersely. "What's up?"

Nick began without hesitation. "There's been a formal inquiry about Joanna from Chicago. They want her for questioning in the death of Enrico Fellini."

"She told me it was ruled a suicide," Ryan said shortly. "He was a very sick man."

"Yeah, but I'm betting she also told you she never believed Fellini would do himself in whether he was sick or not."

Ryan swore liberally. "Who's asking?"

"Gus Forrester. The dective who questioned her originally at the time. And he's not going to be put off indefinitely. He's suspicious and he's smart. He bought the suicide originally because there didn't seem to be any reason to think otherwise."

"And now?" Ryan said.

They'd reached the steps to the house. Nick paused and waited while Joanna and Daniel disappeared inside. "He's got a reason to change his mind." He looked squarely at Ryan. "His investigation has linked Rico's gallery with some very suspicious characters, and he's turned up irregularities in the way Rico did business. 'Irregularities' is Forrester's word."

Ryan frowned. "What did he mean?"

"He wasn't that forthcoming," Nick replied. "But another source in Chicago tells me that some people are very upset over a shipment of diamonds that has somehow gone astray." Ryan swore and Nick went on. "It could be that Forrester doesn't want to tip his hand. He's done enough digging on Joanna to trace her family to Savannah. But whether or not he feels reluctant to trust the SPD with his suspicions, he knows once I'm given an official request, I'm bound by the law."

Watching him intently, Ryan tried to decide if he was here in his capacity as a cop or as a member of the family. The easy relationship he'd enjoyed with Nick meant nothing, he discovered, when measured against Joanna's safety. "Where exactly does that leave us?"

Through the screen of the porch, Joanna and Daniel could be seen moving around inside the house. "If Joanna is spotted in Savannah," Nick said blandly, "I call Gus Forrester. I have no choice. But if she's on Sea Island, for instance—" he shrugged "—she's out of my jurisdiction. That ends at Savannah's city limits."

Without saying any more, Ryan rubbed a hand over his chin, then nodded. "Let's go inside."

Daniel and Joanna were waiting. She looked up, meeting Ryan's eyes. "Did Nick tell you that Forrester is looking for me?"

"Who's Forrester?" Daniel asked.

"Chicago police," Ryan explained, giving the boy a brief smile. "He's the chief investigator who interviewed your mother the day Rico Fellini died."

"They've put it together, haven't they?" Daniel asked eagerly. "They figured out he was murdered."

"Wait a minute," Nick said, frowning at Daniel. "What makes you think Fellini was murdered?"

Realizing he'd opened a can of worms, Daniel gave Ryan a helpless look. "It's okay," Ryan said. "He's family."

Still watching the boy narrowly, Nick waited.

"I don't know that he was murdered," Daniel began cautiously. "I just found it hard to believe that Rico would commit suicide. I knew him pretty well. He wasn't the type to just give up like that." He glanced at Ryan as though for support.

"We've all concluded, more or less, that Fellini didn't take his own life," Ryan said dryly.

Nick's attention was still on the boy. "I'm just interested in hearing how Daniel figured it out. You want to fill me in on that, son?"

Releasing a sigh, Daniel flopped down on the nearest chair. "It's sort of hard to explain." He picked at the shoelaces on his Reeboks. "I just had a feeling."

"Uh-huh." Nick nodded slowly, still preoccupied with something about Daniel.

"How is Shannon?" Joanna asked quickly. "And the baby?"

"Fine." Nick transferred his gaze to her with a smile. "They're both doing just great. She's a little tired. She doesn't get much rest nursing, at least, not yet. When Nicky starts sleeping through the night, it'll be a happy day for everybody. Which reminds me..." He headed for the front door. "I'd better be off. I promised to be home by seven."

"Tell Shannon we'll be in to see the baby as soon as we can," Ryan said quietly, following him to the door.

Nick nodded. "She understands."

As soon as they were through the door, Ryan pulled it closed behind him and went down the steps with Nick. "Do you think you can get anything on that boat? Daniel's right. They were *not* shopping for real estate."

"It'll be difficult with no markings, but I'll check around. Somebody might have seen something, or better yet, might know something. I'll put a couple of men on it."

Ryan released a breath. "I'd appreciate it. I don't like the idea that there's somebody out there watching," he said, his tone hard. "If I have to, I'll hire a couple of guys to patrol the area, especially at night."

"If you decide to do that, let me know," Nick said, walking over to his Bronco and pulling the door open. "I can connect you with some good men."

"Yeah, thanks."

"Take care, buddy." Nick put his hand out and Ryan took it. On the point of getting in his car, Nick stopped, then added quietly, "The boy, Daniel...you're right, he is something else. In fact...something about him reminds me of someone else I know." He looked squarely at Ryan. "If I were you, I'd pay close attention if he gets any more of those 'feelings.'"

CHAPTER TEN

"WE NEED TO TALK."

Joanna was stretched high, putting a serving dish on a shelf. Sliding it into place, she turned slowly and looked at Ryan. "About the boat, the inquiry from Forrester or Daniel?"

"Where is he?" Gazing beyond her, he could see that Daniel wasn't watching television in the family room.

"He's in the studio."

Ryan's expression changed. "Does he have any interest in painting?"

She laughed. "No, he can barely draw a straight line. He's far more at home writing text to go with my pictures. He—" Realizing what she had revealed, she stopped abruptly.

Ryan had moved closer, his eyes watchful. "He likes words," he said softly.

Flustered, Joanna gave the sink a final swipe and folded the dish towel into a neat square. "You know how kids are, they—"

"No, Joanna, I don't know how kids are."

She took a second to collect herself, then met his eyes. "I gather this conversation is to be about Daniel."

"All of the above. Let's go outside, take a walk on the beach. I don't think we want him popping in on us while we're having this discussion."

"I'm not even sure I want to have it," she murmured, aware of the slight tremor in her voice. She would have to be tougher than that with an adversary like Ryan. If she had learned anything while she was married to him, it was that he took instant, ruthless advantage when her guard was down.

"Don't worry, I ran the edge off my rage that first night when I found out. I'll be perfectly civilized, so long as you don't reveal any other dark secrets in our shared past."

"I told you, Ryan, I didn't know that you were Daniel's father. I wasn't sure *who* was." She closed her eyes and pressed between her eyes with two fingers. "Oh, that sounds awful...as though I was some kind of...promiscuous...I don't know what. It wasn't like that at all," she said, her voice rising at the end.

"Let's get out of here," he muttered. Taking her hand, he led her onto the porch and down the steps. Outside, the breeze off the water whipped through her hair, making her wish she'd taken the time to confine it.

"My hair..." she began, trying to anchor it behind her ears with both hands.

"Don't," he said, catching her hands and bringing them down to her sides. "It's okay."

"It's all over the...place...and..." Her words suddenly trailed off at the look in his eyes.

"I like it."

They stood, caught in the intimacy of the moment, both aware that the attraction between them had not diminished with the unexpected appearance of Daniel. Trust, yes, maybe. Probably. But the power of what they felt when they were together was still there. It was in the tension in Joanna's throat and in the fierceness of Ryan's gaze. Joanna had a compelling urge to cradle his cheek in her palm. Just to touch him. They had seemed so close to recapturing something magic...was it only two nights ago?

The cry of a gull overhead broke the spell, and Ryan swung away without another word and began walking. Would they ever be able to work through the tangle of the past? Joanna wondered.

She caught up with him in a few steps. "I'm so sorry,

Ryan," she said softly. "I wish I could think of something else to say, some other significant reason for not having made *sure*..." She suddenly felt sad. "But I can't."

"You want to hear something funny," he began, his eyes on his feet as he walked. "I never thought I would be so fascinated. I've only known that I have a son...what? Two days. Forty-eight hours. Now I completely understand how Nick felt that day when he told us about the baby. It's awe and wonder, pride, happiness. He calls up more emotion in me than—"

He shrugged, as though words were beyond him. "It's like I want to know everything about him, Jo. I want to know what he likes and dislikes, what scares him, what touches him. I want to understand how he can master electronics when it's a mystery to me. I want to know how he looked when he was two and when he was six and...ah, everything. I want to make up for lost time, can you understand that?"

"Yes," she whispered, closing her eyes against a crushing wave of guilt and regret.

"This afternoon on the boat, I kept looking at him with this sense of wonder and disbelief and a...an almost painful ache in my chest." He paused. "I have a son and he makes me happy. I never knew I could feel those things."

He glanced over, bending a little as he walked to peer into her face. "I want to spend some time with him—you can understand that, can't you?"

She nodded mutely, her eyes downcast.

In the face of her cooperation, he became more confident. "I want you both to stay here," he went on, trying to suppress his eagerness. "I mean, for the summer at least."

"At least?" she repeated, looking at him in confusion. Could this be the same brooding, haunted man who had barely been civil when she'd appeared on his doorstep just six short days ago?

"Yeah, I think you owe me that, Jo. He's not in school in

the summer, and you're not going anywhere anytime soon, not the way things are shaping up.''

"He doesn't know you're his father, Ryan," she reminded him stiffly.

"Not now. Look, I know it's not something we can just tell him outright. I wouldn't do that, anyway. But I want to tell him, Jo. Before the summer's over and he goes back to his life in Chicago, I want him to know he's an O'Connor and that he's my son.''

"I can't believe you," Joanna said, her voice rising slightly. "Telling him something like this isn't like suddenly revealing that there's no Santa Claus, Ryan. We're talking about telling him something that will turn his world upside down, something that will change everything he's ever known." She stopped, and made him look at her. "Have you truly thought about what you're saying?"

"Have you truly thought what it means if you *don't* tell him?" he countered.

"It means we'll go back to the life we lived—as soon as we can—in Chicago, where he has friends and a social life and church and sports. You can visit us when you want, anytime you want.''

"He can have all that here," Ryan said quietly, "plus a father."

"You never wanted to play that role before," she reminded him bitterly.

"It's not a role," he shot back. "I didn't count on discovering that I had a son, but now that I have, I'm damn sure not going to just spend a few weeks fishing and sailing with him and then wave him off to Chicago when you decide it's safe to resume your life.''

"Ryan..." She pressed her fingers against her forehead for a second, thinking. "This is ridiculous. It's crazy. And it's...it's an emotional risk that is just too great to take. Can't you see that?"

"I see that I've missed my son's first fourteen years, Joanna.

In the grand scheme of things, that's probably a little better than one-fifth of his life. I don't plan to miss any more of it.''

''And I can see that you've hardly changed in all those years,'' Joanna cried, desperate to keep her world—Daniel's world!—intact. ''You still think of yourself first, what *you* want, what makes *you* feel good, not what's best for the others who might be affected by your decision. Other people are going to be hurt if you do this, Ryan.''

He looked away from her. It was nearly night. The line between the sea and sky blended almost invisibly at the horizon. A full moon shadowed by clouds seemed too large to be real.

''I don't want to hurt anyone,'' he said quietly after a minute. ''But I can't be wrong about this. What I feel, what I think we could share as a family, couldn't be wrong.''

He turned back to her. ''I'll tell you one last thing. Now that I know Daniel is my son, there is no way I could stand by and watch him go out of my life.''

His words were not spoken as a threat. Looking at him, Joanna saw pain and vulnerability, and a certain…desperation.

''For the first time since Pete died,'' he told her, ''I wake up in the mornings and think there's a reason to get up.''

Dear God, she could almost believe him. But she couldn't stand by and let him do this, no matter what.

''You're not going to do anything today, are you?'' she asked him.

He shook his head. ''Not at all, not until we've talked about it and decided how to explain it.'' He put out a hand and tucked a wild strand of her hair behind her ear. ''In this day and age, he knows about babies and sex. Kids do. Hell, some kids at his age have *had* sex. I don't want him to think of it just in those terms. We made love that night for all the right reasons. I want him to understand that.''

He made it sound so easy, Joanna thought, resisting the urge to nuzzle her face against his hand. Too easy. Knowing Daniel as she did—having fielded his questions on every conceivable subject from the time he was old enough to ask them—she feared it wouldn't be quite the smooth sailing Ryan imagined. It would probably be more like negotiating whitewater rapids on a raft. With no oar.

"Just promise me you won't say anything without talking to me first, will you?"

They both understood that she accepted the inevitable. But a line had been drawn. Ryan nodded and they began walking again.

"Tell me about the boat you and Daniel saw," she said, her eyes on the lights of a buoy marker in the distance. She had listened while Ryan tried to dispel Daniel's fears about the incident at dinner earlier. Nothing he'd said had convinced her. Or Daniel either, she suspected. The same genes that fired Ryan's insatiable curiosity ran strong in his son. Again she was amazed at how blind she'd been for so long. Daniel was so obviously Ryan's.

"Do you think they've found me?" she asked.

"Maybe."

She sighed, relieved that he wasn't going to try and fob her off. She needed to hear the truth, whatever it was. "They think I took those diamonds," she said softly. "But I didn't. I put them right back where I found them, although in a different statue." She was silent for a moment. "What do you think we should do?"

"Double up on security. Stay out of boats. Leave Wilderose Cottage only when I'm with you."

"Under the circumstances, I can't imagine wanting to leave at all." With the toe of her sneaker, she kicked at a piece of driftwood. "How do you think they found me, Ryan?"

He shrugged. "Who knows? The airlines, maybe, or through your credit cards. It's hard to say. Gus Forrester managed to get a line on your family in Savannah. If these thugs have a connection to the Chicago PD—and don't think that isn't possible—then maybe there's your answer."

"This puts Nick in a bind, doesn't it?" she asked quietly.

"That's the last thing you need to worry about, Jo. He'll be all over Nick like white on rice, but Nick's family. Besides, as he pointed out, Sea Island's out of his jurisdiction."

Out of the blue, he said, "You mentioned Rico's friend, Sammy...Feldstein, wasn't it?"

"Yes."

"Does he know your background? That Savannah is where your mother lives?"

"Hmm, I'm not sure. Maybe." She looked quickly at him. "But even if he did, he wouldn't tell anyone who wanted to hurt me."

"Someone who wanted to hurt you wouldn't necessarily tell him that," Ryan replied dryly.

"Or," Joanna said slowly, "if they thought he knew and didn't want to tell, they might be ruthless enough to force him."

She stopped suddenly, wrapping her arms around her waist. "I'm scared, Ryan."

He pulled her into the shelter of his arms and held her tight. "It'll be all right, Jo," he murmured close to her ear. "I promise."

She couldn't control the shudder that shook her whole body. "You can't know that," she cried softly, burrowing into his warmth. It felt so good to have somebody holding her, to have somebody share the terror and uncertainty that had been with her since she'd opened that horrible statue and poured out a fortune in diamonds. She rested her head against his chest. "If we could just find those diamonds!"

Ryan tipped her face up. "How would that help? Who would we give them to? You don't know the names of Rico's partners. And even if you did, you don't think they would just take them and say thank you and let you walk away, do you?"

He was right, of course. As always. At least about this kind of thing, he was right. Not about Daniel. But she'd deal with that later, she thought wearily. Somehow.

She must have looked distressed, because with a faint smile, he suddenly bent and kissed her on the nose, just a peck. "Don't worry, baby." But then his lips touched hers, a light, teasing little butterfly kiss, and before she could react, he was talking again. "We've got Nick working this at Savannah PD...." Another quick kiss, this one with a little more substance. Between kisses, Ryan's low voice reassured, tantalized. "The police in Chicago are trying to figure it out from that end..." Another kiss, warm, lush. When it ended, their eyes met, then, as Ryan's mouth came closer, Joanna closed her eyes helplessly.

Ryan tried to remember what he'd been saying, but only her name came out. "Joanna...my Joanna..."

With the full melding of their mouths, the kiss was deep and soul stealing. This was not just something that was good between them. Both knew that, were beyond denying it. In spite of the passing of fifteen years, in spite of mistakes and misunderstandings, they needed only to be together, to touch, to feel all the fire and passion that had driven them as young lovers.

Lacing her arms around his neck, Joanna fell into the kiss the way she always did with Ryan. Nobody else made her heart stop at a touch. No other man could start her blood pounding or send her senses whirling out of control with just a kiss.

At least the feeling was mutual, she told herself dizzily. Somewhere in her heightened senses, she knew that Ryan was as affected by their kisses as she was. She pressed her body closer, and with a groan, he gathered her close until they touched from chests to knees. She flushed all over at the feel of him, warm and hard and powerfully male against her softness. His hand fumbled between them, seeking her breast. When he enclosed it, a familiar melting sensation washed through her, sent tremors from her nipples to her womb. He shifted suddenly, parting her legs with his knee, and drove one hand deep inside her jeans to hold her against his arousal. For a few delicious moments, she rocked in rhythm with his thrusts, while both emitted hungry, urgent sounds.

Dragging his mouth from hers, Ryan dropped to his knees on the sand and pulled her with him. Their impatience drove them to wild, frantic groping. He had his hand inside her shirt, and Joanna's fingers sought the snap on his jeans. Both touched and tasted, panted and murmured meaningless phrases, driven with an almost manic compulsion to rediscover the passion they'd found two nights before.

When Joanna's shirt was stripped away, Ryan fumbled with his zipper while planting open-mouthed kisses all over her face, her throat, the cleft between her breasts. Then, as passion threatened to overwhelm them, the flash of a car's headlights streaked across the landscape.

"Oh, God..."

Confused, dazed, weakened by sexual lethargy, it took Joanna a moment to focus. Then she began to scramble up, pulling on her blouse with frantic little motions, tugging at her jeans. Beside her, Ryan breathed in deep, heavy gasps, but he wasn't watching her. Like an animal sensing danger, he focused on the front gate of Wilderose Cottage, where a car had pulled up and stopped.

With a scowl, he looked at Joanna. "Are you okay?"

"Yes, I...ah...yes, I'm okay."

"Let's get up to the house. We've got company."

DANIEL WAS DESCENDING the stairs as they burst into the house. "Somebody's at the gate," he told them.

With her attention fixed on the unexpected visitor, Joanna barely glanced at Daniel. But somewhere in that special place of awareness common to mothers everywhere, she noticed that something about her son's expression wasn't quite right. But the moment passed with the sudden beep of the intercom.

Ryan pushed the button on the speaker. "Who is it?" he snapped.

Everyone in the room seemed stunned when a feminine

voice replied. "Ryan, darling…" A dramatic sigh. "Punch a button or something and open this damn gate. For us New Yorkers it's humid as hell out here. I'm hot, I'm wringing wet, I'm suffering jet lag, and I need a nice, tall gin and tonic desperately. Please tell me you have a well-stocked bar, otherwise I may throw myself in the ocean." A tiny pause. "Not a bad idea, if I didn't prefer a nice, chlorinated pool. By the way, there *is* a pool in this fabulous place, isn't there?"

"Judith?"

"Of course it's me, darling. Now do let me in."

There was total surprise on Ryan's face as he met Joanna's eyes.

"Judith Mann?" she asked softly. "Pete's wife?"

But Ryan had turned back to the intercom. Something about the way he stood absolutely still, pinching the bridge of his nose, suggested tension. And displeasure.

"The gate has to be opened manually, Judith," he said brusquely. "Give me a minute to get out there." Before she could say more, he released the bar and cut the connection.

Joanna heard his brief oath with mixed feelings. Everyone who knew Ryan was aware that he was alone at Sea Island by choice. Why was Pete Mann's widow here? Did Judith have special privileges? She realized suddenly that Daniel was standing beside her. In his hand was one of Cameron O'Connor's old journals. He'd been coming down the stairs when they walked in from the beach, she recalled. Had he been in the attic?

"I wonder if she brought Joey with her," Daniel said. Joanna gave him a quick look, struck by something in his voice.

"Do you think she might?" she asked Ryan.

"God, I don't know." He raked through his hair with both hands, looking harassed and edgy. "I don't even know what *she's* doing here. I told her—" He stopped, as if reconsidering something he was about to say. With an impatient look around, he muttered, "Where in hell did I put those keys?"

"They're in a tray on the hall table," Daniel told him. "That's where you told me to put them after unlocking the sailing stuff, remember?"

"Yeah, thanks." In a couple of strides, he was in the hall. Without looking at Daniel or Joanna, he scooped up the keys. He had his hand on the doorknob when Daniel suddenly spoke.

"I've been in the attic."

Ryan turned back with a distracted expression. Joanna looked from the old journal in Daniel's hand to his face. For some reason she felt suddenly apprehensive.

"What is it, Daniel?" she asked.

Ryan reached again for the doorknob. "I need to get out—"

"This'll only take a second," Daniel said. Ryan stopped, apparently taken aback by Daniel's tone. Joanna had seldom seen that expression in her son's eyes. What on earth...

"I just need to ask you both something before Joey's mother gets in here," Daniel said.

Joanna put out a hand, thinking to touch him, but he moved a little out of reach. He looked pale. And...shocked, yes, that was it—shocked. But there was something else. Now that he had the attention of both Joanna and Ryan, he seemed somehow...hostile. Had he seen them on the beach? she wondered frantically. Would knowing they were sexually involved outrage him? She knew that adolescent boys were sometimes protective of their mothers. Oh, God, would the string of complications in her life never stop?

Daniel looked at the journal in his hand and then at his mother, but his question was aimed at Ryan. "Is it true that you were once married to my mother?"

For a split second, Ryan felt sheer relief. Once he'd discovered Daniel was his son, he'd wanted nothing more than to tell him everything. Here was his opportunity. He glanced quickly at Joanna, and the look on her face killed that impulse. Now that the moment was upon them, he realized that she had been right to insist on caution. How they told Daniel, what and when they told him, could mean the difference between beginning a relationship with his son on good terms or damning them to a long period of misery. Daniel believed his father had died when he was seven. The only damage control needed now, tonight, concerned his and Joanna's marriage. The secret of his son's paternity could wait.

Outside, Judith began honking her car's horn impatiently. *Damn it to hell.*

Closing his eyes briefly, he leaned against the door. "Look, Daniel—"

"If you're thinking up some dumb story so you won't have to answer me," Daniel said angrily, "it'd better be good." He held up the journal, shaking it at both of them. "'Cause right in here, Cameron O'Connor writes about the wedding. It was at Sea Island, right on the lawn at this house!"

"It's true, Daniel." With a glance at Joanna, Ryan tried to convey to her that he would handle this carefully. "Joanna and I were once married. It was a long time ago."

"I guess you got a divorce." It was more a question than a statement. A bewildered question.

"Yes, we got a divorce, but we're still friends." Ryan reached for Joanna's hand and pulled her over so that they stood side by side. The last thing he wanted his son to think was that they were an embittered, estranged couple.

A million questions lurked in the blue eyes that looked from Ryan to Joanna. "Why did you get a divorce?"

Judith honked again and the intercom began beeping.

Ryan swore. "We'll talk about it after I unlock the gate for Judith, okay?"

"Mom?" Daniel's tone struck Joanna to the heart. Her relationship with her son was special, and the past few moments had brought home to her just how precious and fragile are the threads that hold a relationship together. She did not think she could bear it if she and Ryan couldn't somehow explain their history to Daniel in a way that he could understand and accept.

The incessant beeping from the intercom was maddening. She looked wordlessly at Ryan.

"Later, Daniel, I promise," Ryan said to the boy, then waited, his eyebrows raised. Only when Daniel finally nodded did he leave.

JUDITH MANN DID NOT LOOK as though she was suffering from jet lag. She didn't look hot and sweaty, either. To Joanna, she looked sleek and trim in a Donna Karan original. Her near-black hair was confined in a chignon that hadn't dared to spring one loose strand, not even in the breeze blowing off the Atlantic Ocean.

"Of course I remember Joanna," she said, smiling coolly over the top of her drink. "Pete was forever dropping this or that little tidbit after one of his visits. He admired your work. We both did. And Daniel…" She flashed a slightly warmer smile. "Joey has never forgotten the time the four of you went to dinner in Chicago."

"Is Joey okay?" Daniel asked.

"She's fine." She turned to Ryan. "Actually, Joey is at summer camp for the next six weeks. It was a golden opportunity for me to come, darling, and you know how I never hesitate to seize an opportunity." With a quick glance at Joanna, she spread her hands with a slightly bewildered look. "I thought you were holed up here in utter solitude and what do I find?" She gave a breathy sigh. "I can't tell you how pleased I am that you've started living again."

"He hasn't been dead," Daniel said, frowning. "He's just been alone. You know, to think."

Judith laughed. "That was just an expression, dear."

Joanna held out her hand to Daniel. "Ryan and Judith will want to catch up, Daniel," she said, motioning him ahead of her in the direction of the family room.

At the door, she looked back. Judith had moved closer to Ryan. With her drink halfway to her lips, she was smiling at him like a cat with a secret. It was impossible to tell what

Ryan was thinking. His responses ever since he'd ushered Judith into the house had not given Joanna much of a clue as to how he felt having another unannounced houseguest. They were obviously old friends. It was perfectly understandable, Joanna told herself. The career that Ryan and Pete had built as a team could hardly have excluded their personal lives. That was why Pete's widow could drop in on Ryan and get a warmer welcome than he'd extended to her, his ex-wife.

What she didn't know was why it should matter.

"Mom?"

She nodded and closed the door softly behind her. "I'm coming."

DANIEL FLUNG HIMSELF on the bed and folded his arms beneath his head. He wouldn't get any answers to his questions tonight, he had already figured that out. When Mrs. Mann showed up, his "window of opportunity," as somebody had put it, was lost. Maybe it was just as well, since he could spend a little more time thinking about it. He could have put his mother on the spot when she took him out of the room to give Ryan and Joey's mom some privacy, but he didn't really want to hear the story from his mom alone. He wanted to be filled in by both of them together.

He was still pretty ticked off that they had kept a secret like that from him. His mom, especially. For the first time, he realized that grown-ups, even moms, had some things in their lives that they kept private. He studied the tops of his feet, still in the grungy socks he'd worn all day. Maybe grown-ups had a right to keep some secrets, but not one like a marriage and a divorce. Especially when they were together again in the same house. And especially since they hadn't expected him to show up. Now *that* situation took on a lot of different aspects, he decided.

The fan revolved lazily overhead while he thoughtfully explored a few of those aspects. His mom and Ryan didn't act like any divorced couples he knew about. Some of his friends had divorced parents, and they sure didn't act like his mom and Ryan.

He had seen them kissing on the beach. He hadn't meant to, but he'd been up in the attic and there was a window that looked out over the water, and there they were. At first they'd seemed to be arguing. But then Ryan had sort of held his mom close, and next thing they were kissing. He had quit looking then, because that stuff was private.

But he knew, he just *knew* that wasn't the way divorced people acted.

CHAPTER ELEVEN

"I'LL GET THE GATE!"

The Land Rover rocked with the force behind Daniel's exit as he scrambled out and slammed the door. Ryan and Joanna watched in silence as he deactivated the alarm, opened the gate and then pushed it back wide enough to allow Ryan to drive through. They were headed to a kennel recommended by Nick Dalton to shop for a dog. The idea—conceived by Ryan on the spur of the moment—was a stroke of genius. It took them out of the house for the privacy they needed to answer Daniel's questions, and considering what they needed to tell him, presenting him a dog at the same time couldn't hurt. With her eyes on her son, Joanna had to admit that Ryan seemed to take to fatherhood like a pro. Who would have dreamed it?

"What did Nick have to say about the boat spying on us?" she asked quietly.

"Very little, none of it good." Ryan released the clutch and drove slowly through the gate. "The boat was rented with cash by two men who gave a bogus address in Atlanta. The marina attendant had some choice words for the white spray paint they used to obscure the name and number."

"So the boat's a dead end?"

"At this point, it looks that way."

Eyes straight ahead, Joanna sighed. "I'm not surprised, but I had hoped—"

From his side mirror, Ryan watched Daniel close the gate and reset the alarm. "Nick won't quit until he finds something, Jo. He's like a dog with a bone. He knows now that something's going on, and because it affects his family, he'll be twice as tenacious pursuing it.''

''His family?'' Joanna said quickly, looking at him. ''You didn't tell him about Daniel, did you?''

''No. And I won't until we're ready to tell the world.'' His gaze was steady, holding hers. ''Nick doesn't know about Daniel—at least, I don't think so—but he does know you and I were once married. In his book, that makes it family.''

Watching Daniel make his way back to the car, she was forced to drop the subject. She didn't want to acknowledge in front of him that the boat cruising the waters near Wilderose Cottage was probably stalking her. Daniel would worry about her, and with his special gifts, he might even try to *do* something. Just the thought was enough to terrify her. Closing her eyes, she promised to lead a life of absolute boredom if she and her son ever got out of this crazy situation unharmed.

She couldn't believe the turn her life had taken. Since finding Rico's body, it was almost as though a stranger inhabited her body. She'd unearthed a fortune in diamonds, fled her home with her life in jeopardy, invaded her ex-husband's privacy, *slept* with him, witnessed her child's amazing clairvoyance and learned his true paternity. It was so overwhelming that she could almost sympathize with Ryan's need to hole up somewhere and wait for things to be normal again.

And now Judith Mann had arrived to further complicate things. Joanna kept waiting for Ryan to offer some explanation for the sudden appearance of Pete Mann's widow. Not that Judith had shown herself before they left this morning. Apparently she was not an early riser. If her arrival hadn't caused such a stir, Joanna could almost believe she'd imagined it.

She shot a sideways look at Ryan and felt a tug of sympathy in spite of everything. She was tense, but he looked ten times worse. Between frequent narrow-eyed looks at the rearview mirror, he scowled at the road in front of him. She remembered how relaxed he used to be driving, one wrist draped over the wheel, his left elbow propped in the window. Now his knuckles showed white where they clamped around the wheel.

"Got your seat belt on, Daniel?" Ryan asked when the boy had climbed back into the Land Rover.

Behind them, there was some shuffling and then a loud click. "Got it."

"Then we're on our way," Ryan said, and gunned the powerful four-wheel-drive.

"How far is it?" came the age-old question from the back seat.

"Fifteen minutes, tops. According to Nick, this kennel has the best selection of animals around. We should be able to find just the dog we're looking for."

"Didn't I tell you that cops were the best sources? Man, we really owe Nick for this one." Daniel shifted, chafing under the restrictions of the seat belt. "So, now can we talk about when you two were married?"

Both adults were unable to respond for a moment. Ryan recovered first. "Yeah, I guess this will be as good a time as any," he said with a quick glance at Joanna.

She nodded mutely.

"We were young, Daniel," he began, meeting the boy's eyes in the mirror. "It was the year your mother graduated from college. I'd come home for a visit—I had just been hired by a New York news magazine. Jo and I had practically grown up together, but..." Some of the apprehension seemed to leave him. A faint smile softened the line of his mouth. "You'll probably understand this better someday, but it was like we suddenly saw each other with new eyes. Friendship turned into love."

"Then why didn't you stay married?"

"I've thought about that a lot myself," Ryan said. With his gaze on the road in front of him, he appeared to search for words. "Because we had known each other as kids, I don't think we took enough time to get to know the people we'd grown into as adults. We got caught up in the give and take of marriage right away. Naturally, Jo came with me to New York, both of us were working hard...we began to focus on different things. You've heard people say that a good marriage takes hard work, right?''

"I guess so."

"Well, because we'd known each other for such a long time, I now think that we didn't expect to have to work so hard. Looking back, I see that as a killing blow to a marriage."

"You must have given up pretty fast," Daniel said, looking sternly from one to the other. "Shouldn't you have tried a little harder?"

"Yes, we should have," Ryan said promptly. "We should have sat down and told each other what we were thinking. In fact, Dan, your mother did just that, but I wasn't listening. I'm to blame there. It's not enough to just talk, people have to listen, too. I made a terrible mistake, and it can't ever be undone."

"I have one more question," Daniel said, his gaze steady on Ryan's in the mirror. "Why didn't you tell me about being married to each other? I think I had a right to know."

Ryan seemed at a loss for an answer to that one.

"With all due respect, Daniel," Joanna began softly, praying that she could explain in a way that he would accept, "as my son, you didn't necessarily have that right. We've all had experiences that we choose to keep private, and for me, my marriage as a very young person was one of those experiences. I felt I'd failed. I just wanted to forget it."

"But after I got here," Daniel argued, sticking to his guns, "didn't I have the right to know then?"

"Maybe so," she conceded. "It wasn't that we purposely kept it from you then, Daniel," she said, choosing her words even more carefully. "It's just that—" She hesitated, searching for a way to explain the complex relationship between a man and woman who were once married. "Oh, I didn't plan to run to Ryan for protection when I got into trouble. In fact, it was a very...difficult situation when I first got here. Then you showed up so unexpectedly and it was awkward, Daniel. Can you understand that?''

Daniel, who had been hunched forward, listening intently, leaned back slowly, his face thoughtful. "When you put it like that," he said, nodding, "I can understand it."

He gazed through the side window for a mile or two, apparently deep in thought, then to the surprise of the two adults, he chuckled. "I guess I should feel a lot worse about you getting a divorce than I do," he said, "but if you hadn't, I wouldn't be here today, would I?''

Robbed of speech, Joanna tried frantically to think of something to say to that. Beside her, Ryan kept his eyes doggedly on the road.

"Hey, pull yourselves together. Jeez…'' Daniel rolled his eyes. "I know where babies come from. I even know how they get there. My birth certificate gives my father's name, and it isn't Ryan. So it doesn't take a rocket scientist to know I wouldn't be here if you two hadn't divorced." He gave them an exasperated look. "Right?''

"BUT HE'S A MUTT, Daniel," Ryan said, eyeing the half-grown half-breed who was ecstatically licking Daniel's face. "The trainer has been working the pups from his champion female shepherd. The tallest male looks pretty good to me."

With a happy expression, Daniel averted his face to keep from being licked all over. "This one's tall and he's a male, too," Daniel said, already in love. "Besides, he's the best of Mr. Simpson's champion stock. His prize female golden Lab got with his prize male German shepherd. This fellow's a winner!''

"Maybe, but he doesn't look like he'd be much of a watchdog," Ryan observed, but there was a hint of a smile in his eyes. "He welcomed us like we were long-lost friends."

"He knew we *were* friends," Daniel replied. "That proves he's smart. He won't let a trespasser within fifty feet of Wilderose Cottage, will you, champ? Hey! I think that's what I'll name him." He caught the dog's face in his hands and grinned at him. "Champ...suits you fine, doesn't it, boy? Who needs an old pedigree?"

"Give it up, O'Connor," Joanna murmured, wincing as "Champ" leapt at Daniel's chest and boy and dog tumbled into the clipped hedge separating the kennels from the trainer's house. "You're witnessing a lifetime bonding between those two, I'm afraid."

"I think you're right," Ryan said, shaking his head. "Hell, I should be glad. We can have this one cheap, fifty bucks, max."

Flat on his back, Daniel grinned up into the dog's face. "He can't help it that his mother made a mistake, can you, Champ? He's just as brave and smart as if he had the right parents. I love him already!"

I love him already.

The words lingered in the air. For one telling moment, neither Ryan nor Joanna breathed. From the screen of her lashes, she looked to see Ryan's reaction to Daniel's innocent words and found him watching her, his blue eyes intense.

Out of the mouth of babes...

Joanna felt the involuntary start of tears to her eyes. In front of her, the sight of Daniel and Champ blurred into indistinct, shimmering motion. Her heart lurched as Ryan slipped an arm around her waist and hugged her.

"Never a mistake," he said softly, for her ears alone. "Not when it gave us Daniel."

With a shaky smile, she walked with him to the trainer to close the deal.

THE TRIP HOME to Wilderose Cottage was more relaxed than it had been going to the kennel. Now that the deed was done, everyone seemed happy with the choice made. As soon as the Land Rover stopped, Daniel jumped out, eager to start training Champ as a proper guardian of the premises. The dog scrambled out, ignoring Daniel's command to halt, and took off like a streak of gold lightning in a beeline for the beach.

Beside Ryan, Joanna put her fingers over her mouth, but her eyes sparkled with laughter.

"He's got his work cut out," Ryan muttered, watching Daniel's futile attempts to corral the dog.

"Maybe he'll be a fast learner," Joanna suggested, not believing it for a minute.

"I'll just say this," Ryan said as they headed for the house, "I'm glad the security system is up and running and that Daniel's good with electronics. As a watchdog, Champ's sure to be a great playmate. It'll be—"

He broke off suddenly as he caught sight of movement in a window that faced the front of the house.

Fear leapt in Joanna's throat. In the enjoyment of the outing with Ryan and Daniel, she had almost forgotten the threat hanging over her. But in the next instant, she realized they had not surprised an intruder.

"Judith," she murmured, recognizing the woman's sleek profile. But in Ryan's bedroom? Had she been watching for their return? Or was she just rising after spending the night with Ryan?

A sudden, fierce arrow of pain lodged in her chest. She was used to projecting her thoughts in pictures, and instantly she had a flash of the two of them—Ryan and Judith—in bed. Naked. Is that how he had spent the night—loving her? Doing with her exactly what he'd done with Joanna? She moved instinctively to put some distance between herself and Ryan. Oh, God, was she a fool? Again her fingers covered her mouth, but this time it was not to hide a smile. It was to keep Ryan from seeing them tremble.

He probably wouldn't have noticed, she decided a minute later. As soon as he'd unlocked and opened the door, he muttered something to Joanna and headed directly for his bedroom. Inside, she heard the murmur of voices, Judith's light and confident, Ryan's deep and...stern.

They didn't sound like lovers. Unless they'd fought over something. Judith showing up without warning? Ryan entertaining his ex-wife?

Oh, God. Closing her eyes, Joanna spent a minute trying to pull herself together. Since the night she had gone to Ryan and found him caught in a nightmare, she had avoided thinking beyond the moment. Until that night, she'd been swept along by circumstances that were more or less beyond her control, events she thought had changed her life, but as she went to the window and stared out at Daniel playing on the beach with Champ, she realized Rico's death and the discovery of the diamonds had only been a *complication*. She could have found refuge in any number of places if she had genuinely needed to. She simply hadn't needed to look any further once Nick and Shannon had suggested going to Ryan.

Once they were thrown together, it was only a matter of time before they wound up in bed. Joanna had never been able to resist him. Her heart had known the truth fifteen years ago when she'd spent the skiing weekend with David Stanton. It had taken only one brief sexual moment with David to tell her that she would always be Ryan's. Reasons that had seemed compelling at the time had pushed her into settling for less. That was why the thought that he might be involved with Judith Mann was enough to cut her to the heart.

She was in love with Ryan. Again.

"I GUESSED I'D FIND you here."

"Oh!" With a start, Joanna whipped around, nearly bumping into Ryan, who'd come up quietly behind her. Paint brushes and two tubes of paint fell from the half dozen she held in her hand and went clattering to the floor. "I didn't hear you coming up the stairs," she said, quickly stooping to get them.

Ryan bent over at the same time. "Here, let me—"

"I've got it."

They both reached for a tube, and Joanna snatched her hand

away. "Now look!" she moaned when most of the rest of the tubes spilled onto the floor.

"Wait. Stay," he told her, putting out a hand. Then he reached down and scooped everything up and dumped it onto the table.

"Thanks," she muttered. Without looking at him, she put the supplies back into the storage cabinet in a jumble. She'd tidy up tomorrow. Next week. Whenever.

"Am I interrupting?"

"I was just finishing up for the night." She closed the cabinet door a little too hard, then, with an impatient click of her tongue, banged it firmly in place.

For a moment, there was a taut silence between them. She hadn't seen him since they'd arrived home. She wasn't sure if he'd been avoiding her or if they'd both been wary of each other. If he was worrying that she was going to ask any uncomfortable questions, or even bring up the subject of Judith Mann, he would wait until hell froze over.

"Thank you for making dinner," Ryan said. Leaning against her worktable, he watched her movements as she straightened and stowed her work away. "You didn't have to, but I'm glad you did. It was delicious."

"It was nothing...spaghetti," she said, rolling a length of paper and dropping it down into a storage tube. "I have a teenage son. He has to be fed. It made sense to double the recipe and have enough for everybody."

"We missed you," he said, still watching her intently. "Daniel said you weren't hungry."

"I taste a lot while I cook. It's a bad habit—and fattening." She shrugged and left it at that.

"I just want you to know that you don't have to do the cooking around here. We can all pitch in."

Did that mean he had accepted Judith Mann as a guest indefinitely? She tossed a pen into a drawer. "Somehow I can't see The Judith in the kitchen," she said tartly.

It was a second or two before he laughed. "Somehow I agree."

"Tell you what." She looked squarely at him. "I'll cook and somebody else can do the dishes."

Looking amused, Ryan folded his arms over his chest. "Have you seen 'The Judith's' nails?"

"Actually, I have."

He snickered. That was the only word for it. "Done," he said promptly. "You cook, she washes up."

"Oh, what the heck." With a sigh, she slammed another drawer shut. "Daniel can help. He's supposed to, anyway."

The joke at Judith's expense had dispelled the awkwardness between them. He watched silently for a few more minutes as she cleared away the rest of her supplies. Then, with his hands in his back pockets, he walked over and studied the sketches she'd tacked to a board.

"Judith's appearance was a total surprise to me, Joanna. Because of Pete, and for Joey's sake mostly, I keep in touch by phone, but I haven't seen her since I left New York...after Pete's funeral."

"You don't owe me any explanations about your relationship with Judith Mann, Ryan," she said stiffly.

"I don't have a relationship with her," he said, looking as though the thought startled him. "I mean, other than that she's Pete's widow. Under the circumstances, I feel some responsibility. That's understandable, isn't it?"

"Of course."

Picking up on a note in her voice, he looked quickly at her. "I can't just kick her out." He threw out his hand in agitation. "I mean, if Pete was in my place, he'd open his house to the woman who'd been my wife...even if he—"

He began to pace the length of the studio. Joanna was beginning to wonder if she could have jumped to a wrong conclusion. It sounded as though Judith Mann's presence was not something Ryan was happy about.

He stopped and faced her across the width of her drawing

board. "The truth is, I know why she's here and it's nothing personal. The opposite, in fact. She hasn't owned up to it yet, but she doesn't have to." He stopped in front of the windows and stood for a minute looking out at the water. "Her publisher is pushing her for the book."

"What book?"

With a weary shrug, he replied, "My book."

Joanna's eyes were wide. "I didn't know you were writing a book, Ryan."

"I'm not...at least not anymore."

Reaching behind her for her stool, Joanna sat down. Ryan was writing a book? Of course. Somehow it seemed the next logical step in an exceptional career. She didn't know why she'd been caught off guard. When they were first married, it had been one of his long-range goals. His talent was uniquely suited for writing a novel. There had always been a depth of understanding in his work that went beyond the bare bones of factual reporting.

She looked up to find him studying her.

"You don't seem surprised," he said.

"I'm not surprised at all. At least not to learn that you've been writing a book. In fact, now that I think about it, the surprising thing is that you haven't written one before now."

"How do you know? Maybe I did, but it was so bad nobody wanted it."

She dismissed that with a wave of her hand. "That could never happen."

He paused, then smiled. "Thanks for the vote of confidence," he said, "but it's not quite that simple."

"No, not simple," she agreed, smiling back. "But for you imminently doable. For a moment, they gazed at each other, caught in their own thoughts. Was he remembering how he had once bounced possible plot ideas off her? And how those sessions had almost invariably ended in bed? Research, he'd called it.

"What kind of book is it?" she asked curiously.

It was a moment before he replied, "I don't know…a Tom Clancy kind of thing, I guess."

"With your name and experience," she said, beginning to feel excited, "I can see why Judith's publisher is interested."

"My name isn't what it used to be," he said. For the first time in a couple of days, Joanna heard the old bitterness in his voice.

She touched his arm. "That isn't true, Ryan. As a matter of fact, Judith wouldn't be here if her company wasn't eager to publish you."

"I've told her I'm not interested. If I ever decide differently, she'll be one of the first to know."

"Is that why she's here? Trying to persuade you to reconsider? Or is it something personal?"

"It's nothing personal," he said in quick denial. There was nothing fabricated about his surprise.

"Ryan, she was in your bedroom this morning. I saw her through the window waiting for you when we got back from the kennel."

He was shaking his head even before she finished. "She was in the bedroom all right, but not for that." He moved to her drawing board. "My computer's there. She was snooping, looking for the manuscript. It's the logical place to stash the hard copy. Because I refused to let her look at what I've finished, she just grabbed her chance to read it, anyway, when she woke up and found herself alone in the house."

"And did she?"

"Read it? No, she couldn't find it. What I've written is saved on a diskette and *that's* in my wall safe." With an expression that suddenly made her uncomfortable, he asked incredulously, "You thought she spent the night in my bed?"

"I didn't *know*," she said, feeling ridiculous. "It seemed…possible."

"No, it wasn't possible."

She couldn't imagine what he meant by that. Well, she

could *imagine,* but her imagination had been running away with her entirely too much lately. She let it pass.

Ryan, it seemed, wasn't going to do likewise. He started toward her slowly. "It wasn't possible," he began, "because there was no way Judith Mann could ever be invited into my bedroom. Under any circumstances."

She cleared her throat nervously. "I know it sound-ed...ah..."

"Dumb," he finished for her, stopping so close she could feel the heat of his body. "I can't believe you thought it, Jo."

With Joanna perched on the stool, their eyes were on a level, and he filled her whole range of vision. He must have been outside on the beach. He smelled like the surf, salty and damp. Mixed with the spicy, sharp flavor of his after-shave, the scent of him sent her senses spinning dizzily.

"Because since waking up from my nightmare and finding *you* in my bed," he said in a softly dangerous tone, "there's not a chance in hell that any other woman will ever be there again."

"Ryan—"

"Wait a minute." He held up a hand. "Are you telling me that when we made love it meant nothing special to you?"

"No! Of course not."

"That those moments on the beach last night didn't leave you desperate to finish what we started?"

"That's *not* what I meant!" She slipped off the stool, keeping it between them. "I just—"

"I've been hard ever since just thinking about it."

"Please—"

He was leaning toward her, his hands clamped on the rim of the stool. "Are you telling me that the fact that we have a son together hasn't changed everything—*everything!*—Jo?"

Her heart lurched as he reached out and touched her cheek. "Judith Mann is my partner's widow and nothing else," he said quietly, searching her face as he searched for words. "I can't send her away because—" he shook his head "—because I don't think that's what Pete would have done if I had been killed and he was the one left. Does that make sense?''

"Yes, of course," she murmured, leaning into his caress.

"Maybe she'll get discouraged or bored and head on back to New York."

Joanna gave a tense little laugh. "Maybe."

"We can only hope."

"Or maybe you'll change your mind and decide that writing that book is a good idea." She gazed at a button on his shirt, then said carefully, "Maybe a book about Pete and what happened."

He went utterly still for a moment, then, dropping his hands, he stepped back as if from a blow. He looked shocked and hurt to the heart. With an instinctive need to reassure, Joanna put out a hand to touch him.

"Ryan, don't look so—"

But he was backing from her, turning, making his way toward the stairwell as though he couldn't get away fast enough.

"Ryan, wait! Please…"

As he passed the telephone mounted on the wall, it suddenly rang. Closing his eyes, he swore savagely. Another ring. And then another. Joanna made a move to go toward it, but Ryan stopped her.

"No, you can't. I'll get it."

Without lifting the receiver, he silenced the ringing with a quick stab and barked into the speaker phone. "Yeah, hello."

"Hello." The voice was instantly familiar to Joanna. She would have spoken, but at Ryan's fierce look, the words died unuttered. He put two fingers to his lips and shook his head firmly.

"Who is this?" he demanded.

"Sammy Feldstein," came the friendly reply. "Who is this, please?"

"Who were you calling?" Ryan asked abruptly. Joanna gave him a bewildered look. Who else besides herself would Sammy want to talk to? Surely it was safe to speak to Sammy!

"Actually, this is awkward and may sound completely bizarre," Sammy said in a breezy tone that brought a smile to Joanna's lips. "But I'm looking for a friend of mine and I came across your name and number there on the island and decided to call on the outside chance that she's there."

"What friend?" With his hand braced on the wall, Ryan stared at the speaker phone with a dark scowl.

"Joanna Stanton."

CHAPTER TWELVE

"WHO WAS THAT on the phone?"

Daniel was three steps from the top of the stairwell, watching his mother and Ryan. Champ, scrambling past him on the stairs, catapulted into the room. With a sharp bark, he put his nose to the floor and began sniffing interesting new territory. Sensing the tension between the two adults, Daniel glanced quickly at each, then he focused on his mother. "It was Sammy, wasn't it?"

"How did you—"

"What gave you that idea, Daniel?" Ryan asked, covering Joanna's question with his own.

After studying them both another moment or two, Daniel sighed. "A feeling I had."

"Was this feeling similar to the one that told you Rico was murdered?" Ryan asked.

"Sort of."

"The same feeling that guided you from your grandfather's place to this house?"

"That's right."

Taking Joanna by the elbow, Ryan urged her to the stairwell, dodging Champ underfoot. "Then in that case, you already *know* it was Sammy Feldstein."

"Yeah, I guess." With a whistle, Daniel tried to bring the dog to heel. "I just came up to tell Mom not to talk to him. I don't think she ought to let anybody know where she is until everything's cleared up."

"I couldn't agree more," Ryan said. "And your mother

didn't talk to him. I denied that she was here. I told him I didn't know where she was."

"Good," Daniel said.

"What exactly do you mean by 'everything,' Daniel?" Joanna asked. Out of a need to protect him, she had tried to keep some of the insanity of the past few days from Daniel. But he wasn't an average kid.

Daniel took a step that raised him higher on the stairs and Champ trotted over, tail wagging vigorously. "It's like this, Mom. Rico died because he was doing illegal stuff. His partners are really bad people and they need to find you because they're not sure what you know. Or," he added, "what you have."

"What I have?" she asked, confused.

"Like diamonds. Or something."

Her mouth fell open, and she closed it hastily. "What do you know about diamonds, Daniel?"

He shrugged, fondling Champ's ears. "C'mon, I know, Mom."

"Another 'feeling'?" Ryan asked dryly.

"Yeah, like I told you before, I just know stuff."

"Well, *I* don't," Joanna snapped, "so bear with me a minute, both of you."

"Rico was involved in smuggling diamonds into the country," Daniel said flatly. He grinned suddenly at her shocked look, dodging Champ's tongue. "I didn't get that by way of my special powers. I happened to overhear some of what Nick Dalton was saying to Ryan yesterday." He gave Ryan a slightly sheepish smile.

"Go on," Ryan said noncommittally.

"Well, it's elementary. The crooks must not have the goods, but somebody does. They think it's you, Mom. That's why they're looking for you." He frowned suddenly, chewing on his lip. "There's one thing that really worries me about that boat yesterday. We can't be sure whether or not those guys actually spotted you."

She took a deep breath, her gaze going from Daniel to Ryan and back again. Apparently there was no need to try to keep things from Daniel anymore. In fact, it seemed to be the other way around. To avoid worrying her, Daniel had been harboring secrets of his own.

"And if they did," Daniel said earnestly, "you are really in trouble, Mom."

With her arms crossed, she studied her son. "Do you have anything except special powers and snooping to go on?"

Though chagrined, he met her eyes bravely. "Like proof, stuff like that?"

"Yes, stuff like that."

"No, Mom, but I just *know*. You gotta believe me."

Ryan gave her shoulder a squeeze. "As you say, we don't have any proof, Jo, but we can't take any chances. We know Feldstein and Rico were close. Maybe Feldstein knew more about Rico's little scam than he ever let on. Maybe not. At this point, we can't assume anything."

Joanna was shaking her head adamantly. "He didn't know. Rico told me he didn't. He was doing it for Sammy…so there would be something to leave Sammy besides a pile of medical bills."

"Nice sentiment," Ryan said wryly, "but it doesn't prove Sammy's innocent."

"You heard his voice on the phone, Ryan," she argued. "You heard what he said, how he sounded. Did he strike you as a man who would be involved in the murder of his best friend?"

"Mom," Daniel said patiently. "They were more than best friends. They were, you know, they lived together and all. They also worked together. I don't think Rico could have kept something like this a secret from Sammy."

"Okay, okay." She rubbed her forehead wearily. "It's just— Ryan, surely you don't think—"

"I don't know, sweetheart." With his hand still on her shoulder, he gazed into space for a minute. "We just can't take any chances. You can't answer the phone to talk to anyone, promise me that.''

"I won't."

He looked at Daniel, equally stern. "You too, Dan."

"Yes, sir." Standing quietly beside Daniel, even Champ seemed to sense the gravity of the situation.

Ryan nodded, satisfied. "I've already told Judith that the telephone is off limits. She is not to use it or answer it. She was suspicious, but—"

"Suspicious is hardly the word."

All three gaped at the woman standing at the bottom of the stairs. How long had she been there? Joanna wondered. How much had she overheard?

Judith held up her hand. "Okay, altogether now..." She brought her thumb and forefinger together slowly. "One, two, three, close mouths!"

With a nudge to Joanna's waist, Ryan urged everybody down the stairs. "We didn't hear you knock, Judith," he said.

"Well, I did, but you guys were so busy talking, you didn't hear me."

"So you just decided to listen."

Judith shrugged. "I suppose you could put it that way."

Ryan was coldly furious. He hadn't liked it when she'd searched his bedroom without his permission, but that had been merely irritating. This was different. The safety of his family was at stake. Staring at her, he waited for a plausible explanation.

"Oh, don't be so uptight, darling. I—"

He heaved a sigh. "I'm not your darling, Judith."

Her eyes widened, flicking from him to Joanna and back again. "Oka-a-ay, it was only—"

"How much did you overhear?" he demanded curtly.

Her penciled eyebrows went up. "Enough to tell me that something ver-r-ry interesting is going on around here." She tapped a long red nail against her chin thoughtfully. "I thought I caught a little hint of intrigue last night, but you were so unforthcoming, Ryan...still the quintessential strong, silent male. The only way to get anything out of you is to give you pen and paper or a laptop.''

"How much did you overhear?" he repeated through gritted teeth.

"Everything." She shrugged. "More or less."

Daniel moved a little closer, gripping Champ's collar. "Mrs. Mann, you don't seem to understand that my mom is in serious danger. The more people who know she's here, the more danger she's in. You have to listen to Ryan."

She gave a light laugh. "Of course I'm going to listen to Ryan, dear." She spread her hands wide. "I'm a guest in his house. I came to spend a few quiet days on the beach." She gave Ryan a guileless look. "You did mean it when you invited me, didn't you, Ryan? After Pete...well, you remember."

"Stay, Judith." Ryan's voice was resigned. "As long as you understand the situation."

"Yes, the situation." She studied her nails thoughtfully. "From what I overheard, the situation is very interesting." She paused, then using her fingers, ticked off each point. "A murder, a gay relationship, a woman in jeopardy, missing diamonds...a plot begging for just the right person to turn it into a book."

"Forget it," Ryan snapped.

"It sounds more like the 'Movie of the Week' to me," Daniel said jokingly.

"Hmm, sounds even better." Judith's dark eyes glowed at the thought. "I can see why you've taken to this kid, Ryan. He thinks like an O'Connor." She squinted somewhere off in the distance. "A book contract, movie rights...yes, yes...I can see it."

"What you see is your commission on the deal," he shot back.

"I'm serious, Ryan!"

"I'm serious, too," he replied, "as a heart attack. This isn't

some tabloid scandal for your readers to get off on, this is my
family you're talking about here. My wife and my—''

"It's okay, Ryan." Joanna quickly touched his arm before
he could say more. As it was, Judith was studying the three
of them with narrow-eyed interest. The woman was sharp. As
for heart attacks, Ryan's near slip had nearly given her one.

She managed a smile. "He means ex-wife," she said with
forced lightness. "As for my situation, it probably would make
a good book, but right now I don't need the celebrity. I'd just
like to see an end to the whole mess so that my son and I can
get on with our lives."

Ryan grasped Joanna's arm and began hustling the whole
group toward the door. "Come on, let's get out of here. I need
to get in touch with Nick and let him know Feldstein called
asking for Joanna. Guilty or not, if he's guessed she's here, it
could mean trouble."

Outside, the fragrance of honeysuckle and wild roses mixed
with the smell of the sea. In the distance, the tide was a rolling,
rushing, unceasing constant that seemed to heighten the tension gripping them as they headed for the main house. The
phone call had stripped away the last vestige of her security,
and Joanna shivered, moving a little closer to Ryan. He reacted
instinctively, wrapping an arm around her, enveloping her in
warmth and the illusion of safety.

Unusually quiet, Daniel lagged behind. Caught up in their
own concerns, nobody noticed.

IT WAS THE SAME DREAM. Moaning softly, Daniel saw his
mother in a wide corridor with a high ceiling. It was brightly
lit and spacious. An airport, he thought. The same airport as
before. He tensed, knowing what was coming but helpless to
do anything other than watch. And know.

At first she was nearly lost in the ebb and flow of the crowd,
but then she began to make her way through people, crisscrossing until she stopped at a bank of telephones. He watched
her punch in a series of numbers and then she was talking. As

in his last dream, she became agitated and frightened as she spoke. He felt the frantic beat of her heart and the bone-deep fear that gripped her. With all the power that he possessed, he fought to see the identity of the person at the other end. Somehow, even in his dream, he knew that he must see that person.

Close...he could almost...

But she suddenly gave an anguished cry and dropped the phone. She was gone then, just as before, leaving the receiver dangling. The disembodied voice was still vicious, still threatening. And somewhere he could hear his mother crying.

With a jerk, he came awake.

Champ was whining. Flat on his belly, as close as he could get to Daniel, he nuzzled the boy's neck. His tongue was wet and warm, his nose cold. Murmuring the dog's name, Daniel wrapped his arms around him and buried his face in the pale golden fur.

It was several minutes before his heartbeat was normal again. Beside him, Champ had quieted, too. With his hand rubbing the dog's ears, he thought about the nightmare and what it could mean. With a sinking feeling, he knew his mother would not be safe until the diamonds were in the hands of the people who'd smuggled them into the country by way of Rico's gallery.

He hadn't decided what to do about that, so he let his thoughts drift to the other thing.

Instead of going to his room to bed tonight, he'd detoured and climbed the stairs to the attic. There, he'd spent a couple of hours reading Ryan's journals. His mom hadn't exactly given him permission for that, but she had said it was okay to read the journals of Cameron O'Connor. He couldn't see much difference. When you got right down to it, he thought he had an ironclad right to read Ryan's stuff.

Who had a better right? Ryan O'Connor was his father.

At least, he thought he was. With one arm folded beneath his head, he gazed through the window at the starry night. Champ stirred beside him, getting comfortable again. About

Ryan, he couldn't be sure, because although he'd studied every journal entry as if it were part of the Dead Sea Scrolls, he hadn't found one place where Ryan mentioned being a father. In fact, if he hadn't already heard it from the two people who ought to know, he'd still be in the dark about their marriage. In his journals, Ryan never mentioned Daniel's mom, either.

Something was really fishy about it all.

But for just a few minutes, in spite of the fact that there was no evidence except his gut feelings, Daniel let himself imagine having Ryan O'Connor as a father. He didn't remember David Stanton very well, just little glimpses of somebody big and gentle holding his bike while he tried to ride, a nice face smiling at him over his birthday cake, a hug when he had fallen out of a tree, the smell of a particular shaving lotion. He remembered all that and it was nice. He would always love David Stanton, the only father he'd ever known.

But if, somehow, his real father was Ryan O'Connor, that would be neat.

His eyes fixed on the stars, he reluctantly turned his thoughts back to the situation that endangered his mother. She was safe here as long as she was with Ryan, but sooner or later, people had to start living again. They couldn't stay behind the locked gates of Wilderose Cottage forever. Nice as it was, after a while it could get to feel like a prison. He didn't want that to happen with Ryan and his mom.

He was going to have to do something.

RYAN STIRRED ON THE COUCH and almost succeeded in waking up. This was familiar territory. He knew what was coming. It was the same dream. His first reaction was to reject it. Block it. Keep it from coming. But suddenly Joanna's face was before him and he knew the key to end her torment was in this dream. Willing away his reluctance, he opened himself. Using his power, he welcomed the scene that began to unfold.

It was a 1964 Cadillac. The first time, Ryan had missed that detail. Black and gleaming, it nearly filled the cramped, dimly lit area of the garage. What light there was came from the open door where two men emerged. Between them, they dragged a semiconscious man he now knew must be Rico Fellini. As they opened the door of the Cadillac, Ryan realized someone else was watching from inside the gallery. Another detail he'd missed. Concentrating, focusing with all his might, Ryan strained to see the other man. Frustration made him break out in a sweat. He wanted to get up and go to the door himself, throw it wide, take a look. His legs twitched with the effort to get up. He hated being forced into the role of observer and he groaned with the need to speak.

The car started, emitting exhaust. Instantly, a gray cloud obscured his view of the scene. His heart began to pound as the two men hurried toward the door, the deed done. They would go inside, leave him to watch another agonizing death. And then Joanna would come.

As he lay imprisoned in sleep, the men disappeared into the doorway, brushing past the third man, leaving him to close the door. From his position in the house, he leaned out for a quick look at the dying man in the car and Ryan saw his face. Who... With a leap of his heart, Ryan realized who it was. Sammy Feldstein. It had to be.

With a groan, Ryan rolled up and off the couch. Disoriented at first, he found himself standing in the middle of the porch. Shaking his head, he went to the window and threw it wide, then stood sucking in deep, cleansing breaths to rid his lungs of the acrid smell of the car's exhaust.

Unlike Daniel, he didn't accept these weird glimpses of somebody else's life philosophically. When he woke up smelling exhaust from a car that was nearly two thousand miles away, it bothered the hell out of him.

"I thought you'd be sleeping."

Ryan turned to see Joanna, standing in the doorway to the porch, backlit by the rose-hued lamp left burning in the family room. Obviously straight from her bed, she was sleep-tousled and softly feminine. Her tawny hair was unbound, haloed in the light. She was wearing a well-washed sleep shirt that nearly reached her knees, yet no siren from the sea could appear more seductive to him at that moment.

"Ah, Jeez, c'mere." He held out a hand, beckoning her. Without a word, she went to him and slipped her arms around his waist.

"What is it?" she whispered, her cheek soft and dewy against his chest.

"I just need to feel a real, live person," he said, making room for her silky head beneath his chin.

She chuckled softly, and the sound was nearly his undoing. "What other kind is there?"

"You'd be surprised." Heat pooled in his groin, then settled into an ache that he knew couldn't be eased tonight. His newfound lust for his ex-wife was only one of a dozen surprising things that he was having to deal with lately. He couldn't hold back a pained chuckle.

"What's funny?" Joanna asked, looking up at him.

"You don't want to know, babe."

With a smile, she settled back with her head on his chest. "If I were a true feminist, I'd object to being called a babe."

He squeezed her reassuringly. "You are the best kind of feminist," he told her. "You're sensitive and loving and independent and smart. You're a successful career woman who's raised a terrific kid as a single parent. You fight for principles you believe in and yet you still like it when a man holds the door for you."

She pushed back against him so that she could look at his face. "How in the world can you know all that about me? You haven't seen me in fifteen years, and now only on this island."

"No good reporter ever reveals his sources."

"Let me guess. Your source has known me all his life and he's a blood relative."

He chucked her under the chin and then pulled her back

into his arms. "He is so proud of you that he glows when he talks about you."

"He'd better. I'm his mother."

"Not all adolescent boys think their parents are wonderful."

She smiled against his chest. "Well, the circumstances are a little special with Daniel and me." For a few moments, she rested quietly in his arms. "You never answered me. Why are you out here on the porch?"

"Actually, I was asleep on the couch," he told her, rubbing his chin against her hair. "Then—" he shrugged "—shit happens."

"Another nightmare?" she asked.

"Or something. I'm not sure what to call it. Except damn spooky."

"Daniel calls it his special powers."

"Yeah, well, he's got a better handle on it than I have. I'm not kidding you, Jo, I was wary of this 'special power' from the get-go. I never told a soul. I thought…I thought I was weird. Fortunately I never had a message or dreamed anything that had much signficance. Then Pete…" He shook his head. "I guess it's something that I'll just have to learn to live with."

"Your father did."

He paused, taking it in. "Did you read that in his journals?"

"Yes. But, like Daniel, he seemed to accept it and even value it. The one time he didn't heed it was when he was in Vietnam. It was during the terrifying days of the fall of Saigon and Michelle's family was involved. She was nearly killed as a result. Were you aware that she was pregnant at the time with your sister, Shannon?"

"I knew Dad met and married Michelle there. Her family were French-Vietnamese, prominent in politics. I've often wondered if his source for his best stuff was Michelle's father."

"Actually, it was," Joanna said. "You really should read his journals, Ryan. You have a lot in common."

"He never screwed up the way I did," Ryan said, rejecting her words. "It's incredible when you think about it. He went everywhere, recorded the worst of the world's sins, yet he never got caught up in the hype as I did. I don't see how you can say we have a lot in common."

"Oh, but you do," Joanna said, placing a soft kiss on his throat. "If you don't read his journals for anything else but to put your father in proper perspective, you should read them for that alone. He did screw up. It was during the fall of Saigon, and it nearly cost him the lives of his wife and unborn child. Why do you think he made such an abrupt change from reporting hard news to doing documentaries?"

Ryan was stunned. "I don't know. I never actually thought about it." He shrugged. "Professional growth? His documentaries were as critically acclaimed as everything else he did."

"Read his journals, Ryan," she urged softly. "Do yourself and your father a favor."

He pulled her a little closer. "I will," he promised, burying his face in her hair. "And thank you, sweetheart."

She knew then how far he'd come from the tortured, guilt-ridden man who had opened his house to her just days before. "Do you want to talk about your nightmare?"

"I don't want to scare you, sweetheart, but it's the same thing I dreamed the night before you came."

She was silent for a minute. "Isn't that odd? Your father was warned in a dream about Michelle's safety, and here it is happening to you and me."

"Doesn't that scare you?"

"Should it?"

"I don't know. I'm not sure what to do with what I saw."

"You said before that you saw Rico in his car in the garage and that he didn't kill himself. What's different in the dream tonight?"

"I saw a third person." He paused. "Describe Sammy Feldstein, Joanna."

"Oh, no." Suddenly her knees were weak. "Oh, Sammy... no."

"Short, fat, balding. Wears small-framed yuppie glasses?"

Eyes closed, Joanna nodded. "Rico would be so hurt," she whispered.

"Well, he's beyond being hurt," Ryan said. "I just don't know what to do about what I saw. I'd feel like a fool calling Nick Dalton and telling him that Sammy Feldstein is our man and I know it because I'm psychic."

"He might surprise you," Joanna said, idly tracing a tiny scar she'd found on his side.

"Hmm."

"In the meantime, why don't we sleep on it?"

"We?" He bent a little at the knees to get a good look at her face. "As in us? You and me?"

"Don't look so surprised. Didn't you say you'd been, uh, well...hard ever since that episode by the beach? Ohhhh!" She put both hands to her cheeks. "I can't believe I said that!"

"I can't, either, but you can't take it back, babe." He took her hand, startling her even more, and headed for the door.

"Wait! Where are we going?"

"We can't have any privacy in the house," he reminded her, urging her down the steps, then carefully closing the screen door without a sound. "Even if I wanted to risk Daniel finding out, which I don't until we've told him everything, the idea of Judith discovering us really puts me off."

"I don't want anything to put you off," Joanna said in a sultry tone.

"That's it." He stopped right where they were, not quite halfway to the studio, then hauled her up into his arms and kissed the daylights out of her.

"Mmmm..." For long, delicious moments, the only thought in her head was how right it felt to be exactly where she was. Then she felt the tickle of grass between her toes and realized both feet were on the ground again. In a manner of speaking.

Lost in the blue of his gaze, she whispered, "I don't have any shoes on."

"You aren't going to need any." He bent and tenderly touched his lips to hers again. "I love you, Jo."

"I love you, too, Ryan."

"I never stopped, not really. It seems incredible."

She nodded, giving him a soft little kiss on his beautiful mouth. "I know."

He leaned back a bit, as though he was trying to see into her heart. "Are you sure about this?"

"Yes," she said simply.

"Then come." He took her hand.

CHAPTER THIRTEEN

THE DAYBED IN THE STUDIO above Ryan's workshop was a beautiful brass-trimmed, white wrought-iron antique. In the week that she'd been at Wilderose Cottage, Joanna had spent many hours sitting alone among an excess of throw pillows watching the spectacular view of the ocean it faced. Tonight, the view and all else in the studio was lost to her as Ryan stopped at the daybed and pulled her to her feet. Standing in front of him, she thought she might burst with the love she felt for him. He was so beautiful. Tall and lean, broad-shouldered, his hair rumpled by the wind and her hands, which had stroked its silky darkness on the way up the stairs.

Picking up her hands, he brought them to his mouth and gently kissed her palms. Her breath caught at the warmth of his lips, the erotic touch of his tongue. Her heart felt as though it would burst right out of her chest.

He lifted his head and looked into her eyes. The incredible blue of his irises seemed clouded and dark. They gleamed in the light of the moon that streamed in through the huge windows. "Did you know," he asked softly, "that you're the only woman I've ever loved?"

"Oh, Ryan." Tears sprang to her eyes as she took his words to her heart and treasured them. How different their lives might have been if she had believed, truly believed, in his love all those years ago.

"If this isn't forever, Jo, let's stop right now. You broke my heart when you left me. I don't think I could survive it again."

"No," she whispered, "there's no stopping for either of us ever again." She freed her hands from his and placed them against his chest. He was so warm. Beneath the hard muscle, she felt the deep, rapid beat of his heart. Rising to her tiptoes, she gave him a soft kiss.

His mouth opened instantly at the touch of her lips. She closed her eyes, kissing him back with all the love in her soul. It was a moment rife with promise, a moment of commitment. With a groan, Ryan gathered her close, taking the kiss wider and deeper. Their tongues met and danced an erotic rhythm. His hands began a loving quest, smoothing her hair, fondling her ears, her cheeks, her neck, sweeping up her back and down again, sinking into the softness of her buttocks. Joanna swayed pliantly, luxuriating in his touch. For the longest time, they stood rocking a little, touching, kissing. It was a time of gentleness. Both knew that passion would soon overtake them, but this was a moment to be savored.

Ryan placed his mouth against her temple. "You want to hear something?"

"What is it?"

"I used to dream about you."

"Oh…"

"I'd be in some godforsaken corner of the world, tired, used up, my mind filled with scenes from hell, and I'd finally grab some sack time. Close my eyes and blam…there you were."

With a tiny, inarticulate sound, she held him tight.

"I quit trying to fight you off." Joanna knew he didn't realize his hand was buried in her hair. "One time…one time, I was thrown into a cell somewhere in Central America—I was doing a feature on drug cartels—and for the first time, I really thought I was going to die. I would have if you hadn't been with me. I kept your face in front of me, your voice in my head, imagined the way you looked when we were back at Sea Island. When my editors finally got me out of there and I was on my way home, I felt it was crazy to go to New York. Instead, I should have gone home to you."

When she could finally speak, she said, "I used to dream about you, too."

"After you were married?"

"Yes. I felt so guilty, like I was being unfaithful."

He nodded, and she knew he'd misunderstood.

"Not unfaithful to David," she said in a low, shamed whisper. "Unfaithful to you."

"God, Jo."

"You can't dictate your dreams. I guess my heart knew all along that I really belonged to you."

He wrapped his arms around her, crushing her breasts, rocking her silently.

"I don't want to think of that now," she said, stroking his warm flesh with her hands. Her touch made him tremble, she realized, feeling blessed and lucky, so lucky.

"I like it when you tremble," she whispered, feathering kisses over the dense, dark hair on his chest.

"Your touch has always made me tremble," he told her.

Struck by her incredible good fortune, she burrowed as close to him as she could, weak with the pleasure of feeling his body so totally fitted to hers. "I never want that to change," she said, smiling against his skin.

He suddenly grasped the tail of her sleep shirt. "I want this off," he whispered hoarsely. "Lift your arms."

Joanna complied willingly, stepping back to let him remove it. Left only in tiny white bikinis, she brought her hands up to cover herself.

"No, sweetheart..." Catching her wrists, he pulled her hands away, then cupped her breasts, dropping a soft kiss first on one tight nipple, then on the other. "Don't hide from me, love. Never hide from me."

Then she was on the daybed and he was following her down. Pushing his knee between her thighs, he bent and curled his tongue around her nipple. An almost painful sweetness began to build within her. Throwing her head back, she lost herself in dizzying sensation—his warm mouth pulling and tugging, a corresponding ache low in her abdomen, a restless, near-painful yearning.

"Ah, Jo...you taste so good...so..." He bit her nipple gently, then stroked her breast with his tongue. "Hmm, strawberries...cream... I don't think I will ever get enough of you." Nearly lost in pleasure, she prayed he would always feel that way.

Suddenly he was more intense. His foreplay became more aggressive. His hands skimmed the sides of her breasts, past her rib cage to her belly. Beneath her own palms, she felt the hardening of his muscles. His breathing came in short puffs against her stomach. When his hand encountered the elastic of her bikinis, he hooked his thumbs in them and stripped them off her.

"You, too," she murmured, rising up a little to reach the snap on his jeans. But his hands were there before hers and in seconds he was naked. Beautifully naked, she thought, drinking in the sight of him.

He tumbled to the daybed, catching her up in a tangle of arms and legs and hungry kisses.

"I want to touch you and hold you and taste you," he said, his hands and mouth doing just that. "All over." For a brief, dazzling moment, she was suspended in breathless anticipation. He slid down, kissing the giving plane of her abdomen, her navel...lower.

"Oh!" she whispered, clamping her knees together.

But he wasn't to be denied. "Hush, sweetheart," he murmured raggedly. "I want to love all of you the way I used to dream about it." Cupping her bottom, he lifted her, and in lightning-bright seconds, she was lost.

Her heart pounding, she clutched his shoulders, all nerves and sensation, a mindless receptacle of pleasure. She was on a precipice, about to soar into the heavens. When she tumbled over with a high, piercing cry, Ryan smiled against her flesh.

And then he was above her, his eyes near black as he surrounded himself with her tight warmth. He paused, savoring,

KAREN YOUNG 471

holding back. Looking at him, she saw the pulse beating in his throat. The strain of waiting told in the veins standing out on his neck and at his temple. A rush of love for him rose in her, sweet and fierce. And then it seemed he could wait no longer. Groaning with pleasure, he drew back and then thrust fully, deeply, burying himself within her.

Holding his hips with her hands, she arched. He moved slowly at first, rhythmically, and Joanna matched him on the sensual ride. Then, as their passion built, his pace became more urgent. Every thrust sent them higher. She rose to meet him, murmuring her pleasure, echoing his deeper, male utterances. She was with him when he shuddered, buried his face in her hair, and with a hoarse cry, filled her womb with the very essence of himself.

"WHAT ARE WE GOING TO DO, Ryan?"

"I was just wondering the same thing."

"I wish we didn't have to deal with this right now," Joanna said, turning her face into the warmth of his neck and inhaling his sexy male scent. If wishes counted, she would be happy to lie quietly right where she was, propped on pillows in Ryan's arms, watching the night sky through the studio window. "If only we had the luxury of just enjoying finding each other again, filling in the years we've been apart." With her fingers sifting through the hair on his chest, she murmured, "I wish you and Daniel could spend the summer together, getting to know each other without the threat of murderers and thieves cruising off the end of the dock waiting to—" she sighed "—whatever it is they plan to do."

He smiled against her temple. "Yeah, that pretty much covers how I'd like to spend the summer, too."

The night sky was brilliant with stars. "If only we knew where those diamonds were," she said, frowning. "If we did, we could force them to tip their hand by using the diamonds as bait."

"Not on your life, babe," Ryan said firmly. "And I mean

that. Besides, no matter what, you're still a risk to them. You saw the diamonds, and they know you did.''

They lay in companionable silence for a few more minutes. It struck her that the threat hanging over her wasn't as scary as it had been, and she didn't have to look far to see the reason. She felt protected and secure because of Ryan. It might be a false kind of security. After all, sinister people were still spying on her, her friends might not be friends at all, and it was probably only a matter of time before a showdown. But if she had to choose any place on the face of the earth to be during this time in her life, it would be right here. With Ryan.

"We don't have much choice here, Jo," he said suddenly, his tone telling her he'd weighed all the options and made up his mind. "We'll call Nick tomorrow and ask him to come out. It may be that you should turn yourself in and make a statement to Gus Forrester. Tell him you saw the diamonds and what Rico said when you went to him. We'll see what Nick thinks of that. I haven't decided what to tell him about Sammy Feldstein, but I'll sure as hell tell him something.''

With that, he got up and handed her sleep shirt to her. "We need to get back to the house. We don't want Dan to wake up and find you missing.''

Holding the soft shirt against her, she looked up at him. "Ryan, I'm sorry about all this.''

"It's not your fault, sweetheart.''

"Not exactly, but—''

"But nothing. You and Dan need to be safe and secure and able to resume a normal life. I love you and he's our son. What else could be more important to me than seeing this thing through?''

"Resuming your own normal life?''

For a moment, they looked deep into each other's eyes. "Come on," Ryan said softly, "you know that can't happen without you and Dan.''

"If we find that we can leave here tomorrow, what would that mean to you?''

"First I'd try to persuade you to stay here for the rest of the summer, just to be together, the three of us. You said yourself that was a good idea. And then together we'd decide what to do next."

"You'd leave here?"

"I never planned to stay on Sea Island forever," Ryan said simply.

She took a breath and asked what she really wanted to know. "You're okay with Pete's death?"

"I'll never be okay with it, but I finally have a different perspective on it. I think I can put it behind me now."

"Pete would want you to," she murmured, still holding the sleep shirt wadded up against her chest.

"Yeah, he would." He smiled suddenly. "Are you gonna put that thing on?"

She looked down at it blankly and then gave a little gulp. She was buck naked! Turning, she fumbled with the shirt, trying to put it on. And then she stopped, melting, as she felt his lips on her bare shoulder and his arms slip around her, anchoring just beneath her breasts.

"Whoa, Joanna, Joanna, it's me, the man who loves you. I was just teasing, sweetheart."

Aligning her arms with his, she let her head fall back against his shoulder. "I'm not used to this," she whispered.

"Then you'll have to get used to it," he said, nuzzling her ear. "Because I think we're going to be doing a lot of it."

"Oh, Ryan..."

"Oh, Joanna." He turned her to face him, his gaze running the length of her, blatantly sexual. Then he bent and touched his mouth to hers. "You can definitely count on it, babe."

After about half a minute, the sleep shirt slipped from her fingers and plopped to the floor.

Sometime later they made it back to the house.

BREAKFAST WAS BARELY finished the next day when the security box at the gate sounded abruptly. Ryan was up first, striding to the unit on the wall with a grim expression.

"Yeah, who is it?"

"Kathleen O'Connor."

He had not seen his grandmother in many months. Surprised by a rush of affection, he realized he was very glad to hear her voice. In his need for solitude at Sea Island, he'd closed himself off from the good things as well as the bad. His grandmother was definitely one of the good things.

"Gran, this is a surprise," he said.

"I decided I couldn't wait any longer for an invitation at my age, dear." Her voice was a little quavery, and still flavored with a strong Irish lilt. It made him grin.

"I'll come out and open the gate," he told her, shifting his gaze to meet Joanna's. With her coffee cup poised halfway to her mouth, she was smiling softly. He remembered how much Jo had always admired his grandmother. And then his gaze went to Daniel. What would she think about Daniel?

"Send Daniel to open the gate, Ryan," his grandmother commanded.

"Ah..." Daniel was already out of his chair, looking eager. Ryan snapped his mouth closed. Nick, of course, would have mentioned both Joanna and Daniel, Ryan thought. He shouldn't be surprised that the matriarch of the O'Connor clan wanted a firsthand look when she heard his ex-wife was back at Wilderose Cottage. He wondered just how observant his grandmother would be. "No problem," he said, speaking into the unit on the wall. "He's on his way."

KATHLEEN O'CONNOR WAS in the back seat of a black Mercedes, a really swank, gleaming, *big* Mercedes. Daniel had never been this close to a car driven by a chauffeur. As he neared the gate, he realized the driver was a woman. She gave him a smile.

He threw up his hand in greeting and quickly punched the numbers on the pad that opened the gate. When the powerful vehicle eased past him, he tapped the code to close the gate. The car had stopped. After a moment, he walked to the driver's window, intending to tell the driver that it was okay. She could go.

Whoosh. The back window lowered almost silently. A voice came from somewhere inside. "You may get in and ride with us up to the house, Daniel."

"Yes, ma'am," he replied. He opened the door, eager to check out the car, and climbed into the back seat next to Miss Kathleen.

"Hi," he said, looking right into her eyes. He noticed that she was looking pretty sharply at him, too.

"Hello, Daniel. I'm Kathleen O'Connor, Ryan's grandmother." She held out a papery, thin hand and Daniel took it. He was careful not to squeeze it too hard because it felt so delicate. "My mother's visiting here," he explained in case she wasn't sure who he was. "Joanna Stanton. She used to know you."

The old lady smiled. "She still knows me, Daniel, and I still know her. I'm happy that she's finally visiting Sea Island again. And you, too, of course."

"Thank you, ma'am. I like it here a lot."

"And have there been any more intrusions by sea lately?"

He blinked, surprised that Nick had told Miss Kathleen about that. Knowing stuff like that probably worried her, although she didn't look so much worried as...alert, right on top of things. "Um, no, ma'am. At least, we haven't seen anybody."

"And no more phone calls?"

He settled back against the seat. Nobody was supposed to know about Sammy's call. "Phone calls?"

She gave him another one of those shrewd looks. He'd already noticed something unusual about her: she really *looked* at you. About ninety percent of the people who talked to kids didn't really see them, but he had a feeling this old lady did.

There was something special about her. He felt it with a quickening of something way down inside him.

She was really old, he thought, trying to study her unobtrusively. She had to be eighty-something, but the expression on her face wasn't like that of most old folks he knew. Could be her eyes, he decided. Green as glass. He knew she had come over to America from Ireland, which was called the Emerald Isle. Boy, when you thought of it like that, she really looked the part.

Her hands were in front of her, folded on top of a black cane. A lot of old people needed canes to get around. He was sorry Kathleen O'Connor was one of them. He bet she despised that cane. Jeez, maybe she was ninety-something.

"May I share a little secret with you, Daniel?" she asked.

"Yes, ma'am," he said promptly.

"When you get old," she began in a voice that was sort of whisper-soft, "people tend to think that you must be protected from all sorts of things. I'm afraid my family is guilty of that. I'm sure I don't know why, since all my vital organs are in fine shape. I'm not likely to keel over from worry or fright."

"You're not old," he said quickly, wanting to reassure her. "I mean, well…sure, maybe by the calendar and all, but I don't think there's anything old about the way you think or the way you would cope with…ah, all sorts of things."

"I'm happy to hear you say that, Daniel." She turned her gaze to the view of Wilderose Cottage from the window. "Since you've met me now, and judged me, I know you won't feel any hesitation in answering my questions. Now…"

Daniel felt a little lurch in his stomach. He realized he'd been outmaneuvered. He was wide open for whatever she asked.

"Are the police in Chicago making progress on the case?"

Wow. This old lady was something else. "I think Detective Forrester is pretty much on top of things there," he said cautiously.

She smiled. "Been doing some eavesdropping, have you?"

"Yes, ma'am. You know how it is, they think I'm a kid. It's sort of like you—" he grinned and shrugged "—only opposite."

"And Ryan has adequate manpower to safeguard you all?"

"He's hired some off-duty cops recommended by Nick."

"I see." With her gaze sharper than ever, she added, "The diamonds in question are still unaccounted for?"

"Uh-huh. I mean, yes, ma'am."

"Well, then..." She reached over and patted him on the knee. "Thank you, dear." With a small, imperious nod of her head, she signaled to the woman behind the wheel. "We can continue on to the house now, Ernestine."

"Yes, Mrs. O'Connor." The big car moved forward at a sedate pace along the curved driveway toward the house. Daniel could see Ryan and Joanna waiting on the lawn with Champ beside them. They both looked happy to see the old lady. He relaxed a little, glad to be off the hook. Ryan could answer the rest of her questions.

"You remind me of someone, Daniel," she said just as the car drew to a stop.

His heart gave another lurch. "I do?"

"You do indeed."

"Who is it?"

She smiled softly. "Remind me to tell you one day."

AT HER OWN REQUEST, Miss Kathleen was installed on the screen porch, given a glass of iced tea with a sprig of mint and the undivided attention of Ryan and Joanna. Champ needed a run, so Daniel had grabbed a Frisbee and headed for the beach. After a few minutes, Ernestine had joined them, and to Daniel's delight, proved she could throw a mean Frisbee. As soon as she could, Judith had excused herself.

"It's good to see you back at Sea Island, Joanna," Kathleen said, studying her with the kind of open curiosity that only the very old and very young can get away with. "You're even more lovely now than you were then."

Joanna smiled. "Thank you, Miss Kathleen. You're looking wonderful yourself. How have you been?"

"Well, I like to think I'm hanging in there, as they say." She chuckled softly. "Of course, news of your arrival was a shot in the arm. I just had to drive out and welcome you back home."

"Thank you, Miss Kathleen," Joanna murmured.

"And to tell you how much in your debt we are."

"Debt?" She gave Ryan a quick look.

"I don't know how much longer Ryan would have stayed on here, closed off from his family and friends, if you hadn't come along when you did."

"Oh, Miss Kathleen, I—"

"And for that, I thank you from the bottom of my heart."

Ryan set his glass down with a thump. "You're embarrassing her, Gran."

Kathleen leaned forward and touched her arm. "Do forgive me, Joanna. I'll change the subject."

"Good," Ryan said dryly.

His grandmother directed her gaze to the beach, where Daniel frolicked with the dog and Ernestine. "Your son is a delight," she said to Joanna. "We had a nice chat on the drive to the house. He was good enough to fill me in on some of the goings-on around here."

Ryan's gaze narrowed. "Such as?"

"Don't worry, Ryan, I'm not going to collapse beneath the weight of all he told me. I like to know what's happening with the members of my family."

While Ryan and Joanna tried to imagine what she might know, Kathleen turned her gaze to the drink in her hand. Her face gentled as she touched the sprig of mint in the glass. "I planted this mint in that little plot on the side of the guest-house, did you know that, Joanna?"

"No...no, I didn't. I just remember it always being there."

"Yes, it was the first summer that Patrick bought the place," she said, dreamy-eyed as she thought back. "It was

1946, I think." She looked at Joanna. "I wonder if you would mind cutting a bit of it for me, dear? I'd like to take it back to Wilderose House with me. Ernestine and I will enjoy it immensely."

"Of course." Joanna stood up, aware that she was being told in a very kind way that Kathleen wanted to speak to Ryan alone. "I'll be a few minutes," she said, meeting Ryan's eyes before hurrying away.

To his surprise, the silence between him and his grandmother was comfortable. It was good to see her, he thought. More than good. Between them, they shared a special bond. He couldn't quite explain what that bond was, but it was there. For a while longer, they both watched Daniel's exuberant play. Mixed with the sound of Champ's high-pitched puppy bark was the laughter of his son. He ached, suddenly, to reveal the secret to his grandmother.

"He is so like Cameron," she said softly.

He failed to cover his shock fast enough.

God, how had she guessed?

Kathleen touched him gently. "Did you think I wouldn't know? Cameron was taken from me at birth and it was eight years before Patrick managed to find him and reunite us. There's a look about Daniel that reminds me of Cameron." She laughed quietly. "And, of course, there's his special gift."

"Special gift?" Ryan was aware of a rushing sound in his head.

"His clairvoyance, Ryan. You don't have to pretend with me. He inherited it from the O'Connors, and he has a lot of company in this family—myself, Cameron, Shannon, and you, of course."

He was up and at the window. Confused and almost disoriented, he tried to take it in. "Why haven't you ever mentioned this before, Gran?"

"I knew you didn't welcome your gift," she said simply. "I can understand that. Until Patrick persuaded me that such power was special and wondrous, I felt reluctant about my own Dream Sight.''

He turned, staring at the ocean. ''Dream Sight.''

She smiled. ''That's how Patrick and I came to describe it. It's a positive thing, Ryan. Only good can come from it... unless it's ignored.''

He suddenly went still.

Kathleen spoke gently. ''I think you learned that lesson, and it has caused you great sorrow.''

''Yes,'' he said starkly.

''I'm sorry it has taken you so long to find some measure of peace.''

Still facing the window, he was as tense as steel.

''Pete would have some choice words for you if he were here.''

''So I'm told,'' he said dryly.

''Well, now...'' Her voice became brisk. ''One year of exile is long enough. You can begin to live again. Joanna and Daniel were heaven-sent.''

He turned, smiling faintly. ''Literally?'' he asked, his blue eyes putting her in mind of Patrick's. ''Or was that just an expression?''

''What do you think?'' she asked, and he could see all the affection she felt for him in her twinkling smile. ''I'm old, Ryan. I know a lot of people in heaven.''

He stood for a moment battling an unmanly urge to cry. God, nobody could realize how good it felt to know that his grandmother understood. She knew what had happened that black day in the desert, and yet she didn't appear to consider him beyond redemption. He was damn lucky. And in the back of his mind, waiting to be examined later, was the fact that his strange power wasn't unique in his family.

He walked back to sit down beside her. ''Before this conversation gets any more bizarre, I need to tell you that Daniel doesn't know that he's my son.''

''Your secret is safe with me, you know that.''

As he nodded, Ryan saw a change in her expression. For a moment, it was as though both shared a common feeling. A sinister feeling. With surprising strength, she clasped his hand with both of hers. "Ryan, the threat to Joanna and Daniel is real," she said.

"I know. I'll be careful."

The door was suddenly flung wide and Daniel burst onto the porch. "Boy oh boy, Ernestine flings a wicked Frisbee!" he cried. "Champ! Down, boy!" Diving for the dog, he grabbed him before he could unseat Kathleen and her iced tea, which wobbled on the small table.

With the help of her cane, the old lady got to her feet. "Daniel, you may ride with Ernestine and me to the gate if you don't have other plans."

"Are you leaving already?" he asked. His blue eyes filled with disappointment. Ryan was amused. Surely Daniel and Kathleen O'Connor made an odd couple, but they'd obviously fallen hard for each other.

"Yes, but you must visit me soon. At Wilderose House."

"All *right!*"

"Now, I must be off, but not without my mint. Ah, here she is." Kathleen reached for the plastic bag Joanna had filled with pungent green sprigs. "Ernestine, you may carry this, if you would."

"Come back soon, Miss Kathleen," Joanna requested softly.

"Yes, of course, dear. And you must visit Wilderose House the moment you can." She looked at Ryan. "Promise me, Ryan. You both owe a visit to Shannon to see the new baby."

"We'll be there," Ryan said.

With an imperious nod, she accepted Daniel's support and made her way through the house to the front door. Once he'd installed her in the back seat of the Mercedes, Daniel ran around the car to climb in the other side. Kathleen lowered her window and beckoned Ryan close.

"Use your special gift to protect your family, Ryan."

Almost before he straightened up, the window was raised and Daniel and his grandmother were chattering away like old friends.

CHAPTER FOURTEEN

RYAN HUNG UP THE PHONE after talking to Nick and paused with his hand still on the receiver to gaze through the window where Daniel sat on the beach watching the surf with Champ beside him. It was unusual to see them both quiet. Was Daniel worrying about his mother? Ryan wondered. No fourteen-year-old boy should be preoccupied with threats to his mother's safety. Maybe his call to Nick would be the turning point in this mess, he thought.

In the act of turning away, he noticed movement to his left. Judith Mann was picking her way across the lawn to the beach. Knowing her habits, he frowned. Judith did not enjoy a blustery walk along the shoreline. To his surprise, she went directly to Daniel and sat down. She'd never impressed Ryan as a person who was particularly interested in kids. Women. He was just beginning to understand the one he'd married fifteen years ago. His partner's widow would probably remain a life-long mystery.

"Gotcha!" Soft arms slipped around him from behind.

"I was just thinking about you," he said, pulling Joanna in front of him and gathering her close. He was smiling, something that he found himself doing a lot since Joanna had come home.

"You were not. You were standing here looking like a thundercloud ready to rain."

"It wasn't thoughts of you that made me look that way," he said, resting his chin on top of her head. "Everything but you, if you want the truth."

"I heard you on the phone. What did Nick say when you told him you thought Sammy Feldstein might be the bad guy in this mess?"

"He wanted to know what made me think so."

"Uh-oh. And did you tell him?"

"Yeah, I told him I'd seen Sammy's face in a dream."

"You didn't."

"To tell the truth, I didn't at first. I hemmed and hawed and beat around the bush until he finally told me just to spit it out." Ryan felt her smile against his neck. "You laugh, but it was tough trying to tell a hard-nosed cop something like that."

"When you finally did manage to get it out, what did he say?"

"That my suspicions were right on. He received a phone call from Gus Forrester this morning. At Chicago PD, Feldstein is the prime suspect. Now all they need to do is get a handle on where those damn diamonds are and we may be able to nail him."

"I'll be glad when he's in custody."

"Me, too, but Nick tells me he doesn't want to tip his hand that way. He wants to wait until he has the goods on Sammy before making an arrest, then he'll go for an indictment that'll stick. At this point, if they arrest him they won't have enough to indict him, barring a miracle. And, by the way, he thinks you should stay here until the indictment. Going to Forrester now would put you back in the line of fire."

She nodded. "It makes sense, but I'll feel a lot better when he's finally locked up."

"Yeah, me, too." He rocked her gently, his eyes on the beach where Daniel and Judith were talking.

"However," she said with a smile in her voice, "I do believe in miracles."

"Yeah?" He brushed his lips over her hair.

"Uh-huh. I'm living one."

"Ah, sweetheart..." Tipping up her chin, he kissed her slowly, tenderly, then just held her close.

"Nick surprised me with something else," he said after a moment. "He recognized Daniel's resemblance to my father from some old pictures of Gran's."

Joanna released a resigned sigh. "It's amazing, Ryan. In two days, practically everyone who meets Daniel sees that he's an O'Connor. How did it happen that for the first fourteen years of his life nobody noticed a thing?"

"You kept him away, Joanna." He sensed the upheaval of emotion his remark caused and his embrace tightened reassuringly. "I didn't say that to hurt you, sweetheart. There's blame enough to go around here. Although I'll always regret not being there when Daniel was small, I'm as much responsible for what happened as you. Maybe even more so. Our relationship had already broken down when you found yourself pregnant. With so little honesty and trust left between us, how can I blame you for coping the way you did?"

She gazed pensively at the beach. "I do wish I had brought him to Sea Island earlier," she said softly.

He dropped another kiss on her hair. "Well, he's here now and so are you. We'll make up for lost time, just the three of us."

"Haven't you forgotten someone?" Joanna asked, chuckling. "And I don't mean Champ." She gave a little nod to the scenario on the beach. "We have The Judith to add interest to our reunion."

"And Nick, when he chooses to drop in," Ryan said wryly. "And my grandmother, not to mention the telephone repairman, the security people and the thugs who're probably watching the place around the clock. And don't forget the security people Nick sent to watch the watchers who are watching us." He gave a short laugh. "For a man who barely saw two people a week for nearly a year, I'm beginning to feel as popular as a freak in a sideshow."

Joanna pressed her face to his chest in mute apology.

Ryan snapped his fingers. "Hey, I've got an idea. Why don't we call a Sea Island real estate agent and lease another house? Then we could invite the whole bunch here to Wilderose Cottage. Hell, drinks on me. It'd be worth it." With his lips on the curve between her neck and shoulder, he made a hot spot. Joanna shivered. "I want my privacy back," he growled.

"Me, too."

He chuckled. "You want my privacy back?"

"This is all my fault," Joanna suddenly said with dismay.

"Judith's your fault?"

"Well, not her, but everybody else. You'd still be enjoying complete solitude if I hadn't barged in."

He bent and kissed her once, hard. "Until you came, sweetheart, I'd forgotten what it felt like to enjoy anything. Now my wife is back, I've got a great teenage kid, I'm thinking about new projects to work on...." He hesitated, looking beyond her to the beach.

And then his face clouded over and he added, "You know, it's a hell of a note. I was holed up here alone for nearly a year. I never felt trapped. Now the walls feel like a prison. I can't wait to take you and Daniel away, to show you the world. But I can't. I'm stuck. *We're* stuck.

"We need to get this business with the diamonds settled and behind us, Jo. I like it here on Sea Island—especially now that you're here. Wilderose Cottage will always be special to us, but there's life beyond here and we need to begin living it."

It sounded good to her. With her troubled gaze on Daniel, Joanna hoped it wasn't simply too good to be true.

DANIEL LAY SPRAWLED on the sand, his head propped on his hand, watching the waves roll in. Wave-watching, he'd discovered, seemed to be good for thinking. And ever since that call from Sammy Feldstein, he had been having some pretty heavy thoughts. Everybody knew that the people who were looking for his mom believed she had the diamonds or that she knew who did or where they were. She didn't, of course. So this whole thing wasn't going to go away until something happened to make them realize they were harassing his mom for nothing.

His gaze troubled, he watched a big wave crest and foam, then wash toward him. What he was contemplating was pretty drastic, even for him. He wished he could run it by somebody, but it wasn't something you advertised you were thinking of doing.

Consorting with the criminal element, that's what he was thinking of doing. He just needed to refine a few points.

"Hi, kid."

He looked up with surprise to find Judith Mann smiling down at him. "You look as though you're trying to work out a formula for world peace. Mind if I sit down?"

"No, it's okay."

He watched as she sat down, carefully crossing her legs and bringing them up to wrap her arms around her knees. That way, he guessed, she wasn't in contact with anything gritty and damp except where her behind met the sand.

"So, worried about your mom, hmm?"

"Yeah, I guess so."

"It's understandable, but she's as safe here with Ryan as she would be anywhere. More so. Ryan has some experience in self-defense and he's been in tight spots before. If anything happens, he's capable of protecting her. Since it's Joanna, someone he cares for, he'll be especially watchful."

"I know. I told myself all that." His eyes followed as she meticulously brushed sand off her feet. "We can't stay here on Sea Island forever, though. We have a life—school, Mom's work, you know. That's what I was thinking about."

She studied him in silence as though she was thinking of something entirely different.

"Something else worries me, sort of," he admitted.

"What's that?"

"Well, you know...Mom and Ryan being together here, and they used to be married...and..." He trailed off, feeling ridiculous now that he'd said something like that. But Mrs. Mann was a woman and he sensed she was the kind of person who had been around and wouldn't be shocked by much of anything.

"If you're concerned that people might talk, Daniel, then I don't think you should worry. Actually, very few people even know you and your mother are here. Those who do, like Nick and Shannon and Ryan's grandmother, understand the circumstances."

"Yeah, I was thinking pretty much the same thing," he said, definitely relieved. He fixed his gaze on the water. "But you never can tell."

Judith hid a smile. "No, you never can tell."

Only a few feet away, a lone sandpiper scurried along the edge of the surf in an industrious search for food.

"As a matter of fact," Judith said, her eyes on the sandpiper, "you want to hear something nice?"

"Sure."

"Pete used to say that if circumstances ever threw them together again, he wouldn't be surprised if Joanna and Ryan discovered they still had a lot in common."

He frowned, wondering if he was part of the stuff that they had in common. He was more than halfway convinced that Ryan was his father, but he hadn't figured out how to prove it without asking flat out. It occurred to him that Judith might be able to fill in a few blanks about Ryan and his mom, considering that she was married to Pete.

"I guess Pete knew a lot about Ryan," he said, keeping his voice casual. "Personal stuff, I mean."

"They were very good friends. They worked together very closely."

"Did Pete ever mention anything about me?"

"All the time. Especially to Joey. After seeing you in Chicago, he always told her all about it."

He studied the meandering trail of the sandpiper. "Did he ever talk to *you* about me?"

She turned then and looked at him shrewdly. "I'm not sure what you're asking, Daniel. If there's something in particular you think Pete might have said, I'll do my best to answer."

Here it was. Now or never. He swallowed once, hard. "Did Pete ever say that Ryan might be my dad?"

She stared at him in open astonishment. Daniel didn't know what she was thinking, but he knew the answer to his question wasn't yes. He felt a disappointment so profound that he almost wanted to cry. Jeez, he couldn't do that. He swallowed again, this time around a big lump. It was no big deal, for heaven's sake. He had a father. Or he'd had one once. It wasn't as though he was an orphan or anything like that.

"No, he never said that," she said softly, touching his arm, now wrapped tightly around his knees.

Daniel fixed his gaze on her fingers with those awful red nails. Judith looked straight ahead, as though what he'd asked had started a whole new line of thinking.

"But if it were true," she said slowly, "it would explain a lot of things." She brought her gaze back to him. "What made you think of that, Daniel?"

He shrugged. "Lots of things, but mostly—" he sighed with resignation, knowing how inadequate it would sound "—mostly it's just a feeling I have."

She was studying him intently. "You look like Ryan," she murmured. "Blue eyes, hair a shade lighter, but hair color in most people darkens with age. Mostly around the eyes and nose." Her eyes widened. "What about Kathleen O'Connor's visit? Did she say anything?"

"Only that I reminded her of someone."

"Who? Did she say who?"

"Look, Mrs. Mann, maybe we better drop this. I shouldn't have said anything. It's just that—"

She wasn't listening. "If it were true—" Closing her eyes suddenly, Judith slapped her hand against her chest. "Oh, what a fabulous book this would make! Can you believe this? Oh, I'm— I—'' She scrambled up, heedless of the sand on her sandals and on the hem of her jeans, and began pacing.

"Listen to this. There's the missing diamonds, the murder, the gay relationship, a woman in jeopardy. *But*—'' eyes bright, she propped her hands on her hips ''—not just any woman, but the ex-wife of the guy who's giving her sanctuary on a gorgeous, secluded island. Add to that the appearance of the child he never knew he had and...ta-dum! We've got a killer of a book. A bestseller! And all based on a true story, of course.''

"Mrs. Mann, I don't think—''

"Ah, Daniel, Daniel, don't even think a negative thought about this one, love.''

"This isn't Hollywood, Mrs. Mann. This is real life, and besides, Ryan told you straight out that he wasn't going to write a book about this.''

"He will,'' she said, her expression rapt. "We'll convince him.''

"I'm not. I'm staying out of it.''

"Don't you want to see yourself portrayed on the 'Movie of the Week'?''

"No! Besides, the important thing is getting these people off my mom's case.''

"Hmm.'' Judith assumed a thoughtful look. "That, of course, won't happen until the diamonds turn up. And you're right, we can't do the story until it's played out. Damn it!'' She hit the palm of her hand with her fist, her red nails flashing. "I wish we had a glimmer of a clue, just a glimmer as to where they are.''

Daniel stood up, his eyes on Champ, who got sleepily to his feet and gave himself a good shake. "If somebody knew where they were, I guess that information could be used to flush Sammy out,'' he mused, chewing on his bottom lip.

"Sammy? Do we think Sammy is the key player here?''

He shrugged. "I think it means *something* that he called here looking for my mom, don't you?"

"Yes, yes..." She focused on something in the distance, thinking. "Of course, we wouldn't have to have the diamonds so long as those guys *believed* we had them."

"I gotta go in now, Mrs. Mann."

"Hmm? Oh, sure, right."

With a distracted wave, he walked away. He had some serious thinking to do.

An hour later, using the extension in his mother's studio, Daniel picked up the phone and dialed Sammy Feldstein in Chicago.

FELDSTEIN HUNG UP and shoved the telephone back into its cubbyhole on Rico's desk. Just when he'd almost given up, here it was, dropped into his lap like a gift from the gods.

Thank you, thank you, thank you...

His heart was beating like a drum. He sank into the cushioned chair and stared blindly at his hands. God, he was shaking, and no wonder. Another day or two and they would have gotten mean. Their threats were getting more and more virulent. They didn't believe him when he told them he didn't know where the diamonds were.

But he was saved...by a kid, yet!

Whoever would have guessed it? He'd been combing the whole frigging U.S. of A. looking for Joanna when it was Daniel all along. Cute. Clever. Drumming his fingers on the desk, he moved his head up and down slowly, giving credit where it was due. Something about Daniel was unique; he'd picked up on that almost from the first. More than once, Rico himself had mentioned it. Rico would, Sammy thought cynically. Show Rico a fatherless kid and an oh-so-courageous single mother and he turned into a teddy bear. If Rico only knew!

He sat for a few minutes, thinking. If he called his associates and let them know he'd been contacted, they would insist on traveling with him. Nix that. He was certain, more or less, that they wouldn't just forget about Daniel and his mother once they knew for certain that they had actually seen the diamonds. But how they handled Joanna and Daniel was no longer his concern. He didn't wish them any harm, but he personally wasn't going to stick around once he managed to get his hands on the ice. Whatever happened when he was out of the picture…well, he'd just rather not know.

Shoving the chair back a little, he sat for several moments surveying the tasteful interior of the shop with a pang of regret. He had no regrets over Joanna and her kid, but the gallery was something else. He was going to hate walking away from it. He loved every treasure in it. Passionately. From candlestick to coaster, each piece had been lovingly chosen for uniqueness—in design, in color, in antiquity. One thing both Joanna and Rico had admitted—Sammy was an excellent buyer. Joanna might be good with bookkeeping and such, but he—Sammy—had the eye needed for stocking the gallery. The diamond on his finger suddenly caught his eye. He would have the money to start up another gallery. Perhaps in Rio. Now *that* was a nice city. And blessed with warm weather. The climate would be a major consideration wherever he went. He hated the cold.

He scooted back to the desk, reached for the phone and dialed his travel agent. In three minutes, he was booked to Savannah, Georgia.

JUDITH ENTERED the living room where Joanna and Ryan sat on opposite sides of a game table putting together a jigsaw puzzle. With a muffled whimper, she sank carefully onto the couch and leaned back with a long sigh. An obvious victim of too much sun, she was hardly recognizable as the sleek, tailored career woman who'd arrived only two days before. Her nose was pink and shiny, her arms an angry red. Even the tops of her feet peeking from beneath her flowing pants were sunburned.

"Okay, gang, it's six o'clock," she said, her eyes closed in exhaustion. "Even in Georgia, that's the cocktail hour, isn't it?"

"Judith! What have you done?" Joanna grimaced sympathetically and rose to go to her. "Have you medicated yourself? We've got something—"

Judith waved away her concern. "I've slathered enough gunk on my body to keep me wrinkle-free until I'm ninety. But it doesn't seem to do anything for dehydration. A drink, please, Ryan."

"Coming up." The corner of Ryan's mouth quirked in amusement as he got up and made his way to the bar. "Apparently it's been a while since you've been in the sun, Judith. First rule at Sea Island—don't overdo until you've acclimated."

"There was hardly any sun at all," she said, sounding mystified.

"It was a windy, overcast day," Joanna said. "Wind and sand and ultraviolet rays are a deadly combination."

"Gin and tonic suit you?" Ryan asked from the bar.

"God, yes. And lots of ice. *Lots* of ice."

"Well," she said a few minutes later, accepting a tall, frosty glass from Ryan, "I've learned my lesson." She sipped gratefully at the drink, then set it down on the coaster Joanna provided. "Where's Daniel?"

"Out in my studio reading some old family journals," Joanna replied, smiling, as Ryan handed her a glass of wine. "When Ryan gave him permission, he took a box of them out there and we haven't seen him for hours."

"Family journals?"

"It's sort of a family tradition," Ryan explained with a shrug. "Probably the manifestation of collective giant egos, but there you are. We keep journals—my grandmother, my father, me—even Shannon."

"Speaking of Daniel," he said, setting his drink aside, "I

noticed the two of you in conversation on the beach. Want to tell me what that was all about?"

She sighed, looking injured. "Ryan, have you always been so suspicious? What could I have been talking to Daniel about that you would object to?"

"A book contract?"

She rolled her eyes; then, when he remained silent, she gave an impatient click of her tongue. "Oh, okay, it might have come up."

"Judith, I told you—"

"I know, I know, but this is such a fabulous opportunity, Ryan. For you and your family, it would—" She looked a tiny bit alarmed, but pressed on with hardly a missed beat. "I mean, Daniel isn't your family, but Joanna *used* to be, and from the way things look between you two, she probably will be again. So, looking at it like that, Daniel is family, too." She flashed him a bright look. "Right?"

"None of your damned business!"

She got up from the couch, wincing melodramatically, but she wasn't giving up. Watching them, Joanna guessed Judith probably did her best wrangling on her feet. She wanted to sign Ryan to a book contract and she appeared to be willing to do whatever it took to make it happen. Maybe they should join forces, Joanna thought, hiding a smile. She felt Ryan should write a book, too, but not a silly one based on this mess with the missing diamonds. She wanted him to write the book that would be the catharsis of his experience when Pete died.

"You've got to do it, Ryan," Judith cried. "You promised!"

Ryan drove his fingers through his hair in frustration. "How can I think of writing a book when Joanna's life might be in danger, Judith? Think, woman!"

The red nail polish, Joanna noticed apropos of nothing, had vanished. Judith's nails were pink and natural looking. Actually, the more she was around Judith, the more she liked her.

She would never be sugar and spice and everything nice. She was probably a bit selfish and she was definitely openly ambitious, but Joanna didn't think she would stab anybody in the back to get ahead, even if she would do almost anything to get Ryan's signature on the bottom line.

Judith paused, running her finger around the rim of her glass. "Actually, I've been doing just that."

Ryan looked blank. "Doing what?"

"Thinking how we might just bring this whole fiasco to a head," Judith said softly. "It came to me this morning when Daniel and I were talking."

Ryan crossed his arms over his chest, waiting.

"The thugs think Joanna has the diamonds. If you're convinced Sammy Feldstein is the bad guy in all this, then maybe we could force him to tip his hand. Something Daniel said was pretty shrewd. Maybe we could set up something like a sting, you know what I mean? Set up a meeting with Sammy and Joanna. Naturally we'd have Nick and a whole contingent of cops standing by just in case—"

"Are you crazy!" Ryan flung his hand out, then began pacing back and forth. "Are you completely nuts, Judith?" He shot her an incredulous look. "Do you have any idea what you're suggesting? That I should deliberately put Joanna in danger just for the sake of a goddamn movie plot?"

"It's a book, not a movie," Judith mumbled, but Ryan plowed on, overriding her.

"If I thought for one minute that you were seriously suggesting something like this, I don't...I wouldn't..." He stopped, staring at her, then shook his head. "It was just this kind of crazy stunt that nearly sent me round the bend, Judith. For the sake of a *good story,*" he said with savage humor, "I caused the death of your husband."

"I've never accepted your version of that, Ryan," Judith said quietly. "Pete's death was a tragedy. I miss him more than I ever dreamed I would. But *it's not your fault!*"

Calmer, Ryan went back to the bar, standing with his back

to both Judith and Joanna for a few seconds. "I will always feel some responsibility for Pete's death," he said quietly, "but I've learned one thing. I don't ignore my gut feelings anymore, and my guts tell me to keep Joanna as close as if we were Siamese twins! She can't star in an amateur 'America's Most Wanted.'"

Joanna walked over to him. "She may have a point, Ryan," she said, touching his hand, which was clamped on the bar's edge.

With a groan, he dropped his head back, looking at the ceiling. "Not you, too."

"No, no, wait. Why couldn't I call Sammy and set up a meeting, say...at a mall, somewhere that's large with other people milling around? You and Nick could be close by. Maybe he would say something incriminating. I could wear a recording device of some sort."

"Absolutely not!" He turned and cupped her neck with his hand. When he spoke, his voice was shaky. "I can't take a chance like that, not with you, Joanna. Don't ask me."

For a moment, their eyes clung. Then she nodded and gave him a soft smile. "Okay. It was just a thought."

"But it sure might have ended this stalemate," Judith said with regret. Finishing off her drink, she set it on the bar. "So, if we can't plan a sting operation, how about another gin and tonic?"

Ryan laughed. "Now that," he said, scooping up her empty glass, "I can do."

Judith went back to the couch. Once she'd eased carefully onto the cushions, she looked thoughtfully at Ryan and Joanna. "So, I guess second chances are the order of the day for the two of you, hmm?"

"When we decide our future," Ryan said dryly, "you'll be at least the twenty-sixth to know."

"Daniel being number one, right?" She accepted the fresh drink and leaned back. "Since he already suspects, you might want to consider taking him into your confidence about something else.''

Joanna's wine splashed on her fingers. With an unsteady hand, she set the glass on the bar carefully. ''What are you talking about, Judith?''

''Yeah,'' Ryan said suspiciously. ''What *are* you talking about?''

''Daniel and I didn't just talk about your situation, Joanna, he also asked me questions about the past.''

''What past? You and I have no past, Judith.''

''No, he was asking about Ryan and Pete.'' She drew in a deep breath as though she wasn't comfortable with what she was going to say next. ''His question startled me, but after I thought about it—'' she shrugged, including both in her smile ''—well, it didn't seem so incredible.''

''Spit it out, Judith,'' Ryan growled.

''He asked if I knew whether you were his father, Ryan.''

''God.''

''Oh…''

''You both look as though you've been hit by a truck,'' Judith observed, not unsympathetically. ''I suspect he's reading those journals looking for his bloodlines.''

''He won't find anything in mine,'' Ryan said curtly.

''Or Cameron's,'' Joanna said on a whisper. Her eyes went to his. ''Oh, Ryan, I don't think—''

''We'll go sce him.'' Pushing away from the bar, Ryan reached for Joanna's arm, and without slowing, headed for the door. As he shouldered through, he turned back to Judith. ''Thanks, Ju.''

From over the rim of her gin and tonic, Judith smiled at him. ''What're friends for?''

CHAPTER FIFTEEN

USING A HELICOPTER from Will O'Connor's shipyard, Nick Dalton made it to Sea Island within an hour after receiving Ryan's call. "You're telling me nobody's seen Daniel for more than six hours?" He gazed incredulously at the three adults in the room with him. "And nobody thought to check?"

Ryan stopped pacing and gave his brother-in-law a grim look. "I know how it sounds, Nick." He didn't need a lecture. Joanna's pale face and his own increasing apprehension had his stomach in a knot. "We thought he was in the studio—he *told* us he would be in the studio, not to worry about him for lunch—and when we went up to check on him, he was gone. Your men didn't see him leave, either."

Nick clamped a hand against the back of his neck. "Okay, let's run through it again." He gave all three a penetrating look—Ryan, Joanna and Judith Mann. "Don't leave out a single detail."

"We've told you everything!" Joanna cried, springing up from the chair and starting her own round of pacing. "He's gone. Instead of talking, we should be looking for him!"

"Sweetheart." Intercepting her, Ryan pulled her close. "Nick's right. We need to narrow the field. At this point, he could be anywhere."

The phone rang and both Ryan and Joanna jumped for it. Ryan reached it first, barked a hello and then shoved it at Nick. "It's for you."

Nick's conversation was brief. When he hung up, he looked at Ryan. "I sent a unit to check the neighborhood. At 6:00

p.m., he was spotted at the 7-Eleven. He conned a parcel van driver into giving him a ride into town *and* hauling his bike.''

Ryan swore. ''Did he say where they went?''

''They're checking. The store manager knows the driver. We'll find out.''

''Hitchhiking!'' Joanna cried. ''I can't believe he would do this! He knows how dangerous it is. What could he be thinking?''

''Could he have his own agenda?'' Nick suggested softly.

Ryan looked thoughtful. ''It's the only thing that makes sense.''

''Agenda?'' Joanna asked blankly.

''We're talking about a kid who's smart and resourceful,'' Nick said slowly. ''He managed to get from Montreal to Sea Island on his own. We need to try and retrace his footsteps from this morning—or last night—before we can begin to look for him.'' With a sigh, he sat down at the table, his pen poised over his notebook. ''Until we do, we won't even know where to start.''

Moving away from Ryan, Joanna went to the window and stood gripping her elbows with her hands. ''There was something,'' she said, her voice dropping quietly. With an apologetic look at Ryan, she turned to face Nick. ''Maybe...I mean, it could be possible that he was upset about something he found out...something personal.''

''Like what?'' Nick said baldly.

She closed her eyes. ''We think...I mean, Judith said that he wanted to know if Ryan could be his father.'' In the silence that followed, she gazed intently at the beach until she felt Ryan move to her side and slip his arm around her waist. She turned gratefully into his strength and warmth.

Looking at Nick over Joanna's head, Ryan said, ''I am his father, Nick. Jo and I were planning to tell him when we felt the time was right. With the situation so tense around here, the threat to Joanna, me being a virtual stranger to him...well, we decided to put it off.''

"How is it that he asked Judith about this?" Nick inquired.

"It was just this morning," Judith volunteered. "We were talking on the beach." She chuckled softly, looking at Joanna. "He was a little worried about your reputation, Joanna. I tried to reassure him about that. I reminded him that hardly anybody knows you're here, anyway."

Nobody commented on Joanna's horrified look or the blush that colored her face.

"He'd already given me a lecture on morality," Ryan growled, but he, too, looked uncomfortable.

"Did he strike you as unhappy over the prospect that Ryan might be his father?" Nick asked.

"No, just the opposite. I remember thinking he looked disappointed when I told him Pete had never confided anything like that to me."

Leaning back in his chair, Nick considered that. "He didn't act as if he might be considering running away?"

"Not at all. Absolutely not."

"Did you talk about anything else?"

"Well..." She gave Ryan a sheepish glance, then said, "The book."

Ryan spoke from the window where he stood. "Judith's publisher seems to think I should write a book. I've been reluctant, so she was sent to persuade me."

"A lot of good it's done," she grumbled, rolling her eyes.

"And that's all?" Nick said, bringing them back to the point.

Judith frowned, thinking. "Actually..."

"What?" Ryan demanded.

"Actually, now that I think about it, we talked about the situation that put his mother in jeopardy. The key is the missing diamonds, of course. Joanna is in limbo here until the diamonds are found, or until somebody makes a move on her.

Daniel is bright enough to figure that out. Find the diamonds, his mother's off the hook.'' She looked at Ryan. ''We'd also have the ending to the book.''

She cleared her throat and straightened a little in her chair. ''We brainstormed over it a little, trying to figure out how to make it happen. But we weren't serious...not really.'' She frowned, trying to recall. ''I remember...we decided that if Sammy Feldstein could be flushed out, he would probably lead us to his cohorts.''

She looked at Ryan. ''I told you about it, Ryan. We were thinking a sting would be good. Feldstein would only have to *believe* we had the diamonds. We wouldn't actually have to have them.''

Nick looked at Ryan. ''Would Daniel undertake something like this on his own?'' he asked gravely.

Ryan's eyes were dark with worry. ''He might.''

''You think it's more likely that he's singlehandedly trying to capture a gang of thugs than it is that he's upset over discovering he's not who he thought he was?''

''He can't know that for sure,'' Joanna said huskily.

Nick stood up, tucking his notebook in his shirt pocket. ''Either way, we need to get an all-points out on him.''

''We need to go to the airport,'' Ryan said suddenly.

''The airport?'' Nick repeated. Everyone looked at Ryan expectantly.

''I...I just have a feeling.'' His gaze went to Joanna, who searched his face intently, but said nothing.

''The airport it is,'' Nick said, not missing a beat, then walked to the door. ''I'll radio for backup and they'll meet us there.'' From personal experience, he knew better than to waste time when an O'Connor ''had a feeling.''

AFTER DANIEL WORKED OUT the details, it was a piece of cake to put the plan into action. Timing was the thing, he discovered. He knew what he had to do; the first step had been getting past Ryan and his mom so he could get to the airport. He needed some excuse to be out of sight long enough to allow time to get away from Wilderose Cottage, past Nick's men, and somehow get across the bridge to the mainland and still get to the airport on time.

The journals turned out to be the perfect answer.

He stayed in the studio long enough to make certain that nobody was suspicious. It was good stuff—Ryan painted such a vivid picture of his assignments that Daniel almost felt he was there. Jeez, it was no wonder Mrs. Mann wanted him to write a book. Daniel couldn't help but think, though, that the book he should write ought to be based on his journals—not on a bunch of diamond smugglers.

He had almost lost track of time, but after an hour had passed and nobody had come checking on him, he slipped out of the studio and got on the bike and rode away. He had to go by way of the beach, since using the gate would have registered on the alarm. It had also been tricky getting past those guys that Ryan was paying to watch the property since the fishing boat incident. But he'd done it. Pushing the bike through sand hadn't been an easy task, and he'd emerged at the road sweating and out of breath.

The part that worried him the most was that he'd had to break a cardinal rule. Since it was sixty miles to Savannah, he'd been forced to hitch a ride. Fortunately he'd found a friendly delivery van driver who'd agreed to haul his bike, too.

At any rate, he was at the airport with a little time to spare before Sammy Feldstein's plane was due in from Chicago. He had a couple of things to do. First, the ticket desk. Then the trial run with the tape recorder. It was a voice-activated model, one he'd discovered in a box of things belonging to Ryan along with his journals and awards and stuff. He was curious why Ryan seemed so careless with junk that appeared pretty important. He planned to ask about it, that is if Ryan ever spoke to him again after this caper was finished.

The ticket agent was pretty and cooperative, and so was her cohort. After taking care of business, Daniel headed for the men's room, where he took off his jacket and then pulled his shirt over his head, checking to see that the recorder was still secure in the belt pouch. With his head bent, he punched a button, reversed the tape, pushed Play, and there it was!

Elated, he listened to the conversation between himself and the ticket agent. He even got the voice of her co-worker loud and clear. Now all he had to do was to get Sammy to incriminate himself—on tape—and that ought to be evidence enough to satisfy even Gus Forrester.

Two minutes later, he walked out of the men's room, shirt tucked in, jacket on. It was too hot and humid for a jacket, but he couldn't see any way around wearing one. The recorder was a big lump, even though he'd positioned it to the side, sort of. With a studiedly casual look around, he squared his shoulders and made for the center of the terminal to study incoming flights on the video monitors.

Flight 213. Gate 7B. All *right*. With a glance at his watch, he went to the appropriate gate and took a seat that gave him a good view of the jetway as well as the people waiting.

According to the monitors, the flight was on time, which meant the passengers would start pouring into the terminal no later than fifteen, twenty minutes. He settled down to wait and immediately thought about his mother. She would be worried, big time. And Ryan. Man, Ryan would probably take a strip off him when he got back to Sea Island, but if everything turned out the way he hoped it would—the way he'd planned it—then maybe they wouldn't be mad at him too long.

They could resume a normal life.

He could ask the big question.

Ryan, are you my father?

NICK'S BACKUP, WEARING street clothes, met them at the airport, and under his direction they immediately spread out to look for Daniel. At this point, Nick felt it was better to keep a low profile. Tipping their hand to Feldstein might endanger Daniel. Joanna slipped a hand into Ryan's, took a deep breath and followed him through the automatic doors into the terminal.

A lone fourteen-year-old boy shouldn't be too difficult to spot, Ryan told himself, anxiously scanning every visible nook and cranny. He crushed the doubts that had dogged him on the way to the airport and concentrated on looking for his son, not on questions that had no answers. He had no proof that Daniel was here, but his instinct was strong, and they had no other leads. The van driver had finally been reached. Daniel had slipped out of the van during his first stop in Savannah.

"Which flight is he meeting?" Joanna asked, scanning the monitors with distress. "Which gate?"

"I don't know," Ryan said, squeezing her hand. "But he's here."

With her icy fingers in his hand, Ryan could feel her terror. Suddenly he was swamped with emotion. He wanted to swear, to demand that this nightmare end. He had just found Joanna and Daniel. He didn't want this chance stolen from him. And if something happened to Daniel, he wasn't sure what would be left. Feeling frustrated and more terrified than he'd been since that fateful day in the desert, he pushed those thoughts away and sent a look heavenward.

Where were his "special powers" when he needed them? Where was the famous O'Connor clairvoyance? All he had to go on was an undeniable feeling that Daniel was here. What good was this bizarre "gift" if it didn't help him when he most needed it? Closing his eyes, he imagined Daniel beside him.

Ah, Daniel, please don't do anything crazy.

"We can't even be certain he's here," Joanna whispered, scanning the passengers waiting in line at the ticket counters.

"He is," Ryan repeated, knowing how improbable it sounded. Daniel was somewhere in the terminal. He just needed to find him. But no matter how he tried, he couldn't see any more than Daniel's face in his mind. He just *felt* his son's presence.

"I had this dream."

The memory of Daniel's words that first night rose vividly. He regretted bitterly now that he'd listened without comment as his son confided his unique "special talent." Why hadn't he said then and there that he knew all too well about those feelings?

"My mom was in the airport...talking on the phone."

Ryan stopped where he was and looked at the bank of tele phones not ten feet away from them.

"Sometimes I know things...sense things...as if my mom's in danger."

Ryan put his hand on Joanna's shoulder. "Jo, I want you to go over to one of those phones and call Sammy Feldstein's number in Chicago."

She gave him an astonished look. "What? Now? Why?"

"Let's see if he's in Chicago. If not..." He turned slowly, taking in people, attendants, travelers, agents, pilots. "Just go over and make that call, babe."

Joanna walked to the first booth, opened her bag and took out her address book and telephone calling card. She found Sammy's name and punched the endless string of numbers, then, with her gaze fixed on Ryan, waited for an answer.

"Hello."

"Ah...is this Sammy?"

"Who wants to know?"

She covered the mouthpiece and said to Ryan, "He wants to know who I am." Ryan nodded.

"This is Joanna Stanton."

There was an instant of silence. "Where are you, Mrs. Stanton?"

"I would like to speak to Sammy, please."

"Do you have the diamonds, Mrs. Stanton?"

"Is Sammy out of town?"

"Look, if you and Sammy think you're going to put something over on us, then you'd better wise up."

"How could we put something over on you?"

"Feldstein may think he's pulling a fast one sneaking out of town, but we've got a tail on him and you're being watched around the clock, lady. So, if the two of you are planning your own private party with our merchandise, you stand a better chance of winning the lottery. Take it from somebody who knows."

Her heart was thudding in her chest. Sammy *was* on his way here, or at least these people thought he was headed this way. She felt fear and suddenly another emotion. Squeezing the receiver, she realized that she was outraged. These people, whoever they were, had sent her into exile, fearing for her life. They'd used her business for criminal purposes, they'd spied on her, intimidated her, put her son in jeopardy.

Without another word, she put her hand out and cut the connection. Still holding the receiver in her hand, she looked at Ryan. "You're right, Ryan. I think Sammy's here, or on his way here. Somehow Daniel must have reached him. If you're certain Daniel's in the airport, it can only mean he's here with some crazy idea to force his hand." She rubbed her forehead with unsteady fingers. "Oh, even for Daniel this is just too much! What if Sammy thinks I have those stupid diamonds? What if he manages to kidnap Daniel or something?"

With a frightened, anguished look on her face, she searched the stream of travelers pouring through a gate from an incoming flight. Suddenly the receiver slipped from her hand.

"Oh dear Lord, there he is, Ryan!"

FROM BEHIND A USED COPY of *USA Today*, Daniel studied Sammy Feldstein. He'd spotted him the moment he stepped into the terminal, but decided to wait and see if he was alone before showing himself. Feldstein seemed to be looking for somebody, which Daniel assumed was him. Good, he thought, hoping for smooth sailing. It didn't take a rocket scientist to guess that a situation like this could take a bad turn without warning. He gazed around, making sure that no one else seemed interested in Feldstein. Nope.

Looking good, he thought, pleased.

He also kept a sharp eye on the friendly ticket agent and her co-worker. He guessed nobody actually took him seriously when he'd talked to them, but it wouldn't matter as long as they were there.

Sure now that his quarry was alone, he waited until Feldstein was turned away from him, then got up very casually. Instantly he had to hitch at the bulge beneath his shirt, which seemed to want to shift whenever he made a sudden move. When he had it anchored firmly in place, he headed over.

"Hi, Sammy."

Feldstein jumped a foot high. "Sheesh, kid, are you trying to give me a heart attack?"

"Why would I do that?" Daniel asked innocently.

Feldstein stared hard at him, then looked around as though checking to see that he was alone. "Where's Joanna?"

"She doesn't know I'm meeting you, so she's not here."

"So how did you get away without making her suspicious? It's nearly 10:00 p.m."

"I managed, Sammy."

"Yeah, you seem to be a shrewd little customer."

Daniel shrugged. "Maybe it takes one to know one."

Feldstein caught his arm. "Listen, you little punk, I didn't come halfway across the country to trade wisecracks. You know what I came for. So, where is it?"

"The statue with the diamonds?"

Feldstein glanced around in alarm. "Shut the hell up! Do you want to tell the whole airport? Why don't you run to the control tower and use the mike?" To Daniel's relief, he dropped his arm. "Cut the crap, kid, I mean it. You said on the phone that you had them. I knew it all along. I told the guys no way would Joanna just turn her back on a fortune in gems. She's nice, but nobody's that nice."

"Who are the guys?" Daniel asked, trying to appear nonchalant. "Is it those truckers that Rico signed last year?"

"What is this?" Feldstein asked softly. "Little pitchers have big ears, eh?"

"It *is* them!"

In his head, Daniel tried frantically to think of a way to get Feldstein to identify his cronies. It was then that he noticed two men who were edging closer and closer. One was tall and big as a linebacker with a short, black mustache. He'd been on the same flight as Sammy. The other was average height, wiry like a runner. He'd pegged him for a businessman earlier. He hadn't looked his way, not then. But he was definitely looking now. And looking less like a businessman. In fact, he looked a lot like one of the men from the boat! Daniel's heart began to thump hard in his chest. He glanced at the ticket counter and found the pretty agent watching curiously, but she smiled. He smiled back.

Feldstein spoke through his teeth. "Someday, kid, if you don't watch it, you're gonna find yourself in big trouble."

"I think he's in big trouble already."

By Feldstein's expression, he didn't expect to see these two guys. With his heart in his mouth, Daniel waited to see what would happen. Just that fast, Feldstein started to back away, but something in the big one's face stopped him.

"What the hell game are you playing, Feldstein?"

Daniel had never believed that a person could turn white from fear, but Feldstein looked like a dead man. It was a freaky thought.

"Are you planning to split the diamonds with these guys?" Daniel asked, looking from one to the other.

"Yeah, Sammy," the big one said with an ugly smile. "You *are* planning to share, ain't that so?"

With both hands out, Feldstein began edging backward. "Look, you guys, this isn't what it looks like. The kid called and I—"

"We know, we know. You shouldn't try to keep secrets from your friends, Feldstein. It's a good thing we put that tap on your phone, I guess. Right, Mick?"

"Right, Bejay."

"Tap?" Feldstein repeated, looking sick.

Up close, "Mick" was was even meaner-looking, Daniel decided. "Look," he said, hoping he could bluff his way out of this, "I can see you people have some things to talk about." He gave an elaborate shrug. "Since they don't concern me, why don't I just leave you to it? Okay?"

"In your dreams, buddy," said Bejay. His hand shot out to grab a fistful of Daniel's jacket, then he jerked him over close enough that Daniel could see each hair in the clipped mustache.

"There are some people back in Chicago who are really ticked off at your mother," Bejay informed him. "You said on the phone that you had the diamonds. Well, here's your chance to avoid something really terrible happening to your mother, kid."

"I...I..." Daniel's voice failed him. Clearing his throat, he tried again. "I don't have them with me," he said, opening his eyes wide. "Do you think I'm crazy?"

Bejay simply lifted him by the arms and shook him hard. Daniel felt like a rag doll without enough stuffing. He saw lights, he felt his teeth rattle, he heard a ringing in his ears. And voices. He heard shouts and a lot of loud voices. He couldn't have said who reached him first, Ryan or Nick, but suddenly they were both there amid a jumble of other voices.

"Airport security! Stop!"

"Police officers! Turn the boy loose!"

"What's going on here?"

"Daniel! Daniel, oh my God, Daniel..."

As his head cleared, he recognized his mother's voice. He hated scaring her like that. He tried to speak, to tell her he was okay, but his tongue wouldn't work. She was kissing him all over his face, touching his arms and rubbing him down, checking for blood or something, he guessed. Somebody was holding on to him, otherwise he doubted his legs could hold him up. Blinking to clear his vision, he looked up into Ryan's face. He was unsmiling. He looked like he might never smile again. Daniel hoped he was wrong about that.

"Jeez, Ryan, I didn't expect to see you here," he said weakly, but his words were smothered against Ryan's chest as he was gathered close in a bear hug. For the first time since things got out of hand, Daniel felt like he might cry. With his face mashed into Ryan's shirt, he returned the hug with everything he had.

But when Ryan turned him loose, his expression was so fierce that Daniel's cocky self-confidence suddenly deserted him. He looked at his mother. "Before you both start yelling, I think you ought to know I've got it all on tape."

"When we get you home," Ryan said in a dangerously soft tone, "maybe you can come up with an explanation that will keep you from being grounded until you're old enough to vote!"

Shoving him into Joanna's arms, Ryan wiped a shaking hand over his mouth. It took a minute to bring the roaring in his ears under control. Joanna's arms were wrapped tightly around Daniel. She was weeping softly. He felt weak-kneed with relief, mad as hell, joyous over finding him unhurt, and...fatherly, he finally decided. He felt like a father.

"WHAT'S THIS ABOUT a tape?" Nick asked a few minutes later when he finally broke away from the throng surrounding the suspects.

"Here," Daniel replied, shedding his jacket and handing it to Joanna so that he could lift his shirt up. He startled everyone when he revealed a jogger's belt pouch strapped around his waist. The faulty catch had worked loose again, and he gave it a hitch before pulling out a small, black, voice-activated tape recorder. With his tongue caught between his teeth, Daniel quickly punched the rewind button and held it up with a self-satisfied look.

"If that's a Sony," Ryan said with a stern look, "I'll bet I know where it came from."

"It was for a worthy cause, right?" Daniel said. "Listen up, you guys." He punched the play button and the voice of Sammy Feldstein suddenly sounded, loud and clear.

"Sheesh, kid, are you trying to give me a heart attack?"

In shocked silence, Ryan, Joanna and Nick listened as their suspicions about Sammy Feldstein were confirmed. Joanna pressed her fingers to her mouth. With a sinking heart, she realized Sammy had been a party to Rico's death. Everything about him, his tone, his attitude, his callousness, told her that he wouldn't have hesitated to do whatever it took to get his hands on those diamonds.

He had even been prepared to hurt Daniel.

Her gaze moved to the scene a few feet away, where one of Nick's men had just snapped handcuffs onto Sammy's wrists. Over his head, Sammy caught her eye, then looked away as he was quickly patted down in a search for concealed weapons. Nearby, the two thugs were pushed against the wall and given similar treatment.

"And to think," she murmured, eyeing him in disgust, "Rico was concerned about leaving Sammy saddled with debts from his sickness."

"If he'd gotten his hands on those diamonds," Ryan said,

scowling at Feldstein, "he would have never needed to worry about any kind of debt ever again."

"No chance of that," Daniel said, waggling his eyebrows like Groucho Marx. Dipping into his baggy shorts, he pulled out a small pouch, the type that holds children's marbles. Lifting it up, he let it swing from the leather string.

Ryan's expression turned thunderous. "Daniel—"

"My God, Daniel," Joanna began, "don't tell me the diamonds are there?"

Even Nick Dalton looked stunned.

With a quick laugh, Daniel handed the pouch to Ryan. "Hey, it's no big deal. They're all here."

With another telling look at Daniel, Ryan pulled the string and stared into the pouch. His jaw like granite, he met Nick's eyes. "I don't know how many there are," he said, passing them over, "but I think Feldstein could have lived a long and leisurely life off the contents in this sack."

Her heart knocking against her ribs, Joanna closed her eyes. "Daniel, what you did was so dangerous! Those men were thieves, murderers. How could you?"

"I'm sorry, Mom," Daniel said, awkwardly rubbing her arm. "It's not as bad as you're thinking. I wouldn't just walk up to somebody I thought was a killer without a little prior planning. I had me some insurance." He glanced at the ticket desk, where the pretty agent was again validating tickets and checking luggage. "When I first got here, I went over to the counter. There was an airport security guard on duty with the two ticket agents. I wanted to talk to them for two reasons."

"Two reasons?" Ryan was still unsmiling.

"Yeah, well, first I needed a trial run with the tape recorder and I explained that I was meeting some people who might become a little upset with me. So I asked them to keep an eye out. If I yelled or they seemed to act suspicious in any way, if they turned mean or even if I gave a high-sign, then I would appreciate it if they'd bail me out."

"That's it?" Ryan asked, obviously working hard to keep a lid on his temper.

"Well, yeah." He shrugged. "It worked, too. Because when that guy started to shake me, that's when all…uh, that's when the fur began to fly." His grin broke. "Next thing I know, I'm safe and they're in cuffs!"

Jamming his hands deep into his pockets, Ryan walked in a tight little circle to work off his horror. By the skin of his teeth, Daniel had pulled this off. Ingenuity was a good thing for a kid to have, but when he had Joanna and Daniel safe in his house under his protection, there were going to be some new rules, by God.

Nick put a calming hand on Ryan's shoulder and looked at Daniel. "Okay, tell us about the diamonds, Dan."

"How did you get them, Daniel?" Joanna asked quietly. With her shock and fear fading somewhat, she wanted some answers.

He cleared his throat, knowing this part wasn't going to be easy. "Well, it's probably not gonna earn me anything but ground time, Mom, but I didn't exactly tell the whole truth when I got to Sea Island."

"Tell it now," Joanna said evenly.

"Right. When I first left Grampa Jem's, I flew to Chicago and went to the gallery." He shifted a little beneath the steely-eyed scrutiny of Joanna and Ryan. "I'm pretty familiar with the stuff at Rico's—you remember how I used to work for Rico on Saturdays sometimes? In one of those old desks he likes so much, there's a concealed drawer. He showed it to me once. Sure enough, they were in there in a statue."

"You just walked in, found that desk, popped the catch and there they were." Ryan was perfectly still, watching Daniel with an inscrutable expression on his face.

Daniel stopped dead. The same wordless communication that had passed between them once before happened again. For a moment, they shared more than just a look, a feeling.

"Yeah," Daniel said softly, "it was incredible."

"I'll bet."

"The truth is," Daniel said, watching Ryan carefully, "I had a feeling."

Ryan nodded, and suddenly his features softened. "I figured as much."

Daniel drew in a deep breath and blew it out. A smile played at the corner of his mouth, tilting it in a way that was so like Ryan's. Completely oblivious of Joanna's rapt gaze shifting from one to the other, Daniel said, "Then I guess when we had that talk the first night I was at Wilderose Cottage, you pretty much understood where I was coming from, didn't you?"

Smiling faintly, Ryan said, "Yeah, I did."

"It happens to you, too. You sometimes see things, sense things before they happen? You know things sometimes without understanding why?"

"Yes."

"That's what happened with Pete?"

Ryan nodded once. "Yeah."

Daniel's smile faded a little. "So what did you think when you realized I did that, too? I know this is pretty rare. Nobody else I ever met has this. I mean, Mom doesn't. She doesn't have a clue."

Ryan crossed his arms over his chest, but he was incapable of keeping the emotion from his voice. "How much time do you have?" he asked huskily.

It was a moment before Daniel asked, "Were you happy when you found out about me?"

"Yes."

"'Cause you didn't know before I got to Sea Island, did you?"

"No."

Beside them, Joanna felt as though her heart had stopped. For so long, she'd envisioned this moment. But it hadn't been

in an airport. There hadn't been other onlookers. *Wait!* she
wanted to cry. *We need to think of the right words. We need
to make sure Daniel learns this in a way that he can accept.
We shouldn't take a chance on jeopardizing our future together, the three of us. Wait…wait…*

But the time for waiting was past. Daniel was gazing into
Ryan's eyes, both so alike, so blue, both teeming with
thoughts and feelings yet to be revealed.

"Are you my father?" Daniel asked.

"Yes."

IT WAS LATE, past three in the morning. The trip back to Sea
Island was an experience Joanna would never forget. By the
time they'd given their statements to Nick at police headquar-
ters, she was a mass of nerves. It wasn't the stress of revealing
her knowledge of Rico's illegal activity, or even Daniel's role
in removing the diamonds. The threat that had haunted her
was gone. Until the drive home, she had been nearly wild with
anxiety.

But finally they were on their way, and at last she was able
to try to explain her actions that confused, anguished winter
when she and Ryan had been in the process of separation and
divorce. Joanna had been amazed by his acceptance of her
halting, sometimes murky attempt, to make some sense out of
her behavior.

Now Ryan held her close against him as they lay watching
the mists of early morning from the window of her studio. It
seemed so natural that the moment they'd settled Daniel into
bed they had gone to the studio with its view of the sea and
had made love joyously, thankfully, losing themselves in the
wonder and contentment of knowing that this was a new beginning. A second chance.

"I was so scared," she confessed, caressing the tops of his
arms crossed beneath her breasts. Her voice shook as she said,
"I couldn't bear it if I'd destroyed our chance to be a family."

"There was never any question of that," Ryan told her, rubbing his chin against her temple. "Daniel's childhood as David Stanton's son was happy. As his mother, you had as much to do with that as David. I'm the one who's the winner here. He has a heart full of love and he's ready to open it to me."

"Not just ready," she corrected him, smiling, "it's a done deed. He loves you."

Ryan shifted so that both lay facing each other. "I love you," he said, stroking the side of her face. "I want us to be a family, the way it was always meant to be."

She closed her eyes and felt the sting of tears. "I want that, too," she whispered, nestling her cheek into his palm. "I love you."

"Will you marry me?"

She smiled radiantly through her tears. "Yes."

"When?"

"Whenever you say."

He leaned close and kissed her deeply and tenderly. "It'll be different this time, Jo, I promise."

Against his lips, she smiled. "You won't get caught up in your work? You won't neglect me for days at a time while you slave over your next feature article? You won't drop everything when you get an assignment to die for?"

"No, I—"

Joanna put a finger on his mouth. "Hush. Of course you will, but I'm not the person I was back then, Ryan. I have my work, I have Daniel and a thousand other demands, and I—"

"Wait." This time, he kissed her into silence, then framed her face with his hands and studied her in the shadowy light. "I believe that's the way it would be now, but we'll never know because I'm not going back to New York. At least not for a while. Not unless I can't sell my book. And even then, I'm convinced that phase of my life is over."

She looked delighted. "You're definitely going to do the book?"

"Yeah, I am."

"Judith will be thrilled."

He settled again on his back and tucked her into the curve of his shoulder. "Not that book." He studied the gray-violet hue of the sky. Dawn was just moments away. "I'm doing Pete's story."

"Oh, Ryan."

His arm tightened around her, then relaxed. "Yeah, I think it's time."

Joanna watched the last vestige of night give way to the first gentle tint of the rising sun. Writing Pete's story would bring him peace the way nothing else could. Pressed close to Ryan's warmth, she felt as though the sun was rising in her heart. With a smile, she reached up to kiss him, then settled back, satisfied. His book would be good. His best work yet.

She had a feeling.

EPILOGUE

"RYAN? ARE YOU UP HERE?"

At the sound of Joanna's voice, Ryan dropped the journal he was reading, bolted off the daybed and was halfway to the stairs when he spotted the top of his wife's tawny head in the stairwell. Swearing liberally, he caught her arm as she stepped into the studio and led her carefully to the daybed.

"Why didn't you wait?" he demanded, sweeping books and papers to the floor to make a place for her. "I would have come down."

"Because I wanted to come up." Rolling her eyes, she allowed him to play the indulgent husband. He handled her as though she was made of glass these days, when in reality she felt more like she was made of lead.

"We agreed you wouldn't climb those stairs anymore, Joanna. The doctor said—"

"We didn't agree to any such thing. And the doctor said I was healthy as a horse. Exercise is good for me."

"Stairs are not exercise," he retorted, piling pillows behind her back. "They're accidents waiting to happen if you're pregnant."

"Well, I'm definitely pregnant."

He grinned suddenly. "I'll say." He dropped down beside her and propped himself up on an elbow. With his other hand, he gently explored the mound that nurtured their unborn child. His expression reflected wonder, as usual. When he felt the inevitable kick against his palm, his blue eyes flared.

"What's the matter, little one?" he murmured, placing a kiss on the spot. "Getting impatient?"

Joanna's heart turned over. Had a man ever been more fascinated over the prospect of a child? Or happier? To her delight, Ryan was as caught up in her pregnancy as she was. It was nearly inconceivable to her that she'd once believed he wouldn't care or have time for his child.

"I missed you," she said softly, sifting her fingers through his hair. "What were you doing up here in my studio?"

He smiled up at her. "Oh, it's your studio now, is it?"

They had settled happily at Wilderose Cottage after their marriage. For Ryan and Joanna, it had been a natural choice, but they'd worried that Daniel might prefer the friends and familiarity of Chicago. Wrong. He'd gloried in claiming his birthright as the firstborn O'Connor of his generation. And he was almost as excited about his expected baby brother or sister as Ryan. His Grandpa Jem visited regularly and if Daniel had his way, would soon move to Savannah. Daniel was more than happy.

Ryan teased Joanna about the outpouring of creativity that had followed their marriage. By their first anniversary, she had produced enough paintings to have showings in New York and Chicago. It was only natural, he had remarked, that after a few months she became pregnant. A baby was, after all, the ultimate in creativity.

She was not the only creative one. Ryan's book was in the editorial process. Besides his editor, only Joanna had been allowed to read it. It was powerful and moving, and she believed it would be critically acclaimed. Of one thing she was certain: writing a book about Pete had been the catharsis for Ryan that Joanna had hoped it would be.

Watching his face now, she felt a rush of love. "I bet I know what you were doing," she whispered, her fingers caressing.

Shifting to get more comfortable, he rested his head near

her breast, keeping his hand on her stomach. "Reading his journals," he said, his eyes dark with remembrance.

"Did you find something new?"

"Every time I open them, I find something new."

"Your father was special. Like father, like son," she said, smiling.

"And you're so unbiased," he replied with a soft laugh. Then, sobering, he said, "Dad was flawed, as we all are. Until I read about it in his own words, I wasn't aware of the magnitude of the mistake he made when he nearly lost Michelle and their baby. He was so devastated that he even questioned his honor and integrity."

"Sounds familiar, hmm?" Joanna murmured, her eyes gentle.

"He was harder on himself than anyone else." Ryan's laugh was self-disparaging. "Maybe it runs in the family." He waited a moment, then rose up to look at her. "As someone once said to me, I have more in common with my father than I ever dreamed. More than our experience with personal demons. For a time, we were both immobilized by that, but then we managed to seize the second chances that often come with adversity." He looked pensive. "I can't speak for my father, but as for me…I don't know how long it would have taken without you and Daniel."

Framing his face in her hands, Joanna searched his eyes for the shadows that had haunted him when she first came. Finding only love and trust and the promise of a bright and happy future, she gave him a beautiful smile. "You were nearly there when we invaded your space," she told him.

He sat up and took her in his arms, kissing her with tenderness and mounting desire. The taste and texture and wonder of her never failed to excite him. Holding her close, he whispered gruffly, "You can invade my space anytime, sweetheart. As for second chances…we'll make this one last a lifetime. That's a promise."

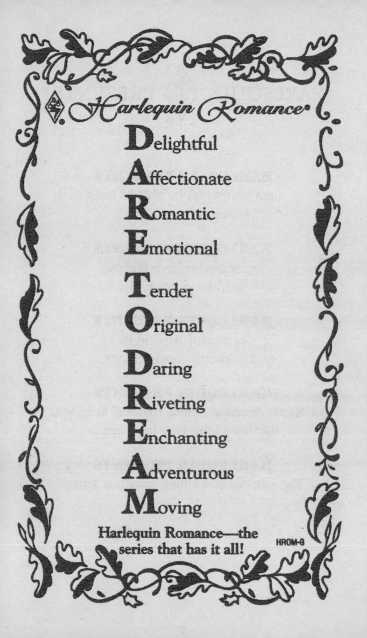

Harlequin Romance®

Delightful

Affectionate

Romantic

Emotional

Tender

Original

Daring

Riveting

Enchanting

Adventurous

Moving

Harlequin Romance—the
series that has it all!

HROM-G

HARLEQUIN 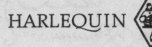 PRESENTS®

HARLEQUIN PRESENTS
men you won't be able to resist
falling in love with...

HARLEQUIN PRESENTS
women who have feelings
just like your own...

HARLEQUIN PRESENTS
powerful passion in
exotic international settings...

HARLEQUIN PRESENTS
intense, dramatic stories that will keep you
turning to the very last page...

HARLEQUIN PRESENTS
The world's bestselling romance series!

Harlequin®
Historical

From rugged lawmen and
valiant knights to defiant heiresses
and spirited frontierswomen,
Harlequin Historicals will
capture your imagination with
their dramatic scope, passion
and adventure.

Harlequin Historicals...
they're too good to miss!

HHGENR

LOOK FOR OUR FOUR FABULOUS MEN!

Each month some of today's bestselling authors bring
four new fabulous men to Harlequin American Romance.
Whether they're rebel ranchers, millionaire power brokers
or sexy single dads, they're all gallant princes—and
they're all ready to sweep you into lighthearted fantasies
and contemporary fairy tales where anything is possible
and where all your dreams come true!

You don't even have to make a wish…
Harlequin American Romance will grant your every desire!

Look for Harlequin American Romance
wherever Harlequin books are sold!

HARLEQUIN SUPERROMANCE®

...there's more to the story!

Superromance. A *big* satisfying read about unforgettable characters. Each month we offer *four* very different stories that range from family drama to adventure and mystery, from highly emotional stories to romantic comedies—and much more! Stories about people you'll believe in and care about. Stories too compelling to put down....

Our authors are among today's *best* romance writers. You'll find familiar names and talented newcomers. Many of them are award winners—and you'll see why!

If you want the biggest and best in romance fiction, you'll get it from Superromance!

Available wherever Harlequin books are sold.